Seafaring Women of the Vera B.

Hearts of Oak Series, Book 1

SUSAN PAGE DAVIS

JAMES S. DAVIS

SUSAN PAGE DAVIS
JAMES S. DAVIS

Published in association with
Tea Tin Press
A Tea Tin Historical

ISBN: 978-0-9972308-0-2

Cover design by Lynnette Bonner of Indie Cover Design – www.indiecoverdesign.com.
Printed in the United States of America

CHAPTER ONE

June, 1854
Port Phillip Bay, Australia

The ship was too quiet. Alice Packard knew something was wrong as they approached the *Vera B.*

The brig lay anchored in the shallow waters of Port Phillip Bay, off the village of St. Kilda. They had left four men on board with her husband's second mate, Mr. McDarby, while Gypsy Deak, who served as boatswain and steward, accompanied Alice ashore for her husband's burial. But no watchman hailed them from the deck as they approached. The brig, with its masts stripped of canvas, rode the gentle waves too quietly.

Alice glanced at Gypsy. The old man had sailed for more than thirty years and knew every timber and crack of the *Vera B.* Did he sense the same peculiarity she did?

"Ahoy the *Vera B.*," Gypsy called.

No one responded.

They reached the side where the rope ladder hung down, but still no one leaned over to greet them or offer a hand.

"I don't like this," Gypsy said. "Let me board first, ma'am."

At fifty-nine years, the old boatswain tended to stiffness, and an old injury gave him a pronounced limp in his gait. Alice watched anxiously as he slowly climbed the ladder. She thought she heard muffled voices and laughter, but it could be from one of the other vessels anchored nearby.

The gate in the bulwark was closed, and Gypsy had to clamber over the rail. Alice couldn't wait any longer, wondering what he had found on deck. She hoisted her skirts and stood in the bow, where Gypsy had tied the dinghy to the bottom of the ladder. She loathed the stunt in full skirts, but years of sailing with her husband had taught her how to conquer ladders quickly and modestly. She made the ascent swiftly and clambered aboard.

Gypsy was several yards away, his back to her, walking past the mainmast toward the captain's cabin at the stern. The door stood wide open, and noise of movement and voices came from within.

Alice's heart lurched. The men were never allowed in the cabin, unless invited by the captain. Had outsiders overrun the handful of men they had left and begun to pillage the brig?

Four men burst from the cabin, their arms laden with guns and other plunder.

"Hey!" Gypsy yelled. He strode toward the ruffians.

Alice caught her breath. The leader was one of their sailors. Where was the mate? She shrank back toward the rail. She wanted to call out to Gypsy, to tell him to be sensible rather than to confront four large, strong young men bent on mischief.

"What do you think you're doing?" Gypsy roared.

Men with any conscience would have quailed before his indignation, but not these four. They jeered at the boatswain. One of them dropped his armful of loot and shoved Gypsy hard toward the mast. Gypsy fell heavily. The men laughed, and one of them aimed a kick at him as they ran for the ladder. Alice crouched behind the lower shrouds and pulled her cloak about her, hoping they would not notice her.

As they climbed over the rail, a tall young fellow called Grimes nudged the man beside him. He nodded in Alice's direction and said something. The other sailor glanced her way. Alice cringed into the shadows.

"Leave her be." The sailor stuck the Colt revolver her husband had bought before they left Massachusetts into his belt and swung up onto the bulwark.

Grimes followed, and she noticed he was wearing Ruel's warm winter coat. Alice's throat tightened. How dare they steal the dead captain's clothing?

A moment later she heard the splash of oars, and their hoots grew fainter. Slowly, Alice stood, her breath coming in short gasps. She peered over the side. The dinghy was halfway to the dock. She turned and ran down the deck to where Gypsy was trying to pull himself to his feet.

"Are you all right?" She offered her hand, and he took it, wincing as he gained his footing. "They hurt you."

"I'll mend." Gypsy's dark expression silenced her. He limped toward her cabin, and she followed. They stood in the doorway, surveying the destruction.

Alice gazed into the cabin she had shared with her husband for the last six months. Its disarray sent her heart plunging. The intruders had made free of the room. Ruel's charts were strewn about the floor, and the bed and wardrobe had been rifled. She turned to the safe, where the captain kept personal valuables, the company's funds for the voyage, and all the small arms. Its door stood open.

"They had the key," Gypsy said, staring at the door of the big iron chest. "They must have got it off McDarby."

"Where is he?" Alice asked.

Their eyes met. "I'll see if he's below," Gypsy said.

Alice's lips trembled as she entered the cabin alone. The gaping door of the large iron safe drew her. Standing before it, she mentally catalogued the weapons Ruel had kept on hand.

Where there had been pistols for all hands in case they were menaced by pirates, the armory now held only five. A musket and Ruel's fowling piece remained, but it appeared the thieves had taken most of the pistol shot. The small strongbox in which Ruel kept their personal funds as well as the company's funds for the voyage was empty.

Automatically, Alice began to straighten the room. She picked up garments, dishes, a small framed photograph, and the bedclothes.

Gypsy's uneven footsteps thumped on the deck, and she turned to the door.

"Mrs. Packard! Ma'am!"

"Yes, Gypsy?"

"It's McDarby, ma'am. He's down in the 'tweendecks covered in blood, and I fear he's like to die."

Alice dabbed at the bleeding wound on Mr. McDarby's head and wrung out her cloth in a basin of water. The gash went deep, and the mate hadn't opened his eyes since they'd found him, though he had moaned when Gypsy lifted him and carried him to his berth.

"I fear he suffered defending my property," she said. Mr. McDarby had reluctantly accepted the added responsibility of being purser for the voyage, which meant he had access to the strongbox. All the men knew that.

"He were doing his duty, ma'am."

That did little to mollify her bruised heart. "Gypsy, what shall we do? His leg is obviously broken, and he may have internal injuries, besides this head wound."

"We'll have to fetch the doctor that tended to the captain."

"Yes. But we've no one to send." Alice met his troubled brown eyes. "You will have to go."

Gypsy frowned. "I don't know where Boardman and the others are. They should have been back last night."

"But they weren't," Alice said. "It must be as the minister told us, though I don't like to think it. They've all deserted us and headed for the goldfields."

"I can't picture Mr. Boardman doing it, ma'am. Not with him knowing of the captain's demise and that you need him to sail this brig."

"You saw how it was in the town. Our men had to take a shovel to dig my husband's grave. Every tool they had at the church was stolen, the minister said. The entire population's gone crazy for gold, just like they did a few years ago in America."

6

Gypsy sighed. "I don't like to leave you here alone with him while I fetch the doctor. Not after this."

"Then let me come with you. We'll take Mr. McDarby to the doctor and then go and search for our crew."

"Then there'll be no one here to mind the ship, Mrs. Packard."

She hesitated. With the lawless atmosphere in this port, marauders could come aboard and steal the remaining equipment and stores, even the rigging and the valuable cargo. But would she be able to withstand such an attack better than Mr. McDarby had? "If we don't find our crew or hire a new one, we'll lose it just as surely as if someone steals it."

Gypsy stroked his gray-streaked beard. "What about the passengers, ma'am?"

"Mrs. McKay wanted to stay ashore awhile, so that she could shop." Alice's husband had accepted a farmer's widow, Hannah McKay, as a passenger in Adelaide, along with her niece and two children. They had paid for passage to their native England. After accompanying Alice to the little churchyard in St. Kilda for the brief graveside service, the family had walked into the village for some last-minute purchases.

Gypsy looked around and then gave a firm nod. "All right, then. Those blighters took the dinghy, but I think we can manage the jollyboat, if we can get MrDarby into it."

He limped out to the passageway. Alice went to the deck and walked with trepidation to her cabin. Facing the upheaval in the room, she sent up a quick prayer. She had one man left of the twenty she had thought loyal. God alone could get her back to Massachusetts.

She laid aside her shawl and hat. In five minutes, she had retrieved the precious charts and taken stock of her belongings. The few pieces of nice jewelry she had brought with her were gone. She touched her bodice, running her fingers over the gold locket Ruel had given her on their first anniversary. At least she'd

7

had that on her person. It now carried a lock of her beloved's hair. Losing the locket would have maimed her.

The rest, she could stand. The company would have to absorb the loss of the cash Ruel had aboard for expenses. More than ever, she was determined to get the *Vera B.* and its valuable cargo back to them. This voyage must not be a total loss for the Collins Shipping Company of Salem.

She washed her face and hands and tidied her hair. Her small, handheld mirror was cracked. Gazing into it, she thought, "I've aged." Or perhaps it was only the fatigue that changed her face. Watching her husband die and knowing he could no longer provide for her and protect her had crushed her, or so she had thought. Now she had a more precarious plight to deal with. She wasn't sure she had the strength.

She knew what Ruel would say. "Trust in God, my dear, and do the next thing."

Alice took a deep breath and laid the mirror aside. Time to get on with it. Later, she would finish straightening the cabin. Her next duty was to Mr. McDarby.

"Nobody's seen Boardman or the others in the village," Gypsy reported two hours later. He had left Mrs. Packard with McDarby at the doctor's place of business while he checked the half dozen pubs in St. Kilda's. "We'll have to look in Melbourne."

Mrs. Packard walked outside with him. "I hope we're not delayed long. The doctor says Mr. McDarby cannot travel in this state. He will keep him as long as need be, and I gave him some money from what I had with me."

Gypsy squinted at her through the mesh of the veil that fell from her navy blue hat. "Are things all right, ma'am? Not meaning to pry, but …"

She patted his arm. "We'll be fine, Mr. Deak. My personal funds are low, what with the doctor and the minister and the

8

theft. But I couldn't ask this man to care for Mr. McDarby for several weeks without recompensing him." She sighed. "I thought we'd be asea and homeward bound by now, and I'd have no more need for something as mundane as money."

"Yes, ma'am. But if we need to hire extra hands to replace those who've ..."

She eyed him keenly. "Do you really think all our men have run off to seek gold, Gypsy?"

He knew the depth of her agitation when she used his nickname. She was such a fine lady. Gypsy had never known her to be seasick, and she was kind to the crew, though not overly familiar. And she was smart. She'd studied navigation on her voyages with Captain Packard. He'd heard her husband boast that his wife could steer the ship as well as he could.

She was good, thick oak stock, Mrs. Packard was. And she was pretty to boot. But would she remain steady without her husband at her side?

"I don't like to think it, ma'am, but it may be they've gone."

"How could they? They've not had their wages yet, and their homes are in Massachusetts. Would they abandon everything in that fashion?"

"Maybe, if they thought they could get rich in the goldfields."

"Mr. Boardman would not treat us thus. And he's to be acting captain for the return voyage."

"It's hard to feature, ma'am." Gypsy looked toward Melbourne, the raw, booming city on the edge of the harbor. "Likely we'll find him and the men sleeping it off in town. Shall I get someone to take you back to the *Vera B?*"

"No," she said firmly. "I'm going with you."

"But, ma'am—"

"No buts, Gypsy. We *must* find them."

He hesitated, but he could see that her mind was made up. He wouldn't want to argue with her under ordinary

9

circumstances, but between her husband's unexpected death and the crew's desertion, some new mettle seemed to sustain her.

"The likeliest place to find them is the taverns, ma'am, though I hate to take a lady as fine as yourself there."

"Perhaps we should split up," she said. "We could cover more ground."

Gypsy scowled. "Nay, 'twould never do, ma'am. The likes of you cannot go about the streets of a gold town alone."

"There's Mrs. McKay." Mrs. Packard raised a hand to wave, and Gypsy turned. Hannah McKay, along with her two youngsters and her pretty niece Jenny were walking down from the village toward the docks.

"I suppose we'd best tell her our situation," Mrs. Packard said. "Should we send them back to the ship?"

"Not alone. We don't know it's safe." Gypsy frowned. He didn't like to send the captain's wife back without an escort either, in case more of the men had returned to steal, or others had heard that the ship was unguarded. "Perhaps you could wait here with them while I —"

"I'm going with you," she said with a stubborn edge to her voice.

"Yes, ma'am. Then you talk to Mrs. McKay. Perhaps they would stay in the village a while longer and take tea here while we search. I'll get a horse and buggy."

"I could have walked," Alice said as she settled her skirts about her.

Gypsy gave a short nod. "Maybe, but you'd be exhausted by the time we got back this evening."

She leaned back against the seat, trying not to think about the cost of the rig and driver. Instead, she pondered where the first mate could be. As to the common sailors, she could well guess. But she was counting on Boardman, as had her husband. Surely he wouldn't abandon her, knowing her distress.

Gypsy gazed back toward Port Phillip Bay. He sat up straighter and leaned out the side. "Look there, ma'am."

Alice followed his gaze. A tall clipper ship was entering the harbor under light sail.

"Don't that be the *Jade Maiden*? Cap'n Howard's ship?"

Alice's heart leaped as she realized Gypsy was right. They had berthed near the clipper at Adelaide just a few days earlier, and she and Ruel had gone aboard to visit his old friend, Captain Josiah Howard. "It is! Oh, Gypsy, maybe the captain can help us. He will at least be able to advise me."

Gypsy stroked his short beard. "It will take them several hours to anchor and settle their business with the harbormaster. Let's go on with our plans. Perhaps you can meet with Cap'n Howard in the morning."

"He doesn't know about my husband's death." Alice stared bleakly at the boatswain.

"There, now, ma'am." Gypsy awkwardly patted her arm. "I'm sure the cap'n will be a comfort to you. And things will look better by then, like as not. As soon as we get Mr. Boardman and the rest back, we'll head for home."

"Thank you." Alice dabbed at the tears that had sprung into her eyes. The buggy turned a corner, and she lost sight of the clipper ship. Gypsy was right. First things first. Without her crew, she was going nowhere. She could consult Ruel's friend tomorrow. Josiah Howard was, in Alice's opinion, an astute, courteous captain. She had met him several times over the years. Her husband had kept up a correspondence with his friend and occasionally ran into him in foreign ports. He had thought well of Captain Howard.

The afternoon was young, and Melbourne's waterfront teemed with activity. While laborers unloaded cargo, sailors on liberty and miners fresh from the goldfields hurried toward the taverns. Alice supposed it would be worse when darkness fell.

11

"Melbourne is bigger than I'd realized," she said, staring about.

"It's grown a lot since the last time I was here," Gypsy said, "and rougher too. It's a jumping off place for the goldfields. I'm thinking you'd best stay outside while I do the asking."

"I don't see many women," she noted.

"Not in this part of town, ma'am. Decent women don't come down here."

He had their driver stop a few yards down the street from a tavern.

"Wait here with the driver. I'll go in and inquire about our men, but it's too boisterous for you."

He returned a few minutes later with a grim shake of his head, and the driver went on. They repeated this routine half a dozen times. At each stop, the quality of the establishment seemed lower and the men within louder.

"That looks like a popular place." Gypsy pointed to a building sporting a sign for the Boar's Tusk. "Maybe some of our lads are inside."

Alice waited in the buggy, shrinking down as dozens of men tramped by, seemingly intent on reaching the tavern. She turned her face away and hoped they would not notice her.

A stocky sailor spotted her and stepped up to the side of the buggy.

"Eh, miss, you want a drink?"

"No!" Her heart pounding, Alice shrank to the other side of the seat. For the first time, she wished she had packed mourning attire for the voyage. A widow's weeds might protect her from unwanted attention.

The driver raised his whip and shook it at the man. "Git along now."

The sailor chortled and moved on toward the tavern. To Alice's relief, Gypsy appeared moments later.

"I've found someone who's seen Boardman," he said, panting. "You need to speak to her, ma'am, and she'll want a

12

coin. But I don't want you going in the front. If we go around back, she'll meet us in the storeroom, where they keep the casks."

Alice took off her veiled hat, pulled up the hood of her cloak, and gave Gypsy her hand. He helped her out of the buggy.

"You wait," Gypsy cautioned the driver darkly. He led Alice swiftly around the side of the building to an alley at the back.

"You said 'her,'" Alice noted. "What sort of person is she?"

"A barmaid. Don't understand much but money."

Alice frowned, wondering if the woman was simpleminded, or if Gypsy simply had a low opinion of the working women of Melbourne.

The back door was locked, and Gypsy rapped on it smartly. It opened a moment later. A blond woman in a low-cut silk dress stood before them. The scent of her perfume mingled with the smells of liquor, tobacco smoke, and sawdust.

"Carrie," Gypsy said, "this is Mrs. Packard, from the *Vera B.*"

Carrie looked Alice up and down as Alice took in the barmaid's lip rouge, powder, and jewelry. The stones in her garish necklace and earrings were too large to be real. From a room beyond the darkened storage area, laughter and shouting wafted to them.

"You're looking for a tall man?" Carrie asked.

"Yes," Alice said. "Our first mate, Mr. Boardman. He's uncommonly tall. American. Sandy hair and blue eyes."

Carrie nodded, setting her earrings swaying. "He was here last night. Him and three others."

CHAPTER TWO

Carrie eyed the woman closely, trying to figure out her role in this drama. Ships' officers often came to the Boar's Tusk in search of tardy seamen, but not ladies, and this woman was definitely a lady. Her clothing, though a bit conservative, was of good cloth and cut—Carrie wouldn't mind having a warm, hooded cloak like that. Her cultured voice took away any lingering doubts.

"How long were they here?" Mrs. Packard asked.

"They had a few drinks, and then your mate and one of his men got into a card game." Carrie glanced over her shoulder to make sure the tavern's owner, Tom Larson, wasn't near the storeroom door. He didn't allow her to waste time talking to people who weren't paying customers. "I heard them say when they left that they'd have enough for a stake."

"A stake?" The grizzled boatswain eyed her sharply.

"I'm pretty sure they were headed for the gold diggings. One of them asked about the ferry to Geelong. That's the usual way they go."

"And you're certain they were men from the Vera B.?" the woman asked.

Carrie hesitated. If this woman was a passenger on the ship, why was she out here with the boatswain? Maybe she had influence with the ship's officers. Carrie had been saving whatever coins she could keep Tom from knowing about, and her stash had grown. She had been thinking it was almost time to make her move. "When is your ship leaving?"

"As soon as we get our crew on board," Mrs. Packard replied.

"Which we'd like to find," the boatswain said tersely.

"Them that was here last night won't be coming back, I can tell you that," Carrie said. "One was a small, Irish-looking fellow. Reddish hair and a full beard." She held back a smile, recalling his snapping blue eyes and winsome laugh.

"Sounds like Radison," The boatswain said.

Mrs. Packard nodded, her brown eyes huge.

Carrie decided to put in her bid. She might not have another chance with a ship that had a decent woman aboard. "Will you take me with you on your ship? I can pay."

Mrs. Packard's lips parted, and she turned to the man.

"Our passenger cabins are already spoken for," he said.

"Please tell us anything else you know about our crew," Mrs. Packard put in quickly. "I'll speak to the officers and see if they couldn't find a place for you."

Carrie threw another glance over her shoulder. "I want to leave this life, ma'am. If you can help me ..."

"The men," the boatswain said between gritted teeth.

Carrie sighed. "That Boardman, the one you said was the mate, he seemed reluctant at first. But he had a run of luck at the table, and when he saw that they had enough for their stake, he agreed to go with the others. I heard them mention that they would meet some friends this morning at the ferry dock. That's all I know."

"Thank you," said the woman.

Carrie could see that she was only marginally interested in securing passage for her. "Ma'am, please don't forget me when you leave here. This life is not my choice. I know it could be worse, but I don't have any say in what I do. And Tom Larson— well, he's not the kind I want to stay with the rest of my life, but he'll never let me go if he can help it."

"Can't you go somewhere else?"

Carrie shook her head. "He's be more than angry. He broke my arm once."

The woman caught her breath. Carrie rubbed her left forearm. It didn't hurt anymore, but the memory was still painful. "If you can ask your captain ... I've been here three years, and I've been saving up. I can't just walk out of here. Tom would find me and bring me back. I need to get clean away. Far away."

"I'll put in a word for you," Mrs. Packard said.

15

The boatswain made a disapproving noise in his throat but said nothing.

Without being prodded, Mrs. Packard opened her purse and took out an English shilling.

"Add that to your stash, Carrie. And thank you."

"You'll let me know if I can get a berth?"

"If it's possible, I'll send a message."

"Thank you." Carrie gazed at the woman. "And when you send word, don't let Tom or anyone else here know."

"We'll be discreet."

It was all Carrie could hope for.

"Carrie? Where you at, love?" Tom's voice rose as he approached the storeroom door.

Carrie shoved the door shut and palmed the shilling. Let the people from the ship draw their own conclusions. "In here. Just getting some lamp oil."

As they emerged from the alley, Alice whirled on Gypsy. "What now? Do you think there's any point in going to the ferry dock?"

"They'll be gone hours ago."

"But all of them? Should we believe that every one of our men is gone, save McDarby?"

"Steady now," Gypsy said. "I fear you should hire new hands and forget about that worthless lot."

Alice sagged against the rough wall of the building. "I still can't believe Mr. Boardman deserted me."

Gypsy glanced up at the cloudy sky. "We might find a few of our men at another watering hole, I suppose, or a few who'll sign on to sail with us. Let's give it another hour, shall we?"

"All right." Alice doubted they would succeed, but they returned to the buggy and went on to the next tavern. Gypsy spoke to men heading inside each establishment or coming out, if

16

they looked sober enough to answer questions. The hubbub of the town seemed to increase. On every street, buildings were under construction. Men shouted to each other. Carts and pedestrians dashed here and there.

"What's all the fuss?" Gypsy asked the driver.

"It's the new gold strike at St. Arnaud. They're all crazed to get there before ten thousand others beat them to it."

Outside a dance hall, Alice pointed out a broadside nailed to the wall. "A new railroad line. They want workers to help build it."

"What's this one say?" Gypsy pointed to another notice.

Alice frowned. "All hands of the *Mary St. James*, return to the ship by June 30, 1854, and you will be pardoned for abandoning your post. Please accept this gracious offer of clemency, as well as triple pay for every crew member upon arrival in Bristol. New crew members welcomed. Signed, Captain Mulberry."

Gypsy stared at her. "Triple pay."

"It seems we're not alone in being short on crew," Alice said. "There's another notice over there, for the schooner *Miranda*." She scanned several more broadsides on the wall. "We're wasting our time. Everyone wants seamen, and I have nothing to pay them."

The old man's mouth twitched. "The ship's all provisioned and ready to sail, ma'am."

"But who shall sail it?" She laughed and quickly caught her breath. This was no time for hysteria. "Oh, Gypsy, I can't just abandon the *Vera B.* How will I ever get a crew?"

"The usual way is to promise payment at the end of the voyage." Gypsy's brow furrowed.

Alice squared her shoulders. "There's someone we haven't considered—someone who can help us."

Gypsy's eyes lit. "Captain Howard, you mean?"

Alice blinked. "No. Well, yes, he might. I wasn't thinking of him."

"Oh. Who, then?"

17

"Why, God, of course."

Gypsy's face fell. "Of course, ma'am. You pray about it. Meanwhile, let's go down to the docks and look for our dinghy."

Alice followed him back to the buggy. Though Gypsy did not share her high opinion of the Almighty, he had shown himself a loyal employee and a true friend. She breathed a prayer of thanks for him and asked for wisdom.

At the dock in St. Kilda, Gypsy helped Alice down from the buggy. She straightened the dusty skirt of her dark blue traveling outfit. They hadn't succeeded in finding either their dinghy or the launch that Boardman and his men had taken ashore the previous day. Shadows lengthened behind the village by the water's edge.

"I'd better wait here for Mrs. McKay and the children."

"I'll get the jollyboat, if no one's made off with it." Gypsy strode away, looking over the boats tied up at nearby slips.

"Mrs. Packard!"

Alice turned and was met by the welcome sight of Hannah McKay, Jenny, and the children walking toward her, with two other women in tow. Eight-year-old Ned broke away and ran to her. Alice smiled, suspecting he'd been longing to run all afternoon and kept in check.

"Hello, Ned. Did you have a nice time?"

"Yes, ma'am. We ate at a teashop."

"That sounds nice."

Hannah, a sturdy woman in her thirties wearing a plain but serviceable woolen dress, bustled up to her, smiling and panting. Her daughter Addie and niece Jenny followed her, carrying small bundles.

"My dear Mrs. Packard, I've brought this lady to meet you." Hannah beckoned to a woman in a light blue moiré promenade dress topped by a deeper blue pelisse in velvet, trimmed with white fur. Her bonnet matched the pelisse and set off her mature but lovely face. Alice supposed her to be in her early forties, and she had no doubt this was the best-dressed woman she had yet encountered in Australia.

"Hello." The woman extended her gloved hand and smiled.

"Mrs. Packard," Hannah said with some importance, "May I present Lady Dunbar. And this is her maid, Miss Lizzie Henshaw." Hannah nodded toward the other woman, who hung back a pace.

"How do you do?" Alice smiled at both of them.

"We're in good health," Lady Dunbar replied, "but in a bit of a difficulty, and Mrs. McKay thought you might be able to help us."

"Oh?" Alice couldn't imagine how she might help this wealthy woman.

Lady Dunbar took her arm and drew her a few steps away from the others. "Mrs. McKay said your ship will embark shortly, and that you take passengers."

"Oh! Well ..." Alice's mind whirled. The cabins they had available were filled, thanks to Hannah's brood, and she wasn't sure she could embark at all, if she didn't get her crew back. Of course, Hannah knew nothing of her problem. "That's questionable. You heard about my husband?"

"Mrs. McKay told me, and I am sorry. But I won't stand on ceremony. I'll tell you the truth, and you can do with it as you like. My husband, the Earl of Dunbar, is a hard man. I'll not mince words—he's not only possessed of a foul temper, but he's taken up with a coarse woman half my age. Right now he's gone to Ballarat to meet with some mining executives. I would like nothing better than to leave these shores before he returns and go back to our estate in England. Can you help me?"

"Oh, dear." Alice chose her words carefully. "I'm so sorry for your distress, ma'am, but you see, we're having troubles over the crew. Several of them have not returned from their liberty. My boatswain and I fear that, on hearing of the captain's death, some of them may have struck out for the goldfields."

19

"Most inconvenient." Lady Dunbar frowned. "I could go by steamship, but they're such a ghastly mess. Will you know more by tomorrow?"

"I should."

"Perhaps Henshaw and I can meet you at the teashop on the high street here in St. Kilda? One o'clock?"

Alice hesitated. She had all but promised any available space to Carrie O'Dell. "I'm not sure. Our space is limited and—"

"Henshaw and I can share a cabin. I'll pay you well. And don't worry about me—I'm a good sailor. I practically grew up on my father's yacht."

"I see." Alice's head swam. The added income would be a blessing, but how could she house more passengers? "I'll discuss it with my officers."

"Good. I'll see you tomorrow then." Lady Dunbar gathered her skirts and turned away. Alice watched as the maid fell in behind her with a flurry of petticoats and taffeta overskirts.

"Well," Alice said as Hannah and eighteen-year-old Jenny came to her side.

"I wasn't certain you could take more passengers," Hannah began.

"Neither am I," Alice said. "I'll put the matter to Mr. Deak."

"There's Gypsy," Ned yelled. He shot off down the quay to meet the boatswain, who limped toward them.

"I've found our launch." Gypsy pointed as he reached them.

"Oh, good," Alice said. "No sign of the men?"

Gypsy shot Hannah a glance and touched his forelock in salute. "A Chinese fisherman saw several men land in it last night. Nobody seems to have seen them since." His smile twisted into a grimace. "The Chinaman also said it isn't wise to let your crew go ashore unsupervised here."

Alice laughed. "It's a little late for that bit of wisdom. Oh, how could I have been so foolish?"

"There's trouble with the crew?" Hannah asked. "I knew the ones on leave hadn't returned this morning. . ."

"It's worse even than that," Alice said. "I'll tell you on our way to the ship. We seem to be deserted, Mrs. McKay."

"There now," Hannah said, patting her shoulder. "You couldn't have foreseen this. But such a shame, and your dear husband only buried this morning."

"Yes." Alice sighed. "We're not certain yet what we'll do. Can we handle the launch, Gypsy?"

"Perhaps, if one or more of you ladies is willing to help row."

"I'm good for it," Hannah said, "and Jenny, too."

Her niece smiled. "Aye, Mr. Deak."

"I can too," Ned piped up.

Gypsy laughed. "Well, then, perhaps we'll make it to the ship, and we can tow the jollyboat behind. May I carry your bundle, ma'am?" He reached for the burlap sack Jenny carried, and as she passed it to him, an odor wafted Alice's way.

"Fish?" Gypsy arched his gray eyebrows at Jenny.

"Yair, we met a girl selling salmon and bream," Jenny said.

"She was a very interesting young thing," Hannah said. "She said she fishes in the harbor and sells her catch on the beach, among the Chinese fishermen. Mr. Deak, I thought you or the cook might prepare it for supper. There's enough for all of us."

"Of course, ma'am. Fresh fish will be a nice change."

They all settled into the boat under Gypsy's instruction. He, Alice, Hannah, and Jenny took up the four oars. Gypsy placed Ned in the stern. Alice let Addie sit beside her on the thwart and hold the end of her oar. She was glad she did, as the work was strenuous, and Addie's effort was a big help. Once away from the docks, they fell into rhythm and soon arrived at the *Vera B.*

Twilight had fallen, and no lantern had yet been lit on the deck. No watchman came to the side. Alice shivered. The boatswain steered them in until the boat's prow thunked against the ship's hull, where the rope ladder hung down. Jenny shipped her oar and grabbed one of the lower rungs.

21

Gypsy secured the launch and let Ned scramble quickly up the ladder. The rest of them followed. Alice went last, but for Gypsy. When she gained the deck, Hannah held the children back, and Jenny looked anxiously about the ship's waist.

"Do you mean there's *no one* on board?" Hannah asked.

"I'm afraid so." Alice had told her the gist of the day's events on the way out, but Hannah seemed to take in the gravity of it as they stood on the vacant deck.

Gypsy tossed the bag of fish over the bulwark and clambered aboard. He looked about to make sure nothing had been disturbed since they'd left.

"Go ahead to your cabins, ladies. I'll soon have supper cooking. Shall I lay the table in the officers' mess, ma'am?" He looked to Alice.

"Yes, thank you, Gypsy. I don't' wish to eat alone tonight, and it will be warmer in the 'tweendecks, anyway." She smiled wanly at Mrs. McKay. "This Australian winter is nothing like what we have in New England, but I do feel the chill these nights. I'll see you in an hour, and thank you all for your assistance with the rowing."

"You're welcome," Hannah said. "Come, Jenny. Ned, come down from there and get washed up."

Gypsy didn't wait to see where Ned had climbed to. He snatched up the sack and headed for the galley. He was concerned about Mrs. Packard. She must be exhausted. She hadn't told Mrs. McKay her financial situation, but she had that to consider. If they couldn't get another crew quickly, she would have to send the McKay family away, to seek passage on another ship. But he was quite certain that Mrs. Packard didn't have enough money left to refund their fares.

He sighed and entered the cook's domain, a small room built on the main deck, and lit a lantern. Not only was no coffeepot simmering, but the cookstove was cold and the galley empty. He limped over to the cupboard.

His bum leg ached after stumping about all afternoon looking for the crew. Years ago, a rogue wave had sent him plummeting from the ratlines, and he'd broken his leg badly. He'd held various positions on sailing vessels since, including cook. He blessed the day Captain Packard had taken him on as his steward and boatswain, in charge of the supplies, as well as tackle and maintenance of the ship, a job he vastly preferred. But he was more than capable of preparing supper for the six souls on board.

Reaching for the tin of lucifers, he stayed his hand. The quick-matches for starting the stove were kept in their protective tin, inside a hanging cupboard. Tonight the tin was partly open. Gypsy lifted it. One of the little fire sticks lay on the shelf behind it. Someone had been careless. Had one of the deserters taken a few lucifers with him? In that case, why hadn't he nabbed the whole tin?

He fired up the stove, which soon ticked cheerfully and put off a welcome warmth. In less than an hour, he had a large pot of coffee ready, as well as the fish, biscuits, and applesauce. It wasn't a feast, but he would do better tomorrow if need be. The cook had run a can of milk over the side on a line yesterday. Gypsy drew it up and set out tankards of milk for the McKay children.

The cook's job was usually one of the easiest to fill when hiring a crew, and he had no doubt Mrs. Packard could find one. If only she could find eight or ten able seamen, but the prospects for that were looking bleak.

CHAPTER THREE

When Alice awoke the next morning, the sky outside the cabin windows was still murky gray. Though she had dozed off and on, she still ached with fatigue. She sat up and gazed at her husband's side of the bed. Ruel! Without him, how would she make it through this day and the weeks and months to come?

She rose and dressed mechanically, putting on a plain woolen dress to ward off the cold. She spent a few minutes straightening the last of the disarray in the cabin, noting more and more items that were missing.

She wouldn't think about that. She would have to decide how to arrange her husband's things. It occurred to her that she might be less comfortable, but she could offer this roomy, pleasant cabin to Lady Dunbar and her maid as passengers. She could take a smaller one below for herself. Of course, if she hired a new crew, the sailing master might expect to have the captain's cabin. That was another matter on which Gypsy, a sailor for more than forty years, might have some wisdom. Only Gypsy knew her dire financial situation. His practical outlook might be helpful.

She found him in the galley, loading a basket with plates and flatware. Jenny stood at the stove, pouring flapjack batter.

"Jenny's cooking breakfast," Gypsy said.

"So I see." Alice smiled at the girl. "Thank you, Jenny. It's kind of you to step in."

"I don't mind," Jenny replied, flipping her long braid back over her shoulder. "I always helped Aunt Hannah at the farm. I'll have everything ready in just a few minutes."

Alice followed Gypsy out on deck and looked out over the harbor, blessedly calm this morning. "Look. See that boat?"

Gypsy stepped to the rail and followed her gaze, squinting into the morning sun. A small boat manned by half a dozen men had made its way between the moored vessels and glided closer. "They're headed this way. Looks like officers in the midst."

One of the men in the boat lifted a hand in greeting, and Alice's heart leaped.

"It's Captain Howard. He's paying a call!" Gypsy's face crumpled. "Ah, ma'am, we're mortified. We've no officers to greet the cap'n."

Alice tightened her jaw. "Nevertheless, we must do what we can to make him welcome. Captain Howard will understand."

"Yes, ma'am."

Alice spied Ned peeping around the mainmast. "I'll send Ned to ask Jenny to bring tea to my cabin. You greet them, Gypsy, while I put everything to rights."

She dispatched the boy and hurried into the cabin, set chairs for her guests, tucked a few items into the wardrobe and smoothed the quilt on the bed. The large chamber served as the captain's bedroom, dining room, study, and when he had guests, his parlor. Alice opened her chest. At least the deserters hadn't taken her good china. She hastily unwrapped three of the cups and saucers she had brought from home and set them on the table. No time to coach Jenny on using her ivy-entwined teapot and silver spoons.

Alice wished she had a black dress, but she had refused to pack one, despite her mother's advice. She had lost a baby six years ago, while Ruel was at sea.

"I won't go prepared to mourn again," she had told her mother firmly. Carrying a full set of mourning attire would be like admitting they might once more suffer loss.

But she had never expected to lose Ruel; to be widowed in a foreign land and have no proper clothing in which to greet his friends who came to console her.

She raised her chin. Ruel would not want her to rush out now and purchase a black gown. In fact, if he were alive, he

25

would tell her to don the bright dresses he loved to see her wear. He would hate it if she wore all black for a year and moped about in sorrow. He would tell her to cry a bit if she wished, but then to go on.

Alice hurried to the wardrobe and took out the gray silk shawl he had brought her from China on his first voyage after their marriage. She exchanged it for the plain blue knit one she'd had on and wrapped it about her shoulders. She strode out on deck just as Captain Howard and his chief mate climbed through the gate in the bulwark.

Alice held out her hand to Josiah with a smile. "Captain Howard! How kind of you to come."

"I hope I'm not too early." He eyed her a bit fretfully. "I heard about Ruel from the harbormaster, and I couldn't delay any longer."

Just the mention of her husband brought tears to Alice's eyes. "Thank you. If you and your mate would step into the cabin, we'll have tea shortly."

"Very good," Josiah said. "I believe you've met my first mate, Mr. Stark."

Alice extended her hand. "Good to see you again, sir."

"It's mutual, madam, but I am so sorry about the captain."

"Thank you. This way, gentlemen."

She led them into the cabin and urged them to sit with her at the small square table where she and Ruel had shared many meals.

"Is there anything I could help you with?" Josiah asked as soon as they were inside.

"How good of you. I wonder ... Mr. Deak might use some help in shipping our launch and jollyboat."

Josiah's eyebrows rose. "Of course. The men who brought us in the boat can help him. Mr. Stark?"

"Certainly." Stark rose and went out, closing the door behind him.

"Of course you're wondering why our own men haven't done it," Alice said.

"I did wonder when we came aboard and I saw no watch," Josiah admitted. "Have you had trouble?"

"I'm afraid so." Alice set silver spoons and linen napkins on the table as she told him about the desertion of the crew and the second mate's unfortunate encounter.

"We took Mr. McDarby ashore for medical aid yesterday," she said. "I fear we will have to leave him here when we sail."

After a brief knock, the door opened and Mr. Stark returned.

"Begging your pardon, ma'am," he said, "but I'm aghast. Mr. Deak told me your mate was waylaid by your own crew."

"I fear so," Alice said. "I was just telling Captain Howard about it."

"I'm appalled as well," Josiah said. "Please tell me what happened to your husband. Surely his death had nothing to do with this mutiny."

"No. He was ill when we left Adelaide. He wasn't feeling well that day, but he thought it would pass when we got out to sea. Over the next two days, his discomfort grew so acute that Mr. Boardman and I decided to put in at Port Phillip and seek out a surgeon." She paused to draw a deep breath.

"Of course," Josiah murmured.

"The physician declared it was appendicitis," Alice said. "Nothing could be done."

"How dreadful for you."

"Yes." Tears filled Alice's eyes as she remembered the way her husband had writhed and moaned. "His last words were, 'Boardman will take you home, my dearest. You must be brave.' He didn't think of himself, Captain, only my wellbeing."

"That's very like Ruel," Josiah said.

Stark nodded sympathetically, his expression dour.

"Well, it's over. If I had known you were so close behind us, I would have delayed the interment another day." Alice sighed. "And now, it seems my crew has abandoned me."

27

"All of them?" Stark said.

"Yes, and I am not alone. Other ships are advertising triple wages for able hands. You must post your most trusted men on guard to make sure your own crew does not leave you. Thousands seem to be fleeing their obligations for the goldfields."

"I left my men under close watch to begin the unloading," Josiah said.

A brisk knock announced Jenny and her aunt. Alice smiled ruefully. "Come in, ladies. Captain Howard, Mr. Stark, may I introduce Mrs. McKay and her niece? We are so desperate for hands that I've pressed my passengers into service this morning."

Josiah and Mr. Stark leaped to their feet.

"Good day, ladies," Josiah said.

Hannah set down the thick ironstone teapot they had used to brew the tea. "Thank you sir, but you must sit. Allow Jenny and me to pour your tea."

They served as well as any steward could have done, with Jenny constantly glancing toward her aunt for affirmation. As soon as all their cups were filled, Hannah looked to Alice, who nodded.

"Come, Jenny." Hannah took the tray and led her niece outside, closing the door behind them.

"So you are without any crew at all?" Josiah asked.

"None but Mr. Deak. He's proved his worth a hundred times to me in the last forty-eight hours." Alice sat back with a small sigh. "I can scarcely believe the rest have betrayed me. Gypsy and I went into Melbourne yesterday afternoon, hoping to find some of them, but it was not to be."

"You've a full cargo?" Josiah asked.

"Yes. Ruel brought a load of lumber and manufactured goods from Massachusetts, and we took on wool and wheat in Adelaide, along with some sundries. A little eucalyptus, some whale oil."

"My cargo is mostly mining tools and supplies," Josiah said. "I left off quite a load of farming equipment in Adelaide, but back in Boston I'd heard about the frenzy here, so I stocked up on picks, shovels, gold pans, boots, tents—whatever the Forty-niners would have wanted a few years ago."

"That was wise," Alice said. "You can get any price you ask, from what I hear."

Josiah nodded. "The harbormaster tells me we can sell it as fast as we can unload it, which is what we'll be doing today and tomorrow."

Alice realized he would not be able to help her immediately. Of course he must tend to his business first. And Josiah would need every one of his men to unload the cargo and take on new. Her vague hopes that he might lend her a few men evaporated.

"What can I do to best help you, ma'am?" he asked.

"I'm not sure you can do anything, sir. Mr. Deak and I will manage."

"But you're without resources. Forgive me, but how will you hire a new crew if you have no funds?"

"I'm not sure yet," Alice admitted. "I shall have to promise good wages at the end of the voyage, I suppose."

"They'll expect a bonus before they'll sign on, I fear." Josiah reached inside his fine broadcloth jacket and took out a wallet. "I don't carry much on me, but let me give you what I have." He took out a few bills and laid them on the table.

"Oh, I couldn't." Alice's face heated.

"You must," Josiah said firmly.

Mr. Stark had the grace to look away and sip his tea.

She realized it would be foolish to turn down this kindness and tucked the money between the folds of her skirt.

"Thank you, Captain. I shall repay you when we meet again."

"Not necessary. Now, dear lady, let me put forward a suggestion. Why don't you sail back to the States with me?"

"But the brig and cargo! I can't abandon Collins Shipping's property. I have an obligation—"

29

"No, my dear. Your husband had an obligation. I dare say you have no contract with Collins yourself."

She was tempted to agree. It would be so much easier. And yet, she knew she would never forgive herself if she didn't try her hardest to honor Ruel's trust. "That may be true, but I can hardly walk away from it. Not only would they lose a great deal of money, but my husband's name would be sullied."

Mr. Stark set his teacup down on the saucer with a clink. "Perhaps Captain Howard and I can help find you a new crew."

"Yes," Josiah said. "If it's within my power, I will do that very thing. As soon as my cargo is attended to."

"Thank you," she said. "I fully intend to man this ship and take her home."

A hasty knock was followed by Ned throwing open the cabin door.

"What is it, Ned?" Alice asked, taking in his tumbled hair and flushed face.

"Gypsy and the cap'n's men are finished with the boats."

"Here," Stark said, frowning. "That's a cheeky lad."

Josiah said, not unkindly, "Mr. Stark is right, boy. You should address Mrs. Packard as ma'am, and refer to the boatswain as Mr. Deak. He is, after all, your elder."

Ned grinned. "I'll say. Sorry, ma'am. But they're all done."

"Thank you, Mr. McKay." As Ned left, Alice gazed at Josiah. "I appreciate the help."

"Think nothing of it." Josiah drained his teacup and pushed back his chair. "Now, let us get on with our business. Perhaps my officers and I can drum up some crewmen for you after we finish unloading."

"I'd be grateful if you could."

He nodded. "I shall come to you again when I'm free. Probably tomorrow evening, if that suits you."

"It suits me fine."

Alice escorted them out onto the deck, where Ned stood beside Gypsy by the rail. She had never seen the boy so quiet.

30

"Your boat is ready, sir," Gypsy said to Captain Howard.

"Very good." Josiah bent over Alice's hand. "Again, my condolences."

"My sympathies, madam," Mr. Stark murmured.

"Thank you, gentlemen. It means a great deal, knowing there are friends in port."

Alice stood beside Gypsy until both men were in their boat and the oarsmen shoved off. She waved and turned away. "Captain Howard has a cargo to unload, but he promised to call again tomorrow evening. I fear it's up to us to fit this ship to sail, though the captain did give me a few dollars. We can try to lure in a few sailors with it."

"Well, ma'am, I know you hoped to weigh anchor today, but that's not to be. Perhaps we can get a few men and sail up the coast to another port, not so near the gold strikes."

Alice's lips twitched. "Captain Howard suggested I abandon ship myself and sail home on the *Jade Maiden*."

Gypsy's eyes narrowed. "You wouldn't."

"No, I wouldn't. Besides, we have those crates to deliver to Brisbane."

"Aye, the special cargo," Gypsy said.

"Now, more than ever, we need to make that delivery. What we receive for it will be my own money, Gypsy. It was my husband's private venture. If we succeed, we'll have funds to replenish our provisions when needed and to meet any emergencies. But first we must find the crew to get us there."

"Ahoy, *Vera B.*!"

"Mr. Deak! Ma'am!" Ned, who had climbed into the ratlines of the lower mainmast, pointed downward into the harbor. "There's a rowboat coming!"

Alice and Gypsy rushed to the rail.

"Ahoy," called a man seated in a dinghy while another plied the oars. "Be there a Mrs. Packard aboard?"

"Aye," Gypsy said.

Alice raised her hand. "I am Mrs. Packard."

31

"I've a message for you, ma'am."

CHAPTER FOUR

Gypsy watched Mrs. Packard's face as she opened the note the messenger had brought. The man stood near the rail, waiting for a reply, but also, Gypsy knew, waiting for recompense. He wasn't sure Mrs. Packard had any coins to give him, and his own pockets were empty.

Mrs. Packard looked up, folding the slip of paper and creasing it with her fingers. "Thank you. Please say that I will do as this says."

The man touched his forelock but lingered.

"Oh!" Color surged to Mrs. Packard's cheeks. "Wait here." She bustled into her cabin and returned a moment later. She passed something into the man's outstretched hand.

As soon as he was over the side, she turned to Gypsy. "It was from Carrie O'Dell."

Gypsy frowned. "Badgering you for a place on board, no doubt. That woman is no good."

"Fares from a couple more passengers might give us some needed funds. Other than what Captain Howard gave me, that fellow got my last cent."

Gypsy sighed. "The mates won't like it if you give up all their cabins, ma'am."

"I know. It may make it harder to sign on officers, if we don't get back those we've lost." She looked him full in the face. "Carrie wants me to meet her at a hotel on the same street as the Boar's Tusk. While I am with her, can you take Captain Howard's money and see about scaring up some new hands?"

"Gladly, ma'am. When are we going?"

33

"As soon as possible. She said eleven o'clock—six bells. We'll have to hire a buggy again, or we won't make it in time, but thanks to Captain Howard, we have the means."

Gypsy had to admire her spirit. "Would you think Mrs. McKay and her brood might stay aboard?" he asked.

"She's willing, but I must get out a pistol for her. Her husband taught her to shoot. We mustn't leave the ship unattended with the rough element among the argonauts."

Gypsy hadn't the slightest idea what she was talking about, and it must have shown on his face.

"The gold seekers," Mrs. Packard amended.

"Ah. Right. If you'll speak to Mrs. McKay, I'll get the boat ready, then."

"My friend is desperate."

Carrie leaned close over the table, and Alice tried not to let her nose wrinkle as the powerful fumes of perfume hit her.

"I'm so sorry. I told you our space is limited." Alice took a bite of the mutton pie Carrie had ordered before her arrival at the hotel. Apparently the barmaid had a good haul the previous evening, and she had insisted on treating Alice to a hearty lunch. Only a couple of other people had come into the dining room for an early meal, and they had comparative privacy, but Carrie flicked frequent glances toward the door. She had chosen to sit facing it, and Alice surmised that she feared her boss or one of his cronies walking in and observing their meeting.

"Yes, but you don't understand. Kate is … Look, she hasn't a penny, nor any family. Con Snyder got hold of her."

"Who is he?" Alice asked.

"He owns the brothel on the next street—Dame Nell's."

"Dame Nell's?" Alice said doubtfully.

She nodded. "Sort of an ironic name, you might say. It's called after his mistress, but make no mistake—Con's the one

34

who runs the business. Nell looks after the girls for him, and she keeps an eagle eye on them."

"About this Kate," Alice said.

"Con forced her to work for him. She hates it, and she'd do anything to leave. She's had a very hard life, even as a child. I could tell you tales."

"I'm sure." Alice sipped her tea, thinking. She couldn't possibly take a prostitute aboard the *Vera B.* Perhaps it would be best to give a flat no to both Carrie and her friend. Bringing a barmaid and a woman of the street on board would cause no end of trouble with the crewmen.

"Miss O'Dell, I don't think we can possibly do it."

"She can pay," Carrie said. "Same as me."

"I thought she didn't have a cent."

Carrie waved a hand in dismissal. "In a manner of speaking. She's put by a bit, but Con would flog her if he knew she'd held out on him. And we'll stay out of the way, ma'am. I know what you're thinking. The sailors would be all over us."

"Well ..."

Carrie shook her head adamantly. "We'd dress plain and keep to our cabin, I promise. You can call us whatever you like. We could dress as widows, maybe, and not speak to anyone because of our wretched grief. That would keep them away from us, wouldn't it?"

Speechless, Alice gazed into Carrie's lovely blue eyes. She couldn't imagine this bird of bright plumage successfully masquerading as a mourning widow for long. Her instincts would have her flirting with the sailors in no time.

"Or nuns even. That might be better. We could do it," Carrie insisted.

"But we don't have another cabin for your friend."

"We'll share. And there's something else." Carrie glanced toward the door. "About your crew."

"You've learned something?" Alice's hand shook, and she put down her teacup. She had no right to feel angry with Carrie,

35

but at that moment she would have enjoyed slapping her. Why had she gone on about her friend when she had important news about the men?

"It's as we feared. They've gone to the goldfields, the whole pack of 'em. I heard it from a fisherman. They left a boat near the Anderson dock. If I were you, I'd go fetch it, or it's like to disappear."

"I'll have Gypsy do that."

Carrie frowned at her. "If you don't mind me asking, what's that old duffer to you? He takes your orders right enough."

Alice looked down at her half-finished meal. "He's the ship's boatswain, and my husband—" She raised her gaze to Carrie's. "My husband was the captain."

"Was?"

"Yes. He died two nights past, and we buried him in St. Kilda."

Carrie sat back in her chair. "Now I understand. You're as desperate as we are, aren't you, ma'am?"

Alice felt her cheeks heat. "I'm sure we'll manage. Now, won't you let me pay for my portion of the meal?"

"Oh, no. That's on me, Mrs. Packard. And I'm sorry, truly, about the cap'n. And now your crew has jumped ship. I guess we women are all in hard times. The one thing I want most in all the world is just to be taken back to Ireland. But you'll be lucky to get home yourself."

Alice hesitated. "I intend to take the *Vera B.* home. I've only to man it, and I have friends working on that. But the ship isn't built for passengers, Miss O'Dell."

"I might be able to drum up a few men for you, if the pay was right."

"That … that would be a big help. I'd pay good wages, but at the end of the voyage."

Carrie sighed. "No doubt they'd want enough for a good lash at the tavern before they came aboard."

"I couldn't. They'd likely take the money and get drunk and never show up to work."

Carrie nodded. "Well, I'll ask about anyway. Might be some boys wanting to go to America who'd wait for the pay." She smiled suddenly. "If you took a few paying passengers, you could use that money to hire more men."

"Yes," Alice said slowly.

"Kate and I, we could tuck up in hammocks on the deck, or even below in the cargo, ma'am. Couldn't be any worse than how I came over."

"Oh, no, it wouldn't do."

"Well, you think on it. And I didn't mention it before, but there's other girls over to Dame Nell's who would work themselves to death to get out of Con Snyder's clutches. If you had room, you could make your fortune taking on passengers." Carrie's eyes darted to the doorway, and she jerked her chin in that direction. "There's your bo'sun."

Alice turned, relieved to see Gypsy limping toward them.

"Sit down," she said. "What news?"

Gypsy took a seat, shaking his head. "I couldn't get anyone, though I tried my best."

Alice's spirits plunged. "Maybe Captain Howard will have more success."

"P'raps."

Carrie pushed back her chair and stood. "I must get back, or Tom will miss me. Get your man something to eat." She dropped two coins on the table and whisked out the door before Alice could protest.

"Well, that's right nice of her," Gypsy said.

"I fear she's trying to bribe me." Alice eyed the coins with misgivings, but Gypsy scooped them up.

"Bribe you to what? Take her on the ship?"

"Yes—and her friend, too. Seems she knows a—a shady woman who also wants to escape her situation."

"Oho! Bad business, that."

37

"Yes, but she did say she'd try to scare up some sailors for us. You might as well eat, Gypsy, since she's gone and we don't want to chase her back to the tavern. Then we must be going, or I'll be late for my appointment with Lady Dunbar."

Alice's meeting with the aristocrat didn't go any better than the one with Carrie, and she came away feeling that she might have better spent her time putting up broadsides advertising for crewmen. She left the tearoom and walked down to St. Kilda's docks, glad to see Gypsy sitting with his back against a barrel, smoking a pipe. When he saw Alice approaching, he scrambled to his feet and doffed his cap.

"I got the dinghy back here, ma'am."

"That's the best news I've had all day." Alice let out a big sigh. "I told Lady Dunbar we couldn't take her, though she offered me double the usual fare."

Gypsy nodded. "Don't ask me where we'll get a crew, ma'am. I asked all around the village, but I heard the same thing everywhere I went. A dozen ships are in the same predicament we are. Hands are hard to come by." He stooped and picked up a string of fish.

"What's this?" Alice asked.

"Oh, I met that fisher girl Mrs. McKay told about and gave her the change I had left from the tavern. Norwegian she is. Apparently the story's true—she lives on her own and fishes for her living. And you'll never guess what she asked me."

Alice eyed him for a moment. "Of course. She wants passage with us."

Gypsy barked a laugh. "You've hit it, ma'am. Even said she could work the sails and rigging with the best of our men if we needed an extra tar."

Alice shook her head. "Why is it that so many women want to leave Australia, and so few men? Lady Dunbar even put in her bit again about sailing her father's yacht. She said much the same thing—she could give a hand in a pinch."

Gypsy's eyes rolled heavenward. "Imagine ladies climbing the shrouds and reefing the sails." He laughed.

Alice put out a hand. "Wait. Maybe hiring the Norwegian girl isn't such a bad idea."

"What?" Gypsy's eyes all but popped out of his head. "Where would you keep her, ma'am? And you can't put girls to work with men! Why, she's no more than fifteen or sixteen. Younger than Jenny McKay."

"But you said she's a good sailor."

"No, I didn't say it, ma'am. *She* did. To hear her tell it, her father drowned a couple of years back, and she's been on her own ever since. Has a dinghy with a sail, and she takes it out every day to fish. Catches salmon and bream in the Rip, if you can believe it."

"Is she strong and healthy?" Alice asked.

"I suppose so, but you can't—"

"Think about it. Gypsy, we won't get Boardman and the others back. All our men are gone. It's time we faced reality."

"No." Gypsy backed away. "Mrs. Packard, if you even think about hiring that girl as a jack tar, you'll have to say good-bye to me. It's not natural, ma'am."

Alice sighed and pinched the bridge of her nose. "I know you're right, Gypsy, but what can I do? We've got half a dozen women practically begging us for passage. If they were willing to work—"

"Women? Sailing the brig?" Gypsy's face was a thundercloud.

"Can you think of a better solution? Captain Howard can't give me any of his men. How many able seamen would we need, at a minimum, to sail the *Vera B.*?"

Gypsy spluttered out a breath. "I suppose a dozen good men would be able to take her home."

"Absolute minimum?"

39

"Well, ten, then, or in a tight spot eight might do it, with the officers jumping in to help in a gale, but it would be watch and watch, and if we lost even one man, or if anyone got sick—and, ma'am, I'm talking about seasoned crewmen who know what they're doing. Not grass-green girls and uppity ladies who've never worked a day in their lives."

"You're right, of course." She dredged up a smile. "We'll figure something out. I'm sure God will not forsake us here on this bleak shore. Now, we must get the dinghy back to the ship."

"Aye. Maybe—" Gypsy broke off and peered down the shore. "There's the girl, ma'am. See her walking at the high water line?"

At first Alice supposed the tall, lithe young person she spotted was a lad, but she soon noticed the long, pale braid hanging over one shoulder.

"Heavens! Is it safe for her to go about so boldly alone?"

"Probably not, but she's done it for some time now. I imagine she has ways of defending herself."

Alice's heart went out to the girl. "I'd like to meet her."

Sonja pulled up short when she heard her name called. She squinted toward the docks beneath the brim of her cap. The gray-haired boatswain from the *Vera B.* was beckoning to her, the one who called himself Gypsy. She hoped he wasn't going to complain about the fish she'd sold him earlier. He'd told her he had only a few cents, and American coins at that, but had added a twist of tobacco, which she knew she could sell. She'd liked him and given him a better price than she normally would for the fresh salmon.

Next to him stood a beautiful woman in a dress of good blue cloth, with a long, gray cloak over her shoulders. Her bright hair gleamed in the sun. Hesitantly, Sonja walked toward Gypsy and

40

the lady. She stopped three paces from them and nodded to Gypsy.

"Hello, Sonja. Mrs. Packard wanted to meet you."

Sonja gulped. This must be the widow of the poor, dead captain she'd heard about. She looked sad, but she smiled graciously.

"We enjoyed your catch yesterday, Sonja. I'm very pleased to meet you."

"How do, ma'am." Sonja felt suddenly self-conscious in her duck trousers and loose shirt. She glanced down at her bare feet.

"Mr. Deak tells me you have your own boat and fish in the bay."

Sonja glanced quickly at Gypsy. Was "Mr. Deak" his true name? She cleared her throat. "Yes'm, I do. Are you with the brig yonder?"

"Yes."

Sonja nodded. "I'd like to sail on her, ma'am."

The woman looked at Gypsy, and Sonja was sure he had already told her this. "We don't take many passengers, I'm afraid."

"But I'd work, ma'am. And I could sell my dinghy. With that and what I've saved from my fishing, I think I could pay for my passage. Whatever I owed, I could work off."

The lady opened her mouth, and Sonja rushed on before she could refuse.

"My father had a little sloop, ma'am. I'm very good at handling sails, though I've never worked on a big ship. I can paint and scrub and mend sail. And I could catch fish for your crew to eat." A sudden thought made her even bolder. "I know this bay better'n just about anyone, too. I could save you the cost of a pilot going out the Rip."

The woman blinked as though startled by this information.

"Are you sure?" she asked.

41

"Oh, yes'm. I know its currents and channels, and how it is when the tide rushes out. I know every inch of the bottom, ma'am. Fishing, you have to."

The woman's lips parted, but it was Gypsy who spoke. "You afraid of heights?"

Sonja's heart leaped. He was actually considering it.

"No, sir, not me. I've mostly been on small boats, but I can climb."

Mrs. Packard frowned. "I suppose you want to go back to Norway."

Sonja shook her head. "I've an uncle in America. He took his family there, and he fishes out of a place called Gloucester. Do ye know it?"

"Aye," said Gypsy. He took a pull from his pipe.

Mrs. Packard added, "I know it well. 'Tis quite a fishing town."

"After Pa died, I wrote, and my uncle said he'd send me money to go there," Sonja said. "But it hasn't come, in nearly two years."

"I'm sorry."

Mrs. Packard's kind voice wrenched Sonja's heart. She hadn't meant to reveal so much. She never told anyone her financial circumstances. She haunted the post office, but even the postmaster didn't know she hoped for funds to take her to America.

"Who do you live with now?" Mrs. Packard asked.

"Meself." It was mostly true. Early on, several locals had helped her after her father died, but since most of the English people were too busy or poor to take her in, she had mostly been on her own until making friends with Jin Laohu, a respectable elder within the shanty community of Chinese fishermen. The generous man had protected her and taken her in like an adopted daughter, but she never felt at home ashore and rarely stayed overnight among the Chinese.

Mrs. Packard's eye's narrowed. "Where do you live?"

42

Sonja clamped her lips together. These people had no business knowing she spent most nights dozing in her dinghy, anchored in a secluded cove.

Gypsy and Mrs. Packard looked at each other, and Sonja held her breath.

Gypsy threw up his hands. "Where on earth would we put 'er?"

The lady seemed to struggle for a moment then turned to Sonja with another of her lovely smiles. "Would you excuse us for a moment? I need to speak privately with Mr. Deak."

"Surely." Sonja walked a few yards away and hunkered down on the beach. She wasn't letting them out of her sight until she had an answer.

Jenny stood near the foremast, watching Ned and Addie race about the capstan. Across the ship's waist, Aunt Hannah emerged from the main hatch. Their sleeping cabins were down there between the decks. The captain's cabin was the only one completely above decks, with actual windows looking out on the harbor. Jenny had been inside it when they served the tea. It was roomy and luxurious compared to the cramped cells they occupied below.

"See anyone?" Aunt Hannah asked.

"Nary a soul." Jenny and Aunt Hannah had agreed that one of them should stay on deck all the time while Mrs. Packard and Gypsy were ashore, in case someone else came to call.

Addie's skirts twisted about her legs, and she stumbled. Ned pounced, slapped her back, and shouted, "You're in!" He danced away toward the cat head, from which the anchor cable fell.

"Do you think Mr. Deak will keep watch all night tonight?" Jenny asked her aunt.

"I wouldn't be surprised. Mrs. Packard might even take a turn. They're determined to keep this ship from being plundered again, and they've a valuable cargo in the hold." Aunt Hannah looked toward St. Kilda. "Now, Jenny, if anyone approaches, send Ned to get me. I'm going to try and get a nap, in case I'm needed tonight."

"Sure," Jenny said.

Ned stopped running and saluted his mother. "Aye, aye, ma'am."

Hannah smiled. "Thank you, McKay," she said in her most formal tone.

As Hannah walked toward the hatch, Addie crept up behind Ned and slapped the back of his head. "You're in!" She darted away.

Jenny smiled and leaned back against the foremast. She hoped it would be warmer tonight. The brig had no heat, and a June night in Victoria could make your toes turn blue.

She was glad the weather was fair, even if it was chilly.

She could barely remember her voyage to Australia as a child. Her family had come full of dreams of a bright future. Her father and his brother had planned to build a farm together that would support their families. Those plans began to crumble when Jenny's mother died on the ship, along with the tiny baby she had birthed. Two years later, when the farm near Gawler was starting to prosper, her father drowned in the river while trying to rescue a heifer calf.

Aunt Hannah and Uncle Alton had become her parents, and little Addie a sister. Later Ned was born. It had been so long ago that Jenny found it hard to remember her mother's face.

Now Uncle Alton was gone, and they were sailing for England. Aunt Hannah had two sisters there, and the McKay brothers had kin, too. Her aunt had assured her their relatives in Yorkshire would welcome them warmly. With a sigh, Jenny gazed toward Melbourne. The city looked raw and dirty by daylight, but last night in the moonlight, it had twinkled with magic.

Jenny hated to leave Australia. She'd loved the farm, and the wildness all around them. Before Uncle Alton died, Aunt Hannah

44

spoke often of the freedom they'd gained by coming here and the blessing of owning land.

Though the farming community was spread out, the McKays considered the closest neighbors their friends. The nearest neighbor's son, Willie Cliborne, flashed through her mind. He was a year younger than Jenny, but they were good friends. Willie had been heartbroken when she told him they were going back to England. She had allowed a quick hug in farewell, but turned away when he tried to kiss her. Now she almost wished she had let him. She'd be nineteen by the time she got to Yorkshire and made new friends—other than sailors, of course. But Aunt Hannah had warned her about sailors. When they reached England, would she be considered an old maid that no men would want to court?

At Addie's cry, she turned and peered toward the prow. Ned was up on the bowsprit, arms extended, walking a precarious path toward its tip.

"Come back," Addie called, her voice higher than normal.

Jenny strode toward them. "You, Ned McKay, get back here! I'll not have you falling in the drink—not on my watch!"

Scowling, Ned pivoted gracefully and ran back down the bowsprit, hopping onto the deck at the bottom.

"Jenny, if the first mate's deserted and the second mate's too beat up to work, who's going to run this ship?"

Jenny hesitated. "I don't know, Ned. If Mrs. Packard can't hire a new crew, I suppose we'll have to move to a different ship."

"Or not go to England after all?" Addie asked, her eyes large with hope.

Jenny considered that. Aunt Hannah had signed over her rights to the farmland and taken money equal to what she and Uncle Alton had already paid on it. "We haven't money to buy another farm. And your mother gave most of what she had to Captain Packard for our passage." She didn't mention Aunt

Hannah's suggestion that they might find jobs as seamstresses or housemaids in England.

"Well, if we have to find another ship, Mrs. Packard will give our money back, won't she?" Addie asked.

Jenny smiled in relief. "Of course she will. Now, stop worrying."

CHAPTER FIVE

"Gypsy, I think we must consider this. It could be the Lord's provision. If Carrie O'Dell and her friend could—"

"What? No! You can't mean it." Gypsy's eyes were a troubled gray, and his mouth held an injured quirk.

"If we could get ten of this girl ..."

"But those women you're talking about, they're not like her. They only know one kind of work, and it's not the backbreaking labor of a ship. They'd give you all sorts of problems."

"They're desperate. Carrie said she and her friend would do anything."

He shook his head and knocked the ash out of his pipe against one of the dock's pilings. "Women like that on the ship? It would never do!"

"Why not?" Alice asked. "We could train them."

"We?" He eyed her suspiciously.

Alice hesitated. "Well, yes. You could drill them for a few days here in the harbor. If Lady Dunbar and Sonja are as experienced as they claim, they can help. I can teach a couple of them to take sightings and figure our position. We could make them mates. Hannah and Jenny could help too. I could refund their passage fare when we reach England. With Lady Dunbar and her maid, Carrie and her friend, that's seven right there, besides you and me. Surely we can find a few more strong, willing women—In fact, Carrie mentioned that several others from the brothel wish to leave."

Gypsy's face was bright red behind his beard, and he seemed to have lost the power of speech.

Alice patted his sleeve. "There, now, Gypsy, I didn't mean to overset you. Think about it, would you? And I shall pray." She had been praying nonstop about the crew ever since the first inkling that some of her men might have deserted, but this new idea was a totally different ball of wax. She gazed into the faithful man's eyes. "One way or another, for my husband's sake, I intend to take the brig home. And I need you, Gypsy."

He let out a long, slow breath. "Very good, ma'am."

"You mean you wouldn't leave me?"

"What? No, ma'am! Besides, what would the likes of me do in the goldfields with this bad leg? No, I'm afraid you're stuck with me, Mrs. Packard, whether I like your scheming or no."

"Don't you think we could sign Sonja?" Alice prodded. She knew Gypsy hated the idea of women working the sails, but in honesty, the plan looked better and better to her.

Gypsy looked toward where the girl crouched, waiting for their verdict. "She'd probably be all right, but the men …"

"Without men, that wouldn't be a problem. You see? It would be much simpler to have a crew of women. We could put them in the forecastle, and you could have the second mate's cabin."

"Oh, I suppose they'd trick the fo'castle out with poseys and ribbons." Gypsy grimaced. "You don't expect the Duchess to sleep in there, do you?"

"You mean Lady Dunbar?" It was a question that had nagged at Alice. "It might be possible to divide my cabin in half."

Gypsy's jaw dropped.

"I'm still thinking about it," Alice admitted. "But if she and her maid had half—Well, I think her sailing experience would be worth it. I've lost hope of getting our men back, Gypsy. If any return wanting their jobs back, they'll have to swear good behavior and adapt to our new conditions—or find another place." Until she spoke the words, Alice hadn't realized the decision was firm.

"It would take a year to train those women," Gypsy moaned.

"Well, we don't have a year. A week at most. What do you say?"

He shook his head. "Since you've asked my opinion, I think it's a mistake."

"Let's invite Sonja aboard so she can see the brig. We might get an idea of how much she really knows. And I can put the idea to Hannah and Jenny, to see what they think."

"But they know nothing about sailing!"

"Not yet, they don't." Alice smiled. "If they sign on as crew, they soon will."

"The kids," Gypsy protested.

"Cabin boys," Alice said decisively. "I'm sure we'd have plenty of able cooks. Come, let's give Sonja the news." Alice walked toward the girl, and to her relief, Gypsy kept pace.

Sonja stood, her breathing shallow and her face a pale mask.

"Would you like to visit the *Vera B.* and see what it's like?" Alice asked.

Sonja's lower lip trembled. "Very much, ma'am. Should I get my things?"

Alice glanced at Gypsy. "I think … yes, you may do that." Her mind whirled with where she would put Sonja if they wound up with a partly male crew after all.

"Oh, ma'am, thank you!"

The agony of Alice's decision splintered before the relieved smile on Sonja's face.

Gypsy put on the cleanest of his two shirts the next morning, trimmed his beard, and combed his shaggy hair—though why he should bother to clean up to pay a call on a barmaid was beyond him. If they had to use females, he wished they could get more young women like that Sonja Frantzen. Now, there was a gal who might turn out to be useful. Her first words on boarding the brig had been, "How much does she draw, sir?" With Jenny McKay joining them, Gypsy had taken her over the ship. While Jenny seemed interested and a little nervous,

Sonja had observed everything and asked a hundred questions. If only every lad who took up sailing started out with such an eager outlook.

No one had disturbed them during the night, and Mrs. Packard had taken a turn at watch with Sonja. Gypsy had taken the midwatch, from midnight to four in the morning, and Hannah and Jenny had taken on the morning watch, with Gypsy spelling them while they made breakfast.

Though he still didn't like leaving the McKays alone on board, Gypsy felt a little easier after the quiet night. He had put a brace of loaded pistols in Hannah's trust, and now Gypsy and Sonja rowed ashore with Mrs. Packard. Great plans were buzzing between Hannah and Jenny to prepare a special meal for Captain Howard's visit that evening. When they touched shore, Sonja secured the boat and hurried off down the beach to where she had left her own dinghy.

"I hope she can get a good price for her boat on short notice," Alice said.

Gypsy watched the boyish form. Dressed in sailor's garb, she would pass for a young tar. He could only hope the other women Mrs. Packard was considering would take to sea life as well.

"She said one of her Chinese friends would likely buy it. She wanted to say farewell to them anyhow."

"Very good. And if she can't sell it, we might consider taking it as an extra boat. We could either pay her later or return it to her when she leaves us." Mrs. Packard squared her shoulders. "Are you ready?"

Gypsy frowned. He would never be ready to strike a business arrangement with the girl from the Boar's Tusk, but the decision wasn't his to make. He would protect and support Mrs. Packard as best he could. He only hoped this course would not destroy them all.

"Aye, ma'am."

He left Mrs. Packard at the hotel down the street and ambled on to the pub to summon Carrie O'Dell. Only a few die-hard drinkers were inside the Boar's Tusk this morning. Tom Larson and a couple of his employees were sweeping the place down and washing the glasses from the night before.

Gypsy knew better than to ask outright for Carrie, so he bought a glass of ale and made it last nearly half an hour. At last one of the bar girls came over to his table and asked if she could get him another drink.

"Be the one called Carrie O'Dell about today?" Gypsy asked.

The girl's eyebrows arched. "You want to see her?"

Gypsy glanced over his shoulder to make sure Larson wouldn't hear. "Not me, but there's a lady would like to speak to her. She's sipping tea at the hotel."

"I might drop a word in Carrie's ear."

Gypsy took this to be a hint for a coin. He gave her one, which Mrs. Packard had supplied from Captain Howard's gift. "I'll tell the lady to expect her." He put on his cap and left the tavern.

He and Mrs. Packard waited some time before Carrie, in rose-colored silk and a lace shawl, entered the hotel. She strode to their table, her face flushed.

"Mrs. Packard! You've found a place for me?"

"I believe I have, if you've a mind to work hard."

"Work? What do you mean, ma'am? Shall I cook on the ship? I'm willing." Carrie sat down and smoothed her skirts.

"You said you had half a dozen or more women who would do anything to leave this place."

"It's true, ma'am." Carrie's forehead wrinkled. "What are you getting at?"

"Are they healthy and strong? Can they do a hard day's work?"

"Most of them, I expect. What sort of work?"

"Sailor's work."

Carrie sat very still, eyeing Mrs. Packard as if she didn't trust her ears.

51

Mrs. Packard folded her hands on the table. "We've been unable to hire a new crew. If your women want to go to England or America, they'll have to work their way there as seamen would. That way, they would save their fares and would have a bit of money on the other end to help them get started in a new life."

Slowly, a smile spread across Carrie's face. She was very pretty, Gypsy realized. With the proper clothes, she might be taken for a lady, though her blonde locks were a bit too bright to be natural.

"I can't speak for Kate's lot, but I'm willing." Her expression clouded for a moment. "Would we have to climb clear up to the top of the masts?"

"That you would," Gypsy said, "but we'd start you out slow, with some drill in the harbor before we set out."

Carrie nodded. "Kate's game, I'm sure of it. She's not afraid of anything. I can't speak for the other women at Dame Nell's."

"It would be strenuous work," Mrs. Packard cautioned.

"I understand. Shall I see if I can go and get Kate to talk to you now? This time of day, most of them are sleeping."

"Are the women allowed to go about on their own?" Gypsy asked.

"Con's away now. He left Nell to keep the girls in line and earning while he's gone. She'd be asleep now, I've no doubt. They close the doors when the sun rises. I could get Kate."

"Is this the best place to meet her?" Mrs. Packard asked. "What if someone saw her talking to us?"

Carrie's lips set in a thin line and she nodded. "You may be right."

"We've got a buggy," Gypsy said. "It's not a closed carriage, but it's got a top. Tell Miss Robinson to wear a veil or a muffler over her face, and we'll drive about while we talk."

Mrs. Packard's face brightened. "Mr. Deak, if you give our driver an extra shilling, can he be persuaded to go and have a drink while we have this conference?"

Gypsy hesitated. He had spent nearly all his life on shipboard. "Who would drive then, ma'am?"

"I could," Carrie said.

Mrs. Packard smiled at her. "That's all right, then."

Carrie rose. "Fix it with your driver, and I'll have Kate back here soon.

"We'll be right outside," Mrs. Packard assured her.

The clandestine meeting seemed a little silly, until Alice reminded herself of the cruel men who held these women in their power.

Kate Robinson was a tall, handsome woman. Her dark hair peeping from beneath a powder blue angora scarf had a reddish glint, and her hazel eyes, though careworn, snapped with passion. She sat in the back seat of the buggy with Alice, while Gypsy sat up front beside Carrie, slouching and trying not to draw attention.

"I'll do anything you say, ma'am," Kate said. "Just get me away from Con Snyder. That man is our ruination."

"How did you come to ... to Dame Nell's?" Alice asked.

"He bought me."

Alice caught her breath. She had heard of such things, but had been shielded from actually seeing it.

Kate glanced about warily and leaned closer. "I was orphaned young, and went from place to place." She hesitated, as if determining how much to tell. "Eventually, a farmer and his wife took me in, but all they wanted was a slave. When the man died, I was mostly grown. Maybe thirteen or fourteen. His wife sold me, and I wound up in Con Snyder's tender care." She shuddered. "If he finds out I'm even thinking of running away, he'll kill me."

Alice gulped. This poor young woman! She couldn't imagine the horrors Kate had suffered throughout her short life. Did she

53

really want to be responsible for several women from abominable backgrounds? Gypsy turned on the seat and gave her a dark look.

"You must understand completely what I'm asking," Alice said. "Mr. Deak is a good man who would do you no harm. He is the only sailor I have left from our crew. The rest jumped ship for the goldfields. My husband died, and I must take the ship home safely. But I cannot hire men for it. They're all off hunting gold."

"Aye, I know about it," Kate said. "I see nuggets most every night. I've managed to pocket a few my customers gave me without Con finding out."

Alice decided to ignore this bit of lurid information. "If you and some of your friends are willing to risk it, I'll carry you and half a dozen more to England or America, whichever you like. We'll discharge our cargo in Liverpool and then cross the Atlantic to Boston. You won't have to pay me. In fact, at the end of the voyage you would collect a small wage."

Kate's eyes gleamed. "I'll do it, ma'am, and I won't disappoint you. I can work hard."

"What about your friends?" Alice asked. "It's not easy work. They have to be healthy and strong. I won't take any sickly or weak ones, or any that won't work hard."

Kate nodded as she listened.

"And they must take orders," Alice continued. "Mr. Deak and I will train you to do the work, but you must all sign a pledge saying you will do as we say until the end of the voyage. Then you will be free to go your ways to live as you please. I promise you, we'll treat you fairly and provide you with food and a bed—well, probably a hammock. It's dangerous work, and the living conditions will be difficult. Are you willing to accept that?"

"More than willing, ma'am. I welcome it."

Carrie swiveled around. "I told you! Kate's a great one for adventure."

Alice nodded, appraising the woman beside her. "Within days, your hands will blister and peel. You'll not wear fine clothes or eat dainty food. The life you leave may end up looking better."

"Not with our freedom at the end of it," Carrie said.

"That's right." Kate gazed soberly at Alice. "I'll work myself to death for you, ma'am, if I don't have to answer to any man."

Alice threw a troubled glance at Gypsy. Would she be able to keep order among a crew of women who had been abused and demeaned? She would need Gypsy's help, especially for the training.

"Mr. Deak will be an officer on my ship," she said carefully. "I assure you, he will not bother you or the other women. At this point, I doubt any of our other hands will return, but if we do take on any men, they will have to sign a pledge not to harm you. You and your friends will have to accept Mr. Deak's presence at least, and his superior knowledge of sailing if you are to learn the trade."

Kate sat quietly for a moment, gazing out the side of the buggy. At last she turned back to Alice. "I suppose so, if you swear no man will touch us."

"Not ... in that way." Alice nearly choked over the words.

Kate nodded. "When do we go aboard?"

"You'll have to get past Nell," Carrie said over her shoulder.

"That's so," Kate replied. "She's a tough one. Came here on a convict transport years ago, and she'd give us a good whipping if she caught us trying to leave. But I think we can manage it with some planning. Tomorrow about this time?"

"If you can be ready so soon," Alice's voice faltered. Why had Nell been transported with a shipful of felons? Had she engaged in crime in England and been deported? What sort of misdeeds had she committed that would make these young women afraid of her?

"We need to go while Con's away," Kate said. "He's gone to see about starting a new house in Ballarat, near the goldfields. If we don't get out before he returns, he'll send half of us there to cater to the diggers. But he'll be back soon. Maybe tomorrow or the next day."

"Then by all means, let's make haste," Alice said, shoving aside her qualms.

"Where do we meet?"

"Our ship is closer to St. Kilda. Can you get the women there?"

"It's a long way."

"It's too long a pull for our boat to come to the anchorage at Melbourne," Gypsy said. "We haven't the manpower."

Kate's mouth twisted. "But if someone saw us together and told Nell or Tom Larson—"

"We'll have to get the girls out by twos and threes," Carrie said. "I'll help you. You talk to them today, Kate. Only the ones who are fit and strong and want to leave Australia for good. No turning back. We'll sneak them out while Nell is getting her beauty rest."

"We'll need several days to drill once you're aboard," Gypsy said.

"We'll work it out, Mr. Deak," Alice assured him. "First we must get the women to the brig and clothe them such that the sailors anchored near us won't realize our new crew is made up of females."

Gypsy muttered something unintelligible.

"Perhaps I can hire a wagon tomorrow," Alice said, planning as she spoke. Sonja would be the perfect accomplice in this maneuver. "Carrie and I will settle on a place where we'll meet."

"Not too close to Nell's," Kate said.

Alice nodded. "A street or two over, perhaps. Send them in small groups. Mr. Deak can wait at the docks in St. Kilda and row you to the *Vera B.* Kate, tell the women not to pack a lot of fancy clothes or cosmetics. Each may bring only what she can carry. Gowns and perfume will do them no good on this voyage."

Kate inhaled deeply, her shoulders straightening. "I'll tell them. I've got four girls in mind for sure, and one or two possibles. We'll be there tomorrow, ma'am."

CHAPTER SIX

"A boy brought word that Lady Dunbar and her maid will board at three o'clock," Hannah announced as soon as Alice's feet touched the deck of the *Vera B*.

"Oh, dear. So quickly." Alice patted her hair.

"What if she won't agree to ship as a sailor?" Hannah asked. "Will you still take them?"

"We can't. That's all there is to it. If she and Miss Henshaw won't sign up, we'll have to turn them down. We'll need our cabins for our mates, not for passengers who won't work." Alice realized that might sound condescending, in light of Hannah's recent change in status. "Forgive me. I didn't mean you and Jenny. As things stood when you came aboard, of course we would have—"

"No need to apologize," Hannah said with a smile. "We understand your situation. Thank you for allowing Jenny and me to hire on. It will save us a great deal of money, and I expect it will be good experience. Of course ..." She flicked a glance toward the hatch. "I don't know how things will go, having Jenny and the children exposed to these fallen women you hope to take on."

"They're all women who want to leave that wicked life," Alice said. "I don't think they'll romanticize it to the young people."

Hannah nodded. "I shall be proud to serve as your carpenter and whatever other duties you put me to, ma'am. But for now, I beg you to take off your hat and sit down in your cabin for lunch. Jenny and I have prepared a meal that I hope you'll find tasty."

Alice squeezed her hand. "Thank you so much. Do you mind helping Gypsy prepare for Captain Howard's visit this evening?"

"We have already begun working on the menu, but you must stop asking me if I mind this and that, Mrs. Packard."

"I —" Alice stopped, not knowing whether to apologize or not.

Hannah chuckled. "I'm your employee now, ma'am. Give me orders as you would a jack tar."

"This is all so new to me, I confess. I never gave orders, you see. My husband did that, and the mates. I just lived among them."

"And that has changed now." Hannah took her arm and steered her toward her cabin. "I'm sure Captain Packard was a fine example of how you must now conduct yourself. I'll tell Jenny you are ready for your luncheon."

"Thank you." Alice entered the cabin, removed her long hatpin, and laid her hat on the bed. Hannah was right. She needed to project authority and confidence. It was an attitude she had never studied, having deferred to her husband and her parents in all things. She had never thought beyond the management of a household, but now she must become a leader, a businesswoman, and the manager of a community of nearly twenty people.

"Lord, thank You for giving me Gypsy and Hannah," she whispered. Sonja, too, would be a great aid to her, and, she hoped, Lady Dunbar.

When Jenny knocked at the door and entered with her aunt, bearing Alice's luncheon, she was already planning how she would explain the situation to the countess.

###

Boarding the brig from a small boat was at best undignified, but Lady Dunbar adjusted her petticoats and hat, after which she approached Alice smiling and offering her hand.

"I'll greet you American style, Mrs. Packard, since I hope your note means we'll be spending several months together."

Alice took the countess's hand, glad she had donned her own gloves. "I hope so too, ma'am."

The maid came over the side. Alice had asked Jenny McKay to assist her in greeting the ladies, and the young woman stepped forward.

"May I help you, miss?" she asked.

Lizzie Henshaw scowled at Jenny and reached for the rail to steady herself, her other hand clapping her hat firmly to her head. "I'm fine."

Jenny nodded and stepped back, but she didn't lower her eyes as a servant would. Miss Henshaw's lips curled downward.

"Won't you come into the cabin out of this wind?" Alice gestured toward her quarters as Gypsy and Sonja, who had rowed the visitors out, climbed aboard.

"Thank you." Lady Dunbar accompanied her across the deck to the cabin, with Miss Henshaw two steps behind.

"Ah, this is lovely," the countess said as she entered and looked around the captain's cabin.

"Snug but pleasant," Alice agreed with a smile. "Won't you sit down? Jenny and Hannah will bring us tea."

The three of them took seats about the small table. Miss Henshaw's gaze darted here and there, lingering on the stern windows, the patchwork quilt on the bed, and the solid safe beside it.

"Miss Henshaw, I'm pleased you could come," Alice said.

"I go where m'lady goes."

"Of course."

Lady Dunbar waved a hand toward the bed. "That's a lovely coverlet you have there."

"Why, thank you. It's one I made while waiting for my husband to return from sea." Alice smiled, but tears pricked at her eyes. "It was the last voyage he took without me. He was gone nearly two years, and I determined not to be left home after that."

"We have something in common then," Lady Sarah said. "When Dunbar said he wished to come to Australia and get a jump on the mining business, I insisted on accompanying him. Much to my regret, I fear. However, you say you made that spread?"

Alice nodded. "In New England, most of the girls make quilts for their hope chests, and after they're married for the family to use. The women trade patterns and gather for quilting bees."

"It sounds delightful. I fear the women in my set in London were more prone to attend card parties and assemblies. Now." Lady Dunbar turned her attention back to Alice. "You have space for my maid and myself on this voyage?"

Alice drew a careful breath. "That depends on you, ma'am. At our last meeting, I told you we were having difficulty manning the brig."

"Have you solved your difficulties?"

"I believe I have, but not in the way I expected." Alice glanced at Miss Henshaw. She'd heard that rich people spoke freely, as if their servants were not present, and she supposed Lady Dunbar expected her to do the same. "I have reached a decision, and I am taking women aboard as my working crew."

Miss Henshaw's eyes widened, but Lady Dunbar seemed to take this revelation as just another bit of information to weigh. In the silence that followed, a rap came on the door.

"Come in," Alice called. Jenny and Hannah entered with the tea tray. Alice had entrusted her ivy-sprigged teapot to Hannah for future use, and so the refreshment arrived in style.

"You've met Mrs. McKay and her niece, Jenny," Alice said. "They have changed their status from passengers to sailors and will be working on the voyage to England."

Lady Dunbar smiled. "How admirable! The Norwegian girl in the boat—she is also one of your new seamen?"

"Yes, that is Sonja. Her father brought her up on a fishing vessel before his death. She would like to join some relations in America and is working for her passage."

Lady Dunbar nodded, as if this were a common occurrence, but Miss Henshaw's expression hovered between disapproval and contempt.

Hannah and Jenny gracefully served the tea, Though Miss Henshaw kept a critical eye on them.

"And you've other women joining you?" Lady Dunbar asked.

"Yes. Tomorrow, I hope." Alice hesitated, not sure how much to impart. "The timing is a bit tricky, I'm afraid."

"Oh?" Lady Dunbar quirked an eyebrow, and Alice saw that she must tell the entire story.

"I assume you will keep my confidence."

"Oho," the countess said. "There's nothing I like better than a bit of scandal, if it doesn't involve me."

Alice chuckled. "Then perhaps it won't shock you too badly when I tell you that most of my sailors are recruits from a—a bordello in Melbourne."

Miss Henshaw spluttered and spit a mouthful of tea back into her cup. Alice pretended not to notice, but though she had rehearsed this speech, she felt the color rising in her cheeks.

Lady Dunbar's smile widened. "Brava, madam. An arrangement of mutual benefit?"

"Yes. These women are eager to escape the sordid life they've been forced into. If I can help them leave it behind, it is worth much inconvenience to me. But truly, I will also gain from it. They say they are willing to take orders and work hard, so long as they are safe on the ship and won't be returned to their enslavement."

"You actually expect them to work the sails?" Miss Henshaw fixed Alice with a dubious stare, then returned her attention to her teacup, as though realizing she had spoken out of turn.

"Yes, we do," Alice said. "I know it's hard work, and dangerous, but my boatswain feels we can train them to do it. And they're willing." She smiled at Lady Dunbar. "You told me you have sailing experience. I'd love to hear your opinion."

Lady Dunbar shrugged. "I suppose girls can climb as well as boys, if they've got the nerve. And the wardrobe, of course. I can't picture them shinnying up a mast in stays and crinolines."

Miss Henshaw blinked rapidly and clamped her lips together.

Alice laughed, delighted at Lady Dunbar's attitude. "You're right. Our crew will have to adopt masculine dress. I hope to keep their gender from being noticed by those on passing ships."

"Yes." Lady Dunbar's brow furrowed, and she sipped her tea. "Those girls would be in danger if the wrong people discovered them. How do you intend to get them aboard without arousing a clamor?"

Alice set down her cup. "So far, that is my biggest obstacle. By the nature of their present employment, they must leave in the daylight hours to avoid detection. We plan to get them away in small groups, but once they arrive at the dock, it will draw attention if people see that many women coming out to the *Vera B.*"

"You must hide them until darkness," Lady Dunbar said firmly. She looked around expectantly, and Hannah stepped forward.

"May I refill your tea, ma'am?"

"Yes, thank you."

While Hannah poured, the countess seemed lost in thought. She picked up the full cup and smiled. "You can hide them at my house until sundown."

Alice stared at her. "Are you sure? Wouldn't that be an imposition?"

"Nonsense. With Dunbar away, I've been bored to tears. How many will there be?"

"Perhaps eight, all told," Alice said, going by Kate's estimate and counting her and Carrie in the roster.

Lady Dunbar nodded. "That's settled, then. Get them to St. Kilda. My house is a large stone affair in Dolphin Street. Dunbar's rented it for the winter, and it's drafty as a Scottish castle. But I can keep your girls warm for a day, and I don't expect anyone would look for them there."

"I'm so grateful," Alice said. "If the owner of the establishment were to find out—"

Miss Henshaw gasped. "M'lady, forgive me, but you can't really mean to bring those—those women into the house and have brothel owners beating on the door?"

Lady Dunbar turned a cool gaze on her maid. "Yes, Henshaw. I shall welcome these women as guests. I'm all for helping the unfortunate improve their lot. As to the owners, they won't have the slightest clue where their women have gone. We can't put a stop to prostitution, but if we can help six or eight women leave that profession, we'll be doing the world a favor. You could even call it the Lord's work, if it makes you feel better."

Miss Henshaw stared downward, her cheeks flaming.

Alice's throat ached, and she feared she would shed a few tears. Her confidence in her course grew. She smiled and sent up a quick, silent praise, having no doubt Who had sent this lady into her life.

"I cannot thank you enough."

Lady Dunbar brushed it aside. "It's nothing. A mere diversion, so far as I'm concerned. I'm glad to do it. *But*—" She looked meaningfully into Alice's eyes. "You have not yet told me your thoughts on my sailing with you."

"I wanted you to be aware of the situation first," Alice said.

The countess nodded. "You'll need women who know something about sailing."

Alice cleared her throat, not quite able to meet Lady Dunbar's gaze. "You did say you have sailed on yachts, and that you took part in some of the work."

"I did. My father treated me as one of the crew when I was a girl. He said it would serve me in good stead to learn how to sail. But surely you've been afloat enough yourself to teach these women?"

"I can plot a course and find a position," Alice said. "I've never done the actual work of raising and lowering the sails, or trimming them to take best advantage of the wind. My husband taught me much, but without Mr. Deak, I would not dare to undertake this voyage."

"I know about winds and such," Lady Dunbar said slowly. "I expect I could lend a bit of muscle to the halyards. I've never climbed a tall mast. I'm not sure I'm limber enough. I hope these women you're getting are young and strong."

"I hope so too." Alice glanced at Jenny, who stood near the small side table that held the tea tray. "Mr. Deak had Jenny and Sonja up the mainmast this morning, and they did very well."

"Are you asking me to ship as a seaman?" Lady Dunbar asked.

Alice felt her cheeks flush. "Oh, no, I couldn't ask that of you. However, I'll admit it crossed my mind to invite you to become a mate—a ship's officer. You have authority, Lady Dunbar. The girls would listen to you. And you have the knowledge to supervise a watch."

"M'lady, you couldn't," Miss Henshaw cried. "You wouldn't!"

Lady Dunbar eyed her coolly. "Oh, wouldn't I? You surprise me, Henshaw." She turned to Alice with a smile. "I'd be happy to accept, ma'am, in whatever capacity you decide to put me, and I'll take your orders and Mr. Deak's."

Miss Henshaw made a strangled sound in her throat.

65

"I'm so pleased," Alice managed, and held out her hand. The countess shook it firmly.

"As to Henshaw," Lady Dunbar continued, "I shall leave it up to her whether she wishes to accompany us or not."

Alice looked at the maid.

"I – I—" Miss Henshaw looked from Alice to her mistress and back. "Perhaps as a passenger. I could still attend her ladyship that way."

"I'm afraid we won't have room for passengers," Alice said. She and Gypsy had discussed the matter earlier, including Hannah in the conference. Ned and Addie would be the only two aboard who were not signed sailors, and even they would be given chores. Hannah and Jenny would keep the two small cabins they had, together with the children. The other two cabins below would be assigned to Gypsy and one of the mates Alice chose. If necessary, Alice would divide her cabin and give half to the first mate, but space was in such high demand that no idle passengers would be accepted.

After a moment's silence, Lady Dunbar said, "Why don't you think on it, Henshaw? I'm sure you could do a sailor's work if you *wanted* to. We must go home now. You will pack my trunks, and if you decide to come along, your own as well. I shall confer with the housekeeper about the guests I expect tomorrow. Luncheon for ten, and tea and sandwiches at dusk, before we set out."

CHAPTER SEVEN

Alice was calm when Josiah Howard arrived for dinner with his first mate in tow. Having made the critical decisions and seen several matters fall into place, she felt she was indeed doing the right thing. Josiah wouldn't like it, but she had to follow her instincts on this.

"I should be done loading in four or five days," Josiah said as Gypsy and Hannah served their first course of fresh salmon with dill sauce. "I'll be glad to make sail. Even with all our precautions, four of my men have deserted."

"And what course will you take?" Alice asked.

"I'll go east with the trade winds. I have a stop planned in Bombay to take on some hemp for the rope trade, though it will extend our trip by a month or so. I hope it will be profitable."

Alice decided to be forthright. "I don't expect you've had time to inquire about my business?"

He smiled ruefully. "I have made a few inquiries among other ships' masters I ran into, and Mr. Stark asked about in town this afternoon. We weren't able to learn anything about your crew, and nobody has men to spare. I'm afraid we haven't found any hands for you. I'm sorry."

Alice nodded soberly. "Thank you for your efforts. I've found a few seamen, and I believe I'll be able to set sail within a week, perhaps sooner."

"What's this?" Mr. Stark perked up. "You've found a new crew, ma'am?"

"I've signed several hands and hope to complete my roster tomorrow," Alice said.

"Indeed." Stark looked at his captain.

"That's marvelous, Alice," Josiah said. "Where on earth did you find them?"

"Oh, we met one on the beach, one at a tavern, others from ... " She felt the warmth rise in her cheeks. She couldn't bring herself to say the word "brothel" in front of Captain Howard and his mate. "From various places. I found several from the British Isles who want to leave these shores."

"Not former convicts, I hope?" Josiah eyed her keenly. "You must be careful, Alice."

"Oh, I will. And Mr. Deak will help me keep them in line and train those who need training."

"Do you have a mate?"

Alice smiled and reached for her water glass. "In fact, I do, or I'm quite sure I do. I interviewed a candidate this afternoon, in this very cabin."

"Congratulations. I thought it an impossible task."

She smiled at him. "So did I. But God has provided."

"Well, then." Josiah pushed back his chair and stood, his expression a bit stiff. "I wish you a swift and pleasant voyage."

Kate cracked open the door of her chamber and listened. All was still. She slipped into the corridor in her dressing gown and crept along until she came to Nell's door. With her ear against the panel, she stood, willing her heart to slow down.

She heard nothing from inside. Nell must be asleep, although she wasn't snoring. Nell's snoring was notorious. Brea, the Irish girl whose room shared a wall with Nell's, had complained about it often.

Kate tiptoed back to her room and removed her dressing gown. She was fully clothed underneath, and all she had to do was cram the gown into the top of her satchel. Kate was fortunate to have a piece of luggage. Con had taken her to Van Diemen's Land at times, and had bought her a nice leather bag and cosmetic kit for traveling. Most of those going with her today had no bags, but had crammed their belongings into flour sacks from the kitchen or satin pillowcases they had stripped from their beds.

Back in the hallway, she went to Anne's door and opened it stealthily. Anne sat on the edge of her bed, waiting. One of the youngest girls at Dame Nell's, she looked frightened and vulnerable. Kate beckoned, and she picked up a sack and joined her in the hall. Emma was next. She, too, was waiting for the summons.

Without a word, they tiptoed down the stairs.

Emma had attempted to escape twice before. Both times, Con had caught her and beaten her severely before returning her to work. Her fear and the scars she bore had prompted Kate to put her in the first group.

At the bottom of the stairs, she held up a hand. Leaving her bag in a corner, she stole to the front door and carefully slid back the first bolt. The second bolt clicked, and she held her breath, but no one stirred upstairs. The other girls who were going today had been warned to keep still until Kate came for them. She turned the last lock and opened the door a couple of inches. The hinges moved silently, thanks to some grease Anne had sneaked from the kitchen.

The street was quiet this time of day. She pulled the door wider and looked left and right. Fifty yards away, a woman dressed in forest green waited near a tinsmith's stall. She had covered her hair with a hood, and her face was in shadow, but Kate knew it was Carrie. She put a hand up to shade her eyes, their signal. Carrie deliberately shifted the basket she carried from her left arm to her right. All was well.

Kate turned and wiggled her fingers at Emma and Anne. The two girls hurried forward. Kate opened the door wider. "She's there. Don't run. Just saunter over to her and fall into step. She'll tell you where the wagon is waiting."

Emma and Anne scooted out the door and down the two steps to street level. Kate watched through a crack until they had gone half the distance. She closed the door and turned back to the stairs.

Polly and Fiona were next. Kate had paired them because Polly was timid and appeared somewhat helpless, while Fiona was the opposite. Polly had only been at Dame Nell's a few months, and had cried every day. She had confided to Kate that Con won her in a card game in Geelong. Kate believed it. The color had quickly gone out of Polly's cheeks, and she hardly ate. Nell had browbeaten the poor girl, compelling her to use more rouge and threatening a whipping if Polly didn't act more cheerful and inviting when their customers came around. Kate took a risk by including her. Mrs. Packard had insisted on strong, hard workers. But she couldn't leave Polly here.

Fiona would watch out for Polly on this dash for freedom. While she herself was cowed by Con's brutality, Fiona hated anyone who took advantage of someone weaker. That had landed her in trouble with both Con and Nell more than once, when Fiona tried to befriend new girls and make them feel welcome and less empty inside.

As she and the two girls reached the front door, a stair creaked. Kate whipped around, her heart racing. Brea. She exhaled and shut her eyes for a moment. Brea, as usual, was impatient. Perhaps it was best to send her away now, rather than in the last group. She put a finger to her lips and beckoned the Irish girl to her side.

Mrs. Packard should be glad to see Brea. She was tall, strong, and fierce. Brea was the only one who had fought back when Con tried to beat her. She might cause a few headaches, but she would put every bit of her strength into all that hard work the lady had mentioned, and if there were any fights, Brea was a good one to have on your side.

Kate looked out the doorway. Carrie had returned to her place by the tinsmith's booth. A few people moved about the street, but no one approached Dame Nell's. She and Carrie exchanged signals, and Kate took a deep breath. Two were safe, or at least away from this evil place. She waved Fiona and Polly forward. Fiona's knit hat didn't completely cover her bushy red hair. Kate tugged it down. "Don't rush. People will stare."

Brea whispered, "I'll keep her in line."

The three girls eased their sacks through the door and headed out. Fiona's shoes clopped on the steps, and Kate cringed. Hastily, she shut the door and stepped away from it. If Nell heard, she mustn't find her peering out the door.

No sounds came from overhead, and after waiting motionless for at least a minute, Kate tiptoed to the stairs. At the landing, she saw Lucy's door open a few inches, and the girl peeked out. Lucy's heart-shaped face and snub nose made her look like an innocent child, but Kate knew better. Lucy was a favorite among the miners and sailors who frequented the house.

Kate put a finger to her lips and pointed to the stairs. Lucy opened her door and tiptoed out, carrying a worn canvas bag. Kate moved along to Mary's door.

Mary sat waiting on the edge of her bed, her dark eyes huge in her pale face. She swallowed hard. "Ready?"

Kate nodded. Mary rose and reached for her pillowcase. The flounce of a petticoat stuck out, and she tucked it back in and pulled in a deep breath. Kate turned and glanced toward Nell's door. Nothing seemed amiss, so she waved Mary forward.

Lucy waited for them at the bottom of the staircase.

"Wait here," Kate breathed. These were the last two, and she would go with them. She cracked the door open and peeked out. Carrie was farther down the street than before, not yet back at the tinsmith's. Kate hesitated. It probably wouldn't hurt if they set out now. She turned back to find Mary and Lucy close behind her. A movement on the stair landing turned her blood to ice.

"Well, now! What do you suppose you're about?" Nell's blat could probably be heard on the street. She stood on the landing in her shimmering nightdress and lamb's wool slippers, the

71

puzzlement in her eyes hardening to anger as she noticed the girls' sacks.

Kate's pulse lurched, and she glanced at the girls. Mary ducked behind Lucy, as though the slender girl could hide her.

Kate stepped forward. "We're just going to the sweet shop, Nell. We wanted some bonbons. We'll be back in a few minutes."

Nell eyed her narrowly and plodded down a few stairs. "I know you, Kate Robinson. You don't get up before noon and traipse off to the shops, and you don't go taking sacks with you. What's going on here?"

"Nothing." Kate took another step, so that she was closer to Nell and the two girls were between her and the door.

"You girls go to your rooms." Nell fixed them with her steely glare. "If you need something, you tell me, and I'll arrange it."

"We just wanted some fresh air," Lucy said, smiling like a little cherub.

"I said get upstairs."

Lucy's gaze shifted to Kate.

"Go," Kate hissed. She whirled to face Nell. Behind her, the door opened and Mary gasped as Lucy yanked her outside.

"You sneaking little—"

"Easy, now." Kate put granite in her voice. "You know I can thrash you, Nell. It would be easy. Don't make me do it."

Nell whipped her hand from between the folds of her nightdress. Kate found herself staring at the business end of a small, bejeweled pistol.

CHAPTER EIGHT

"You get upstairs!" Nell's face had gone a dull red. "I'm locking you in your room while I chase down those two no-good shrews."

Kate stood her ground. The gun wasn't a toy—she had seen it before and heard how Con had given it to Nell as a birthday present, so she could protect herself when he wasn't around. But Kate also knew Nell wouldn't set foot outside in her nightclothes.

She forced a smile. "Be reasonable, Nell. By the time you change and put up your hair, they'll be back with their lollies."

Nell snorted. "And with their baggage tucked under their arms, I suppose?"

Kate's mouth went dry. She should have gotten all the bags outside first, out of sight.

"What happened?" Nell snarled. "Did someone else offer them money to come and work for him? I'll bet it's Andy McNeil. He's tried to lure girls away from us before. Just you wait until Con hears about it! He'll have Andy by the throat."

Kate raised her chin. "It wasn't Andy. They want a better life, Nell. You know Con's a hard master."

Nell's eyes flickered. "What sort of better life can they get? Surely they don't think they'll find decent husbands?"

"No. They want to get clean away, to where they won't have to answer to Con or any other man."

Nell gazed at her for a long moment, then waved the glittery pistol. "Come, now. Even if I can't find those two, I'm not losing three. Con likes you. He'll be pleased that I stopped you from tagging after them."

Kate tried to swallow the lump in her throat. "What about the others?"

"What others?" The confusion that crossed Nell's face gave Kate some satisfaction.

"The others who have gone."

Nell's lips trembled. "You traitor. You worthless piece of garbage." The pistol slid from her hand and thudded on the carpeted step. She sat down abruptly. "Con will kill me."

A shred of pity kept Kate from fleeing out the door. "Surely not, Nell. You're his favorite."

"Not anymore." Tears streamed down the older woman's face. "He's been carrying on with you young sheilas, and he's got a woman in Geelong. He thinks I don't know, but I've lost favor. He'll beat me senseless and leave me somewhere to die."

Kate frowned. "Surely he wouldn't harm you, Nell. You've been together a long time. Who would run the business when he's gone? Who would watch the girls?"

"Oh, that's rich! You help them all run away and then ask who will watch them."

"Not all," Kate said. "There's still Jane and Tildie and Elspeth upstairs."

Nell raised her head and sniffed. "They didn't want to go with you?"

Kate grimaced. "We didn't tell them. We've got jobs, you see, and it's only for women who'll work hard."

"Harder than here?"

"Yes. But not this kind of work. We'll have our souls back, Nell. We'll work with our hands. We'll be free—and no one will take away the money we earn. No one will take advantage of us."

Nell gazed at her. "Sounds like heaven."

"Well, it's not that, but we think we'll be better off than we are here. Besides, we ... we didn't trust the others."

"You knew they'd tell me."

Kate shrugged. "I'm sorry about Con. We didn't mean to get you in trouble."

"They'll find my body in the bay, like as not." Nell stood. "Take me with you."

Kate stared at her. "I … I can't."

"Why not? Am I too old and weak?"

"I know you're strong, Nell."

"What, then?"

"Who will look after the others?"

"I don't know. They can look after themselves until Con comes home, or they can leave if they please, same as you. What kind of work is it? Farming? Weaving?"

"No, it's … it's a ship."

Nell's eyes widened. "You're sailing somewhere to work?"

"No, I mean we're going to work on the ship."

"One of the steamers? You said you wouldn't be pandering to men."

"No, we're going to help sail it. All the men have run off to the goldfields. We'll be sailors, and we're going to England."

"Well, I never!" Standing on the first step, Nell was almost eye to eye with Kate. "Whatever you do, I can't stay here. Con's tired of me, and if he finds I've lost most of his women, he'll kill me. I don't know if I can sail a ship, but I'll try."

Kate stooped and picked up the little pistol. Straightening, she held it out to Nell, butt first. "Hurry, then. My friends won't wait forever."

"You'll wait while I change?"

"Yes, but I'd better go tell the lookout we'll be another five minutes, so she won't worry."

"You won't leave me?"

Nell sounded so fearful that Kate laid a hand on her sleeve. "I promise. But be quick, and don't wake the others."

Nell scurried up the stairs, and Kate let out a long breath. Had she done the right thing? She could have overpowered Nell easily, or wrested the pistol from her. And Nell was past forty. She couldn't be suited for sailing. For a moment, Kate considered dashing off and leaving her. But if she did that, Nell would raise an alarm. And she had promised. Kate Robinson may not be good for much, but she kept her word.

She opened the door and looked down the street. To her relief, Carrie was pacing halfway between Dame Nell's and the tinsmith's stall. Kate stepped onto the stoop and put her hand to her brow.

Carrie stopped pacing. She switched the basket to her other arm and stared anxiously. Kate looked back inside and then closed the door softly. She hurried toward Carrie.

"What happened?" Carrie demanded.

"Nell is coming with us."

Carrie's jaw dropped. "No!"

Kate nodded. "She threatened to shoot me, and I think she might have, but she lost her nerve when I told her Lucy and Mary weren't the only ones. She'd rather go to sea with us than face Con."

"You told her? What if it was a trick, and she tells someone where we're going?"

Kate huffed out a breath. "She won't. She's getting dressed. I'll go wait for her and make sure she doesn't pull any tricks."

"You do that," Carrie said. "I won't let you ruin our chance, Kate."

"I'm not!" Kate's chest ached. Carrie was her only true friend. "I wouldn't ruin this."

"I know you wouldn't *mean* to." Carrie looked anxiously toward the house.

"Wait here," Kate said. "We won't be long."

She ran back into the house. Had she betrayed them all, as Carrie feared? She pulled up short at the foot of the staircase. Nell was coming down, wearing a gold satin dress, a heavy shawl, her favorite hat decked with ribbon flowers, and leather shoes. She hadn't stopped to put on her powder and lip rouge, but she carried a bulging leather travel case.

"Are you ready?" Kate asked.

Nell's laugh quavered. "Not really, but I didn't dare stop any longer. Let's go see this ship."

76

"Fine, but first we're going somewhere else." Kate followed her out the door, hoping Lady Dunbar was prepared to receive one of Melbourne's most notorious madams.

Carrie could barely make out Lady Dunbar's form on the thwart ahead of her. She struggled to catch the others' timing with her oar. To her left, Gypsy Deak's profile was silhouetted by the faint lights from Melbourne. Boats gently bobbed on the low waves around them. Mr. Deak's scraggly whiskers shone silvery in the murk. She could follow his rhythm as he bent to row, so she matched her oar's tempo to his.

"Pull, pull," Sonja chanted just loudly enough to be heard. The lanky fishing girl stood easily at the helm, one bare foot resting on the thwart ahead of her. "Fore, aft, fore, aft, dip an' pull, ladies." She paused. "You too, Mr. Deak." She moved the tiller slightly to the left, comfortable in her task of steering the launch.

Carrie had felt chilly in the cool breeze as she entered the boat, but now she began to sweat, putting her back into the rowing. Her chest ached, and it was hard to draw a deep breath.

"Look sharp, crew. We approach the brig." Sonja looked forward, and Carrie allowed a quick glance over her shoulder. The hull and rigging of the *Vera B.* loomed close now. She felt a strange sensation in her stomach. Sure, the daring escape had been nerve-wracking, but what was this new trepidation? She looked up at the towering masts and shivered.

"Frantzen, we be heading to the brig's stern, correct, lass?" Mr. Deak said. Carrie wondered how the old sailor felt about working side-by-side with women.

Sonja adjusted the tiller and put both feet on the bottom of the boat. "Aye, sir. Port, stay your oars." She looked toward those on the left side of the boat as she faced forward. "That be this side."

Carrie clumsily followed Lady Dunbar's lead and held her oar still in the water, while Mr. Deak and Brea, seated on the starboard side of the boat, continued rowing. The boat swung gracefully to port.

"Do you see the anchor, Frantzen?" Mr. Deak asked. "Did they get it up?"

"I see it, sir. Pull now, port. Fore and aft, dip and pull."

A sound from the bow made Carrie start. Someone was retching. She glanced behind her. Polly leaned over the gunwale. Seasick already? The waves were barely enough to notice. Carrie turned back and kept rowing.

Sonja guided them expertly around to the ship's stern, where a pair of lanterns illuminated Alice Packard and several other women on deck near the back rail. Carrie recognized Nell, Kate, and a couple of others she had helped escape among them.

Sonja steered them in until their boat's stern was right behind the *Vera B.'s* rudder. She stood on the stern thwart and looked up at the women on the brig. "Hold us steady, crew," she hissed.

"Ready, Sonja?" someone called down.

"Aye."

One of the women dropped a rope over the rail. Sonja swiped at it but missed. "*Svart bjørn,*" she muttered, stepping off the thwart to grab a boathook from the bottom of the boat.

"What'd she say?" Carrie whispered as Sonja reached over the side with the boathook and snagged the rope.

"It's her own language," Mr. Deak said. "That's how they cuss in Norway." He shook his head. "I'm not used to women black-mouthin'."

Carrie sighed. "I suppose you'll hear more of it. Some of us girls are as bad as sailors."

Mr. Deak grunted, and Carrie wondered how things would shake out on board the *Vera B.* Sure, sailors used bad language and simple ways, as a rule, but how would Alice Packard take to a crew of—well, women of the world? Carrie's position in the tavern was more socially acceptable than that of the brothel women, but that said little, and no mistaking. Mrs. Packard and Lady Dunbar were women of social refinement. So far, they had shown amazing kindness to the beleaguered women. Could the crew live up to their standards?

"Very good, ladies, we be tied in." Sonja straightened after securing the tow rope from the brig to the launch's stern. "Mr. Deak, shall we double on the oars?"

Deak gazed around at the other occupants of the boat. "Aye. Ladies, we'll be towing the ship out of the anchorage, and it's strong work, so all of you need to come alongside us and help row."

Carrie scooted over to allow Polly and Emma to clamber between herself and Mr. Deak. Polly squeezed in beside her and adjusted her skirt.

"Are you all right?" Carrie whispered as Polly gripped the end of her oar.

"No," Polly whimpered. "But I shall make do."

Ahead of them, Lizzie Henshaw sat gracefully beside Lady Dunbar, while Lucy wedged in beside Brea to help man her oar. The brig, though not a large ship, loomed large from their viewpoint in the boat, like the wall of a castle.

"Ready?" Sonja asked.

"Aye," Mr. Deak said.

"Ready—drop and pull, dip and pull. Dip and pull."

The women pulled clumsily at first as the four additional rowers found their pace. They moved out from the brig, and the boat was brought up short as the towline tightened. Sonja slowed the rhythm of her cadence, allowing the rowers to pull hard at the oars.

Polly gasped and nearly fell backward off the thwart as the end of Carrie's oar hit her in the chest.

"Sorry!" Carrie hissed. "You'll have to lean back with each stroke!"

79

Polly whimpered something in return, clearly miserable. "You can do this, Polly. We'll survive. And we'll be the freer for it."

Polly said nothing, but applied what strength she could to the oar. They rowed for fifteen or twenty minutes. Carrie's arms ached, and her chest hurt as she grabbed each breath, but the *Vera B.* followed them slowly through the calm water. Carrie heard murmurings from the thwart in front of her. Lucy and Lizzie were starting to gasp and whinge a bit. Her own hands felt tender. She flexed her fingers when she was able, and changed her grip on the oar to keep from forming blisters. She wondered if her thin gloves were helping or hurting. By the time the night was out, they would probably wear through.

Sonja stood on the thwart and peered over the rowers' heads, gazing left, right and center. The *Vera B.* trailed them a hundred feet astern until they had towed it beyond the other vessels.

"Stay your oars." Sonja stepped down and rummaged beneath the thwart for a thin rope. She uncoiled the line and lowered the weighted end over the side.

Carrie was glad for the rest. Her back, shoulder, and stomach muscles ached something fierce.

"What's the reading?" Mr. Deak asked.

"Four fathoms," Sonja replied. She bounced the line up and down on the bottom of the bay. "We'd best stop here. It shallows up after this, and there be places we could go aground. We're beyond the channel, so no one will run us down."

"Very good," said Mr. Deak. "I allow these women be ready to board."

Sonja untied the towrope and guided them to the side of the *Vera B.* She called out to the brig, and the big anchor plunged into the bay. Alice Packard and the other women stood at the rail. A sturdy woman in men's clothing dropped a rope ladder as Sonja tied the boat alongside the brig.

"First things first, ladies," said Mr. Deak. "Climbing a rope ladder isn't as easy as it seems."

"Allow me to demonstrate," Lady Dunbar said. She stood in the boat and grasped the ladder. She deftly hauled herself up rung by rung and made it through the gate in the bulwark.

Lizzie followed her mistress without floundering, if a little less expertly. Brea was next, her skirt billowing in a gust of wind. One by one, the women moved forward to climb the ladder.

"Go ahead, Polly." Carrie patted the queasy girl's shoulder.

Polly clambered over the luggage in the bow and headed unsteadily up the ladder. Carrie suddenly dreaded that the girl would swoon and fall off. She tried to formulate a plan to catch her if she missed her footing, but Polly made it to the top and was received aboard by those on deck.

Carrie made it up the ladder without incident. Alice Packard reached out to help her onto the deck.

"Carrie, I'm glad to have you aboard at last!"

"Thank you, Mrs. Packard. We did it!" Carrie sighed, and looked about the deck in the lantern light.

The women from Dame Nell's gathered and stood nervously by the rail, looking expectantly to Mrs. Packard. Carrie stepped in beside them.

"Ladies, thank you for coming to my ship. We should be quite safe here for the night. We shall keep watch while you rest. In the morning, we shall sign you in as crew members—assuming you are determined to sail with me." Mrs. Packard smiled. "Now it is late, and I feel we ought to get some sleep. It's been a strenuous day for all of us."

The woman who had thrown down the towrope and the ladder now hauled on a line that led down to the launch. A pretty young woman helped her pull it up.

"Hannah and Jenny McKay are helping Mr. Deak and Sonja get your bags up," Mrs. Packard said. "They'll have them on deck shortly. Then Sonja and the McKays will show you to the

81

forecastle and 'tweendecks, where we have hammocks hung for you. We'll get you rested up, and see to business in the morning."

Lady Dunbar cleared her throat. "Ma'am, if everyone has been exhausting themselves all day, who shall take the first watch?"

Alice exhaled. "I thought we would let you ladies sleep, after all you've been through today."

Kate stepped forward. "That's very thoughtful, Mrs. Packard, but if I may speak freely—"

"By all means, Miss Robinson."

"Some of us were able to take a brief nap at Lady Dunbar's house today. Most of us—we are accustomed to staying up all night. This is our daytime, when it's dark. I don't think I could sleep if I tried."

Mrs. Packard was quiet for a moment. "We will establish our regular watch schedule tomorrow, and eventually I am sure you will adjust to it. Tonight, Miss Robinson, if you and one of your friends would like to stand the next watch with Sonja, you may. I would like as many of you as possible to try to rest, though."

"I'll help watch." Fiona stepped forward. "Might as well start now."

Mrs. Packard nodded. "Very well. Sailors on watch, stow your baggage and then report to Sonja Frantzen. She will show you your post."

Carrie's bag was one of the last to come over the side. As she waited, Lizzie Henshaw said anxiously to Lady Dunbar, "Our trunks, milady?"

"They will bring them," her mistress said.

"Very good, milady."

Hannah turned away from the ladder with a long, slender stick in her hand. "Whose is this bow?"

"That's mine." Lizzie snatched it from Hannah's hand and followed the group Jenny was leading down the stairs in the middle of the deck. Carrie's bag was next, and she took it from Hannah.

"Thank you."

Hannah smiled. "You're welcome, lass. We're glad to have you aboard."

As she passed Lady Dunbar, Carrie heard Mrs. Packard say to her, "If you don't mind, ma'am, I need to speak to you. After you see Miss Henshaw settled below with the others, could you come to my cabin for a few minutes?"

"Of course." Lady Dunbar's eyes crinkled at the corners. "I'll be with you straightaway, ma'am."

What was that about, Carrie wondered. That afternoon, Lady Dunbar had said she and her maid intended to sign on as sailors too. Carrie found it hard to believe an aristocrat would willingly submit to manual labor. Maybe Mrs. Packard would tell her she wasn't suited for the work. Or maybe it was something to do with stowing their excessive baggage.

Carrie quickened her steps. So long as she didn't have to share her hammock with anyone, she didn't care what the rich women did.

CHAPTER NINE

"Thank you so much for coming to speak with me." Alice led Lady Dunbar to the table, where they had sat the previous afternoon. "Is Miss Henshaw settled?"

Lady Dunbar's mouth quirked. "Yes, though I won't say she's happy."

"I was rather surprised to see her tonight." Alice smoothed her skirts as she sat down.

"She didn't really want to come, but she fears her lot would be worse if she stayed here without my protection. She would have to find another position, and there aren't many spots for ladies' maids in this area."

"I hope she can come to terms with things. If she won't sign the articles, I can't keep her on board."

"I know, and I've explained that to her. I think she was expecting a stateroom for the two of us."

"That I cannot give her." Alice smiled wearily. "I cannot thank you enough for all you've done today. The girls seemed quite pleased with your role in their escape, and with your hospitality. I heard several mention the delicious the food served at your house."

"I was glad to do it. They were so frightened."

"I hope they'll be safe here until we weigh anchor." Alice met her gaze. "Lady Dunbar, I must—"

"Please. If I'm to be a sailor and you are my captain, you must stop calling me that."

Alice paused, unsure how to respond. "The problem of address has gnawed at me."

"How do you intend to address your crew?"

"Normally, the sailors would be called by their last names. The mates would be addressed as "Mr." But most of these girls know each other well, by their Christian names, and we've four McKays aboard, and our mates will be women. I'm at a loss how to handle the problem."

Lady Dunbar cocked her head to one side. "And how will the women address you?"

"I – I don't know. Perhaps you could make a suggestion."

"I think you should be called 'Captain.' It will establish your authority from the start."

"It seems so masculine."

"Everything we do will be masculine. You must keep a distance between yourself and the crew. That is not to say, aloof, but with these women it must be clear that some are in authority and their orders must be obeyed."

"Yes. But ..." Alice frowned. "You don't suppose 'Mrs. Packard' would do? I couldn't bear to hear them call me Captain Packard, so soon after Ruel's death."

"Perhaps 'Captain Alice,'" Lady Dunbar said gently.

Alice's lips quivered, but she managed a smile. "I like that."

"Good. That's one problem solved. And your mates? Perhaps they could be called 'ma'am,' and go by last names. Miss Frantzen, perhaps?"

"Oh, Sonja's too young to be a mate, don't you think?" Alice studied the older woman's features. "She does have more knowledge of the sea than the others, but I don't know if they would respect her."

"You may be right. It might be wise to choose one from among them. One whose lead they'll follow."

"I've settled on my first mate," Alice said.

"Mr. Deak?"

"No, I offered him the position, but he said he'd rather not, with the crew being women. He'll keep his post as steward and boatswain, though, and train our new hands, for which I am most

85

grateful." Alice drew in a breath. "No, I meant you, ma'am, if you're willing."

Lady Dunbar sat still for a moment, her expression unreadable. When she raised her chin, she met Alice's gaze. "I am honored. I'm happy to accept."

A huge weight lifted from Alice's shoulders. "Thank you so much." She turned and waved toward a stack of boards lying on the floor between the wardrobe and the bulkhead. "This lumber is for a partition. We've only four small cabins below. Most of the women will sleep in the forecastle by turns, according to their watches. Hannah McKay and her family were assigned two cabins when they came aboard as passengers, and I thought it best to keep them, with the children, separate from the rest."

"Probably wise," Lady Dunbar murmured.

"Exactly. Gypsy, of course, will need a cabin of his own. The last one, I thought I would offer to the second mate, whoever she may be."

Lady Dunbar waited, her eyebrows arched.

"Hannah McKay will be our carpenter," Alice went on. "She gained some building experience on the farm with her husband. With her guidance, we can put up a partition to divide this cabin in half."

"Surely you don't want to do that," Lady Dunbar said. "It would be quite cramped for you after enjoying this spacious room."

Alice shook her head. "With my husband gone, everything is different. I don't need much space. And I would like you near me, if you don't mind."

"I don't, and I am touched. I hope the offer is not driven by the idea that I must have finer surroundings than the unfortunate women below."

"Not at all. I think it's appropriate, and it will free the last cabin below. And now ... what shall I call you? And the others, how will they address you?"

"What would you prefer? Lady Dunbar is out of the question, I think."

Alice thought for a moment. "Lady Sarah, perhaps? Or Mrs. Fiske?"

"Let's drop the 'lady' altogether, if you don't mind. Its use in any capacity could be divisive."

"Perhaps."

"And just between us, I'd like you to call me Sarah, if I may presume to call you Alice in private."

"I would like that."

Sarah's smile warmed Alice. "Good. 'Mrs. Fiske,' I suppose, when necessary. It is accurate. 'Ma'am' in most cases."

Alice nodded. "That's settled, then. Do you think we might call the women by their first names?"

"Why don't you ask them?"

"Perhaps I shall."

Sarah rose. "My dear, you have dark circles under your eyes. I'm sure you're exhausted. I shall sleep beside Henshaw tonight. I'm sure she's terrified, being left alone with a roomful of harlots."

"I'm so sorry. I should have thought of some way—"

Sarah chuckled. "No, my dear, you shouldn't have. You are doing a good thing. Henshaw has been with me four years, and she's very skilled at what she does. In a way, I'm fond of her. But if she wants to be part of this voyage, she must take her rightful place among the sailors—and if anyone knows about station and keeping one's proper place, it is Lizzie Henshaw."

Kate followed Sonja up the steps to the *Vera B.'s* quarterdeck, and Fiona brought up the rear. Sonja ambled over to the ship's wheel and grasped one of the handles.

"Here's the wheel," she said. "I've not manned it yet, but Mr. Deak assured me everyone on board will have a go at it eventually. All my sailing has been with a tiller."

Kate nodded, stepping up to grasp the wheel. She rotated it a little to get the feel. The big wooden circle, its rounded handles extending from the rim, turned harder than she had expected. She heard a low creak, back behind the cabin, and jumped.

"It's only the rudder," Sonja said, her eyes drifting sideways in amusement.

Fiona snickered and stepped up to the wheel. "We should have greased it, like we did the door hinges at Nell's."

Kate exhaled sharply. "Not amusing, Fiona."

Fiona shrugged, her fiery hair gleaming in the light that reached them from the distant Williamstown Lighthouse. "Relax, Kate. We're safe. A night with nae men!"

Kate grimaced, glancing at Sonja. How much did the young girl know about the ways of the world? No stranger to tough work, the fishing girl at least had been spared the horrors of the brothel. Caught between shame before Sonja and irritation with Fiona, Kate bit her tongue.

Her expression must have betrayed her. Fiona changed the subject, her thick Scottish accent barely concealing her awkward tone. "So. Sonja. I hear ye ken how to sail."

"A little."

"A little?" Fiona giggled. "From what Carrie said, you've practically sailed alone from here t' Bombay every year since you were three."

Sonja grinned. "Miss Carrie must believe in tall tales. I've never been to Bombay, and I've never gone beyond the Rip alone. But I have been sailing since I was two."

Kate raised her eyebrows. "What? Since you were two?"

"Aye, but I didn't do anything useful until I was about four, when my papa taught me to tie weights and floats." Sonja chuckled. "I wasn't very good at first. We lost a few off the nets."

Fiona stared at her. "You went to sea at two years old. On a fishing boat with your father?"

"Aye. There wasn't anyone to care for me after me mam died. He used to tie me to the sloop's mast so I couldn't fall overboard."

"Oh," Fiona cooed. "That's sad, Sonja."

Sonja shrugged. "I don't remember, really. I wish I had a mother, but I miss my pa more. It's been over two years now. I lost him off Apollo Bay."

Kate turned away, her own memories crowding in. Though Sonja's childhood had been much different from hers, they had some things in common. She gazed through the rigging to the distant lights of Melbourne, suddenly wishing to be alone.

Fiona was in a conversational mood, however. "At least you had a father, Sonja. I lost mine when I was a wee thing. He went to India with the army, and they say he died of the tropical fever. Was your father good to you?"

"Aye, very good. We worked hard—me, him, and Bob, and he didn't take no excuses, right? But he was all I had, and now he's gone. And Bob too—that was Pa's partner. I wouldn'a learned English if it weren't for Bob."

Kate faced the ship's bow and grasped the rail tightly. Tears? She knew what had prompted them—the vague memories of her own early life, and the dim faces she barely recalled. Countless times she had wished she could remember how her mother looked. But why had she allowed herself to be overcome by it? No tears! Tears meant weakness.

"Kate?" Fiona called from behind her. "Are you all right?"

Kate whirled around. "I'm dandy," she growled. "Fine as silk. I—I've never been better!" She glanced at Sonja in time to see her wince.

Kate slumped backward against the railing. "I'm sorry, Fiona." She looked at Sonja. "I lost—both my parents when I was young. I was shipwrecked, and I don't really know where. I don't know how old I was, or even my true name. I just

89

remember a big ship, like this one, and then I was choking in the surf on the shore. Some natives found me and took me in."

Fiona stared at her. "You never told me that."

Kate brushed her hair back from her face. "I suppose none of us ever tell our whole story." She didn't plan on telling anyone what had happened after she had been "rescued" from the aborigines several years later by the troopers out of Geelong. The English farmer she had been sold to as an indentured servant had made the primitive ways of the black bush people seem noble and refined by comparison.

"You're lucky those blacks didn't kill you and chuck you down a wombat hole," Sonja said soberly. "That's what happened to the folks who got shipwrecked from the *Maria* up off Cape Jervis a while back. People still talk about it in the harbor."

"I heard about that," Fiona said. "I had a customer a few months ago who talked about it. Twenty-five men, women, and children, he said. They survived the shipwreck and made it to land, and the abo's slaughtered them! Them natives are dangerous, especially the ones out in the bush!"

"They are not!" Kate lunged toward Fiona and looked her in the eye, their faces barely a foot apart. "I've heard about it, too, but I can't think the natives killed them without cause. You weren't there, Fiona. You don't know."

Fiona held up her hands as though to ward off Kate's harsh words.

Kate pulled in a ragged breath. "The Girai Wurrung not only saved my life, they raised me. A couple who couldn't have children took me in. I was with them for several years. They fed me and taught me the ways of the bush. No one has ever shown me more kindness than they did. They are peaceful people, Fiona, and I don't ever want to hear you say 'abo' again, you hear?"

Fiona's green eyes widened. "Very well, Kate. I spoke hastily. I didna know about your past."

"I wouldn't be here without them."

90

Fiona nodded and looked at Sonja, who had been gazing at the deck with her mouth skewed to one side. "So, Sonja, when we're on watch like this, what exactly are we to do?"

Sonja looked up. "It's only my third time. When we're at sea and under sail, there will be a lot more to do, but when we're at anchor, there's basically three things. Watch for any problems with the ship, watch for any big changes in the wind or current, and be alert for any boats or ships approaching. Here in the harbor, there shouldn't be much to worry about."

"It's that last thing you mentioned that concerns me most. Boats approaching," Kate said.

"Because somebody might be after you?"

"Yair."

"You'll be safer once we get you out of those big skirts." Sonja eyed Kate's dress in the dimness.

"Could be. I'd feel safer with a gun, or a sword or something."

Sonja nodded. "We probably should be paying more attention to our duties. Maybe you can stay here on the quarterdeck, Kate. Fiona, you could go keep watch up in the bow, and I'll make the rounds."

Sonja and Fiona walked off. Kate looked around and shivered, wishing she had a warmer mantle. A nice guernsey like some of the sailors wore would keep out the chilly breeze. She paced toward the port rail, leaned over, and scanned the side of the ship. Clouds blocked the starlight now, and the beacon from the lighthouse shone at an angle that gave her little aid, but she could make out the hull's curve by the glimmer of lights on shore. Nothing seemed amiss.

She headed back to the wheel and clasped it, then moved to the binnacle, the stand that housed the compass. She'd seen one before, when she sailed with Con to Van Diemen's Land. The lantern beside it wasn't lit, so she couldn't see the compass needle, but from the position of Melbourne's lights, she was pretty sure the brig pointed east.

91

A slight clunk drew her attention toward the stairway. She thought maybe Sonja had returned, but she saw nothing. Heart pounding, Kate sneaked along the rail, keeping low. She whirled around the newel post and saw a small figure perched on the top step.

The McKay boy's eyes flared and his mouth flopped open as Kate grabbed him by the shoulders.

"What in thunder are you doing up, boy?" she hissed. "I thought you were an intruder." She hauled him to a standing position and shoved him back against the rail, which came to his shoulder blades. "Well?"

He trembled. "I—I'm sorry! I was just, you know, looking for stuff."

"Stuff? What kind of stuff?"

"You know, things people don't need." Ned sniffed.

Kate looked at his hands. In one he held a small rag, and in the other, a block of wood. "Well can't it wait until morning? Why aren't you asleep?"

He sighed. "Ma left some coffee in the billy, and I wanted to know if it tasted good."

Kate stifled a guffaw. "Did it?"

"Not until I dumped sugar in it. Then I drank it all."

Kate snorted. "So now you can't sleep. Well you'd better go back to your cabin, Mr. McKay. Your mother will miss you."

"Not for a while. I told her I had to go to the head. It wasn't a lie!"

Sonja came up the steps, having heard some of the exchange. "I'm sure it wasn't a lie, if you drank a whole pot of coffee." She grinned over the boy's head at Kate.

"Only half a pot."

"Even so, Ned McKay, you'd best be off to bed."

"That's right." Kate tweaked his ear.

"All right, but. . . ."

"Yes?" Kate asked, trying to put an ominous note in her voice.

"It's dark down there. Do you have a candle?"

Kate looked at Sonja, whose brows knit in response.

"No," Kate said. "We don't."

Ned scowled. "I don't want to fall down the ladder."

Sonja put a hand on his shoulder. "Candles are too dangerous on ships, Ned. You'll have to get used to finding your way in the dark."

"Never mind." Ned turned toward the stairs.

Sonja smiled wryly. Kate grasped the rail with both hands and watched as Ned crossed the deck. He stopped to look up at her and Sonja.

"Get!" Kate said.

He disappeared down the hatch, and Kate shook her head. "Men. They start out cute and harmless, but then. . . "

Sonja bit her lip. "I wouldn't know."

Kate sighed. "I'll feel better when we leave the bay."

Sonja leaned on the binnacle. "I don't know what you've been through, but I'm sure things will get better."

Kate realized she was making an overture. Eventually, she might get along all right with Sonja, but right now she couldn't think about making new friends. Her mind might drift to other things, but it always tore back to Con Snyder and what he would do when he returned from Ballarat. She shrugged. "As long as we can escape without getting caught."

CHAPTER TEN

"You've all signed your name or made your mark. You're now officially crew members of the *Vera B.* Welcome." Alice stood at the quarterdeck rail as she addressed the women lined up below. "At this time, I will introduce your officers. As you know, I am captain of this ship. You may call me Captain Alice, ma'am, or captain." She waved her hand toward Gypsy, who stood to one side, near the bulwark in the waist of the ship. "Mr. Deak you have all met. He is my steward and boatswain. That means he has charge of all the cargo, stores, and tackle of the ship. You will follow any orders he gives you. He will also instruct you in all matters pertaining to sailing."

Most of the women glanced toward the slight, graying man.

"My first mate," Alice went on, "is Lady Dunbar, who insists on relinquishing her title for this voyage. You will address her as ma'am or Mrs. Fiske. She will assist in your training, and she will be in charge of the first watch. You will answer to her in all things."

Some of the young women frowned, but Anne and Polly smiled outright, and most of the others gazed at Sarah with carefully neutral expressions.

"Mrs. Fiske, would you like to say anything?" Alice asked.

"Thank you, ma'am." Sarah turned to face the group. "I know you are all glad for this opportunity, as am I. I am sure you'll make the most of it. We come from different stations in life, but that does not make me a better person than any of you. I was asked to take this position because I have experience sailing. While I have never worked on a square-rigged ship before, I trust I can help you learn the basics of your new tasks. This is a new venture for all of us, and I trust it will be a roaring success."

Alice smiled. "Thank you. Because of our unusual situation, we shall try to keep the crews of other ships from discovering we are nearly all women. To that end, I shall address you as hands, sailors, or crew, rather than ladies. I mean no offense."

Elfin Lucy, with the snub nose, giggled.

Alice looked over them all, standing on deck in the light breeze, their tresses fluttering and their skirts waving gently. Most of the girls from Nell's wore low-cut bodices, and some sported gaudy jewelry. Not for long.

Alice continued, "As you came aboard last night, I got to know some of you and asked some questions. I have decided to appoint Nell Tillman as cook for the voyage. I've been told she has a gift for cooking, and I feel we are blessed to have her. Some of you will be assigned to help her as part of your watch duties, but Miss Tillman will sling her hammock in the galley at night, and she has full sway there."

Watching the young women carefully, Alice saw no resentment on their faces, and she was thankful for that. Last night, the appearance of a middle-aged woman who had obviously been pampered for years had taken her by surprise. A few years older than Sarah, Nell was not nearly as fit or agile as the countess. Nell would almost certainly be unable to scale a mast or take part in most of the strenuous shipboard duties.

Alice's instinct to turn Nell away had been quashed, however, when Kate took her aside and explained the circumstances under which the madam had joined her party. If the girls would accept her as cook, perhaps all would go smoothly. They would no longer have to take orders from Nell, and she could contribute to the effort in a way that would help them all. Her conversation with Kate led Alice to believe it might be best to give Nell sleeping quarters separate from the others. Some of the young women no doubt harbored resentment for the role she had played in their servitude to Con Snyder.

"Our next order of business will be appointing a second mate, who will command the second watch. She will also have other duties, which I will discuss with her. Since I don't know all your abilities, but you know each other, I ask that you look about and nominate one of your number as second mate. Think carefully and choose someone who is strong, steady, and fair. Someone you're willing to follow."

The young women stared at each other in silence. After a few moments, a few put their heads together and whispered. Henshaw and Sarah stood without moving or speaking to anyone else. A moment later, Carrie turned toward the quarterdeck and timidly raised her hand.

"Yes, Miss O'Dell?" Alice said.

"I'd like to name Kate Robinson, ma'am."

Alice looked at the taller young woman beside her and nodded. "Does anyone else have a nomination?"

After a few seconds of silence, Alice said. "Kate Robinson, step forward."

Kate took a step, looking up at her. Until this morning, Alice had not seen her in full daylight. The statuesque woman looked about five-and-twenty, with handsome features, hazel eyes, and rich auburn hair, plaited and tied with a green satin ribbon. This was the woman who had gotten seven others out of the brothel at her own peril. Knowing the story of Nell's threats and Kate's bravery, Alice felt the girls had made a good choice.

"Miss Robinson, I am proud to name you second mate of this ship for the voyage. When we dismiss, Mrs. Fiske's watch will be on duty until eight bells—that is, noon. Your watch will also remain on deck for instruction in sailing. While they begin, you may lay below and move your gear into the empty cabin at the end of the passageway."

Surprise flickered across Kate's face.

"Do you have any questions?"

"No, ma'am. Thank you."

Alice nodded. "When you have settled your things, please meet me up here on the quarterdeck, at the ship's wheel."

"Yes, ma'am."

Alice was satisfied with Kate's responses and her calmness. She gazed at the full group. "You hands will address the second mate as Miss Robinson or ma'am. She is an officer of this ship and is to be respected and obeyed as such. Now, we have one more question that must be settled immediately. That is, what shall I call you? Do you wish to be known by your surnames, as is common on shipboard? Or do you prefer your Christian names?"

A murmur ran through the ranks. She let them consult for a minute, then called, "Miss Fiona Campbell, what say you?"

The redhead raised startled eyes toward her. "Ma'am, we already call each other by our first names."

"So, you are proposing that I call you Fiona, not Campbell, and Miss Frantzen be Sonja, and Miss Henshaw Lizzie?"

Miss Henshaw jerked her head up and stared at Alice.

"It seems more natural, ma'am," Fiona said. "I've been with Brea and Kate and Lucy—most of these girls—for a long time."

Alice nodded. "Any objections?" She waited a moment, but no one spoke, though Lizzie's cheek twitched. "That is how we shall do it, then, but I remind you that Miss Robinson, as mate, must be addressed as such."

"Yes, ma'am," Fiona said, and several of the girls nodded. Kate looked down at the deck, seeming embarrassed. Alice made a mental note to ask her later if she was uncomfortable with this separation from the other girls. It might mean some resentment, but if Kate could put up with that, this might be an opportunity that would do her a world of good. A letter of reference at the end of the voyage might help her secure a respectable position on land.

"Those on the first watch, under Mrs. Fiske, are: Hannah, Lizzie, Jenny, Brea, Fiona, and Mary," Alice said, consulting a list she had put together earlier. You will work together and have your leisure time together. Miss Robinson's watch is the second and shall consist of: Carrie, Sonja, Polly, Lucy, Anne, and Emma." The young women eyed each other with speculation. Alice cleared her throat. "Now, about our clothing."

That got their attention. Alice placed both hands on the smooth rail.

"If we are to remain incognito, and if you are to perform your duties efficiently and modestly, we must make some changes in wardrobe. How many of you can sew?"

Nell, Carrie, Lizzie, Emma, and Jenny raised their hands.

"Very good. I'll now ask Hannah to tell you our plans for altering and sewing clothing."

Hannah, who had stood as part of the group, stepped to the front and turned to face them. "Some of the sailors that deserted this ship left belongings behind them. We have moved all of that out of the forecastle, into the 'tweendecks. Captain Alice decided that whatever they left behind, we could use. When you are not on watch, you will come below and see if any of the trousers, blouses, caps, and so on, fit you. They're not the prettiest bits you've ever seen, but we will no longer be concerned with fashion. Anyone who cannot find working clothes will have to alter some of their own clothing or stitch new from the bolts of cloth Captain Alice has provided. As you can see from my trousers, a flannel petticoat can be turned into a pair of loose pants without too much trouble. I will render you any assistance..."

Alice drew a deep breath of sea air. The women paid attention to Hannah's every word. This would work. It had to. She would send the hands to Gypsy next and let him explain their daily duties. Then the sail drill would begin. They would sail within a week, if all went well.

Not *if*, she told herself. All *would* go well.

Gypsy leaned against the upturned hull of the *Vera B.*'s jollyboat, which was stowed neatly on the main deck behind the foremast. He took his cap off and wiped his brow, even though it wasn't more than seventy degrees. A little over an hour after the crew's signing in, he still waited for the women to return from the 'tweendecks, where they were supposed to be improvising some decent sailing garb.

The ship's bell struck three times. Gypsy looked up to where Mrs. Fiske stood at the wheel. She at least knew how to keep time for the vessel. He hoped, as promised, she knew a lot more. The first mate made sure the hourglass sat firmly in its bracket and glanced curtly in his direction before looking out to the bay.

Gypsy wouldn't admit it to anyone, but he was within an inch of letting the dinghy down and bolting for it. The task he was about to attempt would likely be the most difficult, awkward trial of his life. Even worse than preparing Captain Packard for burial.

He shook his head and exhaled. What good was running away? He was old, and partly crippled to boot. No doubt he could find work in this port so starved for labor, but shore work was not his cup of tea. He belonged at sea. And besides, there was no way he could let Alice Packard down. He wasn't like those mangy mongrels who had deserted their posts for the goldfields.

But this was going to be so . . . hard. Gypsy didn't mind teaching new sailors, but men were one thing. Women? They were a rare species to him. He didn't know their ways, or their capabilities. And they sure didn't belong on yardarms, where they'd be as useful as zebras or hippopotamuses.

Ned McKay wandered by with a handful of wood chips and stared at him. "Does your face hurt, Mr. Deak?"

"No," Gypsy said, though his head was beginning to ache.

"I only wondered, 'cause you were wrinkling it up."

Gypsy stared back at Ned. "Your face will look like this too, when you're my age. Especially if you have to deal with calamities like I do."

Ned made a face. "I'll see you later, Mr. Deak. I'm collecting chips from where Mum was working in the cabin."

Gypsy watched him amble off. Like many boys, Ned was fascinated with chips and sawdust and blocks of wood. Ah well, what was the harm in it, as long as the kid didn't leave things underfoot?

Gypsy went down to his new cabin. He had only slept in it for two nights. He didn't keep a lot of kit. He did have one thing, however, that might come in handy for teaching the girls. He opened his sea chest and pawed under his odds and ends until he came to his knot panel. He lifted it out and closed the chest. Yes, this might help. On his way back to deck, he took a dozen clew lines from the ship's stores.

When he came back out on the main deck, Sonja and four other crew members waited at the foremast.

"Very well, er, sailors," Gypsy greeted them. "I see you're all trimmed out for duty."

Sonja already had a decent sailing outfit, and the others wore cast-off get-up left behind by the deserters. Some of the pants and shirts were too loose, or worse yet, a little too tight. Gypsy tried not to look.

"How long'll we have to wait for the others?" he asked.

Sonja shrugged. "It could take a while. These clothes did for Brea, Fiona, Mary, and Anne. The others . . . who knows."

Gypsy squinted. "Very well. Let's just practice a little while we wait. Sonja, I believe you know your knots?"

Sonja shifted her jaw. "I know a lot of them, but I don't know what they're all called."

Gypsy showed the girls his knot panel. "On this shingle, I've tied a great many knots. By the end of the voyage, I reckon you'll be able to tie most every one of them. But we don't use them all every day. These seven here, at the top, are the most important. Bowline, square knot, clove hitch, sheet bend, figure eight, rolling hitch, and the round turn and two half-hitches."

"I know them," said Sonja.

Gypsy handed her a line. "How about if you demonstrate." He handed out lines to the other four, as well.

Sonja patiently showed the other girls how to make the seven knots. They followed her a bit clumsily. Gypsy stood back and observed how each one learned. He needed to determine who could be relied on to tie a good knot.

Miss Robinson and another sailor came up through the hatch. Kate wore a jacket discarded by a former crew member and a pair of hastily made trousers of a sleek, red material. Gypsy raised his eyebrows. He had seen some variety in what sailors wore over the years, but this was a bit flashy. Some of them must have taken Hannah literally about altering their undergarments. The other girl, Emma, appeared to have modified a gingham skirt into an awkward-looking pair of pants to go with a blue shirt.

Miss Robinson and Emma attended Sonja's knot tying class with keen interest. Gypsy observed with minimal input, except when Sonja asked him to remind her of the knots' names. He noticed that Kate and Emma quickly mastered the knots, whereas the other four girls were lubbers at it.

As the rest of the women were fitted with working clothes, they emerged from below. Hannah McKay came on deck last with Lizzie Henshaw, who blushed and scowled, obviously humiliated to be seen in trousers. She wore a bizarre white and blue sailing outfit that had surely once been a go-to-meeting dress. Gypsy looked away, not sure whether he was in more danger of chuckling or retching at the sight of the huge middy collar and tailored bodice.

"Very good, crew, I see we have all sailing hands assembled," Mrs. Fiske said, approaching the group. The girls all looked to her expectantly. Sonja paused in the middle of demonstrating a round turn and two half hitches around one of the foremast halyards. "Now that we are all here, Mr. Deak, how would you prefer we proceed with the training?"

Gypsy supposed he'd better make a speech of some kind. He had trained a lot of sailors in his day, but usually only one or two at a time. He hardly knew where to start, because he had no idea what they already knew. Basics, he decided. He stepped back toward the rail. How could he make this lesson as simple as possible?

101

"Ladies—crew—this. . . is a ship. A brig, actually. A ship would have three masts, a brig has two. But if I call it a ship, it's only because we sometimes call any big vessel a ship. The front end of the ship is called the bow, or the prow. The hind end of the ship is called the stern. The left side, as you face the bow, is called port. The right side is starboard." He paused. Was he being too elementary? Surely everyone knew these things . . .

"This mast here, the front one, we call the foremast. The other mast is the mainmast. It's very important that you remember, because any time we yell out an order that has to do with the rigging and sails, you need to know which one. Almost every line, halyard, sheet, sail, spar, and so on, is part of either the mainmast or the foremast rigging. When we call 'all hands' and you come up on deck, you will always be posted to the same mast. The first watch, Mrs. Fiske's watch, will man the mainmast. The second watch, Miss Robinson's watch, will man the foremast. Am I clear so far?"

Several of the women nodded. "You're doing fine, Mr. Deak," Mrs. Fiske said.

He nodded. "Most of the time, only one watch will be on duty. During those normal times, all the sailors of that watch will do all the work. We only call 'all hands' when there is an emergency or a special task."

Over the next half hour, Gypsy led the crew on a full tour of the decks and taught them the names of everything in sight. Probably the girls wouldn't remember a tenth of what he told them the first time around, but it was a start. And besides, it delayed the inevitable. As long as he could forestall taking the women into the rigging, he would.

They ended up on the quarterdeck, at the wheel.

"Anyone on watch who is experienced enough can man the helm," Gypsy told them. "Steering the ship is not too difficult, but learning your compass points, and how to maintain them, that's different. Also, it's one thing to hold the wheel fast on the open sea in a fair wind, but it's something else entirely to man it in a storm, or in a straight passage, such as the Rip here, leading out of the bay. That's where a skillful mariner earns his salt." He looked around at his audience. "Her salt."

He gestured to the hourglass, which was a few minutes away from running out of sand. "Every half hour, we ring the bell. We're almost to eight bells now, and at noon, eight bells, the captain normally takes our reading with the sextant, to see where we are in the world and to know exactly when noon is. When he—I mean she—determines this, then we start the hourglass again, and our new day begins. At noon, not dawn."

The crew looked around at each other. Some of the girls seemed to understand, but others wore baffled frowns.

As if she had been listening to his speech and suddenly reminded of her duty, Mrs. Packard came up the stairs carrying the sextant under her arm.

"Good day, crew," she said. "I hope you are learning well from Mr. Deak."

"The crew is attending earnestly to his every word," Mrs. Fiske assured her. Gypsy wished he could concur, but he had noticed a bit of distraction, especially from certain individuals. That Lizzie Henshaw, in particular, seemed out of sorts. He feared her scowl was infecting some of the others. He had begun to make a list in his mind of people who might cause trouble in the months to come, and Lizzie was at the top.

"Mr. Deak was just telling us how you would be coming out to shoot the sun with the sextant," Mrs. Fiske said.

Mrs. Packard smiled. "Indeed. This is a task the captain and mates perform every day. Mrs. Fiske, are you already proficient at taking sightings?"

"It has been a while, Captain, but I believe it will come back to me."

"Very well. Over time, we shall train Miss Robinson, but that will be another day. Would you like to take the sighting, Mrs. Fiske?"

"Certainly." The first mate eagerly received the sextant from Mrs. Packard and put it to her eye.

The girls crowded around to watch.

"Give the first mate a little space," Gypsy admonished.

The crowd retreated a little. In the shuffle, Lizzie bumped into Brea. The surly, dark-haired Irish girl's eyebrows shot up. "That's me foot you're on. I'll thank y' to stand upon your own, you manicured maggot."

"I didn't do anything," Lizzie snapped, backing away.

"Avast there," Gypsy roared. Shocked at himself, he looked quickly toward Mrs. Packard and the first mate. Surely the captain must have some idea how all this tried his patience.

Mrs. Packard cleared her throat. "Crew. You must be patient with each other. Mrs. Fiske, when you've finished taking the sun, record your sighting in the log, and the first watch may lay below for lunch."

At her words, Gypsy realized an appetizing aroma from the galley had been teasing his nose for the last quarter hour, and he was very hungry.

"Aye, aye," Mrs. Fiske said, "but Lizzie, you'll remain behind."

"But—" Lizzie caught the mate's withering gaze and clamped her lips together.

CHAPTER ELEVEN

Josiah Howard quickened his steps toward the harbormaster's shack on the dock. He pulled out the pocket watch he carried when going ashore and grunted. Nearly three o'clock—six bells. The sun was already headed westward and would set in two hours or so. He hoped Stark had gotten the rest of the cargo unloaded. They could begin lading in the morning.

As he approached the rough shed, Josiah heard a voice raised within. The strident tones made him pause.

"Whatever you do, you mustn't let them leave the harbor with those women aboard," roared a man with a heavy British accent.

Josiah hesitated. Women? Aboard a ship? What was going on here?

"Settle down, sir," said the harbormaster, Mr. Eddleston. "Unless you can prove there's something shady going on—"

"Shady? You can't let those women leave Port Phillip Bay without their master's permission, or you'll be abetting in illegal transport."

"They're not slaves, are they?" The harbormaster sounded a little testy.

"Slaves? Naw!"

"Convicts serving a sentence?" Eddleston asked.

"No, but they're property of Con Snyder."

"Oh, Snyder."

"You needn't dismiss him, sir," said the complainer. "Snyder's away on business, but if he comes home and finds you've let his women slip off, he'll take it out of your hide, believe me."

105

"Let me tell you something, Larson," the harbormaster said. "Snyder can't own those women, understand? They may be his employees, so-called, but unless the constabulary tells me it's illegal for them to book passage on a merchant ship, I'll stay out of it, and I'd advise you to do the same. I don't know why you're so concerned about it, anyway."

"There's one of my girls with them, that's why. From the Boar's Tusk. She's worked for me three years, and I've been good to her."

"Oh, so that's why she wants to leave."

Josiah had decided to walk away and return when the argument was over, but Larson's next words pulled him up short.

"They've moved that brig today, getting ready to make sail. If you don't stop the *Vera B.* from leaving port, I *will* bring the law down on you."

Josiah's heart turned to stone. What had the *Vera B.* to do with this dispute over a group of soiled women decamping from Melbourne? Surely Alice hadn't accepted a bevy of harlots as passengers on her brig. The crew would go wild—and she'd said she had found a new crew. Maybe she didn't know her passengers were of the worst ilk. He really ought to have checked on her this morning.

"You do that." The harbormaster didn't seem too worried by Larson's threat of legal action. So far as Josiah knew, the rough towns in Australia were still far from civilized. Perhaps Eddleston knew Larson would have difficulty getting the police to overstep his authority when it came to the harbor.

"You don't think they can run a ship with a crew of sheilas?" Larson snarled.

Josiah could hardly trust his ears. He walked toward the door. Before he reached it, a middle-aged man strode out, his hands shoved in the pockets of his wool coat. He rushed past with his head lowered and face so full of wrath that Josiah did not try to stop him. He stepped into the harbormaster's shack.

"Hello, Mr. Eddleston."

The harbormaster, a retired sailing master himself, sat on a stool, hunched over a ledger. He looked up at the greeting. "Oh, hello, Captain. Help you, sir?"

"Yes, I've sold the rest of my cargo to Wilton and Company."

Eddleston nodded. "They supply the mining camps."

"Yes. What I didn't sell here, they'll carry to St. Arnaud by bullock dray. I'll be lading tallow and other goods, starting tomorrow. Here's the new manifest."

The harbormaster took the paper and scanned it. "Very good. Let me know when the lading is complete."

"I'll do that."

Eddleston turned back to his books, but Josiah lingered.

"Forgive me, but I couldn't help overhearing a bit of what passed between you and the man who was just here. Larson, was it?"

Eddleston gave a snort. "Aye, Tom Larson, from the Boar's Tusk. Do you know it?"

"No."

"It's a pub in Rawson Street. He's madder than a soaking wet emu. Seems one of his bargirls up and left him, and he thinks I ought to go out to the ship she's sailing on and haul her off."

"Surely she has a right to go if she wishes," Josiah said.

"Ah, yes, and the others that went with her."

"I couldn't help but hear. Several women of the night, I take it."

Eddleston rubbed his chin. "Best stay out of it. If those girls can get away, God bless 'em. I won't help those brutes take them back."

"I should think not."

"I said to Larson, they're not slaves, but the truth is, some of them are close to that. They're forced into it, and then they can't get away. I'm thinking a lot of them would rather be anywhere else. So if the *Vera B.*'s master is determined to help them, I say huzzah."

"But, the *Vera B.*—her captain is dead."

Eddleston nodded. "The steward came by and said they've signed some new hands. They've changed their mooring, but so what? They didn't take on any new cargo here—just put in because poor Packard was dying. They can weigh anchor anytime they want, and I shan't try to stop them."

"This new crew," Josiah said uneasily. "I heard Larson say they'd sail the ship with women."

"I wouldn't put much stock in anything that man says. He's been drinking anyway, probably heard a pack of rumors. Nobody would sail a brig with females in the rigging. Preposterous." Eddleston frowned and scratched the side of his jaw. "Now, if Snyder were here—him bein' the owner of that establishment—well, he's a tough customer. But the word is he left on the steamer last week, so I'm not too worried."

"I see. Well, thank you." Josiah stepped outside and hurried toward the shore, where his boat crew was to meet him.

"Cap'n," the boat chief called as he approached.

"What is it, Murphy?"

"Mr. Stark sent word to bring you out as soon as we can. It's something to do with the last of the cargo, sir. There's some water damage, and the buyer doesn't want that part."

Josiah huffed out a breath. If this matter concerning the cargo kept him, he would have to put off calling on Alice until morning, when he hoped he would find out exactly what was going on. He admired Alice, but at their last meeting, she'd shown a bit more independence than he liked to see in a woman. He hoped she hadn't gotten herself into a mess—especially if he had to extricate her.

He climbed into the boat and nodded to Murphy to shove off. Whatever Alice was up to, it would have to wait.

###

Sonja stood on the foot rope of the fore mainsail, bending over the yardarm, with Polly on her right and Carrie on her left. She reached over to help Carrie. "It's just a clove hitch. You can do it."

Carrie fumbled to tie her gasket to the spar. Her nails still held a chipped coat of red varnish. That wouldn't last long.

"I'm sorry, Sonja, I'm just nervous. We're so high up."

"You'll get used to it. I haven't done much tall rigging either, but it will come to you." Sonja glanced up at the three furled sails above. When they got underway, they would have to go farther aloft and loose those sails as well. The highest yard was at least 100 feet above the sea.

"I can't tie the knots," Carrie whimpered. "I can't even untie them."

"Stop that. You're tough, and we both know it. I'll practice with you. You'll learn the knots." Sonja looked across to the foretop, the platform partway up the mast, where Mr. Deak stood supervising. His face was grim but calm. She knew his climb had been painful.

Polly was also struggling with a knot. Sonja had doubts about Polly's usefulness in the rigging. The girl was neither strong nor brave. She also couldn't tie a knot to save her life. Between her and Carrie, Sonja feared they would have the weaker of the two watches.

"Sonja, come here, lass." Mr. Deak beckoned from the foretop.

"Aye, sir." Sonja stepped sideways on the foot rope. "I'm gonna pass you, Polly."

"Oh dear," Polly gasped.

"Steady now." Sonja didn't see the crossover as too big an ordeal, but evidently Polly was scared out of her wits. Sonja edged sideways, hugging the yardarm until she was near enough to touch Polly. "Hold that yard, Polly. You're all right."

Sonja reached around her with her right arm and grabbed the jackstay on the other side. She swung her right leg out and

109

around Polly and found the foot rope. A gentle swell rocked the ship, causing the yardarm to pitch.

"Oh!" Polly exclaimed as her foot slipped off the rope. Sonja quickly let go of the yard with her left hand and grabbed Polly around the middle to keep her from falling.

Polly shrieked, but Sonja held her firmly until she found her footing again.

"Are you all right?" Sonja swung around Polly as she had originally intended, and looked her in the eye.

Polly shed a tear and gasped. "I'm scared," she whispered.

"You'll be fine." Sonja patted her shoulder and edged along the foot rope toward the foretop. Something wasn't right about the way Polly was shaped. Maybe she was just overweight. Sonja wouldn't know about such things, having always been as thin as a spar. She didn't make a habit of grabbing people around the middle, so maybe it was nothing.

When she scrambled up the jacob's ladder to the foretop, Mr. Deak let out a long huff. "What do you think, Sonja?"

She grasped a halyard for stability as another swell rocked the vessel. "We're learning, Mr. Deak, but not everyone's learning very quickly."

Mr. Deak nodded. "That's what I've seen, too. What do you think of our plan? Can we get to your hiding place before dark?"

Sonja bit her lip. She had just heard six bells. "Swan Bay's too far."

Mr. Deak shifted uncomfortably against the mast. "We've seen an awful lot of craft go by today. They've been a ways out, but sooner or later, folks'll get curious and start looking at us with spyglasses and such. Tomorrow's the Sabbath, and Captain Alice would like us to be away from prying eyes while we observe the Scriptures. Especially since we don't know when the girls' master might come looking for them."

Sonja thought about it. "There's a closer place. Over past Point Cook. Wind's from the north, though. Will she do all right? We don't have to set many sails, do we?"

"It's a beam reach," Mr. Deak said. "That should be fine, and the spanker will help splendidly." He peered around the mast to the other end of the spar, where Kate Robinson worked with four other women. "Make sure all gaskets are tight to the spar, sailors, and then lay alow on the deck." He turned to Sonja. "Miss Robinson is doing quite well with her knots and climbing. I think she'll be a good second mate."

"I agree, sir." Sonja was secretly glad to have Kate as her mate, because she could relate to her a little better than to Mrs. Fiske.

"You better get back on the starboard yard and check their work, sailor."

"Aye, sir." She turned to the yard. "Polly, is your knot tied?"

"Yes," Polly's reply sounded like a moan.

"Come off the yard and climb down. Carrie, you too."

Polly shakily crabbed her way to the shrouds and grasped them, her eyes wild.

"Take heart, lass," Mr. Deak said, reaching a hand to boost Polly onto the foretop. "First day in the rigging is always the roughest."

"Carrie, come on back," Sonja said. Carrie was a good ten feet out on the yard, blocking the way for Fiona and Emma, who were closer to its end.

Carrie didn't reply, but trembled visibly.

"You'll have to go get her," Mr. Deak muttered. "I'd do it, but. . . ."

"Aye sir." Sonja swung herself down onto the foot rope. She edged along to Carrie. "Carrie, we can get down now."

"I can't move!" Tears ran down Carrie's face, and her blond hair fluttered in the breeze.

"It's all right. We're done." Sonja put her hand on Carrie's back. "Come on. I've got ya. Just move one hand or foot at a time. You're safe."

Carrie groaned, but released the jackstay with one hand to grasp it a few inches nearer the mast.

"That's it. We need to hurry, because there's somewhere we need to go."

Sonja guided Carrie back to the shrouds. The Irish girl moved a little quicker then, but still breathed heavily.

With Carrie safely on the ratlines, Fiona and Emma made their way off more easily. They were a little shaky, but able to get on in the heights. Sonja looked along the spar. All the gaskets were properly tied and the sail was free from the yardarm.

"Lay alow, crew," Mr. Deak said.

The women climbed down the shrouds and from there to the bulwarks. Fiona and a couple of the other more adventurous girls jumped the last few feet down to deck. Sonja did the same.

Mr. Deak made his way down the shrouds and gently eased himself onto the deck. He looked at Captain Alice and Mrs. Fiske, who stood watching. "Sonja says we can't get to Swan Bay, tonight, but she knows another place that's more private than here. We can make it if we hurry."

"I'll trust her judgment," Captain Alice said.

"Very well," said Mr. Deak. "With your leave, ma'am, I shall present the crew orders to Mrs. Fiske."

"You have my leave."

"Man the foresail halyards," Mr. Deak said.

"Man the foresail halyards!" Mrs. Fiske boomed.

Mr. Deak reminded the sailors which ropes she meant, and the girls grabbed on. Ned and Addie McKay seized the ropes as well.

"Heave, ho!" Mrs. Fiske commanded. It was hard work, but the girls managed to hoist the sail. "Belay it!" Mrs. Fiske said.

Sonja helped Kate and Emma fix the two halyards around wooden pins so they wouldn't shift.

"Good work." Mrs. Fiske's voice held a touch of pride. "Look aloft, crew, you have set your first sail!"

Sonja looked up with the others and grinned at the billowing sail. It was a grand thing, but there was no time to celebrate.

112

"Prepare to lay aloft the mainmast," Mr. Deak said to Mrs. Fiske. "Not everyone, only six."

"Lay aloft the mainmast to set the main course," Mrs. Fiske bellowed. "Only the first six up the shrouds need attend."

Sonja bolted for the port main shrouds and barely beat Fiona to them. She scrambled up the ratlines, glancing across the ship's waist to see Kate and Jenny ascending the starboard shrouds, with Hannah right behind. A glance down showed Brea and Emma fiercely following Fiona. This made seven, not six, but Sonja was in the lead and she wasn't stopping.

"Lay along the yard!" Mrs. Fiske ordered.

"What does that mean?" Fiona gasped behind her.

"Go out on the yard, like we were on the other one." Sonja climbed to the mainsail yard and headed out to one side, her feet feeling the rope that sagged a couple of feet below the long wooden arm. The other women spread out all along it.

"Set the mainsail!"

Sonja and the others loosed the gaskets, freeing the furled canvas, and retied them around the bare yard.

"Lay alow on the deck!"

The sailors headed down the shrouds. Sonja's heart soared as her team all had their feet on the deck before Kate's. When they were down, Mrs. Fiske gave the order to man the main course halyards.

"We raise it now," Sonja told Fiona. After some exhilarating tugging and heaving, the main course was stretched taut, and they belayed the lines.

"Bravo," said Mrs. Fiske. "Not bad, not bad a'tall."

Mr. Deak showed them the brace lines, and they practiced hauling on these ropes to pivot the sails around the masts. "We'll be doing this a lot," he advised. "People think you only use the wheel to steer the ship, but trimming the sails is even more important when making a sharp turn. You need to know which sheets control which sails and be ready to man them."

They unfurled the outer jib. It was a bit of a dicey prospect, since it involved walking out on the nets along the bowsprit, but Sonja didn't mind. This was much more like the work she had done on her father's sloop, the *Pen Mary*. She led Kate and Jenny out onto the bowsprit to untie the sail. She noted there were three additional headsails, but they only needed the outer jib today. It took a couple minutes to accomplish their task, and then they made their way back to the foredeck, where Mr. Deak showed them how to haul on the proper line to set the outer jib flying taut.

He led the crew back along the rail and gathered them around the mainmast. "Last one for today—the spanker. It's easy."

Sonja held back and let some of the less experienced girls take part. In two minutes flat, they had the spanker rigged and taut.

Mrs. Fiske had Ned turn the hourglass and ring seven bells.

Mr. Deak looked at Sonja. "Are we ready? Do you have a course for Mrs. Fiske?"

"Follow the coast west, and stay half a mile off shore," she replied. "We'll go past Point Cook and find a place to anchor."

"Very well. Crew, to the capstan."

They inserted rods in the round frame of the capstan to make handles.

"Isn't this where we sing?" Fiona asked.

"If you wish." Mr. Deak shrugged.

"Come all ye young fellows, who follow the sea," Fiona began, and the next thing Sonja knew, all the women from Nell's were singing. Evidently they had learned a number of sea chanties from their customers. All she knew were a few Norwegian songs her father had taught her.

Singing boisterously, they hoisted the anchor. It was not hard with all hands trudging around the capstan, pushing the rods. Even Nell and a sullen Lizzie came from the galley to throw their weight into it.

". . .give me some time, to blow the man down." The anchor clanked into the cat's head, and it was clear the brig was already making headway in the light breeze. Mrs. Fiske sent them running to the braces, where she gave them instructions on which way to trim the sails to catch the breeze best.

"I declare, we're making five knots," Mr. Deak said as the brig headed west across Port Phillip Bay. "Not bad for so little sail." He glanced at the sun, which approached the northwestern mountains. "Sonja, how's our depth, lass?"

Sonja ran to the bow and found the lead line. This she could do well. She coiled the line so it wouldn't foul and tossed it out ahead of the ship so that the line would be vertical by the time they approached it. When it hung straight, she pulled it up and counted.

"Five fathoms!"

Gypsy waved in acknowledgement.

Sonja had to keep an eye on the depth. She knew the bottom well, but every once in a while a chance sounding would take her by surprise. She coiled the line for another toss.

"How do you do that?"

Sonja whirled around to see Carrie standing behind her. "You startled me."

"Sorry." Carrie grasped the rail, cringed, and pulled her hand back to look at it. "Blisters."

"Yair. Your hands will toughen up like cow hide before long." Sonja held out her own hand.

Carrie grasped it. "Astonishing. Your hand feels like a man's."

A pang went down Sonja. She had always performed a man's work, but she didn't like to be compared to one. She glanced at Carrie, one of the most feminine women on board. She could see how a man could be attracted to Carrie. But what about herself? Could any man ever like her? Sonja had not given it much thought, but now it disturbed her. She had not seen her reflection in years and didn't even know what she looked like.

115

She smiled. "Your hands will be like this. You're on my watch. Stick with me, and I'll teach you everything I know."

"I don't know if I can do it, Sonja. You saw me. I want to learn everything and be a good sailor, but I don't know if I can. On the yardarm . . ." Carrie glanced up at the spread sails and shook her head.

Sonja gazed at her evenly. "When you're up there, don't think about fear. Think about freedom."

Carrie sighed. "You're right, and no mistake. I'll try." The *Vera B.* plowed on across the bay. Sonja wasn't sure, but she felt they might even be making six knots. The wind held steady, and the sails were kept trimmed in place. A thrill ran over Sonja. She was part of this big ship, and for the first time since Pa died, she belonged somewhere.

She stayed in the bow and dropped her lead line every few minutes, checking the depth. She knew there were a few trouble spots to avoid.

The sun set as Point Cook loomed ahead to starboard. The solstice was near. Today might even be the shortest day of the year—and it was the day they chose to set out on a new life.

Four bells sounded, and Kate called to her from the waist. "Tea time, Sonja. Our watch is going below to eat."

Sonja reluctantly stowed the lead line. If they traveled too far while she was eating, they could get into some treacherous waters.

CHAPTER TWELVE

Alice left her cabin wearing her good bombazine dress on Sunday morning, with Ruel's Bible in the crook of her arm. A fine rain splashed on the deck, and she had instructed Sarah to assemble the crew between decks for their church service.

Kate's watch was now on duty. She would stay on deck with Gypsy and two sailors from her watch, to keep lookout while the rest were below. Alice shivered and pulled her cloak about her for the short walk from the cabin to the main hatch, and to the open space below. In New England, she would think this temperature quite warm in winter, but her new crew would quail before the severe weather Massachusetts endured.

The women waited, seated on blankets. Some had their backs to the bulkhead or bales of wool that were stacked on one side, and Sarah had let them chatter until she arrived. Ned and Addie sat with their mother and Jenny. Alice nodded to Sarah and removed her damp cloak. She took her place before the small group with a smile that belied her nervousness. Would these women accept her message, or would they disdain it? She sent up a prayer that God would open their hearts.

"Good morning. This is our first Sunday together, and I am pleased to mark it as such in the log. I don't know what you normally do on the Sabbath, but my husband always held services for his men, and we shall do the same. Afterward, you may rest, read, sew, or enjoy other quiet pursuits when you are not on watch. Though I don't like to put you to work unless necessary on Sunday, we plan to do more sail drill a little later. You must master the basics so we can leave harbor soon."

Several of the women nodded.

"All right, then. Do you know any hymns?"

Several of the girls looked blankly at her or eyed one another with suspicion.

"Does anyone know 'My Faith Looks up to Thee?'"

Most of them shook their heads.

"Perhaps 'Rock of Ages?'" Sarah suggested.

"Oh, yes, that's a good one," Alice said.

Sarah, Jenny, and Hannah sang through the first verse with her. When they had finished, Alice held up her hand.

"I think we should sing through that stanza again, and if you ladies would like to join in, that would be marvelous. We sing hymns to bring praise and glory to our Lord, and we shall learn a new one each week."

They sang through the verse twice more, and halfway through the second time, Alice was gratified to hear several hesitant voices fill out the melody. At least half the girls' lips moved, and sweet strains blended together. With some practice, she was sure they could form a creditable choir.

After the singing, she offered a brief prayer and opened the Bible. "I have looked out a psalm to share with you today. I am not much of a sermonizer, but the Bible has much to say to us, and I am glad for a chance to share it with you. Did you know God says some things about sailors?"

Most of the girls watched her intently, though Brea leaned back and closed her eyes, and Lizzie looked slightly bored.

"These words are found in the one-hundred-seventh psalm. *They that go down to the sea in ships, that do business in great waters; these see the works of the Lord, and His wonders in the deep. For He commandeth and raiseth the stormy wind, which lifteth up the waves thereof. They mount up to heaven, they go down again to the depths*—"

"Boat ho!"

Everyone's eyes jerked toward the hatch, from which they had heard the lookout's cry. Alice nodded at Sarah, who stood and walked quickly toward the companionway.

"*They go down again to the depths*," Alice continued, knowing the women were listening more to the steps and voices overhead than to her. "*Their soul is melted because of trouble. They reel to and fro, and stagger like a drunken man, and are at their wits' end.*"

Emma laughed.

Alice looked up and smiled. "Quite a description of a sailor during a stormy time, isn't it? I'm afraid we shall experience that all too soon. The psalm goes on, *Then they cry unto the Lord in their trouble, and He bringeth them out of their distresses. He maketh the storm a calm, so that the waves thereof are still. Then are they glad, because they be quiet; so He bringeth them unto their desired haven. Oh, that men would praise the Lord for His goodness, and for His wonderful works to the children of men!*"

She closed the Bible. "I have often read that psalm and meditated on it during stormy weather. God is always there, and He is the one who is able to calm the waves. For today, I wish you to remember the part that says, *so He bringeth them unto their desired haven.* Ladies, God will go with us in this ship. I am trusting Him to bring us to a safe haven. I urge you to trust Him too."

More noises drew their attention overhead, and Sarah appeared on the stairs.

"There," Alice said, knowing she had lost her audience. "We shall meet again next Sunday."

Sarah came to her and said in a low voice, "It is Captain Howard, ma'am. He has come aboard, and wishes to have a word with you."

"Thank you." Alice looked back at the women, who shifted restlessly. "I shall go and greet our visitor. I request you to stay below, since Captain Howard doesn't know we are mostly of the fair sex. Perhaps you can find something useful to do until his boat leaves, and then those of the second watch will lay above. You are dismissed."

She donned her cloak and took her Bible beneath its folds. When she stepped onto the main deck, Josiah, looking a bit bedraggled, left Gypsy near the rail and came toward her.

"Good morning, Captain," she said. "Please come in out of this wet."

"Alice!" Josiah strode toward her. "What's this I hear on shore? Have you really taken aboard a bevy of lewd women?"

Alice stopped short and squared her shoulders. "Please, Josiah—not out here."

###

Josiah closed the cabin door behind them and turned to face Alice. He blinked.

"You—you've changed the cabin."

"Yes. We needed more accommodations, so we partitioned it."

Josiah took off his soggy hat. Bad enough that it had taken his men an hour to find out where she was anchored and another hour to get him over here in the rain. Everything on the *Vera B.* seemed topsy-turvy.

"Now, what did you hear ashore?" Alice asked.

"Ridiculous things. That you've stolen all the women from a brothel and are using them to sail the brig."

"I've stolen nothing." She met his gaze almost defiantly. "It's true several women have signed on with me as crew. That's not illegal."

"But—you can't do this."

"Desperate times call for desperate measures, Josiah."

They stood for a moment, eyeing each other. Josiah almost feared to speak. The walls of the shrunken cabin closed in on him. How could a woman as sensible as Alice do something like this?

"Won't you sit down and discuss it?" Alice waved toward the small table that was now crowded between the safe and the bed.

"You're determined to do this?"

"Yes."

"Then you should know that I heard a man complaining to the harbormaster."

"What man?"

120

"His name was Larson, I think."

Alice's eyes clouded. "That would be Tom Larson, Carrie O'Dell's boss at the Boar's Tusk."

"Yes, he mentioned that one of his employees had run away, and several from a—a house of ill repute had gone too. He pressed the harbormaster to board this ship and get them back, or at least stop you from leaving port."

Alice caught her breath. "He named the *Vera B.*?"

"He did. Apparently someone saw a group of women embarking."

Alice frowned, obviously disconcerted. "We must make haste."

"Indeed, if you insist on doing this."

"We must leave on the next tide."

"How many men have you?"

"There's Gypsy."

"Ruel's steward?"

"Yes. He's the only one who stayed with me."

Josiah shook his head. "I wish I could lend you a few hands, but you know I can't."

"I appreciate the thought, but now I've settled on my course of action, it would only be disruptive to bring men aboard."

"Give it up, Alice. Come over to the *Jade Maiden.* Please!"

"I can't. These women's freedom is at stake."

He lowered his gaze to the deck. "Shall I speak for a pilot for you?"

She hesitated. "We'll take care of it when we are ready."

"So, you think you may not be ready tomorrow? Do these women know the first thing about sailing?"

"I'd say they know the first thing, and some of them know the second. It will be a challenge."

"Yes. Especially if the brothel owner returns. Larson indicated this Snyder is a dangerous man."

"So I understand. Forgive me, Josiah, but I must confer with my mates."

"Alice." He put a hand on her wrist. "Don't do this. It could end tragically."

"I am aware of the risk. But I thank you for your concern."

"Then there's nothing I can say to dissuade you?"

"Nothing."

He let his hand fall to his side. Almost he invoked her husband's name, to ask what Ruel would think of this scheme. But she was so adamant, he might as well try selling ice to an eskimo.

"Very well," he said. "We begin loading tallow this afternoon. It will take two days at least, perhaps longer. If you can wait, I'll sail with you."

"If Tom Larson knows our plans, it would be foolish of us to stay."

Josiah bit back a retort about the foolishness of the entire plan. He nodded and put on his hat. "Then I wish you Godspeed."

As he crossed the main deck, he glanced at the lookout on the quarterdeck. A young woman, if he was not mistaken, in sailor's clothes. It was indecent. How could Alice do this?

He wanted to be angry, but inside he knew he had never seen her more lovely than when she spoke her mind. He hoped he would see her again in this life.

Josiah's news called for an immediate change of plans. Alice called Gypsy and her mates to the quarterdeck. The rain had let up, but the sky still lowered.

"We need more drill before we dare take them outside the harbor," Gypsy insisted. "And that's not to mention running the Rip with a green crew."

"We may not have time to practice." Alice tried to keep her voice even, but her insides were in turmoil.

"Mr. Deak is right, I think." Sarah smiled apologetically. "Can't we try a practice sail around the bay, keeping as far from the anchorage as possible? The hands need to know what to do at a moment's notice."

"That will only come with time," Gypsy said.

Kate kept silent during the discussion, and Alice respected her for that. She knew the least about sailing of them all—and yet, she knew best the consequences if they were caught. Alice eyed her closely. Kate's face was white, and she clenched her fists at her sides.

"What is it, Miss Robinson?" Alice asked.

"Nothing, ma'am. I'm just awaiting your orders."

"You think Mr. Larson will make more trouble."

Kate nodded. "Him and Con are pals. Larson wants Carrie back. He knows Con would fight for him if he was here. Larson will do whatever he can to stop us."

Alice exhaled. "You're right, of course. All of you. So we'd best get on with it."

Gypsy scowled. "I say we follow Mrs. Fiske's suggestion. A sail around the outer rim of the bay, without passing too close to shore or other vessels. Then we'll know if we're ready to run for it. If not, we'll need to keep drilling until the women are ready."

"Ma'am?" Kate said to Alice.

"Yes?"

"The crew on watch heard what Captain Howard said—that he'd heard about us in town. They're scared. We all are."

Alice touched her shoulder. She hoped she hadn't made a mistake in choosing Kate as her second mate. The young woman would need to keep her head when they got into bad weather—or difficulty with the local authorities. "I know. I'm not well versed on the Australian law, but I don't think those men have a right to force you to go back. And Mr. Larson certainly has no right to claim Mr. Snyder's employees. We will do everything we can to prevent that."

"We'll have to get out of Port Phillip Bay before they can act," Sarah said.

Gypsy nodded. "I'll call all hands."

Under other circumstances, Kate could have fallen in love with nautical charts, but the possibility that Con could show up and haul her back to Dame Nell's and beat her senseless dampened her delight in seeing the maps.

Captain Alice had called her into the cabin to examine the charts while Gypsy stayed at the wheel and Mrs. Fiske issued orders. It would take Kate a while to learn the nuances of sailing. When to loosen a line, when to turn a sail just a whisker—or a point. Each section of the ship's wheel was a point. What on earth did that mean? She was beginning to grasp the fact that navigation was a mathematical study, and she had never had the privilege of learning much figuring. Lady Alice had promised to tutor her, once they were free of Port Phillip. That would be something—if it ever came to pass.

Right now, she reveled in the chart. Kate had caught on quickly to the way it pictured the coastline, as though from above. A bird's-eye view, Captain Alice had said. Kate liked that thought. Her Girai Wurrung parents would like it, too—the idea of Kate soaring above the bay, looking down on where the land jutted into the water.

"This is our position right now." Captain Alice pointed to a dip in the line that represented the inner coast of the bay. "We're a little west of Point Cook. When we go on deck, you should be able to see this headland clearly." She sighed. "It would be nice if we could take the chart out there, but it's too damp. I don't want to get it wet."

Kate nodded. She could see how important the chart was to their escape.

"We're sailing eastward around the bay," Captain Alice continued. "You understand about the compass?"

"Mostly."

"Mrs. Fiske is making sure we don't get too close to shore or to where the other ships are anchored."

"And the wind just blows us where we want to go?" Kate felt totally ignorant. She wished she could offer her new boss more promise, more knowledge. Given the chance, she would learn this trade, no matter how complicated it seemed.

"There will be a point soon where they will have to change tack. We'll get too close to the wind."

Kate frowned, not sure what that meant.

"I can see I need to explain that a little better. When we go out, I want you to take particular note of the angle of the sails and where the wind is coming from. If we always went where the wind was going, we'd end up aground. We change the angle at which the sails meet the wind, and we change the rudder's position. They change the ship's direction. You will soon be used to it, but I know it's overwhelming at first."

Kate swallowed hard. "Do you think I can learn all this?"

"Yes, I do. You're a quick learner, Kate. I was pleased when you were chosen as mate. Look at the chart. See the way the shore curves? We can't go straight east. We have to keep adjusting the sails and the rudder to make the ship follow a path that bends, like the shore does." Captain Alice looked up and smiled. "Come. Let's go out and see it. Mr. Deak can explain better how we adjust the sails to make the brig go precisely where we want it to."

On deck, Mrs. Fiske stood at the rail of the quarterdeck, yelling and gesturing to the crew members. All but Nell were on the main deck or in the rigging, responding as best they could to her commands.

She turned toward Kate and the captain as they approached the wheel.

125

"Mr. Deak, I think you should take over. The sailors are learning, but it's by inches when we need to take giant steps."

"You take the wheel, ma'am." Gypsy released the handles, and Mrs. Fiske took his place. He turned to the captain. "I'm thinking it's time they learned how to change tack without putting the ship dead in irons."

"I agree." Captain Alice looked at Kate. "He means facing the teeth of the wind. If we do that, the wind will push us backward until we can steer one way or the other with the rudder."

"That could be deadly if it happened in the Rip," Gypsy said. "We can't make the passage out of the harbor safely unless these girls—I mean the crew, ma'am—can tack quickly."

The captain frowned. "Gypsy, do you think you could tell Kate what to give as an order and have her relay it to the crew? There's much she needs to learn before she can supervise a watch alone, but she may as well start feeling her role now."

Gypsy nodded. "Come with me to the rail, Miss Robinson. If there's time, I'll explain each maneuver to you. If not, I'll just tell you what to say and we'll do it—explanations to follow."

Kate nodded. Gypsy seemed like a good sort, and she didn't mind taking orders from him. Not once since the women had come aboard had she seen him leering at the girls or heard him use an obscenity. Of all the men Captain Alice might have been left with, Gypsy was all right.

"Good. Now, we have to make a turn in the Rip, or we'll never get out. We need to practice that tack as nearly as we can before we ever get there."

The *Vera B.* had made a circular run in the middle of bay, allowing the women to experience trimming the sails in various points of the wind. Kate thought her head would explode. Every time she learned something, she saw or heard a thousand other things that baffled her.

They broke for dinner when eight bells rang at noon, with Mrs. Fiske's watch going below first. While they ate, Kate's watch practiced their knots and competed to see who could climb to the tops first—the small platforms partway up the masts. Kate was surprised by the girls' agility. She had expected Sonja to excel, but on the second run, Carrie nearly beat her up the rigging. Emma and Lucy had found their balance on the ratlines, and they were learning almost as quickly, with Anne not far behind them. Polly was the only one who seemed to hold back, and Kate couldn't help worrying about her. She hoped she wouldn't regret bringing her.

She was famished by the time her watch got to eat. She hadn't even been working the way they had, but her throat was dry and her voice hoarse from the dozens of commands she had shouted.

Nell brought her meal to her at the small table between decks, where the officers ate. Kate wouldn't mind if she ate when the others did, but Mrs. Fiske, Captain Alice, and Gypsy were still up on deck. Would it make a huge difference if she carried her plate along the passageway to where the girls enjoyed their lunch?

"Think you we've made a change for the better?" Nell asked as she poured a cup of strong coffee for Kate.

Kate eyed her in surprise. "I do. Don't you?"

"I don't know yet. Most of the girls have blisters, and I shouldn't wonder if someone breaks their neck before we're done."

Kate put a bite of fish in her mouth and closed her eyes for a moment. "Nell, you do have a way with cooking."

Nell's smile changed her face, and for an instant Kate saw the beguiling beauty who had conquered Con Snyder. "I haven't baked much for a long time, but I'm enjoying it. I guess I have the best job on the ship."

"You wouldn't want to go back, would you?"

Nell shook her head. "We can't. He'd never forgive us. And you know Tom Larson'll tell Con the minute he steps off the steamboat from Geelong. No, we're in it now, all of us. I just

127

think it's going to be harder than some of the girls bargained for."

"They knew," Kate said. "What waits for us at the end of the voyage will make it worth all the blisters and bruises."

"It may not be all you think."

"I trust Mrs. Fiske and the captain. They've both said they'll help us find jobs. Good honest jobs, so we can support ourselves without catering to men."

"I hope it's so." Nell smiled. "That Mrs. Fiske. She as much as told me she could get me a place with a milliner she knows, or as a cook if I'd prefer it."

"I believe she will," Kate said. "Or you can go on to America with Captain Alice. She said there are lots of opportunities for women there."

Gypsy came down the companionway and limped toward them. "Got anything for a tired old sailor, Miss Nell?"

Nell laughed. "So long as it's only food you want, Mr. Deak."

Gypsy pulled up short. "I mean no other."

"I thought not. Sit down, sir. I'll bring your plate."

Gypsy sat down opposite Kate. "We've started another course around the bay. As soon as I fill my belly, we'll call all hands and get your watch up there again. I'll have you in the rigging, too. Are you ready for it?"

Kate scrunched up her face. "Do you think I'm learning anything, Mr. Deak?"

"Oho, what kind of question is that? You know fathoms more than you did a day ago."

"Thanks, but now I've got to learn to feel the wind and just how to tweak the sails, and even mathematics and how to plot a course, and—"

"Avast there." Gypsy held up a hand. "It'll come to you, Miss Robinson. All in good time."

Kate had barely time to finish her lunch and freshen up—or, as Gypsy bluntly put it, visit the head—before they were called back on deck. She joined her watch members at the bottom of the foremast. Mr. Deak called the orders to set the topsails on both masts.

Kate had climbed to the top of the second sail only once before, and her stomach felt a bit queasy as she clung to the yardarm and untied the knots holding the foretopsail in place.

Once the two large topsails spread out and grabbed the nor'-nor'west wind, they sailed anticlockwise around the bay at an impressive clip. Eight knots, Mr. Deak declared proudly. When Kate's feet hit the deck once more, she stood for a moment with Carrie, Lucy, and Emma, gazing up at what they had done.

Anne missed a step on the ratlines, losing her cap on the way down. She joined them at last, a look of triumph in her eyes. "There, I made it again."

"Good work," Kate told her.

"Thanks." Anne raised her eyes to the stretched canvas. "We're really going, aren't we?"

"I can hardly believe it," Lucy said.

Kate put a hand on each girl's shoulder. "Believe it. We're going to be free."

A mighty blast sounded off the starboard side of the ship. Kate jumped and turned to see a steamboat the size of the *Vera B.* bearing down on them. Its engines rumbled as it approached, barely a quarter mile away.

"Steamboat to starboard!" Gypsy shouted.

"I see it," Mrs. Fiske replied.

"*Blekksprut!*" Sonja muttered beside Kate. "How did we miss seeing the *Vesta?*"

Kate sprinted to the quarterdeck and vaulted up the steps, her watch pulling up to wait below the rail. "Will we miss it?" she asked Mrs. Fiske. The steamboat from Geelong was closer than Kate had expected, and closing the distance. She caught her breath. They were near enough for the *Vesta's* crew and passengers to spy the girls' long hair. She whipped around to tell Anne to get her cap on.

"She'll pass astern of us," Mrs. Fiske reassured her as Captain Alice hurried over from the port rail. "No danger of collision."

"They'll see us, though!" Kate glanced down at the main deck where the sailors of both watches stood transfixed, watching the steamboat.

"Second watch below," Gypsy roared.

Carrie, Sonja, Polly, Lucy, and Emma ran for the hatch, while Anne scrambled across the deck to retrieve her cap. Her golden brown hair had come loose, and it waved in the breeze like a pennant.

Kate looked back toward the approaching steamer. Her heart clutched. On deck with a dozen other passengers, staring toward the *Vera B.*, stood the tall, bulky form of Con Snyder.

CHAPTER THIRTEEN

Alice gripped the bulwark, gazing at the steamboat. Sarah was right, the boat would easily miss the *Vera B.*, but it was closer than she liked. She was certain Ruel would have been angry at the watch if they had allowed their ship to pass so closely in front of another vessel.

"Con!" Kate stared toward the *Vesta* and put a hand to her mouth.

Alice looked at the crowded rail of the steamboat, where a big jowly man in a gray suit, red waistcoat, and tall hat pranced angrily in place, gesticulating wildly toward the *Vera B.*

Gypsy whistled. "That's the man you're running from?"

Kate nodded, her face taut. "He sees me."

"Lay below with your watch," Alice said. It was too late for secrecy, but it seemed best to get Kate out of sight.

"If you're not back. . ." Alice heard Con's voice rise briefly against the steam engine's thunking. ". . . and I'll hunt you down and thrash you like a. . . ."

The rest of Con's tirade was lost to them as the wind ruffled in the sails overhead, but Alice saw a glint of metal in the ruffian's hand. A second later, a flash of fire and smoke appeared from his hands and a shot rang out. The bullet hit the hull below Alice and Kate, making them both jump.

Alice's hair stood on end. She and Kate ducked below the bulwark, but Gypsy craned his neck to watch the steamboat. "They've passed astern," he said, motioning for them to get up. "Nobody's a good shot at that distance, anyhow."

Kate looked at Alice, her eyes fierce. "How fast can we leave? He means it. He will follow us."

Alice stood slowly and glanced at Gypsy and Sarah. The first mate looked unperturbed, but Gypsy breathed rapidly. She knew they all needed her reply, but she didn't know what to say.

"I don't see how we could leave the harbor without at least another day or two of training." She watched for Gypsy's reaction. "The crew is learning, but they still have a long way to go. Especially to make it out through the channel safely."

Gypsy sighed. "You saw that man, Mrs. Packard. How long will it take him to come after us, if we stay in the bay? There's nowhere to hide this brig."

Alice shook her head. "Kate, please go fetch Sonja. And Nell," she added as Kate bounded down the stairs. Kate looked back and nodded.

Alice turned to Sarah. "How's our course?"

"We are heading due south, ma'am. Sonja assured me this course will be safe until after we pass the headland." She gestured at the distant shore off the starboard bow.

"Very good." Alice looked aloft at the sails. They filled properly with the wind, and the rigging looked as it should.

"Hannah," Sarah called down to the main deck, "I'd like to see a little more vigilance. Distribute the crew about the deck, and I want a lookout posted in the foretop. We mustn't have any collisions."

Hannah dispersed the watch to various positions. Lizzie started up the ratlines toward the foretop.

Kate returned with Sonja and Nell. The grim lines of Nell's face revealed that Kate had told her about sighting Con.

Alice gathered them around Sarah, who stayed at the wheel, eyeing the sails. "We need to decide what to do." She made an extra effort to keep her voice calm. "Con Snyder has seen us, and it's plain that he will come after you women. I wish I knew how long we have."

Sarah let out a deep breath. "The steamboat will take a little while to get to dock. Then it would take some time for the brigand to find someone to bring him after us in a boat."

Nell frowned. "He has someone though, as long as the bloke's in town. Bluey Glenn. He has that schooner, the *Lorelai*. Kate and I have been on it. Bluey owes Con a chunk of money, and Con lets him pay it off with passage."

Kate shook her head. "I hated those trips. Van Diemens Land, Adelaide. Newcastle. Uhh." She shuddered and looked away.

"Con would take some of us out for special occasions," Nell explained. "Special for the customers. Not for us."

"We got Anne in Van Diemens Land," Kate said. "She was so scared, she cried in the hold the whole way."

Alice grimaced. "I'm sorry you experienced that. We must get you away from them."

Kate lifted her chin. "Captain Alice, there's no time. I know we signed your articles, but. . ."

A chill ran through Alice's body. "Yes, Miss Robinson?"

"Please—don't let us be caught. What can we do if we stay with the ship? We'll be captured. But if we sail to Geelong, I could take the girls into the bush and hide. I know how to live out there. Maybe we can get away—" She broke off, her face crumpled.

"Kate! Please don't panic." Alice grabbed Kate's shoulder and looked her in the eye. She couldn't have Kate desert her, but a reprimand might work against her. She mustn't strengthen the beleaguered woman's resolve to abandon the ship with her troupe. Kate said nothing, but returned Alice's gaze with guarded eyes.

Alice looked at Gypsy. "Mr. Deak. Is there any way we can get out of the bay? Can we possibly do it?"

Gypsy grimaced. "Without dying, or running aground?" He turned to Sonja. "The pilot's down yonder at Queenscliff, right?"

Sonja nodded. "We can signal for him when we get there. But if time's short. . . ."

Alice looked at the fishing girl. "You know the channel, don't you? Do you think you could guide us out?"

133

Sonja let out a long sigh. "I know the channel. More than one, in fact. There are several that lead to the Rip, but once you're in it, there's only one place you can go. I've watched hundreds of ships go in and out while I was fishing in the shallows."

"So you can get us out?" Alice wasn't sure about the legal ramifications of leaving port without clearing with the harbormaster—especially, heaven forbid, if the *Vera B.* ran aground and blocked the channel.

"Aye, ma'am. I know the bottom, that's for sure. And the depth. I think I have a feel for the ship's handling—enough to be safe."

Alice looked around at their faces. Gypsy gritted his teeth. She supposed he would veto the idea. More than anyone else, he knew the condition of the crew, and Alice was under no illusion of the girls' sailing skills.

"I'll tell you what." Gypsy paused. "It's a matter of life or death. If we stay here, there's little hope. If we attempt the channel, there is a small hope."

Alice wasn't expecting this opinion from the old sailor, but she was glad to hear it.

Sarah smiled softly at Kate. "Even if you were to take the girls into the highlands, I'm sure Con would find you eventually. You could evade him by yourself, maybe, but with nine of you, there's no way you could be quick enough and cover your tracks."

Nell nodded. "Plenty of men with hounds to track people down, and most of those girls have never been off in the wild. They wouldn't have any more idea what to do than they have right here. I say we stay with the ship."

Kate's shoulders slumped. "Forgive me, Captain Alice. I spoke hastily."

"I forgive you. I understand how frightened you must be. If you stay the course, we have a chance, but everyone on this ship will have to work together."

"You can count on me, Captain." Kate set her jaw, fierce determination glittering in her eyes.

"Me too," said Nell. "Once we explain it to the girls, they'll all put in with a will. I reckon they'd rather go down with the ship than face Con now."

Gypsy nodded. "We may not live to tell about it, but we're leaving this port today, Captain Alice, with your command."

Sarah raised her hand in salute. "Huzzah, Captain Alice, let us make sail for the Rip!"

"Let's do it," Sonja said. "We may have three or four hours on Snyder, in which case, he won't be able to leave until morning. Nobody goes out at night." She glanced at the sails. "The wind is with us now, but if we wait until it shifts, we'll be trapped."

Gypsy grinned and looked at Alice. "I remember Captain Packard mentioning that the prevailing winds would work in our favor, going up the east coast, ma'am. That's good for another reason, too."

"What's that, Mr. Deak?"

"If that rascal is chasing us in a schooner, we'll have the advantage. Especially if we get our topgallants and royals up. Schooners sail good upwind, but before the wind, you can't beat a good square rigger like the *Vera B.*"

"Then we really have a chance?" Kate's eyes were wide. "What do we need to do?"

Sonja stood on the *Vera B*'s bowsprit, lead line in hand. She glanced to starboard, where the village of Queenscliff lay beyond half a mile of water. Shortland's Bluff, it was called, when she lived there with her father. Now the growing fishing village and lighthouse point had changed its name, and she hardly knew the inhabitants anymore. She turned away. It wouldn't do to reminisce now. Straight ahead was the Rip—the only way for vessels to leave Port Phillip Bay. Beyond were the Bass Straight and the open sea.

"Sonja, I don't see any cutter approaching," Mr. Deak called from the bow.

She glanced back at him. "I know. The pilot must be somewhere else. Or doesn't think we should leave with this tide." The tide rushed in through the Rip at more than four knots, slowing the *Vera B.*'s headway considerably.

"Is it safe?" The old sailor eyed her gravely.

"The Rip is never safe, sir." Sonja looked beyond him to see Kate, Lucy, and Carrie on the main deck. The masts blocked her view of the helm, but Captain Alice had taken the wheel to spell Mrs. Fiske. She swallowed hard. If she made a mistake and they ran aground, all of them were in mortal danger. And if they survived, what would happen to her? From the things she'd heard Anne and Emma saying, Con Snyder might kidnap her too, and force her to work in his den of evil. Anne was Sonja's age. A year ago, Con had tricked her aboard his boat in Van Diemen's Land and carried her back to Melbourne to work for him. Sonja might not be as pretty as Anne or Lucy, but she reckoned Con wouldn't care.

"If we're ready, I'll call all hands." Mr. Deak turned and headed for the hatch.

Sonja threw the lead again and bounced it off the bottom. Four fathoms. She knew this part of the bay. It was not the primary shipping channel, but a smaller channel running along the western shore, too shallow for bigger ships. By taking it, they would save at least an hour.

She looked up to the foretop, where Emma kept watch. "All clear, Emma?"

The waifish lookout shaded her eyes, her blond hair teasing from under her cap in the wind. "All clear, Sonja! No boats."

Sonja chewed her lip and fidgeted with the lead line's weight. It was all well and good to say she could pilot them out the Rip, but the responsibility pressed down on her like a chunk of ballast.

Lives depended on her judgment and experience. She wished her papa was beside her.

A clamor on deck broke her reverie. The first watch sailors had arrived on deck, along with the McKay children.

Mr. Deak came to the bow. "Sonja, you just tell me what we need to do, and I'll relay the orders to Kate, and she'll relay them to the helm. Mrs. Fiske is taking the wheel again."

"Very good, sir." Sonja glanced at the undulating waters ahead. "The tide's pretty strong, but the sun will be down in another hour or so. The problem is, if we can't make it out by sunset, we won't be able to see."

Mr. Deak's eyes shifted. "Another two knots would make a world of difference, wouldn't it?" He looked aloft. "Wind's light. I think we should shake the topgallants out."

Sonja nodded, though she hated to send the girls up to their highest climb yet in waters as perilous as the Rip. "Can you do it one mast at a time?" she asked. "We need sailors on deck to trim sails at any time."

"Very good," said Mr. Deak. "You stay there and call out if we need to change course."

Over the next few minutes, Sonja guided the *Vera B.* into the main channel of the Rip as her watch went aloft to the fore topgallant yard, over seventy feet above deck. Sonja wished she could assist. She hoped Carrie and Polly were all right. *Hang on tight!* At least Kate was with them. Hannah stepped in to take the second mate's role as messenger on deck.

In the middle of the Rip, the tidal current was even stronger. Sonja's throat went dry as the brig started slipping backward toward Port Phillip Bay. She glanced at the rigging, where her watch was descending the ratlines. The fore topgallant sail flopped loose in the breeze. Her watch had done its duty.

"Haul on the fore topgallant halyards!" Mr. Deak said, not waiting for the sailors in the rigging to reach the deck. The sailors of the first watch scrambled to tug on the lines, setting the topgallant firmly in place.

Sonja perceived an immediate difference. The vessel began to make headway again. She checked their course. They were right in the middle of the channel. "Starboard two points!" she called out. They would need a lot of small corrections as they went.

Mr. Deak had the crew trim the sails as soon as the second watch was back on deck. Then he sent the first watch up the mainmast shrouds to release the main topgallant.

The foremast sails obstructed Sonja's view of the women's effort. She concentrated on keeping the *Vera B.* in the middle of the channel. Slowly, they progressed. "Four points to port!" she called out as they approached a bend in the channel.

Slowly, they gained on the Rip. The lighthouses on the two headlands, Point Lonsdale and Point Nepean, beckoned to Sonja. The channel lay right between. They were heading too close to Point Lonsdale. "Two points to port!" she shouted.

After relaying her message, Mr. Deak gave word to raise the main topgallant. The first watch came wearily down the ratlines as the second watch heaved the halyards, securing the topgallant sail. Sonja felt an increase in speed, but the brig still veered too close to Point Lonsdale. She knew the channel was only safe for the middle third of the stretch of water between the two headlands. The ship was veering outside that middle third.

"Hard to port!" she shouted back to Mr. Deak.

She stooped and held on to the netting on the bowsprit as the ship lumbered around. After a moment, Mr. Deak called, "The mate says we're close-hauled, and we'll have to tack."

"*Stinkend Rotte,*" Sonja muttered under her breath. Smelly rat. They wouldn't have time or space to tack, and the first watch still wasn't down from the rigging. Jenny was making her way down, with Brea following. The sails shivered in the wind. Sonja knew what that meant. If the angle of the wind hitting the sail got smaller, they would be dead in irons—at the mercy of the wind and current until they could straighten the vessel out and try

138

again. Meanwhile, they could be dashed against rocks or stranded in the shallows.

"Can we heave to?" Sonja asked. She knew that once sails were set, there were only certain ways a vessel could be stopped quickly. Dropping the anchor was not an option.

"Soon as the crew is down from the shrouds," Mr. Deak promised. "We'll tack then. Can't until everybody's on deck to man both sets of sheets."

Sonja exhaled and looked forward. They were nearly to the submerged ridge at the entrance to the harbor, where ships could easily run aground. She could tell that Mrs. Fiske was expertly holding the brig on the edge of losing the wind. There would be no time to tack. All she could do was hope that the tide was high enough for the hull to miss the shoal wherever they crossed it. The channel was to their left.

"Crew's almost down," Mr. Deak said, "Lizzie being the last."

Sonja tossed the lead line. It came up at three fathoms. If they were in a clipper ship, they would already be aground. She looked left and right. Cape Nepean and Cape Lonsdale were even—she was right between the two headlands marking the entrance to the sea. Had they cleared the bar?

The *Vera B.* shuddered violently, causing Sonja's foot to slip off the bowsprit. Her leg plunged through the netting attached to its side, which stopped her painfully at the point her thigh was too large to continue through. A loud shriek sounded from the rigging.

Sonja swore and scrambled to free herself from the net.

CHAPTER FOURTEEN

Lizzie landed with a thud on the oaken deck and lay still for a moment, dazed.

"Lizzie! Are you all right?"

Slowly she raised her head. Hannah and Fiona knelt beside her.

"Are you hurt?" Fiona asked.

Lizzie swallowed hard and struggled to sit up. "My hip. And my arm." A moment later, a fierce burning in her hands caused her to gasp. She held them out, palms up.

Hannah took her left hand gently. "Those are bad rope burns."

Gypsy had reached them.

"All right, sailor?"

"I ... don't know. Did we hit something?"

"We scraped bottom," Gypsy said, "but we're clear now."

Lady Dunbar squeezed in between Fiona and Gypsy. "Lizzie, my dear, are you all right? I heard you scream, and—" She fell to her knees and reached for Lizzie's other hand. Lady Dunbar could be graceful, even in made-over sailor's trousers.

"I don't think I've broken anything," Lizzie managed. She glanced up at the ratlines. "Unless I broke something on the ship."

They all chuckled. The other girls closed in around her.

"Can you stand?" Hannah asked.

Lizzie nodded, teeth clenched in pain.

"Bring her to my cabin," Lady Dunbar said.

Lizzie was glad of that. She hated the dark, cramped forecastle she was forced to share with the other women. The sleeping arrangements were intolerable. Half the crew was on

140

watch all the time, and the other half could retire to the forecastle if they wished. But while Lizzie was on duty, that whiny Polly Marsh slept in her hammock. The idea that she, a lady's maid of the first standing, shared her bedding with a harlot revolted her. She had begged Captain Alice to let her sleep out in the 'tweendecks, but had been courteously turned down.

She took Hannah's hand and pushed up off the deck. Pain screeched through her hip and down her leg. She staggered and leaned heavily on Fiona.

"All right?" Lady Dunbar eyed her closely.

Lizzie nodded.

"Small steps then," Hannah said. "Fiona and I will help you."

"All right, back to your posts, the rest of you. The sun's setting, and we've work to do." Gypsy clapped his hands, and the other women's footsteps pounded on the deck.

Lizzie glanced toward shore. The sun spilled red, pink, and mauve hues on the low clouds in the west, and the lighthouses on both headlands had fallen behind them.

Hannah and Fiona helped her to the cabin, and Lady Dunbar let them in. Lizzie looked around. She hadn't been inside since the board partition had been built. This new cabin was tiny, but held a comfortable-looking bed, a chest, and a small chair. Near the chair, a shelf could be folded down from the wall for use as a table.

"Sit down, my dear."

"Thank you, my lady."

"We're not using that now, remember?"

Lizzie grimaced and nodded. How she wished to have their original roles restored.

Lady Dunbar lit a lantern. "Fiona, our watch goes on duty at four bells for the second dog watch. Get your supper quickly so you're ready for duty when the watch changes. Remember, the dog watches are only two hours."

"Yes, ma'am," Fiona said.

"And tell Captain Alice I shall take the wheel again shortly."

"I think she put Kate on it, ma'am."

Lizzie stared at her. Kate Robinson, that brazen girl, was manning the wheel? Lizzie still couldn't believe Kate had been chosen as second mate. Hannah McKay would have been better—or even herself.

"I'll get the salve and bandages," Hannah said. "Is your hip all right, Lizzie?"

"No, but it will get better, I suppose." Lizzie pushed up her sleeve and crooked her right arm so she could see the part she fell on and grimaced.

"That'll need a bandage too," Hannah said. "I'm amazed you didn't break every bone in your body." She left the cabin, and Lady Dunbar raised Lizzie's arm toward the lantern and scrutinized it.

"It's bruising up quickly. I'll speak to Mr. Deak when we're done. You won't be in the rigging for a few days."

"I don't think I could climb up there now if my life depended on it."

"You won't need to. If they need extra hands, I'll go up myself."

"Oh, you mustn't do that, my lady!"

"There, now." Lady Dunbar patted her hand. "Rest here through the dogwatch, and then if you're able, we'll help you below."

"Oh, my lady, couldn't I go back to my former duties?" Tears pooled in Lizzie's eyes. "I want to take care of you, as before. This sailor work is too hard."

The countess smiled kindly. "I'm sorry, Lizzie. That was the condition of our sailing on this ship. I do miss your pampering and deft touches, but I'm learning that I can comb my own hair and dress myself when I have to. It's probably good for me."

"Oh, my lady, please!" Tears flowed steadily now. "I'll do anything if you'll let me out of that forecastle! It's horrid being in there with those strumpets!"

Lady Dunbar was quiet for a moment, then she met Lizzie's gaze. "I know this is a trial for you. I cannot get you excused from either your berth or your duties. Lizzie, you must look within yourself for strength. If you do, I am sure you will find it."

Lizzie sobbed.

"I saw you in the rigging today," Lady Dunbar said. "You were frightened, and yes, a bit clumsy. But you did it. And I was proud."

Lizzie sniffed. "Truly?"

"Yes. Very proud. I know this isn't what you want to hear, but we shall go on as we have been. When we get to England, I'll be happy if you wish to remain in my employ. If not, then I will support your decision. You may find after this voyage that you are capable of many things you never considered before, and you may choose a different path."

Hannah came in carrying a small tin, some strips of cloth, and a pair of scissors.

"If you have everything in hand, Hannah, I'll go back on deck." Lady Dunbar said.

"Yes, Mrs. Fiske. I'm sure we'll be fine. And Nell is fixing Lizzie some willow bark tea."

"I'm sure that will be soothing."

"Oh, and Jenny and Brea went below to scout for leaks in the hull. Captain's orders," Hannah said.

"Thank you." The countess went out.

Lizzie opened her hands so Hannah could apply the salve and bandages, and then leaned back in the chair so she could dab at the blood on her forearm.

If only she could believe they would make it safely to England! She'd been lucky today. How many more times would they force her to climb into the rigging? She could be killed in an instant.

Compared to this nightmare, England was heaven. As Lady Dunbar's personal maid, Lizzie had gone to many of the social events her mistress attended. She had friends among the other upper echelon servants, and even a few among the aristocracy. Last year she had been the toast of several summer house parties when she won the popular archery contests. Some of Lady Dunbar's friends had even asked to borrow her so she could show their own maids how to execute an elaborate hairstyle.

But now Lizzie was a common sailor, a pair of hands that could haul on a rope when needed—and an expendable one at that.

"There we go," Hannah said, closing the tin of salve. "Let's get you over to the bed."

Two hours on the featherbed her ladyship had brought from her house to use on her bunk, with fluffy, clean-smelling blankets, was almost worth the fall.

Lizzie's next conscious sensation was of something tickling her nose. She batted at it groggily. The nuisance continued. She opened her eyes and blinked in the glare of a lantern. The throbbing in various parts of her body was eclipsed only by the annoying sight that greeted her. The McKay boy stood next to the bed, grinning and holding a gray-tipped white feather.

"What are you doing here, you little brat?"

Ned laughed and danced in place. "Mrs. Fiske said to wake you up. It's tea time, if you're hungry."

Lizzie groaned. "Send me a woman, I need help. And don't touch me with that filthy feather."

"It's not filthy. I thought you might like it for your arrows."

"That's not the type of feather used on arrows."

Ned's face crumpled. "It's from a seagull."

"We use goose feathers. And wing feathers only."

"Oh." He looked down at his treasure and sighed. "I don't suppose we'll see any geese on the ship."

"I highly doubt it."

"I was hoping ..."

"Yes?" she asked sharply.

"I hoped if I got you more feathers, you'd teach me to shoot the bow."

Lizzie shook her head, but that only made it ache. "Listen, you dunce, there's no place to shoot on a ship, and if the arrows went over the side, you would lose them. Besides, I don't make my own arrows."

"Oh." The boy's chin drooped.

"What do you want to learn for, anyway?"

"For when we meet the pirates."

Lizzie tried not to gape. Was he repeating things the adults had said, or making up his own adventure tales? "What do you know about pirates?"

"Only what Gypsy said. He's fought pirates before, and he says we might see some before we cross the line."

"The line? You mean the equator?"

Ned nodded. He headed for the door, his feet dragging.

"Send me a girl," she called after him. "And don't you even think about touching my bow."

A moment later, Addie appeared in the doorway.

"Miss Lizzie? Ned said you need help."

Lizzie sighed. "I suppose you are better than nothing."

Addie smirked. "Boys are no good at all."

"You speak truth." Lizzie pushed herself up. "I am bruised from toe to crown. If you could just come closer and let me grasp your hand …"

Addie complied, and with a moan, Lizzie sat on the edge of the bed, her feet dangling.

"Does it hurt?" Addie asked.

"Fiercely."

"The girls said you fell ten feet off the shrouds."

"That's about right."

Addie nodded. "Miss Robinson said she feels bad for you, all banged up like that."

"Hmpf. Help me stand." Lizzie pushed down on her shoulder, and Addie pulled on her arm. After rocking back and forth a couple of times, Lizzie stood. The pain burned in her hip, and she sucked air through her teeth.

"You all right?" Addie asked.

"No. Help me to the head." The floor lurched beneath Lizzie's feet, and she grabbed Addie to help keep her balance. "Ugh! Why is it so rough?"

Addie grinned. "We're outside the bay now. In the ocean."

Alice tried to sleep during the night watch, but wound up on deck with Gypsy an hour before midnight, while he patiently coached Kate in steering. Now that they were in the open water of the Bass Strait, with little likelihood of ramming another vessel or running aground, Kate's practical navigation lessons had begun.

Off the port bow, she could make out the dark shore of Victoria.

"Good evening, captain." Gypsy tipped his hat as Alice approached.

"Ma'am," Kate said with a quick glance.

"How do we fare?" Alice asked.

"We're making good speed." Gypsy looked up at the vast canvas spread above them. "I was tempted to set the royals, but—"

"The women had trouble with the height of the topgallant yard today."

"Yes, so I won't send them higher just yet. We're catching plenty of wind. I just don't like to think of Snyder coming after us."

"Surely he won't try to leave the bay tonight," Alice said.

"Nobody runs the Rip at night. But tomorrow ..."

"He *will* come after us," Kate said grimly.

"I think we can outrun him, if this wind holds," Gypsy said.

Alice looked at the compass by the light of the binnacle lantern. "Southeast."

146

"Aye. We'll hold that course until we spot the lighthouse on Wilson's Promontory. By morning we'll be a good way from Port Phillip." Gypsy walked over to the rail and looked down on the waist. "I've put the crew to coiling the lines and practicing their knots. Perhaps you have another duty for them?"

"They've all worked hard today," Alice said. "Could we let half go below?"

Gypsy looked doubtful. "Not good for discipline, ma'am. They should stay on deck during the watch. Besides, the first watch have their hammocks."

"All right, then, I'll bring them up here and teach them the points of the compass."

The women seemed glad of the distraction, and Alice quizzed them to see what they remembered from their lessons the day before. To her surprise, Carrie had learned the thirty-two points almost perfectly—even better than Sonja.

"You've been practicing," Alice said.

"Yes, ma'am."

Alice nodded. "The hourglass has nearly run out. You may turn it, and Sonja may ring seven bells."

Gypsy spelled Kate at the wheel, and she joined their lesson. Alice asked who could point out the Southern Cross. Most of the girls knew the constellation. She took them through several others they could use as reference points on these winter nights. She would soon start a mathematics class for those most advanced. Kate, Carrie and Sonja, surely, and possibly Lucy. From Sarah's watch, Jenny was a likely student, and Fiona, if she could concentrate. Brea was smart enough, but Alice wasn't sure she would deign to sit under her tutelage. The bare show of respect the black-haired girl paid her and Sarah bordered on insolence.

When eight bells approached, Alice thought she might be able to sleep. She walked over to the wheel. "When will you sleep, Gypsy?"

147

"I can bring my blanket up. Once Mrs. Fiske is comfortable with the course, I'll catnap in the launch."

Alice shook her head. "All right, but call me after the midwatch. I'll take the morning watch with Kate, so you can get a good rest. We'll need you during the daylight hours."

Josiah put his spyglass to his eye and focused on the men at the dock. Confound this delay. The barrels of tallow should have been stowed below hours ago. Apparently the rendering plant was as low on laborers as he was.

"Mr. Stark."

"Yes, sir?" Stark walked toward him across the quarterdeck.

"I'm going ashore to see the harbormaster. Finish this up so we can get under way."

"Yes, captain." Stark called to the crew on the deck below, "Prepare the captain's launch."

Josiah handed him the spyglass and headed for the waist. He shivered and nearly went back to his cabin for gloves.

He climbed out of the boat at the small dock where longshoremen were loading barrels of tallow for his cargo onto lighters. Dozens of boats lined the docks in the harbor. Anchored a short way out was a trim coasting schooner, the *Lorelai*.

Josiah's steps faltered as he caught sight of a man he recognized on the dock. It was Larson, the one he'd heard on Saturday, arguing with Eddleston about the *Vera B.* Now Larson was deep in conversation with two men. One was dressed for sea and could be the schooner's captain. The other was a large, florid man he'd never seen, but it didn't take Josiah long to guess his identity.

"They won't get away with it," the big man said.

"Easy now, Con. Bluey will help us," Larson said.

"How much will you pay me?" the sailor asked. "I hadn't planned to put out again so soon."

148

"You owe me, Bluey Glenn," the big man growled. "If you take us out after them, I might mark out your debt. If you won't, I'll crack your skull."

Josiah hurried past them.

"Morning, Cap'n," the harbormaster said when he stepped into the shack. Eddleston's tiny office was warm from a small coal-burner set up inside.

"Good day. I hope to finish my lading and weigh anchor soon."

"You won't make it out the channel today, sir."

"At dawn, then."

Eddleston nodded. "Might."

"I must," Josiah said. "I fear the *Vera B.* has sailed. Did Mrs. Packard or her steward stop by here?"

"No, but there was no need. Didn't see it myself, but I heard they struck out just before sunset. They seem to have cleared the channel without a pilot. Plucky move."

"No pilot? That's mad!"

Eddleston chuckled. "Mad, or they have someone clever aboard."

The boatswain, Josiah supposed. "What about those women? Have you heard any more?"

"Nope. Just Larson and Snyder in here last night trying to bully me into doing something. I told them I had no reason, nor any means, to stop the *Vera. B.,* and no interest in who they'd taken on board. Snyder threatened to bring the constabulary, but that's a bluff."

"All bluster and no bite, is he?" Josiah asked.

"Oh, Snyder can bite all right, but this time his bone was too far out of reach." Eddleston chuckled. "I don't know what those women's plans are, but I wish them luck."

Josiah frowned and looked out at the harbor. "So do I."

He really must make sail. He would go back and try to hasten the last of the loading.

As he strode along the waterfront, he saw that Snyder and Larson were now on the schooner's deck with Bluey Glenn. They wouldn't make a run for it tonight, would they? A small vessel like that could get up a lot of speed, if it had the right wind. And this captain knew the local waters.

If only Alice had waited for him. He could scarcely believe she had done something so foolish. Apparently she had formed new plans with old Gypsy Deak as soon as he left her brig yesterday. And not using a pilot! Had they really made it out safely? He hoped Eddleston was right—he wouldn't wish her aground.

He would order the *Jade Maiden's* sails loosed at morning tide, and she would fly after the *Vera B*. He couldn't stay near Alice's brig all the way home, and he wouldn't endanger his ship to help her, but the *Jade Maiden's* presence could give her some protection until she was beyond Larson and Snyder's reach. They wouldn't follow her far. Up the coast, maybe, but not across the Indian Ocean.

The thought of Alice taking her brig into the dangerous waters around the Indies sobered him. He had tangled with Malay pirates. They had no mercy. But those butchers would be unlikely to attack two American ships sailing together. Yes, he'd better make way at first light.

CHAPTER FIFTEEN

The wind blew cold against Carrie's left cheek. It had picked up soon after she came on deck for the afternoon watch. She wished she had the warm woolen coat she had worn when she left the pub, but the captain had told the crew they must wear short jackets that wouldn't interfere with their work. Carrie was lucky to have fallen heir to one left behind by a deserter. It was too big, but she wore an extra shirt under it, and two pairs of long stockings beneath her trousers.

She shivered and waited for orders from Kate, who stood on the quarterdeck with Mr. Deak. He looked spry for such an old fellow. Carrie hoped he'd had a good sleep during the morning watch. Kate had gone easy on them during the darkness, changing the lookout in the foretop every time the bells rang, so that they each had at least one turn up there alone at night, but didn't have to endure it too long in the cold.

She had found the rigging eerie in the dark, and yet wonderful. With the huge sails above her and stars glittering like jewels in the inky winter sky, Carrie had felt a sense of grandeur. Then Kate—probably at Captain Alice's instigation—had ordered them to scrub down the deck in the predawn grayness. She'd said they would do it every morning before they could get their breakfast. In warmer weather, it wouldn't be so bad, but getting on your hands and knees on the wet planking in this chill and rubbing the deck with a holystone until your hands chafed and your clothes were soaking wet—Carrie had never worked this hard at the Boar's Tusk.

The very thought gave her pause. She didn't want to go back to being a pub girl, ever, even if it meant holystoning a freezing cold deck every morning for the rest of her life. Even though the

151

pub customers were not allowed to manhandle the girls, she still had to be friendly to them, and more than friendly to her boss. That was the worst of it. She'd considered leaving, but Tom had let her know that wasn't an option, so far as he was concerned, and so she stayed, longing for freedom.

She had it now. Aching knees and chilblains were better than serving beer to drunken sailors half the night and being at Tom Larson's beck and call the rest of the time.

"We'll reef the topsails," Kate called. Lucky Kate. She didn't have to join them in cleaning the deck, but she usually went into the rigging with them. "Polly, call all hands."

The first watch stumbled on deck yawning and rubbing their eyes at the lowery afternoon sky. Kate gave the instructions quickly. She must have memorized what Gypsy told her to say, and she sounded confident.

Carrie joined her watch mates in climbing the foremast shrouds. Emma, who was on duty as lookout in the foretop, made it to the foretopsail first. Carrie glanced over at the mainmast. The first watch women were reaching their posts about the same time. Those on her watch spread out along the yard, to the positions needed to perform the task. Some of these girls bickered constantly back at Dame Nell's, Carrie knew, but here they had to work together or suffer dire consequences. Anne placed herself next to Polly and let her stay closest to the mast. They all, by unspoken agreement, kept an eye out for Polly.

Once the reefs were taken and the sailors climbed down, Kate dismissed the first watch. She went up to the wheel, and Mr. Deak came down into the waist.

"Now we will begin our gun training. We'll start with pistols and then go on to the swivel gun and the bow gun."

Carrie looked at Emma, who stood beside her. The pretty girl's blue eyes widened. "Guns. Is he training us in case Con catches up with us?"

"That or pirates," Carrie said. "Sonja says they're thick where we're headed."

Carrie had never held a pistol in her life. She didn't like it, but with the prospect of being captured by Con Snyder or a band of Malay pirates, she swallowed her apprehension. Kate handed out wisps of wool to stuff in their ears while they practiced.

Hitting the marks Mr. Deak set up across the deck was a real challenge, with the ship moving up and down as they took aim. Carrie surprised herself by actually hitting the target scrap of wood once out of the four times she shot. At least her misses went high, and she didn't put any holes in the bulwark, like Lucy did. Only Kate did better than Carrie, hitting hers twice and sending the chips flying off the rail and into the sea.

The bow-mounted two-pound gun frightened Carrie more. It boomed each time they fired it. Having no targets on the tossing waves, Mr. Deak divided them into two gun crews and had each crew load and fire the small cannon only twice.

"Just so you're familiar with the process," he explained. "Now, on to the swivel gun."

This weapon was a smaller gun that could be moved about easily and mounted on the bulwarks with clamps. Once it was securely in place, they could turn it wherever they liked to follow the target. Carrie could see how it would be handy in defending the *Vera B.* against pirates attempting to board.

"All right, men," Mr. Deak yelled when they were finished. "Er, sailors. Stow the powder and shot in the launch's sail locker for next time."

As Carrie picked up one of the bags of shot, Ned darted from the shadow of the mainmast and fell to his knees below where they had last mounted the swivel gun. He took a small piece of paper from his pocket and bent close to the deck.

"Ned, what are you doing?" she asked.

He jumped and folded the paper quickly. Stuffing it into his pocket, he rose with a guilty look on his face. "Nothing."

Carrie frowned, but her watch mates were already gathering amidships. She quickly stowed the shot in the locker and joined them.

153

"We've a sheet to the wind on the main topsail," Mr. Deak told them. "I need two sailors to go up and secure it." He scanned their faces. "Lucy. Carrie."

Lucy beat her to the shrouds, and Carrie followed her up to the platform that formed the main top. Lucy paused, panting and looking up at the next part of the climb.

"How are you doing?" Carrie asked.

"All right. But I can't say I like going up there. It's so tippy!"

"I know." Carrie swallowed hard. "I'll go first."

"Thanks," Lucy said.

That meant Carrie would be the one to go out to the extremity of the yardarm and actually grab the flailing rope while holding on to the yard with one hand. There was no backing out now. She hauled in a deep breath and began climbing the ladder-like ratlines toward the heights of the topmast.

Below her, the deck of the Vera B. plunged up and down with the waves, and the mast swayed like a pendulum. The girls' faces were little white specks, staring up at her.

Carrie reached the yardarm and clung to it, groping with her feet until she felt reasonably secure on the foot rope. Gingerly, she inched out along the length of the spar, holding on firmly with at least one hand at all times.

A rogue wave made the ship dip, and the mast flew toward the horizon. Overcome with nausea, Carrie closed her eyes. Several of the girls had been seasick since they left the bay, but so far she had kept her gorge from rising. Now she clung to the jackstay and prayed she wouldn't retch on those below.

"Carrie?"

She opened her eyes. Lucy was only a foot away.

"You going to make it?"

She nodded and looked toward her goal. She was only a few steps from the loose line that flapped from the corner of the sail.

She stretched toward it, hoping she could catch it without going any farther, but it danced cruelly beyond her grasp. She took another cautious step, but the mast swung back just then,

154

and she missed her footing. She screamed as she fell, clawing for the foot rope.

By the time Carrie's muffled scream reached those on the deck below, Sonja was climbing the shrouds. Carrie somehow found purchase on the foot rope and hung upside down beneath it, clinging with her feet and hands.

"Sonja! Wait," Gypsy called. She paused and looked down at him. He grabbed a coiled line and thrust it into Anne's hands. "Lay aloft with that."

Anne dashed to obey. She passed the rope up to Sonja, who shouldered it and continued up the shrouds.

Gypsy could only stand and watch. Bless their hearts, these women! How long would it take them to learn to hold on?

Sonja didn't pause at the maintop, but scrambled on up the ratlines. Anne climbed as far as the top and waited on the platform. Gypsy shifted his weight, trying to ignore the pain that stabbed his left knee. If he were fit, he'd be the one up there now.

While Sonja climbed, Lucy edged out toward Carrie. The ship rolled—not too drastically, but Gypsy knew that sixty feet above the deck it would feel like the world was ending. He wanted to tell Carrie to hang on, but his throat was too tight to squawk.

"Carrie, I'll g-get you." Poor little Lucy sobbed so hard, it was a wonder she didn't shake herself out of the rigging, but her plaintive voice wafted down to them.

Sonja reached the level of the topsail yard, and Lucy looked back toward the mast. Gypsy couldn't hear Sonja's words, but he was sure she was calming Lucy. Thank heaven for a girl not afraid of heights!

Slowly, Lucy inched toward Sonja, standing on the rope and moving each foot deliberately. When she reached the topmast shrouds, Sonja maneuvered around her and started out along the

155

foot rope, toward Carrie. She stopped and fiddled with the coiled line she carried.

"Hurry," Gypsy wanted to say. Carrie's arms would be burning now. The brig pitched, and he swallowed hard. No one could survive a fall from that height.

His heart seized a moment later when Carrie's legs began to move, but she kept her hold as Sonja passed her line around Carrie's upper body. At tortoise speed, they shuffled back toward the mast, Sonja with tiny steps and Carrie wriggling backward along the rope. Lucy waited on the shrouds. She reached out with Sonja, and somehow the two of them got Carrie safely on the ratlines.

They came down slowly, Lucy first, then Carrie with Sonja's line still around her, and finally Sonja. When Lucy hit the deck and jumped out of the way, Gypsy reached up and lifted Carrie down to the deck.

"Well, now," he said, surveying her milk-white face. She looked terrified and vulnerable—so different from when he and Alice had met her at the Boar's Tusk.

"I'm sorry!" Carrie covered her face with her hands, but not before he saw tears flowing down her cheeks.

He gave her shoulder an awkward pat. "Don't be. You lived through it, and you'll be a better sailor now."

Carrie gave a little hiccup and squared her shoulders. "Thank you."

Sonja dropped her end of the rope, and Gypsy undid the knots and took it off Carrie. Lucy began coiling it.

"Are you hurt?" Gypsy asked Carrie.

"No, sir. A little sore."

"Lay below for the rest of the watch."

"Aye, aye, sir," Carrie whispered. She headed for the main hatch.

Gypsy glanced at the mast. Sonja had headed back up the shrouds.

"Where are you going?" Gypsy roared.

Sonja paused and looked down. "Up to the yard, sir, to secure that loose line."

He had forgotten all about the loose sheet he had sent Lucy and Carrie up to bring in.

"Sonja."

"Yes, sir?" She waited, hands on the ropes, ready to continue.

"Don't you dare ..." He shook his head.

"I won't sir."

Jenny laid the scissors on the worktable and straightened. It would be eight bells soon, and they would have to hop up on deck. She looked around the cramped workspace and assessed the first watch's wardrobe progress. Mrs. Fiske had let the off-duty sailors leave the hatch door open, allowing light into the 'tweendecks so they could work on their sewing. She, Hannah, Addie, Mary, Fiona, and Brea had managed to cut and stitch three pairs of canvas pants in the past few hours. They had also patched, mended, and altered several shirts and jackets left by the *Vera B.*'s former sailors.

"That will have to do," her aunt said, holding up the last pair of trousers. "You might have time to try them on, Mary."

Mary took the pants and scurried into the forecastle.

Jenny flexed her sore fingers. Since Addie was still a little shaky with the shears, she and Hannah did most of the cutting. The other three girls couldn't do it, with their hands blistered and tender from the ropes. Jenny was glad she had come to the brig already calloused. She helped Hannah put away the fabric and supplies. Fiona gladly lent a hand, but Brea seemed aloof. The dark-haired girl hadn't said much all day.

The ship's bell sounded from up on deck.

"Addie, can you finish cleaning up?" Hannah headed up the companionway.

"Aye, aye, mum."

"I'll help," said Ned, emerging from nowhere.

Jenny scowled. "Since when have you volunteered to help with anything involving sewing? Or cleaning up, for that matter?"

Ned shrugged. "I don't mind."

Jenny didn't have time to think about it. She followed Hannah, Brea, and Fiona up into the bright sunlight. Polly, Lucy, Emma, and Anne waited for them to come on deck, then went below.

Mrs. Fiske greeted them from the quarterdeck. "Good afternoon, first watch. It appears we have some fair weather today, and we are making good speed. Mr. Deak will train us in gunnery, as he did with the others earlier." She paused and looked around. "Where's Mary?"

"She should be along," Hannah said. "She was trying on her new trousers."

"Very well," said Mrs. Fiske. "I just checked on Lizzie. I believe she will mend, but I'm keeping her on rest at least until tomorrow. Mr. Deak went below, but he will return shortly. As soon as he and Mary are here, we will begin gunnery practice. I might add that I am quite looking forward to it."

Jenny looked at Brea and Fiona. Brea's eyes sparkled at the word "gunnery," and Fiona seemed interested too. Jenny loved guns herself. She knew it wasn't good to brag, but she had shot her first kangaroo when she was twelve, and had lost count of how many dingoes, crows, magpies, and galahs. Aunt Hannah, if anything, was even steadier.

"While we're waiting for Mary, I need a lookout in the foretop." Mrs. Fiske glanced up toward the foremast and frowned. "I think Sonja's still up there. Probably waiting to be relieved. Jenny, I believe it's your turn."

"Aye, ma'am!" Jenny stepped briskly toward the foremast shrouds, disappointed that she would miss the weapons lesson.

"Keep a sharp lookout," Mrs. Fiske called after her. "We are in the main shipping lane between the northern colonies and southerly ones, don't forget."

"Yes, ma'am!" Jenny hopped up to the rail and grabbed the shrouds. She actually enjoyed climbing in the rigging. Her muscles and hands were a little sore from the exertions of the past few days, but she was no stranger to hard work. She scrambled up the ratlines, gloating inwardly that she was one of the more agile sailors. She may not be as good as Sonja, but Jenny took to this new life quickly.

She looked up at the foretop. Sonja knelt gazing forward, her head just visible past the edge of the platform.

"Hello, Sonja," Jenny called. Sonja looked her way but didn't answer.

Jenny climbed the rest of the way, her heart pounding from the exercise. She came to the jacob's ladder and climbed the few rungs to the foretop.

"Sonja?" Jenny came up behind the kneeling girl. "Are you all right?" Sonja turned to gaze at Jenny, her sea-gray eyes filled with tears. She scooted over, and Jenny pulled herself up. "What's wrong?"

Sonja put her head between her knees. Her shoulders shook. Jenny hesitated, then cautiously put her arm around her. "It's all right."

"I'm sorry, Jenny. I—forgot how it makes me feel, to have the sea all around. Look at it. It's everywhere!"

Jenny frowned and looked around. Beyond the masts and sails, it was true, there was nothing to see on any side but the ocean and sky.

Sonja sniffed. "I hate the sea."

Jenny shook her head, confused. "You didn't hate it yesterday."

"But today it's all there is. Only sea. No land. Nowhere to swim to. If—the ship goes down."

Jenny gawked at her. "That's it? You don't mind the water if you can see the shore?"

159

Sonja hid her head again. "It was like that when our sloop wrecked. Nothing but waves around me." Sonja wiped away a tear with her cuff.

Jenny didn't know what to say. "Come on, I'm here to relieve you. Go down and get some rest."

Sonja exhaled. "I'm sorry, Jenny. I never knew I would be scared again."

"How long since your dad died?"

"Two years." After a long pause, Sonja raised her chin. "It was my fault."

"Surely not," Jenny said.

"It's true. I forgot to take the soundings that day. The *Pen Mary* crashed on a rock under the surface. Papa and Bob drowned when the boat turned over." She wiped her nose on her sleeve. But I lived. And I was all alone in the water. I couldn't see land."

At last things began to make sense. "It will be all right," Jenny said. "And I don't really think it was your fault. You couldn't have known about the rock, even if you did take a sounding. Some things happen. Like when my father drowned in the river."

Sonja smiled with one side of her face, the other side looking doubtful. "Thanks, Jenny. I didn't know your papa drowned, too. I'm sorry." Slowly she moved toward the edge of the platform.

Jenny watched her climb down. She doubted that her words would take away Sonja's feelings of guilt. She wished she could erase her friend's awful memories, but that was beyond her power.

CHAPTER SIXTEEN

"A sail!" shouted a lookout from the stern. Alice turned to see Mary standing at the taffrail, pointing abaft, her sunburned face sober. "What do you think, Captain? I hope it isn't Con!"

Alice crossed to the taffrail. A sail hovered on the horizon, but she couldn't make out any details of the vessel. "Good eyes, Mary. I sincerely doubt it could be his ship, though. We have a good start on him, and Sonja assured me no one would brave the Rip at night. I don't believe he could catch up so quickly."

Mary grimaced. "You don't know Con. When he wants something bad, he gets it. If there's any possible way to go faster, he'll find it."

"Keep an eye on that sail, Mary, but don't forget to watch for others. A clipper ship like Captain Howard's can beat us by three or four knots, but hardly anything else can."

Alice hurried to her cabin for the glass. "It appears to be a British ship," she told Mary and Sarah a moment later.

Mary exhaled in relief. "Good!"

"The wind is slacking off a little, don't you think?" Sarah asked.

"It is," said Alice. "But it may be temporary. I've been eyeing those clouds off the starboard bow. I wondered if we should get the royals up to take every advantage over that Con Snyder. If Ruel were here, he would probably have the stuns'ls out, too. But with those clouds…"

"If you want my advice," Sarah said, "wait until morning, and then we'll set the royals if we have avoided the squall."

Alice shivered. "I despise squalls and storms. I believe I shall nap until dinner, in case we're up all night."

"Very good," said Sarah. "I'll watch the weather."

Alice hastened to her cabin and closed the door. Dread clawed at her stomach. This would be the women's first experience at sea during a storm, except those like Nell, who was old enough to remembering coming here by ship. "Lord, what I have I done?" She dropped to her knees beside her bed. "I have been presumptuous, Father. I have relied on my own wisdom and taken all these lives into peril. Give us mercy, Lord God. I beg you to spare us and bring us to that safe haven of which you speak."

Sonja lay in her hammock, unable to sleep. Over and over, her mind replayed the days she had spent in the water, clinging to a water cask and fearing she would die.

The door to the forecastle opened, letting in a dim light from the 'tweendecks. Hannah stood in the opening. "Sonja, can you come with me?"

She rolled out of her hammock and walked woodenly with Hannah to the worktable, where they sat down.

"Jenny told me you took a bad turn up in the top, and I asked Nell to bring us some hot tea," Hannah said gently, sliding a thick ironstone mug toward her. "Can you tell me what happened?"

Sonja swallowed. "I'm sorry, Hannah. I just got thinking about a bad day. When my papa's boat wrecked. I hadn't been out away from shore since that time, and it hit hard today."

Hannah fixed her with an even look. "We all have bad moments. Won't you tell me about it?"

Sonja didn't really want to talk about it, but she felt she had to. She lifted the cup and sipped the tea. It was good and strong, with sugar in it. She looked at Hannah, who waited patiently.

"It struck me of a sudden, like an oar to the back of the head. I never expected it. You know I used to fish with my papa."

Hannah nodded.

"One thing I did on the boat was take the soundings. But I got busy fishing and forgot to throw the lead line. We wrecked on a rock. Papa and his mate Bob went down and never came up. And I was all alone."

The pale light drifting down from the hatch caught the glimmer of tears in Hannah's eyes. Sonja swiped at her nose with the cuff of her sailor's blouse. She had spent very little time with women. Had she made Hannah cry, or was it normal for a woman to tear up when she heard a sad story?

"I can't remember me mum." Her words dangled in the air awkwardly.

Hannah leaned toward her. "It appears that most of you girls in the crew don't have mothers. But we're your family now, Sonja."

"Thank you. That's kind of you."

"It's normal to think back about the loved ones you've lost, but don't blame yourself. That won't help. It will only make you feel worse. Instead, think of the good times you had with your pa."

"I'll try." Sonja sipped the tea again.

Hannah smiled. "We have a long voyage ahead of us. Captain Alice and the mates and I are very grateful for your skills and experience. We're counting on you. You got us out the Rip, and you've helped the rest of us learn the ropes. I'm sure that fear will pass once you're used to the open ocean."

Sonja's stomach churned, but Hannah was probably right. Just as her sorrow had faded with time, her fear would too, once she got used to the open sea. "I hope so."

She looked up and saw Carrie standing in the doorway to the forecastle. "I'm sorry," she said. "I wasn't trying to eavesdrop, but I couldn't help but hear."

Sonja exhaled and shook her head. "I'm sorry, Carrie. I had a bad mind in the foretop."

Carrie approached and sat down on the protruding edge of a bale of wool. "You helped me today, and I want to help you too, if I can."

Sonja shrugged. "It was just that when I saw the sea everywhere, and no land, it made me remember when Papa and Bob and I wrecked."

"How did you survive?" Hannah asked. "Were you far from land?"

"The *Pen Mary* sank only a mile or so from shore, but the current carried me out to sea. I grabbed the water keg, 'cause it floated by, about half full. I was in the sea for three days, and I could drink from the keg, but I got so tired of holding on, I almost let go a dozen times. Do you know what it's like to know you're going to die? To know there's no one around to help you? To just wait?" She sobbed.

"Oh, dear," Hannah said. She and Carrie moved in and put their arms around her.

Maybe this was what it meant to have a mother, a sister— family to care for you. Her father had never given her anything but a quick hug around the shoulders, and that on rare occasions. Feeling the soft pressure of Hannah and Carrie's embrace was both scary and soothing. It meant she belonged.

When Carrie stepped back, tears glistened in her eyes. "You gave me courage to face the rigging, Sonja. It's still scary, but I remember what you said the other day. To think of freedom, and getting away from Con and Tom, so I can get past my fear. I'm going to help you with your fears, too. You can do this."

Sonja smiled. "I don't like to admit being scared. But I guess everyone is afraid of something."

"Believe me. We're all scared sometimes," Hanna said. "But how did you get to land, after the wreck?"

"I got picked up, finally, by a packet from Hobart Town. They almost didn't see me. I'm glad they had a kind captain. Some ships wouldn't have stopped."

164

"You were fortunate indeed," Hannah said. "God was looking out for you."

"They were going to Sydney, but the captain paid my fare back to Melbourne when we got there. But Papa was gone." She fell silent as the sadness washed over her.

"Well you're safe now," Carrie said. "And Hannah's right. We'll be your family, and no mistake."

"What's that?" Hannah whirled sharply and sniffed. "Is that smoke I smell?"

Gypsy stood observing the first watch trim the foresail when Sonja poked her head up through the forward hatch.

"Mr. Deak, can you come quick?"

He limped over to the head of the ladder, glad to see that Sonja had recovered some of her spirit. "What is it, lass?"

"Smoke, sir. I thought maybe it came from up here, but it's not..." She looked about the main deck. "It must be down below."

"Go on down," Gypsy said. One thing after another. He followed Sonja down as quickly as he could. Before his feet touched on the 'tweendecks, he smelled it.

"Gunpowder."

"What?" Sonja's gray eyes were huge in the dimness.

Gypsy wrinkled his nose. "I don't think I'd mistake it. It's coming up from below." He strode across to where the hatch leading down into the cargo hold stood open. "This should be closed. Who opened it?"

"I don't know," Sonja said.

Hannah and Carrie crowded in close. "The second watch are mostly in the fo'castle," Hannah said. "Addie and Ned were playing down here while I – " She broke off, a stricken expression freezing her face.

"Fetch a lantern," Gypsy said.

165

Carrie turned and dashed for the main hatch. Gypsy didn't wait, but started down the ladder. The smoke grew thicker. At least there was no flicker of open flame down here. He coughed and looked about the hold crammed with grain bags and wool bales, but couldn't see anything. His eyes watered.

"Who's down here?" he yelled. He had heard of wool combusting in ships' holds. If that happened, they would have to steer for shore and pray they made land. Fire was the worst thing a sailor could face on a ship.

A yellow light above snagged his attention.

"Here!" Carrie leaned down over the hatch, passing a glowing lantern.

The smoke seemed quite small, now that he had some illumination. It mostly hung in the air near the ladder. Gypsy went carefully down the last few steps and hitched a few paces forward. Where was it coming from?

A small cough gave away his quarry. Gypsy held the lantern high and edged around a row of casks held in place by cargo netting. The acrid smell of gunpowder grew stronger. Ned McKay huddled between a barrel and a bale of wool, his shoulders heaving and his hands over his face.

"Well, well." Gypsy crouched beside him. "Uncover your face, boy."

Slowly, Ned obeyed.

"What are you doing? Setting fire to the *Vera B.*?"

"No, sir. I—I put it out."

"You put it out."

Ned gulped and nodded. "I didn't think it would jump like that. And then I thought—I thought it had got away from me. But I put it out." He squared his shoulders with a remnant of pride.

"We'll see about that." Gypsy stood and raised the lantern. A charred spot on the floor and a blackened scar up one side of a bale showed him where the blaze had been. He stooped and

166

picked up a bit of burnt wood. "Have you been playing with quick matches?"

"Only one. I just wanted to see what would burn the quickest of my bits, and if the powder would catch them all."

Gypsy drew in a deep breath. "You've no idea what you could have done. If you'd struck the lucifer near a keg of powder, we'd all be fathoms below now. Do you understand?"

Ned nodded, quaking.

"Short of that, you could have burned the whole ship, cargo, people, and all." Gypsy realized he was shouting. "Get upstairs," he said more quietly. "If your mother doesn't tan your hide, I will."

He followed Ned to the ladder with the lantern. "Sonja, bring down a bucket of water. We need to make sure nothing's smoldering down here." If the wool bales caught, fire could lurk deep within the hold and not go out. He only hoped Ned had thoroughly extinguished it.

"What have I got myself into?" he muttered. "I must be a grand fool to've signed on for this voyage."

Kate glanced at the hourglass just in time to see the last bit of sand flow into the bottom. "Quick, turn it over!" she said, keeping a firm hold on the ship's wheel. The *Vera B.* lifted and dropped rhythmically on the waves as the telltale glow of the sun gleamed over the northeast horizon, bathing the brig in an eerie light.

Addie jumped up off the deck, where she had been leaning against the binnacle, and flipped the hourglass over.

"Six bells, Addie."

The young girl enthusiastically rang the bell six times, then stooped to pick up the blanket she had dropped. "Brr, it's cold, Miss Kate." She wrapped the blanket around her narrow shoulders and scrunched against the binnacle.

"It'd be a lot warmer down in your cabin." Kate glanced at the compass. When she had taken over the watch at four in the morning, Mrs. Fiske had told her to alter course at six bells if everything went as expected. Cautiously, she steered the *Vera B.* one point to port, watching the sails for change in the wind direction.

"I couldn't sleep," said Addie. "Jenny was snoring. And Ned was crying again, next door."

"Your mum didn't whoop him that hard," said Kate. "I was afraid Mr. Deak was going to bring out a cat-o'-nine-tails."

"What's that?" Addie asked.

"It's a—" Kate stopped, remembering Addie's impressionable age. She had seen the scarred backs of British sailors who had survived a lashing in the Royal Navy. That sort of men were all too frequently customers at Dame Nell's.

"A what?" Addie persisted, her eyes gleaming in the dawn's first rays.

"Nothing you need to know about."

As the sun's first sliver peered over the horizon, her range of visibility increased. Kate noted with relief that the clouds from the previous evening were gone.

"Steamer dead ahead!" Anne shouted from the foretop.

Kate frowned and looked forward. The masts blocked her view directly ahead, but she saw a cloud rising from the water near the horizon just to the left of them. She decided to allow the distance to close more before altering course. The other ship was still many miles away.

"Addie, go see if Nell needs a hand," said Kate. Breakfast would be served to the first watch in only half an hour, and the children had been told to be helpful in the galley.

"Aye, aye, ma'am." Addie clattered down the steps.

Kate looked all around. The wind was from the port quarter. Mrs. Fiske and Mr. Deak had taught her that wind from the quarter was best for speed and control. She hoped she was remembering everything important. She glanced behind her and saw Emma leaning over the taffrail. "Are you all right, Emma?"

Emma turned. "I see a sail back there."

Kate frowned. "Come hold the wheel."

When Emma had taken the wheel, Kate turned and grabbed the clew line on the spanker boom for support. She looked astern and saw a white speck in the distance. "I don't like that."

"We don't know it's Con." Emma bit her lip.

Kate grabbed the wheel beside her, and they both held it for a while.

"It could be, though."

Emma shuddered. "He wouldn't have much trouble rounding up some men in Melbourne. They'll be armed like pirates. Do you think he would trade any of us to them, for reward?"

Kate stared at her. "No doubt—if he didn't kill us."

Emma clenched her teeth.

Kate looked ahead. The steamer was a lot closer now. She turned the wheel a point to starboard to give the steamship more room. "Emma, I hate to wake Mr. Deak, but we'd better tell him about the sail."

Alice woke to a loud whistle outside her cabin. She sat up in bed and looked out her window, but there was no steamship to be seen, only wide open ocean and the sun like a glowing tangerine on the horizon.

Life at sea had taught her to dress quickly. In less than two minutes, she stepped on deck. The first person she saw was Sonja, standing by the mainmast. The lanky girl turned when she heard Alice close the door.

"Good morning, ma'am," she managed, looking a little startled.

"Good morning, Sonja." Alice knew captains didn't ordinarily speak to their crew members, but things were far different on the *Vera B.* than they had been a few weeks prior. "Did we just pass a steamship?"

Sonja nodded. "The *Nottingham.* It goes from Sydney and Newcastle to Melbourne."

"It sounded terribly close." Alice craned her neck to look up at the quarterdeck, where Kate manned the wheel. "But I don't feel her wake, so I suppose we weren't as close as I thought."

"I think we passed a quarter mile from her, ma'am."

Gypsy and Emma came up the companionway. "Good morning, Captain," said Gypsy, rubbing his eyes. "Emma says we might want the spyglass."

"There's a ship gaining behind us," Emma explained.

"Very well." Alice ducked back into her cabin and retrieved the telescope. She heard Sarah stirring next door, but didn't take the time to confer with her.

When she arrived on the quarterdeck, she found Gypsy and Emma at the taffrail and Kate at the wheel.

"My old eyes can't see nothing," said Gypsy. "There might be a sail, and I wouldn't know. Do you see anything, Captain?"

Alice put the telescope to her eye and leaned against the taffrail for support. She could just make out two masts with broad fore-and-aft sails staggered port and starboard, and a small topsail on the foremast. She lowered the telescope. "It's a tops'l schooner."

"A schooner?" Emma's blue eyes widened.

"Then again, there are thousands of schooners on the sea," said Gypsy.

"Kate, have a look," said Alice. She walked over and took the wheel.

Kate spotted through the telescope and grunted. "I can't be sure, but it looks like Bluey's schooner. His does have that one funny sail at the top."

"The tops'l," Gypsy supplied.

"I've never seen it look quite like that though," said Kate. "The big sails—something's weird about them."

Gypsy had a look in the spyglass. It took him a while to find the schooner. "Ah yes. That's because he's stuck his mains'l to port and his fores'l to starboard. It's hard for a schooner to get enough sail out, running before the wind. But he's making good time. He might be gaining on us."

Alice shook her head. "We'll have to put on more sail, won't we, Gypsy?"

He sighed and handed her the telescope. "I s'pose we knew the day would come. I hope these sailors are ready for the royal yards."

Alice caught her breath and looked up at the mast tops. The royals were the highest sails of all.

CHAPTER SEVENTEEN

"All hands on deck!" Mr. Deak's voice boomed through the *Vera B.* Lizzie exhaled sharply as pain shot through her body. Her hands still burned, and her hip, back, and ribs still ached from her fall three days earlier.

"Aw, crikey," Brea groaned, rolling out of her hammock. She, Fiona, and Mary fumbled around for shoes and piled out into the 'tweendecks, leaving the door open.

Lizzie moaned and stretched. There was no helping it, she had to go to the head, and she may as well do it while no one was around. She didn't feel proper being seen entering the necessary—this was something you shouldn't acknowledge to others.

Once inside, she was appalled by how filthy the head had become. Disgusting! What on earth had she gotten herself into? The Blackwall frigate she and Lord and Lady Dunbar had traveled on to Australia had been confining, but it was much bigger than the *Vera B.* and at least had sanitary first class accommodations.

A few minutes later, Lizzie made her way up on deck. Mr. Deak shouted orders from the quarterdeck as the sailors from both watches climbed the rigging. Lizzie grabbed the bulwark for support and craned her neck.

"Did you eat a lemon?" Lizzie looked down in disgust and saw Ned McKay staring at her.

"What are you talking about?" she demanded.

"You look like you ate a lemon. Chicken Dawson had a lemon tree on the farm next to ours. Addie and I thought they were oranges, so we ate them. You made a face like Addie did."

"You vicious little brat," Lizzie spat out. "Get away from me. You almost killed us all yesterday, playing Guy Fawkes."

Ned scowled and stalked off. Lizzie shuddered. If there was anything she detested, it was little boys.

She looked up, tipping her head back so far her neck hurt. The sailors spread out along the royal yards, like rag dolls pegged to a clothesline. Only five sailors manned the main royal yard, but seven, including Kate, were on the fore royal yard. She knew she belonged up there with her watch, but she didn't mind missing this excursion. The royal yards were at least one hundred feet above the deck. She hoped that even when she healed up, she wouldn't ever have to climb all the way to the top.

The tiny figures in the rigging swayed back and forth with the movement of the ship, silhouetted against a small tuft of cloud. Sailing wasn't for women. Especially respectable women. Those women had sold their honor for money back at the brothel. Now they had sold their safety. And she had sold her own safety, too. Not for money, but because she was compelled. Blackmailed by Lady Dunbar. If she hadn't joined this voyage, her mistress would have left her to her own resources in St. Kilda. She growled softly. When she got back to England. . .

A shriek from above interrupted Lizzie's thoughts. A dark shape swooped at the sailors on the yards.

"What's that?" Mr. Deak shouted from the quarterdeck. "A crow?"

"A magpie," said Lady Dunbar from the wheel. "They're terrible—they dive right at you. One knocked my hat off once. I'm surprised to see one so far out to sea."

Lizzie hated magpies. Australia had some beautiful birds, but the ugly magpies were atrocious.

The large black-and-white bird flew screeching around the mast tops. One of the girls took a swipe at it—Sonja, maybe. The magpie was in the fanatical, territorial mood so common to its species.

173

"Mr. Deak, can you do something?" Captain Alice said. The old man headed for the stairs.

That did it. Lizzie might not be too impressed with her fellow sailors, but she didn't want a berserk magpie to make them fall from the rigging. Her heart pounding, she dashed to the hatch, scurried down the ladder, and rushed to the spot where her trunks were stowed. It took her a minute to find her bow and quiver. She hesitated only a moment as she gazed at her two dozen treasured arrows. She pulled in a deep breath and closed the trunk, clambering back on deck just in time to be shocked by an ear-splitting report from the quarterdeck. She looked to the rail, where Mr. Deak held a smoking firearm.

He shook his head and said mournfully, "I never could hit birds."

Lizzie strung her bow and looked up. The magpie wheeled and screeched around the sailors, who still struggled with the royal sails. One of them screamed as the obnoxious bird swooped toward her.

"Lizzie, don't hit Mum," Ned yelled from across the ship's waist.

"Hush, brat." Kneeling on the deck, she grabbed an arrow from her quiver and drew the bow. She nearly lost her balance as the ship rolled. This would not be easy. If that dirty little beggar would fly down to her level, she knew she could put an arrow through its gizzard.

The magpie did not oblige. Lizzie relaxed the bowstring, waiting until the bird flew away from the mast. Now or never. She pulled back, aimed carefully, and released. The arrow missed by about a foot. The bird screeched in surprise. Lizzie grimaced as the arrow plummeted toward the sea a hundred yards away.

"You missed," Ned yelled.

"Hold your tongue, rodent!" Lizzie nocked another arrow and aimed. She realized everyone was watching her. With a huff of determination, she steadied her aim and released the arrow. Before it reached the mark, she knew she would hit the bird. The arrow pierced it where one wing met the body, and the magpie spiraled screeching and twitching to the deck, where it landed just outside the open galley door.

Nell poked her head out in surprise and looked at the magpie. "What's this?"

"Brava!" Lady Dunbar cried from the wheel. "Flawlessly executed, Henshaw."

Lizzie exhaled and stood up. A searing pain drew her attention to her right hand. Pulling the bowstring had reopened the rope burns on her fingers.

The women in the rigging got the royal sails unfurled and started down the shrouds. Lizzie stowed her bow and quiver below deck. When she returned, the sailors were dropping off the bottom ratlines one by one.

"That was good shooting," Hannah said. "I hate those magpies. At the farm, they ate our seed, harassed the stock. We couldn't get rid of them."

Lizzie smiled. For the first time since boarding the *Vera B.*, she felt as if she had done something useful.

A flurry of movement drew her eyes to the quarterdeck, where the officers huddled in an agitated conference.

Kate lifted the spyglass and gazed astern. "That's him all right," she shouted. "He's gaining."

Mr. Deak turned toward the main deck. "Haul away at those royal halyards! We can set more canvas than Bluey Glenn, and so long as this wind holds, we can outrun him."

Josiah's steward brought him his jacket and hat. He donned them and hurried to the quarterdeck.

"Sail in sight, Mr. Stark?" he asked the first mate.

"Aye, sir." Stark handed him the spyglass. "You can see it from here now without the glass. Two points to port. He's keeping within sight of land."

Josiah raised the glass to his eye and focused on the scrap of white far ahead. "Schooner. You think it's the *Lorelai*?"

"Don't know yet."

Josiah's nerves urged him to stay on deck and pace, but it would be hours before they closed on the schooner. He didn't make a habit of haunting the deck when the mate was on watch. He glanced up at the full sails and handed the glass back to Stark. "Let me know when you can identify her, or when you're within half a mile."

"You wish to speak her, sir?"

"Oh, yes, if she's the *Lorelai*, I have much to say to her captain." Five days since Alice had left port, and four since Bluey Glenn's schooner had put out. Patience was one of Josiah's virtues. If he caught up with the *Lorelai* before she overtook the *Vera B.*, the long pursuit was well worth it.

He went back to his roomy cabin. At least they had a good breeze and fair weather. The *Jade Maiden* ought to be able to overhaul that schooner today.

He found sleep impossible. He hadn't expected Snyder and Larson to follow Alice this far. Together, those two made a formidable force. If they wouldn't listen to reason, he would find another way. His six six-pounders and four swivel guns could blow the *Lorelai* to splinters. The schooner's captain would realize that, even if Larson and Snyder didn't.

He studied the charts. They'd passed Twofold Bay. Would Alice go all the way up the coast with the prevailing winds and veer westward for the Cape of Good Hope and home? She was going the long way around, but the trade winds justified the course. He had chosen this route because he was committed to stop in Bombay.

He hoped Alice would tear for home without stopping. If she had a seasoned crew, she needn't worry about the schooner pursuing her. But with green hands, and women at that … Josiah shook his head. Unthinkable.

He strode to the cabin door and flung it open. His steward jumped up from his seat on a hinged board that folded down from the bulkhead.

"I'd like some tea if you can manage it, Chase. If the galley's cold, then a glass of port."

"Yes, sir." Chase hurried toward the galley.

Josiah went back to his desk and scanned the chart of Australia's southeast coast. He did hope he'd find Alice. But even if he didn't, he could keep those vile men from chasing her halfway to the Torres Strait.

After his tea, he napped for a couple of hours, but rose when the watch changed. He went on deck just as Reiner, the second mate, relieved Stark.

"How close is that schooner?" he asked the first mate.

"We'll catch her within an hour, sir. She's dead ahead of us, tacking to take advantage of the land breeze."

"Thank you. You may go, Stark, but I'll have you on deck when we make contact."

"Very good, Captain."

In half an hour, Josiah read the name *Lorelai* clearly through the telescope while he stood in the bow. He had Reiner send a man to get the first mate and call all hands.

Josiah met Stark on the quarterdeck.

"Got them rattled, have we?" Stark grinned.

"I'd say so," Josiah replied.

Stark chuckled. "No doubt their captain is leery of this big merchant ship bearing down on him—and with good reason."

"Move all the swivel guns to the lee side," Josiah told him. "Load with canister."

Stark smiled as he carried out his orders, ensuring the swivel guns were in position to rake the *Lorelai's* side if the situation demanded. Josiah watched with satisfaction.

"Come up alongside her," Josiah told his second mate. Reiner quickly gave his men orders. They swung even with the *Lorelai* on the windward side.

Reiner looked over at the captain. "Do you wish to speak, sir?"

"Get them to heave to and tell them Captain Howard wishes to speak with Captain Glenn."

Five minutes later, Josiah and Bluey Glenn faced each other across a short expanse of water. Tom Larson and Con Snyder flanked the schooner's captain. Even from fifty yards, Josiah could see that Snyder was hard as nails.

"Be you looking for a brig out of Melbourne?" Josiah called through the speaking trumpet.

"Aye. The *Vera B.*" Glenn pushed his cap back to reveal a shock of red hair.

"Belay that," Josiah said.

"Beg pardon, gov'ner?"

"Give up your pursuit."

Glenn glanced at his two cohorts. "Can't do that, sir."

"Oh, I think you can." Josiah gestured, and four sailors stood forward to aim the swivel guns.

"Now, look here," Bluey Glenn sputtered. "You can't attack me. I'm commissioned to help these men recover stolen property."

"Last I knew," Josiah said distinctly, "human beings were not property in the British Empire."

"What do you know about it?" Snyder screamed without benefit of the instrument, but Josiah had no trouble hearing him.

"I know plenty. My men and I are armed and will not hesitate to bring our six-pounders to bear on your hull. I expect the swivel guns will cut most of you to ribbons first. What do you say, Captain Glenn?"

The three men huddled for a minute. Josiah glanced up at the counter-braced yards. Reiner and his men were doing a splendid job of maintaining their position.

"Mr. Stark," Josiah said.

"Yes, sir?"

"I don't want bloodshed unless it's necessary. If they menace us, shred their sails."

"With pleasure, sir." Stark's eyes glittered as he walked amidships to instruct the men.

Josiah couldn't hear Bluey Glenn, but he appeared to be pleading with Snyder and Larson. He thought it was Larson whose "...blasted Americans..." drifted over to him.

Snyder shouted and turned toward Josiah, a long-barreled pistol in his hand. Josiah pulled his own Colt revolver from inside his coat as he ducked. A ball threw splinters off the bulwark. Stark barked an order and the four swivel guns let loose. The Lorelai's sails quivered. Slashes appeared in the canvas, and a couple of lines snapped. The foretopsail sagged like a bedraggled petticoat.

"Reload," Stark yelled. "If we fire again, aim lower. Show 'em we mean business."

Glenn raised his speaking trumpet. "Enough, gov'ner! We'll turn back."

Josiah straightened, smiling, and said softly, "I thought you would. Outmanned and outgunned. Only a fool would persist."

Snyder wrenched the trumpet from Glenn's hand and yelled, "Ya barbarian! You'll regret this!"

"I don't see how, Mr. Snyder," Josiah replied. "My men are ready to resume fire if you do not comply at once."

"I'll report you to the Admiralty!"

Josiah laughed. "Who are they going to believe, you or me? Captain Glenn, come about immediately, if you want your vessel and crew to survive."

"Aye, gov'ner." Bluey waved and strode to his ship's wheel. "Haul the mainsail round!"

Josiah let out a big sigh. "Well done, Mr. Reiner. Mr. Stark. Carry on."

###

179

Alice stepped outside her cabin and looked around. The sun shone brightly on the eastern horizon, and a smart breeze brought a welcome respite. They had sailed out of the chilly winter to the south into warmer latitudes. The *Vera B.*'s sailors all seemed to be topside, enjoying the pleasant day.

Gypsy called to Alice from near the shrouds and chains, "Good morning, Mrs. Packard!" His grizzled face split into a grin as he limped toward her. "As you can see, ma'am, we're hard at work sprucing up the ship. Do you think we'll make Moreton Bay before sunset?"

Alice smiled. "I believe we will, in fact, we should arrive by noon, if the wind continues from this direction." She bit her lip. "I want Sonja to look at my charts. We need to change course now, to north by west. It won't be long before we hit shallows, and the channel into Moreton Bay will need close attention."

"Very good, ma'am." Gypsy looked up to where Kate and Sarah stood at the wheel, talking. "Change course to north by west!"

Alice nodded in approval as Kate and Sarah turned the wheel to swing the ship around to port. "After you trim the sails, send Sonja and a smart girl from the first watch. I want Sonja to teach the lead line to others, because we'll be using it frequently on the next leg of our journey."

"The Great Barrier Reef." Gypsy looked at her, his eyes smoldering. "It was either that, or Cape Horn."

"I did not wish to take this crew through that dangerous passage."

Gypsy shrugged. "So we'll face the Barrier Reef, the Torres Strait, the pestilence of the tropics, crocodiles bigger than a boat—not to mention pirates. We don't know for sure if we've lost Snyder, either." He grinned. "It's six of one, or seven of the other. I'm fine with the warm and toasty route."

Alice sighed. "What would I do without you, Gypsy? The crocodiles and pirates can wait. Today I'm just concerned about getting into Moreton Bay without wrecking the brig."

"Yes, ma'am. Before I send Sonja, there are a few issues that have come up with the crew. I wonder if you ought to have a man-to-man talk with some of these women. . . ."

Ten minutes later, Alice sat in her cabin awaiting the first of three sailors Gypsy would send her for "man-to-man" talks. She leafed through her Bible, praying silently. Tensions had developed between various crew members over the past few days, and Gypsy pointed out dilemmas she already perceived. She asked the Lord for guidance and strength.

A knock came at the door, so quiet she might not have noticed if she were not expecting it. "Come in." Alice stood.

The door creaked open, and Polly Marsh gingerly looked in. She locked eyes with Alice, timidly entered, and closed the door behind her.

"Sit down, Polly." Alice showed her to a chair. The young woman's face was pale.

Polly eased herself onto the cushioned chair, and Alice sat on her bed. "Polly, Mr. Deak says you haven't been well, and Hannah also has said so."

Polly stared at Alice, her big brown eyes panic-stricken. "I— I—"

"It's all right, Polly, I want to help you. We are heading into port today. If you are ill, maybe we can get some medicine."

"M-ma'am, do you s'pose—it could be scurvy?"

"Scurvy?" Alice pursed her lips. "Have you lost any teeth?"

"N-no, ma'am. But—my gums are swollen, and they were bleeding."

"Sailors usually don't get scurvy until they've been living on biscuits and salt pork for months." Alice sighed. "But—it is possible to get scurvy without being on a ship. Mr. Deak says you've been lethargic and inattentive compared to the others, and those are symptoms of scurvy, too." She frowned. "I've found our sailors' diet to be better than what the crews of many vessels enjoy, though it certainly isn't the governor's table."

Polly said nothing, but looked a little guilty.

"Mr. Deak fears for you when you go aloft. I believe I'm going to keep you out of the rigging until you're feeling better. I'll see if I can obtain some fruits or vegetables when we put into Brisbane. Meanwhile, I want you in the fresh air on deck as much as you can stand, help as you're able, but don't hurt yourself. Don't go aloft. If the fo'c'sle is too stuffy, you have my permission to sling your hammock in the 'tweendecks."

"Thank you, ma'am."

Polly left, and Alice let out a deep breath. So. She had a feeling Polly wouldn't recover soon. She was thankful that Kate had brought her only one who wasn't in reasonably good health. Alice didn't question why God had brought Polly to the *Vera B.*, but rather how she could best bless Polly.

A minute later, Lizzie Henshaw glided in. "You called for me, ma'am?"

Alice decided against offering Lizzie a seat. "Lizzie, how are your hands? Are you quite recovered from the rope burns?"

Lizzie primly extended her hands, palms up.

"I can still see the marks, but they seem to be healed sufficiently for you to be back about your duties. Can I count on you to take your place in the rigging?"

Lizzie grimaced in a way that was quite unbecoming. "Ma'am, I'm not sure that's wise. I fell once. I may fall again. I don't believe I am cut from that sort of cloth."

"Lizzie, no one forced you to sign on with this crew. Being a sailor is hard work and dangerous. But I don't have room for passengers on this vessel. And I certainly don't have room for people who constantly criticize others."

Lizzie looked at her askance. "I beg your pardon, ma'am?"

"I have been told that you make a habit of snubbing the other sailors, and that you maintain some sort of blood feud with young Ned McKay. Don't you think you're old enough not to allow the antics of a child to bring out the worst in you?"

Lizzie's eyes bugged out. "Excuse me, ma'am? That *dear* child is a changeling, demon fury. You know he tried to burn the ship down! If there's someone you shouldn't have room for, it is he!"

Alice eyed her keenly. "I expect childishness out of him. I don't expect it from you." She paced the cabin, carefully framing her words. "I have spoken to Mr. Deak, and I will speak to Mrs. Fiske. Today, we should put into Brisbane, where we will offload some cargo. I have a proposition to make you."

"Ma'am?" Lizzie frowned.

"If you do not wish to accompany us back to England, we can write up letters of recommendation for you, emphasizing your domestic skills, which, Mrs. Fiske assures me, are exemplary. I have little doubt someone in Brisbane will want you."

"Want me, ma'am? As—a maid?"

Alice did her best not to smile, and looked away. "My husband's business contact in Brisbane is one of the chief men of the colony, an assistant to the governor. I doubt that a lady's maid position will be possible to find. But I'm told there are five men for every woman in Australia. I'm sure Mr. Hainsworth and his wife will help you to find a husband."

"What!" Lizzie huffed. "I couldn't be married. As a lady's maid, I—"

"Things are different in Australia. The rules of the old country are going by the wayside here. There are probably hundreds of men in Brisbane looking for a wife. I'm sure you could have your pick of them."

"Isn't this—Brisbane—the same place they call Moreton Bay?" Lizzie's voice might have been that of a cornered wildcat.

"Yes, indeed."

"The penal colony where they send the convicts who are so evil that hanging is too lenient? That Moreton Bay?"

"I don't know if I'd go that far—"

"Well, Captain Alice, it appears I have no choice. I must remain with you, rigging or no rigging."

"Very good, Lizzie. Now do the best you can, take on your tasks with a will, and try to get along with the others."

Lizzie nodded solemnly and left, her eyes flashing.

The third knock on the door was loud and abrupt. Alice braced herself. "Come in."

A muscular, sun-tanned woman entered, her black locks flowing around her beautiful face, her blue eyes piercing the dimness of Alice's cabin like the beacon of a lighthouse. "Ma'am?" The alto voice carried an edge.

Alice repressed a shudder. This one made her nervous. If she had a mind to, Brea could do some damage. "Brea McDonovan. We have something to discuss."

"Indeed." Brea shifted her weight gracefully to her other leg. The woolen sailor's blouse she wore draped her torso artfully, and her claret sash might have come from a fine haberdasher's front window display.

My very own pirate, Alice thought. "First of all, Brea, I've been largely satisfied with your performance as a sailor. You're one of the best, to be sure."

Brea raised an eyebrow. "But?"

Alice bit her lip. "But I'm not pleased with your lack of respect. On this vessel, we must respect each other. Above all, respect must be shown to the officers. Without it, we cannot function. The morale of the entire crew has suffered from this, and it must end."

Brea grimaced, her eyes hard. "I do what I said I'd do, ma'am. Respect runs both ways. I don't ever see you out there pulling on ropes and climbing the shrouds."

Alice was dumfounded. What should she do in the face of such audacity? In spite of the anger that roiled within her, a verse entered her mind: *A soft answer turneth away wrath.*

"Brea, where were you born?"

"Munster, Ireland. I was just a girl when I hit a constable, and they transported me."

Alice could well imagine the scene. But still, transportation was harsh punishment. "I suppose that was your only other time on a ship. I can't expect you to know how it's supposed to be,

184

but the captain of a ship must be the one in charge, and no one is allowed to show dissent."

Brea's eyes narrowed. "Aye, that's how Con was, and no mistaking."

"I'm not talking about beating you into submission, and yet many ships' captains have resorted to it. Does a person have to beat you and threaten to shoot you, like Con did, to have your respect? Is that all you understand?"

Brea snorted. "You think Con has my respect? Only when he's looking. If you don't mind me saying so, true respect is from the heart, and no rule or law can command it."

Alice studied Brea's face. "There's merit in that. But I need to have you show some deference to myself and the other officers, for the sake of morale and discipline on this vessel. We've a long voyage ahead of us." Alice took a slow breath to calm herself. "I know you've been through a lot in life, and I am sorry. I'll do all within my power to get you back to your homeland. But I want you to know, Brea—I cannot respect you until you show respect for others."

"The life I've lived doesn't know the word respect."

"It's one of many things you need to learn. You also need to learn about love. God loved you and sent His Son to die for you. You are loved. I want you to know that."

Brea frowned. "I'd listen more if you'd quit talking about God all the time. God this, God that. Sunday church. Love, respect, sin. It's too much, your going on about how we should live pure lives. It's not me. But you did get me away from Con Snyder, so I will try harder to be on my best behavior, or you can lock me in the bilge."

"I'd rather have you in the rigging doing your job than in the bilge. I need you there. Do what you can, Brea, and I will do my best to earn your respect, if you will show me some. Otherwise. . . ."

"I understand, ma'am."

185

As Brea left, Alice couldn't help feeling that she had lost a major battle. She should have handled the confrontation better. This girl was probably not done causing harm.

When another knock sounded at the door, Alice was relieved to find it was only Sonja and Jenny, come to look at the charts.

CHAPTER EIGHTEEN

Gypsy yelled up at the sailors on the foremast, "Look lively, now. You there, Carrie! Get that clew line."

Though he growled and barked at them all day, he watched with satisfaction as they put the sails in order to enter Moreton Bay. Three weeks of practice and drill had made a huge difference. His crew performed better with every turn of the watch, though they were still awkward at reefing the sails, and some balked at climbing above the topsails. They hadn't the strength of men, it was true, but several of them were smart and quick. Overall, he felt they carried out their duties as well as a crew of green boys would have.

Most of these women were on their own for the first time and stretching toward the future that beckoned them. The fresh air, strenuous work, and regular meals and sleep had most of them looking healthy. A few had started to chafe at the confinements of ship life and close quarters with people they didn't necessarily like. Gypsy reminded them now and then that they weren't clear yet. They had to earn their freedom. At the voyage's end, and not a minute before, they would be their own mistresses. For now, they had to answer to him, Captain Alice, and the mates.

Sonja and Jenny stood in the bow together, taking soundings. All the other hands were on deck except Nell. The women who had not cut their hair concealed it beneath their caps, and they knew they must go below as soon as they had anchored. They would be close to other ships in the harbor and must stay out of sight.

Alice came out of her cabin and joined him on the quarterdeck. Her expression was grave, and fine lines etched the corners of her eyes. No doubt the responsibility she had shouldered accounted for that. "All well?"

"Aye," Gypsy said.

"You'll be ready to go ashore with me?"

He nodded. "We'll make the arrangements for unloading as quick as possible, but first these lubbers have got to anchor safely."

"Can they do it, Gypsy? We don't want to overshoot our berth and plow into another ship."

"Don't worry, Cap'n. They'll do just fine." Inwardly, he had his own misgivings, but unless the harbor was crowded, they should have ample room to maneuver. They needed to get in where they could unload their cargo with a minimum of fuss, but they also needed to avoid anything that would call attention to the *Vera B.* He wouldn't voice his doubts, however. Captain Alice needed to hear confidence, and that was what she would get.

Sonja shouted the depth as they sailed smoothly between Moreton Island and Point Lookout.

"Right in the middle of the channel." Gypsy smiled at Alice.

"Ruel's chart indicates there are wharfs on the inner shore of Moreton Island," she said.

"Well, you'll need to see the superintendent, anyway," Gypsy replied. "We'll go in closer to the mouth of the river and send word that his cargo has arrived. If he wants it unloaded at the island, that's what we'll do."

Alice sighed. "You're right. I shouldn't fret about it. If we can offload the gin closer to the river, it will save them a lot of work, but it will mean sailing in amongst the smaller islands in the bay."

"We'll manage, Cap'n." Gypsy walked over to where Kate stood. "Have your crew reef the topsails. We'll take her in slowly."

"Aye, sir." Kate shouted the orders, and the women leaped to obey.

"Your watch has greatly improved, Miss Robinson," Gypsy said.

"I'd thank you, sir, but it's mostly due to your diligence." Kate shot him a tentative smile.

Gypsy chuckled. "You've worked hard, too. You're learning faster than most."

Kate ducked her head at his praise. "Can I ask you something, Mr. Deak?"

"Surely."

Kate sucked in a breath. "Did I hear Captain Alice say our cargo for Moreton Bay is gin?"

He laughed. "Not what you think, missy. It's a cotton gin. Machinery, all in pieces in crates."

Kate chortled. "I couldn't imagine Captain Alice making her living selling liquor."

"Nay, and her husband wouldn't have either, though he did allow his sailors a bit of grog now and then."

Her eyes widened. "Will we have rum when we have something to celebrate?"

"I doubt it," Gypsy said. "Captain Alice will likely save it for medicinal purposes, or for when we have a bad storm and need to fortify ourselves."

Kate eyed him carefully. "Are you making fun?"

"Not at all. I like my ration as well as the next man. But we don't need it, do we? I don't expect these girls would be the better for it."

"Most of them are used to having a beer with a gent," Kate said.

"Hmm. Well, some of them would probably go off their heads with the first dram. We'll abide by Mrs. Packard's rules and be happy, eh?"

"I am happy, Mr. Deak. Very happy to be here, and not back at Con's. I may not sail again for the rest of my life, but it's much better than what I left behind."

An hour later, Gypsy alternately yelled orders and held his breath. Alice and Mrs. Fiske stood by, ready to jump in if needed, but the crew executed the maneuver well enough. They had a bit too much headway and had to back the main topsail. For a moment, Gypsy feared a collision with a schooner, but they corrected soon enough. He mopped his brow when the anchor dropped. They'd done it.

He grinned at Kate. "Well done, Miss Robinson. Send all below except the two needed for the watch while the captain and I go ashore." He had previously selected Brea and Sonja as the two most likely to pass for men from a distance. Some of the women had a combination of sweet features and softness to their figures that made them obviously feminine, despite their masculine garb.

"A couple of them are disappointed that they won't get to put on dresses and go ashore," Kate said.

Gypsy's eyebrows shot up. "What about you?"

Kate shook her head. "From the tales I've heard about Moreton Bay, I think we're all safer on board. I don't want to take any chances." She gave the order for the sailors to go below. The women scrambled down the hatches. Kate had orders for them to push the crates destined for Brisbane over beneath the main hatch, where they could hitch onto them with a crane and hoist them.

"Ready?" He asked Alice.

"As I'll ever be." She wore a voluminous, crinolined skirt in a shiny material with stripes. Some sort of silk, Gypsy supposed. He hoped her lovely appearance would distract any men she had to deal with from scrutinizing the crew too closely.

They weren't far from the nearest dock, and the water in the bay scarcely rippled. Gypsy rowed the dinghy ashore, leaving all the women but Alice on board. After some discussion, they had agreed that they were all better off if the other women stayed on the ship. Alice sat demurely astern of him, observing the other vessels as he rowed.

"I hope none of them want to get friendly and visit us," she said.

190

"I left orders that if anyone tries to talk to our crew, they're to wave and be silent if possible. But if they can't avoid talking, they're to say the captain's steward will bring them an answer later. Brea has a low voice. I think they'll be all right."

Alice nodded. "I hope all goes well with the governor's man and we can be away on the morning tide."

Gypsy glanced over his shoulder. The sun was already far down the sky. "I don't know if we can unload before dark."

"Do what you can, Gypsy. We understand one another."

"Aye." They were close to a low wharf where other small boats were moored, and he eased up on the oars.

A laborer near the dock directed them to the ferry that would take them up the Brisbane River a short distance to the town. The twenty men on board the ferry stared openly at Alice, and she kept her gaze lowered. Only one other woman shared the short voyage, and she appeared to be the wife of the stout farmer beside her. She never attempted to approach Alice. Gypsy didn't blame her. Alice looked so grand, he doubted most women in this place would dare speak to her, though they might mock her behind her back for thinking she was their better. Humble Alice would never think such things, but the women in these parts lived hard lives. In Gypsy's mind, that meant they despised those who had things easier.

The short walk from the ferry dock to the superintendent's house gave them a quick view of the town.

"I'm surprised," Alice said as they walked past a chemist's shop and a general store. "It looks almost civilized. You hear such lurid tales of the place."

"They closed the penal colony, but I'll warrant the place isn't all tamed yet." Gypsy led her to a comfortable-looking brick house and knocked at the door. A manservant ushered them in and went to fetch the superintendent.

The furnishings, while not luxurious, would not embarrass the householder—all brought from England, no doubt.

191

"This is the house we've brought the fine china for," Alice whispered.

"Aye. And the cotton gin."

A gentleman of about forty entered the room. He wore a somber suit of black with a snowy white linen shirt, and his face held an air of confusion.

"Mrs. Packard?"

"Yes, sir." She walked toward him, extending her hand. "And this is Mr. Deak, the steward of the brig *Vera B*. We've brought your cotton gin, the seed, and the household goods you ordered."

"Ah. Welcome. I'm Edmund Hainsworth." He clasped her gloved hand for a moment. "When I heard an American brig had anchored, I expected the captain."

"My husband became ill after we left Adelaide," Alice said. "He passed on and is buried in St. Kilda."

"I'm so sorry." Hainsworth shook Gypsy's hand. "Mr. Deak. Won't you sit down?"

They took seats on the plush upholstered sofa, their host facing them.

"We hoped we could unload this afternoon," Gypsy said, "but I fear we've not enough daylight."

"I think you're right," Hainsworth said easily.

"Can we get up the river?" Alice asked. "I saw some good-sized steamers at the dock."

"Their draft is very shallow. I don't think you'd want to risk it, especially if you're heavily laden."

Gypsy nodded. "We'll unload at the bay, then."

"I'll arrange a place for you at Helmsley's dock at first light," Hainsworth said. "Can your crew handle the offloading?"

"We'll get it to the top deck, and we've a windlass and can get it over the side," Gypsy replied. "If you can have a crew on the dock to take it from there, we'll finish as quick as we can and see if we're able to make sail before nightfall."

"You don't wish to stay in our fair city a few days?" Hainsworth smiled. "My wife would be happy of some genteel company, Mrs. Packard."

"Thank you, but we must make haste."

"Pity. At least stay for tea."

Alice arched her eyebrows at Gypsy.

"Why don't you stay, ma'am?" he said. "I'll make the arrangements with Mr. Hainsworth's man, and I'll let the mate know our plans. I'll come back for you in ... three hours?" He looked expectantly at Mr. Hainsworth.

"That would be fine. Unless we can persuade Mrs. Packard to spend the night here. We've a spare bedroom." For just a second, Gypsy saw a wistful look in Alice's eyes. A private room on land, and perhaps a bath. But she shook her head. "You're most kind, sir, but I have a few female passengers on board, and I'll feel better if I'm on board tonight."

"Would any of them like to shop tomorrow during the unloading?" Hainsworth asked. "My wife could show you the best shops."

"Perhaps a few would," Alice conceded. "I would like to get some fruit if I can, and one of the ladies said she'd like some thread."

"We'd like to refill our water casks," Gypsy added, "and restock our ammunition. We're headed into pirate waters."

"Indeed. I can help you with that." Mr. Hainsworth looked up as a fair-haired woman about his age entered. "Ah, my wife is here." He and Gypsy jumped to their feet. "Dearest, this is the widow Packard, off the *Vera B.*, and the ship's steward."

The woman came forward. "I heard that a lady had come to call. Dare I hope we'll have an overnight guest?"

"Mrs. Packard will take tea with us, while her steward arranges to unload our cottonseed and the gin tomorrow."

"Oh!" Mrs. Hainsworth clasped her hands together. "Is my china here?"

Alice smiled. "Indeed it is. We shall unload that first."

193

"Joy!" Mrs. Hainsworth said. "My dear, you *must* stay the night."

Gypsy left soon after Alice had let her hostess convince her to stay. She spent an enjoyable evening with Mr. and Mrs. Hainsworth, learning much about the town and its origins as a prison colony. Ruel would have loved hearing Mr. Hainsworth's tales, though some of them made Alice shudder.

Even in the well-furnished bedchamber that night, she was on edge, and not only from the grisly convict stories. Thinking of Gypsy and the crew on board the *Vera B.* kept her awake. Had anyone in the harbor taken note of their sailors on watch? Had Gypsy been able to make all the necessary arrangements so that they could leave on the afternoon tide? She hoped he and the women had been able to hoist all of Mr. Hainsworth's crates to the deck under cover of darkness. She had hoped that the shore crew could board and take them off in the morning without laying eyes on any of her women, but Gypsy feared they would think it odd if not a single one of their sailors helped with that stage of the unloading. He thought he could manage with Brea and Sonja's help, and she hoped he was right.

Though she knew Hannah and some of the others longed to set foot on land again, they had all agreed to lower the risk by having Alice handle the shopping. Reluctantly, she renewed her decision to keep them all on board. Even if the unloading went well, Alice's nerves wouldn't settle until she was sure Bluey Glenn's schooner wasn't waiting for them outside the bay. She rolled over in the comfortable bed a dozen times, thinking about the voyage ahead.

She missed Ruel. Her loss hit her harder than it had since they took the women aboard. On the brig, the divided cabin tricked her senses into thinking it was a different room than the one she had shared with him. She had packed all his clothing in a trunk and sent it to the cargo hold, so she didn't have to look at it every day. Even so, the furnishings of her cabin spoke loudly of her husband. His charts. His navigation books. The quilts they had shared.

The whole business of hiring the women and escaping Port Phillip Bay had distracted her. Every night she fell into bed exhausted. But this was different. Her first night on shore since Adelaide. Ruel should be here with her. She reached out and touched the cool slip of the unused pillow beside her. At last she drifted off.

She slept for hours. When she awoke, she lay for a few minutes under the warm coverlet, thinking of Ruel and her family in Massachusetts. Would they hear of his death before she reached home? Perhaps she should have written a letter to her parents and sent it with Josiah Howard. His clipper might well beat her home, since she planned to stop in England. Sunlight streamed through a crack between the drawn velvet drapes. She ought to rise.

Quickly she doffed the nightdress her hostess had loaned her. Mrs. Hainsworth had laid out a brush and comb, a pitcher of water, soft soap, and towels. Alice washed and rubbed some scented lotion into her roughened hands. She ought to take better care of her skin on board ship, but it seemed like too much trouble when she lived from watch to watch. Once she got home, she would pamper herself.

Her doubts assailed her as she pulled on her petticoat and dress. They would get out of Brisbane today and skirt the Great Barrier Reef, soon leaving the coast altogether. With only the briefest of training, she was taking the women into the unknown. She had watched them wrestle the canvas yesterday as they anchored and furled the sails. Even in calm weather they struggled, and much of the work was carried out high above the deck. Would they all survive the voyage?

If only she had gotten Boardman back, and one or two able-bodied men. What a difference that would make! Experienced

195

men not only had the strength needed, but they would know what to do without being shown every detail. As it was, they lost time during every maneuver while Gypsy or Sarah showed the women what to do. She could hardly believe they had outrun the schooner.

Maybe she could hire a few men here in Brisbane. She scuttled the thought as soon as it occurred. She couldn't add men to the mix now. Where would she house them? And she would have to explain the situation before signing them on. Trouble would surely follow. No, it was out of the question.

Somewhere in the house, a door closed. Alice took a final look in the mirror and hurried into the hallway. Mrs. Hainsworth came up the stairs, looking fresh and beautiful in a dress of figured mauve barège.

"Good morning, Mrs. Packard. Cook has breakfast ready. Do you fancy creamed eggs and scones?"

"I should adore them," Alice replied with a smile. She felt almost guilty going down to an ample breakfast of delicacies. She wished she could share it with the women on the brig.

"I've spoken for a bushel of oranges for you to take with you when you go," Mrs. Hainsworth said. "That and a firkin of raisins. I'm sorry I couldn't get any apples."

Alice smiled. "The crew will be very happy. And do you know if I can buy a few dozen eggs?"

Jenny stood in the bow of the *Vera B.* and pulled the lead line up out of the water. She carefully counted the knots on the rope. It seemed like the weight had plunked on the ocean floor a good bit shallower than the last time.

Above the billowing sails, thousands of stars lit the cloudless sky. Unfamiliar constellations hovered over the horizon. They were three days out of Brisbane. Captain Alice said they would turn north soon and cross the Tropic of Capricorn within a few days.

The lead weight clunked against the ship's hull as Jenny pulled it up. Seventeen fathoms. The depth had been more than her twenty-five-fathom line when she took the last sounding.

"By the mark, seventeen," she yelled back toward the quarterdeck. She heard Lizzie repeat the message from the waist, relaying it to Mrs. Fiske at the wheel.

Not two minutes later, the *Vera B.* shuddered and groaned. Jenny almost lost her footing. A loud profanity boomed down from the foretop, as if from the night sky overhead—Brea's voice.

"Back the sails," Mrs. Fiske shouted from the wheel, her voice shrill. "All hands on deck!" Someone lit a lantern back beyond the mainmast.

"All hands on deck," Hannah yelled down the forward hatch. She was nearly thrown to the deck by a lank, shadowy figure vaulting from the companionway.

At first Jenny thought a kangaroo had sprung up from the 'tweendecks, but an outburst of frantic Norwegian identified the new arrival. Sonja advanced toward Jenny, eyes gleaming in the starlight.

"*Gyselig brenning* wombats!" She marched up to Jenny. "I told you, take the sounding every five minutes!"

The motion of the waves lifted then dropped the *Vera B.*, and the hull rubbed once more against the underwater obstruction, more gently this time. Hannah hastened toward them, and Kate sprinted to the bow carrying a lantern.

"What's going on?" she demanded.

"We hit a reef because Jenny didn't take the sounding!" Sonja sputtered. "We could have all died. We might still." She gave Jenny a withering look and snatched at the lead weight she held.

Jenny felt she would explode. "I did take the sounding! I just took it!" Sonja's ferocity frightened her. She and Sonja had grown

197

quite close since her friend's bout of depression a few weeks earlier. This personal attack hurt.

"Jenny did take a sounding, right before we struck," Hannah said firmly. "It was seventeen fathoms. And it was only a minute ago."

Kate said, "It can't be too bad."

Jenny hoped she was right, but what did Kate know, anyway?

"Back the sails!" Mrs. Fiske bellowed again.

Sonja grimaced, and stalked off toward the waist. Kate gestured for Hannah and Jenny to follow.

Gypsy was on deck now, rubbing sleep from his eyes. "Man the foremast braces!"

Jenny hurried to her post. By now they knew how to back the sails to stop the brig's forward motion.

The off-duty sailors had come from the forecastle, and the whole crew hauled on the sheets and braces to trim the sails of the foremast, counteracting the wind forces on the mainmast. When the last line was secured, the groggy sailors looked around at each other, nervous and edgy. The *Vera B.* no longer hit the reef, but bobbed in place on the waves.

The officers conferred around the ship's wheel for a moment, then Mr. Deak approached the quarterdeck rail with Kate and looked down at the crew. "The wind will blow us sideways for a bit, and we don't know how big that reef is. When we get a decent sounding, we'll anchor for the night so we don't drift into it."

Sonja eyed Jenny testily. Jenny bit her lip. "I'll let you do it."

Sonja nodded and strode toward the bow.

Kate came down the stairs with the lantern. "Someone come with me and check the hold for leaks." Her eyes locked with Jenny's, and she nodded toward the hatch.

Jenny followed Kate down the companionway, then down the ladder leading below the 'tweendecks, to the cargo hold. When they reached the bottom of the ladder, Kate shined the lantern around. Big bales of wool, alternating with barred-in stacks of grain bags, dominated the scene. A narrow passage led forward ten feet to the base of the mainmast, which blocked their view farther ahead. Another narrow passage led back toward the stern.

Kate looked at the decking below their feet. Through the cracks between the boards, Jenny saw the glint of water reflecting a couple feet below.

"There's always a little water in the bilge," Kate said. "I don't think it's any higher than usual. We'd better go forward and look, though. We struck on the port bow, and that's probably where any damage would be."

Jenny nodded. She had come down to check for damage after the *Vera B.* scraped the bottom while exiting The Rip. She followed Kate forward and around the mainmast. She ran her hand along the bales of wool, wondering if any of it had come from her uncle's sheep.

Kate stopped on the other side of the mainmast, and they both peered ahead toward the foremast base. "I think we're fine," Kate said. "If we'd bashed a hole in the hull, we'd all know it. But I want to tell you something."

Jenny searched Kate's eyes in the flickering lantern light.

"You're not on my watch, so I don't get to talk to you much." Kate squinted. "I want you to know, I think you're a good sailor, and you've been a great sport. But more than that, you're an example to the rest of us. Some of the girls are a little jealous of you, because they feel you've had an easy life. You haven't gone through a lot of the grief we have. You lost your parents, yes, but you had your aunt's family to take care of you. Some of the others feel a little awkward about you, but most of them like you. They—we all wish we could go back to being like you. If we ever were."

Jenny wasn't sure how to take this. Aunt Hannah had explained to her a bit about the horrors the girls had experienced, but the whole business was still a big mystery. She was sure

199

Hannah hadn't told her everything, especially about the men, and how all that worked. Aunt Hannah and Uncle Alton's marriage had been a good one, as far as it went—Jenny had heard of people having bad marriages, where they fought all the time and hurt each other. But the whole thing about being with men was something she wondered about, though she guessed some of the details. She shivered and gave Kate a hesitant smile.

Kate exhaled. "Look, don't fret about Sonja. I don't think she meant what she said tonight. She's scared. Remember what happened to her father."

Jenny nodded. "I know. If the ship sank tonight, she'd blame herself, even though she'd yell at me."

"I'm going to talk to her. She wouldn't want to hurt you. Sometimes—when people hurt—a lot—inside. . . ."

"They do things that are hard to explain." Jenny sighed. "I understand."

Kate grimaced kindly. "I don't think there are any leaks. Why don't you just work your way along to the bow and take a butcher's. Listen for any trickling water or anything like that." She handed Jenny the lantern. "I'm headed back on deck. Come on up when you're done, and let us know what you find."

Jenny stepped carefully along the narrow passage between the wool bales, steadying herself with one hand and gingerly carrying the lantern with the other. After Ned's performance in the hold, she was mindful of safety. Wool was easy to light on fire. She remembered how Ned had nearly burned a neighbor's shearing shed down when Uncle Alton had taken him along to help the tar boy. They used hot tar to stop the bleeding when they nicked a sheep. Ned had been fascinated with the fire that kept the tar pot boiling while the men sheared the sheep. Though she hadn't been there, she could just see her cousin feeding little wisps of wool into the flames, until one thing lead to another.

She stepped around the base of the foremast, squeezing along the narrow passageway. The sailors and dockworkers who

200

had loaded the cargo had used nearly every bit of available space. Wool and grain bags were wedged in from deck to ceiling.

When she was nearly to the bow, she stooped and looked through a crack in the decking at the bilge water. It looked the same as ever, and smelled just as bad. She straightened and stood listening, feeling the gentle rise and fall of the vessel on the waves, hearing the slosh of the bilge water, but no trickling. The wool in the hold had a strange damping effect on all the sounds. A muffled clanging above caused her to jump, but she recognized it as the sound of an anchor being dropped, distorted by the walls of wool.

Jenny was about to head back to the ladder when she heard a slight scurrying sound. Her scalp tingled, and she looked to the bow, where several large barrels of whale oil were secured. Probably a rat, but it was her duty to investigate. She stepped forward, putting a hand on one of the barrels. She peered around it, and saw nothing.

The closeness of the hold, the eerie lantern light, and the strange muffling of sounds made her heart beat fast. She had never feared the dark, or dingoes yipping in the distance, nor native men skulking in the woods, but here in the most isolated part of the hold, she felt that she could hear her own breathing, as if she were outside her body. Her flesh crawled. She gritted her teeth and held her breath, gazing wide-eyed at the boards and beams that formed the brig's frame.

There it was—the breathing. But it was not hers. Jenny still held her breath, but something, or someone else, was breathing. It stopped, as if sensing that she heard. Jenny's heart thundered. She looked all around, certain she was being watched. She turned to bolt along the narrow passageway, but checked herself. She was a grown woman of eighteen years, and a sailor to boot. She couldn't be scared of her own shadow.

Grudgingly, she turned to look behind her and nearly dropped the lantern. A pair of eyes glinted at her from above the oil barrels. Her head swam, and she sank to the deck.

CHAPTER NINETEEN

"Gently, gently, precious maiden," a voice whispered.

Jenny felt someone wipe her face with a damp handkerchief. She opened her eyes and saw the handsome features of a man within arm's length. He smiled and quit dabbing her face.

Jenny screamed, but even as she did, she doubted anyone would hear her. The sound was absorbed into the stalwart wool bales on every side.

"No, no, precious maid," the man said. "Please you not to wail. I am not harming you."

Jenny gritted her teeth and forced herself to look at him. He was older than she was, but still young, and had pale eyes, blond hair, and a light beard. In the lantern's rays, she couldn't tell the color of his tattered cotton shirt.

"Who are you?" she gasped.

"Allow me to introduce myself," he said in a clipped accent she couldn't place. "My name is Jakob Zeemer. I am pleased to make your acquaintance."

Jenny sat up, and he scrambled out of her way. "What on earth are you doing on our ship?"

Zeemer grimaced sheepishly. "It seemed the safest place for me."

Jenny glanced at the lantern sitting upright beside her on the planking. "It didn't break."

"No, I catch it."

She pushed herself to her feet, wincing from a new bruise to her hip and a crick in her neck.

Zeemer eyed her garments critically. "You, a woman, are working on the ship?"

She glanced down at her blouse and trousers. "Yes, sir." Suddenly she felt embarrassed to be seen in her work attire.

Zeemer met her eyes, and she thought he looked kind and gracious. "You caused me to scare, miss. For you fell and I mistook you might—perish."

Jenny gawked at him, amused at his diction. "Where are you from?"

A shadow passed over the man's face. "I was born in Rotterdam. Then—with mine father I sailed for Batavia, where we made a life. Yes. But he is starved now. I mean perished."

"Dead?" Jenny supplied, arching her eyebrows.

"*Ja*. Correct. He died until—he was dead. Very sad."

Jenny exhaled. "But you cannot be here. Captain Alice never said you could come on board."

Zeemer huffed. "Perchance he is a reasonable man."

Jenny smirked. "No. Captain Alice is a woman. Her husband was the captain, but he died. Perished."

Zeemer looked bewildered. "Your captain is a woman. You are a woman. You are English, perchance. But English folk do not cause the woman to work as sailor. Or captain."

Jenny shook her head. "Not normally. But this ship is unusual. The whole crew—" She stopped, realizing the man before her was a criminal, since he had stowed away. Should she mention the female crew?

"The whole crew. . . is women?" Zeemer studied her face incredulously.

Jenny scowled. "I need to tell Captain Alice about you. You must have gotten on the ship in Moreton Bay. We'll have to take you back." She knelt to pick up the lantern, her heart pounding. How could he have come aboard in a port where they had all stayed on the ship? But it had to have happened there. Brisbane was the only place they had anchored.

"*Zeker niet!*" Zeemer grasped her firmly but gently by the shoulders and raised her back to a standing position.

Shivers went down Jenny's spine. The sensation of his hands on her, even through her woolen blouse, was electrifying. Her lungs felt squeezed as she met his gaze.

"My dear maiden." Zeemer's eyes implored her. "*Dood*—that is, death, awaits me in Moreton Bay. For the misdeed that I did not *doen*. I am *schuldeloos*."

"What does that mean?" Jenny frowned.

"That means—I did not ever do—the deed." He squinted for emphasis.

"You're innocent."

"*Ja*, innocent."

"But they're going to kill you."

"*Ja*, yes." Zeemer clasped his throat to mimic a noose.

Jenny fought back tears. The Dutchman seemed so polite and sincere. With one hand, he still clung tenderly to her shoulder.

"I have to tell Captain Alice. It would be wrong not to. Maybe she—"

"*Nee, mejuffrouw*. You must not tell the captain. I beg for you. It is mine life." His eyes flickered in the lantern light.

Jenny gasped. "If I don't say anything. . ." She tried to imagine what would happen if Captain Alice discovered later that she had lied and had helped a stowaway. But if he was telling the truth and was accused of something he didn't do ... "Someone could find you later. Then they will wonder why I didn't find you now."

"*Mooie meisje*, fine maiden. Swear for me. It is mine life."

Jenny sniffed back tears. "Why did you help me when I swooned? Why didn't you keep hidden?"

"You did see me, and the light did fall. And I had fear for fire-brand. I did see the face of you, how fine." He shook his head sadly. "I cannot have you *klikken* to the captain for me. He—she—must not know."

"We're going all the way to England. Are you going to stay down here in the cargo hold for months?"

"England! Bad. Nay. I will go to shore at a separate land."

"Captain Alice said we will sail near the Dutch East Indies."

Zeemer brightened. "Batavia! *Ja,* for I can go to shore at Batavia."

Jenny frowned. "Maybe. If it works out, but I don't know. What are you going to eat down here?"

Zeemer looked around. "A little the grain, a little the rum. You have vats of the water." He glanced toward the barrels. "Perchance I find the rat, one rat, two rat."

Jenny squirmed. "No, no, not rats. Ugh! I—maybe I can bring you a little something—sometimes. . . ."

Jakob Zeemer sighed. "You, maid, are the angel." He smiled, and released his grip. "Go—and tell of nothing!"

Kate looked up from the chart she was studying in the captain's cabin when someone knocked on the door.

"Come in."

The door opened a few inches, and Fiona peered in, blinking. Even with her red hair cropped and stuffed under a knit cap, she would never be mistaken for a man.

"Well, then?" Kate asked.

Fiona stepped inside and held out a rolled chart. "Mrs. Fiske asked me to bring this back t' you."

Kate nodded and smoothed out the paper. She laid the chart flat in the chest where the captain kept them—dozens of them, all neatly labeled for the different parts of the sea they would sail on.

"Are y' learning them maps?" Fiona asked.

"They're charts." Kate smiled. "I love them. Captain Alice lets me come in here and look at them when I'm off watch."

Fiona stepped nearer and looked at the one spread on the table. "Looks like a map to me."

"It is, but for some reason when they're for sailing, they're called charts. It's all new to me, but there's something wonderful about them." Kate felt suddenly exposed. She eyed Fiona closely, but the red-haired girl didn't laugh.

Fiona squinted at the diagram. "Are those islands?"

"Yes. We're somewhere near here, and there's a lot of reef all along the coast, under the water."

"Do you think maybe I could learn charts someday?"

"I'm sure of it. Captain Alice mentioned having a class on Sunday afternoons, now that things have settled down a bit."

"What do you think of our Sundays?" Fiona cocked her head to one side.

"You mean ... church?"

Fiona nodded. "Some dinna care for it. Brea said Captain Alice is trying to make us all feel guilty. But—I kind of like it. And I don't think Captain Alice really wants that. She's so nice. I never knew anyone like her. She's not soft on us, but she acts like she thinks we're worth something, and she's given us a real chance, don't you think?"

"I do," Kate said. "Look, you know a little about what happened to me."

"Just what you told me and Sonja that first night on board."

"Well, I honestly don't remember much about my folks—my real folks. I do remember being on the ship, and my mum holding me. And other people around us. But when we wrecked ... " Kate gave a little shake of her head. "The Girai Wurrung had their own ways. They were kind to me, but they didn't have charts. They had other ways of knowing where things were. But there was so much they couldn't teach me. And all this talk about God ... well, I didn't hear about God or church until after I was at the farm a while. I saw a church once and asked what it was. But I didn't understand. I'm not sure I understand now."

"My folks used to go to church," Fiona said slowly. "But after Con got hold of me ..."

"Yair," Kate said. "The man who sold me to Con never went to any church, you can be sure of it. But I think church and

God and that Bible she reads from … there's something good about them."

"Captain Alice thinks we ought to know about it," Fiona said. "Maybe it's something we can learn, like the charts."

"Maybe. And I don't think it will hurt us," Kate said.

"I like the day of rest." Fiona's green eyes held a faraway look.

"Hey!"

They both looked toward the cabin door, where Brea stood scowling. "Are you shirking, Fiona? The mate sent me after you. You're needed."

"Sorry." Fiona threw Kate a smile and scampered toward the door.

"Think you're special?" Brea snapped, gazing around the small cabin and effectively blocking Fiona's exit by standing squarely in the doorway.

"N-no." Fiona came to a halt and glanced over her shoulder at Kate.

"Go back to your posts, both of you." Kate tried to keep her voice even, but Brea glared at her.

"You got it easy, don't you?" Brea held Kate's gaze for a moment, through slits of eyes, then turned and walked out on the deck.

Fiona hurried after her. "Brea, you oughtn't to talk to Kate like that!"

Brea's response was lost to Kate. Were they headed for a standoff? Brea McDonovan always had a thorn in her paw. Today she seemed resentful of Kate's position and the fact that she was allowed to study in the captain's quarters. It was a practical matter, that was all. They didn't take the charts out on deck very often, lest they get wet or be caught by the wind and lost overboard.

Maybe Brea was jealous. Not for the first time, Kate wondered why fortune had fallen upon her when she was chosen as second mate. Carrie had put her name forth. They were friends, and she appreciated the gesture. But would Captain Alice have so quickly accepted one of the others? Perhaps Sonja should have had the post. Brea probably thought she would be more capable. She was certainly stronger than Kate. Maybe she could read better too.

An officer needed education. Captain Alice had made that clear when she encouraged Kate to study the charts and learn navigation. Kate had learned to read some and do simple arithmetic while living at the farm, but some of the others were more proficient. Both Mrs. Fiske and Captain Alice had sat down with her once to work mathematics problems that would help in navigating. It was slow going, but Kate was determined to learn.

She put away the chart and walked out into the brilliant sun. When her eyes had adjusted, she spotted Sonja. Though her free time was her own, Sonja had chosen to sit near the jollyboat and pick apart tarry old ropes to make oakum, the material they used to caulk the seams in the ship's hull. Sonja had a true sailor's heart. If they survived this voyage, it would be because of women like Sonja.

Kate ambled over and sat down beside her. She reached for the bundle of worn rope pieces and took a short length.

"You don't need to do that," Sonja said.

"I know. But it will help us get to England, right?"

Sonja smiled. "That's what I figure."

They worked in silence for a few minutes. Kate's hands grew sticky as the tar coated them.

"How do you think things are going for the girls on our watch?" She picked up a stick to scrape the frayed fibers into Sonja's bucket.

"All right."

"Do they complain in the fo'castle?"

"Some. But nothing like Lizzie and Brea do. I'm happy to be on second watch." Sonja glanced at Kate. "What do you think about Polly?"

"What about her?"

Sonja shrugged. "Most of the women are getting stronger, but Polly ... she's getting worse. She throws up over the side. And ... I don't know. She can't climb, but she seems kind of stout for a frail thing. I've been watching her."

Kate took another piece of rope and picked at it, unraveling the fibers. Fiona, always looking out for the weaker ones, had also mentioned Polly's state to her. "Some of the girls from Dame Nell's had it hard there."

Sonja grunted. "Seems to me you all did."

"In a way. Some of us were more ... privileged. Nell, for instance. Con trusted her and gave her a lot of responsibility. He also gave her gifts and luxuries. I wasn't treated so badly myself, once he and I understood each other."

"But you still had to—" Sonja looked down at her work.

"Yes. We all had to earn money for Con. But you can fight your situation every step of the way, or you can get used to it. After a while I learned to make Con happy, and he didn't beat me after that. Well, not much."

Sonja's eyes widened. "He beat you all?"

"Sure. Men do that. At least—" Kate shook her head. "Well, some men."

"My papa would never. Mr. Deak wouldn't, either."

"I expect you're right. I heard Mr. Deak tell Mrs. Fiske in Brisbane that he would guard the main hatch, and if any man tried to hurt us, he would kill him."

Sonja frowned. "He carried a pistol the whole time there were strange men about."

"Yes," Kate said. "And he made Ned run errands for him. When Captain Alice wasn't here, he wouldn't allow anyone but Mrs. Fiske on deck, and she in her skirts. He could explain her away as a passenger, but he didn't let anyone see our women."

"He's a good man," Sonja said.

"Aye. A proper one."

"Almost like a father to us."

Kate considered that. She didn't know how a decent father would act toward his daughters, or even if there really were such men. Did they all abuse girls and just not talk about it? Somehow she knew Gypsy had never been that way.

She met Sonja's gaze. "Anyway, I'll see to Polly."

"If she's sick …" Sonja arched her eyebrows.

"Yair. We'll take care of her." Kate plopped a wad of oakum in the bucket and stood.

"Good luck cleaning your hands, Miss Robinson."

Kate grinned. "You know, this job is hard, but it's the most fun I've had since those troopers took me out of the bush."

Her fingers were sore from the rough hemp, and she would have to pull out a few tiny fibers that had pricked her skin. Kate headed for the galley.

"Well, look at you," Nell said as she entered. "Got your hands dirty, I see."

"Yair. It may never come off."

"I've got hot water and lye soap."

"Thanks, Nell." Kate let down a shelf seat on the inner wall of the galley.

Nell poured water into a basin. "It ain't boiling, but it's steaming. The captain doesn't like me to keep the stove going, in case we hit a rough spot. But I got my damper and beans cooked for tea this evening."

"You're doing a great job, Nell," Kate said.

"Beats the old one, though I can't say the work is easier."

"No, but you're doing it because you want to."

"Hmm. Never thought I'd give up my fine gowns and jewelry to scrub pots and pans. And yet, here I am, and I can call my soul my own." Nell eyed her shrewdly as she held out a small scrubbing brush and a bar of soap. "So what were you and Sonja putting your heads together over?"

Kate hesitated. Nell was used to watching over the women with a sharp eye. Chances were she had already drawn conclusions. "Polly, actually."

211

"Polly? Where is she?"

"I expect she's below in her hammock, poor thing." Kate soaked her hands in the warm water and took up the soap. "What's your feeling on Polly?"

Nell snorted. "She's increasing for sure." She turned to her worktable, where she was mixing something in a large wooden bowl. "If she'd told me a month ago, I could have helped her."

Kate swallowed hard. Helped her get rid of it, Nell meant. That was standard for brothel girls who got in the family way. Babies simply weren't allowed. She was glad Polly hadn't gone to Nell before they embarked.

"What'll we do now? We'll not anchor again for months."

"We should have put her off in Brisbane," Nell muttered.

Kate couldn't picture putting Polly off the brig in her condition in a vile place where she knew no one. She'd be back in a brothel inside a week.

"I should never have brought her, but I thought she'd be safer with us."

"So she is," Nell said. "But Captain Alice should be told. I suppose she'll take Polly off duty completely. And the captain won't hear of doing anything about it."

"I wouldn't even suggest it to her. She's such a good woman. I'm sure it would shock her to think someone would do that. That *we* would do that."

Nell shook her head, frowning as she stirred. "A baby on a ship. What next?"

212

CHAPTER TWENTY

The ship's bell rang eight times. Jenny pulled up the lead line and checked it. Sonja appeared at her side and waited for her to finish. When the line lay in a neat coil on the deck with the weight in the middle, Jenny nodded at Sonja, then looked toward the waist, where the first and second watch exchanged roles.

"No bottom this time," Jenny said.

"It's been deep lately." Sonja looked out over the twilit expanse of the Coral Sea. "I can tell from the way the waves roll, there's little to worry about here."

Jenny nodded. "I hope we won't run into more shallow water and have to anchor for the night again."

"Aye." Sonja glanced at her. "The charts look safe through tomorrow, I think."

"Captain Packard must have got the newest charts before he set out," Jenny said. "Even so, Mr. Deak said a lot of the small islands and reefs in these parts aren't on them."

Sonja grunted, thinking about that. "See those clouds off the windward quarter? They don't look too friendly."

"I suppose there have to be storms sometimes. We were always glad for rain at the farm." Jenny turned to go.

"Jenny—I'm sorry. About what I said before. I know you took the sounding."

She smiled. "You were wakened suddenly. The first half minute after somebody wakes up doesn't count."

Sonja grinned. "If you say so."

Jenny walked back to the galley, where Nell was cleaning up. She poked her head in the door, her heart beating quickly. "Miss Nell?"

"Yes, Cocky?" Nell had taken to using the nickname for Jenny and her aunt. Usually city folk called farmers "cockies" as a derogatory term, but Nell seemed to use it as an endearment. At least Jenny hoped so. The older woman glanced over at her while scouring the big griddle.

"I was wondering if there were any leftovers."

Nell stopped scrubbing for a moment, then continued her circular motions. "Hmm, maybe a few. What you doing, girl? Keeping a pet rat for a poppet?" She chuckled.

Jenny's throat went dry. "N—No ma'am. Just a little something for later, when I'm on the middle watch."

Nell snorted. "Hungry as a drayman. Well, here's what's left of the damper. The pork rind, I best leave for Sonja. I reckon she wants to fish tonight."

"Thank you, Nell." Jenny wrapped the unleavened bread in her handkerchief and stuffed it into the little leather bag on her belt, where she had stowed a few other bits. She left the galley and headed for the rear hatch, her heart beating in her ears.

She climbed down the stairs, catching her balance as the brig lurched. She hoped the scraps she had collected would be enough to stave off Jakob Zeemer's hunger.

Groping in the dark of the 'tweendecks, Jenny scrambled to the ladder leading down to the hold. She stumbled against a small figure kneeling by the open hatch.

"Hey!" At the high-pitched shriek, Jenny nearly jumped out of her skin. Ned. "You almost knocked me down the hole," he cried.

She grabbed him by the shoulders and pushed him against a bale of wool. "You little yabby, why aren't you in bed?"

"Ma said I could go to the head."

"Is this the head?"

"No."

"What are you doing, looking down in the hold?"

"I wanted to go down there. It's fun."

"Why in blazes aren't you scared of the dark, like other children? Now you listen to me, Ned McKay. Your mum told you, and Mr. Deak told you. Stay out of the hold. You remember the licking you got when you tried to burn the ship down."

"I am so too, scared of the dark!" he retorted.

"Don't change the subject. If your father were here, he'd bullwhip you. Now get back to Aunt Hannah and don't you ever let me catch you hanging around the hold ladder again."

Ned whimpered and scrambled off. Jenny waited until she heard the door of Hannah's cabin open and close. Quickly she climbed down the ladder. She caught her breath at the bottom, fighting the wretched guilt that washed over her. Bad enough she was down here, but she had treated Ned badly due to her nerves. His father had never bullwhipped anyone, and it was not fair of her to say that. She sighed and began to grope her way along the narrow passageway between the bales and sacks.

When she made it past the foremast, she stopped. "Mr. Zeemer!"

"Ah, mine maid!" She heard a thump, and then rustling as he approached in the pitch dark. She realized he could bump into her in the blackness. For some wild reason she didn't understand, she stood still, hoping it might happen.

"Maid?" The word was barely a whisper, but it sounded only a couple feet away.

"I'm here." She inched forward, anticipating his touch in horrid fascination.

She was not disappointed. His hand suddenly grasped her side, just above the hip, then let go, as if excusing itself. "Ah! Maid. You are returned."

"Yes," she squeaked, feeling a little dizzy. "I brought you something."

"Good! I was beginning to find the rat."

Jenny gasped. "No, Mr. Zeemer. No need for rats. I brought you some food."

"Good, good."

215

She brought out the contents of her leather bag. "Here."

Zeemer's hand found her outstretched arm, and he scooped up the food. Jenny had managed to save a total of three and a half ship's biscuits and half her salt beef from lunch, as well as the damper.

Zeemer munched away. "Ah, good sailor food. Better than most."

Jenny sighed. "It doesn't seem so great to me, but they say Nell is a good cook."

"This Nell is a woman also?"

"Yes, sir."

"Hmm." He chewed for a while. "In all my days at sea, I never saw the ship with women in the crew. Is this new for English people?"

Jenny snorted. "Very new. It is never done." She tingled with fear and adventure. What would Aunt Hannah say if she found her alone in the dark with a strange man? She was sure the outcome would not be good. As for Captain Alice—she dared not think it.

"So, this crew of women. How long have they been sailing?"

"Oh, just since June. We sailed out of Melbourne almost four weeks ago, I think. None of us had ever sailed before."

Jakob choked. "What? Four weeks? All of the women?"

"Yair, hard to believe."

He found her arm and clasped it. "You hit the—the—rock with the ship?"

"The reef, yes."

"Oh. Mine head. But it was not hard—we did not go down." He paused, still holding her forearm. "We are going north?"

"Yes, sir."

"Amazing. Not good, not good."

"I thought you said you wanted to go to the Dutch East Indies. That's to the north."

"*Ja,* only I want to get there alive, not killed to death. With the rock, with the shark, with the disease, with the crocodile. And mostly, with the *zeerover*. Because the ship with these women, is not able to sail without hitting the rock. Already, you see. Up north—many rock."

Jenny gulped. "I hope we'll be all right."

Zeemer grabbed her hands again, and felt her callused palms. "You are truly a sailor, like myself. Maid, what is your name?"

"Jenny."

"Jenny. Very English. Jenny, listen to me. You pay attention and don't cause the ship to hit any more rocks, you hear me speak?"

"Yes, sir."

"You are a good angel to bring the food to me. You must go, to not be found here."

"Very well. I—will come again." Jenny squeezed his hand and pulled away. Not particularly wanting the time together to end, she asked, "Why are they trying to kill you in Moreton Bay?"

"Oh, the devils, those English Royal Navy." He sighed. "They believe I did become a *zeerover*. Which was not of my choice. I did not become willing."

"Sea rover? A—pirate? They think you're a pirate?"

"*Ja.*"

"But, surely you're not one?"

"Nay, not inside. But the bad ones, the pirates of the Indies. They conquered—no, captured me. They caused me with the blunderbuss, for to sail the little ship. Very bad. But I was saved by the Royal Navy of England, and then they decided I was a pirate with the brown men. So—they decided to kill me."

Jenny's heart thumped, like a prisoner beating his cell bars. Zeemer was a pirate? Had he killed people? English people?

"Maid. Jenny." Zeemer groped for her, and found her shoulders. "I am a good man. I never will hurt you. Only, I am accused." He released his grip.

She exhaled. "I believe you, Mr. Zeemer. I must go now." She turned and stumbled along the narrow gap between the stacks of cargo.

She climbed the ladder, her heart in her mouth. She really should tell Captain Alice about the stowaway. It wasn't right to conceal him. On the 'tweendecks, she felt her way toward her cabin. When she came even with Aunt Hannah's door, it opened and Hannah stepped out.

"Jenny?"

She drew up short. "Aunt Hannah. Good evening."

Hannah grabbed her arm, pinching it more tightly than Zeemer had done.

"Where have you been, dear?"

Jenny's pulse raced even faster. She was glad it was dark so Hannah could not see her face. "At the head. . . ."

Hannah exhaled loudly. "You don't seem right lately. Something's bothering you. Ned said you snapped at him."

Jenny sighed. "I'm just tired, Aunt Hannah. I need my rest. I didn't mean to go crook at Ned."

"You're shaking, child. You might be ill."

"I'm not ill!" Jenny pulled her hand away. "And I'm not a child. And I don't want to talk about it." She stepped past Hannah and went to her own cabin, where she slammed the door.

Addie, in the lower berth, made a startled sound. "Jenny?"

"It's me. Go back to sleep."

"You're proper cross."

"No I'm not. I'm just—weary."

"The *Vera B.* An American brig. Have you seen her?" Josiah had met Superintendent Hainsworth at the customs house in Brisbane and was now enjoying a glass of wine with him in Hainsworth's parlor.

"Yes indeed. In fact, Mrs. Packard spent the night here with us."

"Thank God," Josiah said. "I've been keeping a lookout for her since I left Port Phillip Bay. I'm glad she made it this far safely."

"She seemed fine," Hainsworth said. "In as good spirits as a woman can be, I suppose, if her husband's not been dead a month."

"Yes. Packard was an old friend of mine. I came across the widow in Port Phillip the day after she buried him. Very tragic."

Hainsworth frowned. "Her steward came ashore with her. I didn't think much of it, but later on, the men unloading my cargo said they never saw any of the rest of their crew, just him and the ship's boy. They thought it odd, that their crew all kept below. I hope they weren't ill."

Josiah hesitated. Had Alice possibly kept her female crew a secret? If so, it wasn't his place to reveal it.

"I'm sure that's not the case. How long ago was that?"

"Oh, let's see. It's been three days—no, four," Hainsworth said. "I had ordered a cotton gin and some Texas cotton seed. This climate is perfect for it."

"Really?"

"It'll be our main crop within a few years. Bigger than wool, I declare. Captain Packard had brought everything I ordered, including some china and textiles for my wife. Of course, I was happy to do business with Mrs. Packard once I knew the captain had died. More wine?"

"No, thank you. I should get back to my ship. I wish I'd known the *Vera B.* was stopping here." Josiah sipped the last of the wine from his glass.

"You might catch them."

Josiah smiled. "That's what I've been hoping. I put in at Port Jackson to see if they'd stopped in Sydney. I did meet one ship's mate there who said his schooner had passed the *Vera B.* several days earlier." It appeared the *Jade Maiden* had lost a lot of time as they tacked about and checked harbors.

"Is it urgent that you overtake them?" Hainsworth asked.

"Not really. I feared for Mrs. Packard's safety at first and thought to sail with the *Vera B.*, but she wanted to weigh anchor before I was ready. If they've come this far safely, they'll probably be fine."

"Why wouldn't they?"

Josiah shook his head. "No reason. She was a little short on crew, is all, and with her bereavement … I tried to persuade her to sail to Boston with me on the *Jade Maiden*, but she declined. The cargo she had for you was probably one reason. She wanted to fulfill her husband's obligation."

Hainsworth raised his glass. "To Mrs. Packard. May she keep clear of the reef and pirates."

Pirates. Those women had no idea what they were sailing into headlong. Josiah rose and extended his hand. "I thank you for your hospitality, sir. I'll leave you now."

The wind howled around the *Vera B.,* making the sails snap. The charts showed reefs to port, but how far? This relentless wind pushed the brig ever closer to the unseen coral beneath the waves. Unable to sleep, Alice stood watch with Sarah on the quarterdeck, praying for safety as six of her crew struggled to control the vessel.

"Reef those sails!" Sarah yelled. She grunted as she threw her weight against the wheel.

"Let me help you." Alice pushed in beside her.

"Thanks. It's all I can manage," Sarah said.

Alice added what force she could as rain began to pelt them. "Maybe you should call all hands."

"I hate to. Kate's watch is exhausted."

Gypsy hobbled up the stairs and over to the binnacle. "Soundings?"

"No bottom," Alice shouted grimly.

"Best put out a sea anchor."

"Aye, aye," Sarah said.

"Let me take the wheel." Gypsy took hold of two handles. "Call the second watch up. If we hit that reef, we'll be done."

"I'll call them." With the raging wind at her back, Alice almost ran across the quarterdeck. Seizing the handrail, she made her way down to the waist. The rain increased, blowing in sideways torrents. She could barely hear Sarah's shouted commands. How could the girls on the masts hear her? Alice looked up and made out two dark figures against the canvas of the topsail. How easy it would be for one of them to miss her footing and plunge to the deck or into the roiling sea.

She reached the main hatch and descended several steps into the comparative quiet of the 'tweendecks.

"All hands on deck!"

A moment later, amid the creaking of the vessel and the muted howl of the wind, scrambling footsteps came toward her. Alice quickly regained the main deck, so they wouldn't run her over in the darkness. She stood against the bulwark as six women emerged. Kate, Sonja, Carrie, Lucy, Emma, and Anne. She couldn't distinguish them all, but Kate and Sonja were taller than the others. Emma's pale blonde hair streamed out behind her in the wind, and Anne's long braid bounced against her back.

Polly, of course, would be no use now and only slow them down. They could only try to assure that her baby had a chance to live. Alice leaped to the braces to help the women there adjust the sheets as others hauled up and furled the fore topsail. She found herself with Jenny and Fiona, from Sarah's watch.

"Pull now," Jenny cried. Alice put all her meager strength to the task.

Hauling on the wet lines in the pouring rain sapped her energy. She and Fiona hung all their weight on the sheets to keep them in place while Jenny tied them.

"Done," Jenny screamed, and Alice let go, limp and bedraggled. What she wouldn't do for a cup of hot tea now, but that was impossible. Nell couldn't keep the stove going today, because of the danger of spilling coals during the foul weather.

Gypsy came down from the quarterdeck and lurched between the small groups of women, instructing them on what to do next. Who held the wheel, Alice wondered. She pushed against the wind and forced her way up the steps. When her eyes came above the level of the quarterdeck, the lamp in the binnacle gave just enough light for her to see Sarah and Nell's faces as they grappled the wheel.

"Do they need help?"

Jenny clung to the railing on the step below her.

"I think they're holding it," Alice replied.

"Then we must help with the sea anchor," Jenny said.

Gypsy brought four more women to the stairs.

"Captain! Open the locker," he shouted.

Alice hurried to the bin against the taffrail and unlatched it. She and Jenny struggled to pull the lid up, but the gale worked against them.

"This wind," Jenny gasped.

"Aye. If only we had an able-bodied sailor or two," Alice puffed out. "Take hold. One, two, three!" They both yanked, and the lid flew open and banged against the rail.

Gypsy was at her side. "Come, sailors. Grab on. We've got to get this over the side."

Soon after the bulky canvas anchor hit the water, Alice felt the ship's forward motion slow as the dragging anchor resisted.

"Will we be all right now?" she yelled to Gypsy.

"I don't know how far we are off the reef. We need to take in the mainsail too. Anything that catches wind drives us leeward."

"I hate to send the girls aloft in this."

"It has to be done," Gypsy said.

Alice watched helplessly as he sent four women from Sarah's watch up the mainmast. As the brig plunged back and forth, Sarah and Nell worked the rudder, trying to counter the force of the wind. Aloft, Brea, Fiona, Mary, and Hannah struggled to furl the sail.

"When they're done, can we send Sarah's watch below to rest?" Alice asked Gypsy. "They're chilled to the bone."

"Not yet." Gypsy walked toward the foremast, where Kate's watch was making sure every line was secure.

"Captain Alice?" Jenny stepped from the shadows.

"Yes?"

"May I ask you something?"

"Of course. Step into my cabin, won't you, out of this wind?"

Once they had shut themselves inside, Alice thought she would swoon from the quiet and the warmth. She felt her way about her tinderbox and struck a lucifer. Carefully she braced herself and lit the wick of a pierced tin lantern. If it fell, the lantern wouldn't break and was less likely to spread fire than globed lanterns. She shut its door and hung it securely on the hook over the table.

"Now, Jenny. What can I help you with?"

Jenny's eyes were huge. She opened her mouth and then closed it.

"Well?" Alice asked.

"I—I heard what you said about needing a man or two."

"I'm sorry. I'm afraid I was feeling my own weakness. But we women did all right, didn't we?"

"Y-yes. But, ma'am?"

"What is it, Jenny?" Alice could see the girl was distressed, and she reached out to touch her sleeve. The woolen blouse was saturated with water. "Go on."

"Mr. Deak said if we crash on the reef, we'll all drown."

"I wish I could say otherwise," Alice said, "but it's a very real danger. We're in God's hands."

"But as you said, if we had a man or two …"

Alice smiled wearily. "There are times when we could use them."

"What if ..." Jenny's eyes went wide, and she sucked in a quick breath.

"What is it, Jenny? Are you frightened?"

"No. Well, yes. It's just ... Ma'am, I can give you a man. An able-bodied seaman who can do all this."

Alice stared at her in the dim light. "Are you saying ..." She shook her head, unable to make sense of the girl's words. "What *are* you saying?"

Jenny lowered her eyelids. "There's a man." She looked at Alice from beneath her thick lashes. "In the hold, ma'am. He—he knows how to sail. And he's healthy and strong."

Alice put a hand to her brow. "I need to sit down." She plunked into the chair that was screwed to the floor beside her table. Had one of their deserters skulked aboard and hidden himself? She fixed her gaze on Jenny. "Who is this man?"

"His name is Jakob Zeemer. He ... he says he came aboard in Moreton Bay. The night you stayed ashore, ma'am."

Alice's throat constricted. "And how many of you knew this?"

"Only me, ma'am, I swear. I found him when I went below to check for leaks."

"You—" She sat still for a moment then rose. "Can you produce him now?"

"I'm sure I can. Do you want me to?"

"Yes. Bring him straight here to the cabin."

"Aye, aye, Captain."

"And, Jenny, we'll have more to say about this later."

"Yes, ma'am," Jenny whispered.

She left, and Alice followed her onto the main deck. The rain still pelted them. Alice shuffled against the wind to the mainmast, where she found Gypsy. She plucked at his sleeve. "Mr. Deak, I need you at once."

He followed Alice into her cabin and closed the door. "What is it, ma'am?"

"Jenny McKay just informed me that we have a stowaway."

"What in blazes? How? When—"

"She says he came aboard in Moreton Bay. And yet all of the women were below decks the entire time." Alice shook her head. "I don't see how he could have done it, but according to Jenny, he sneaked onto the ship the night we anchored, while I was at the Hainsworths' house."

"Aye, he might," Gypsy said. "We kept only a couple of hands on watch that night, so we'd have less chance of discovery."

"I suppose he could have slipped down the fore hatch," Alice said.

Gypsy nodded. "And we'd carried those crates for Hainsworth in the 'tweendecks, so no one had to go down into the cargo hold. I'd had our crew move the crates over just below the hatch, so we could haul them up quick next morn. And they stayed below while a couple of Hainsworth's men came aboard to help take the crates off. ... Yes, I can see it. When did Jenny discover him?"

"That I don't know. I believe I sent her down after we hit that reef ... Jenny and Kate, if my mind serves me. But surely— Gypsy, it's been days!"

He frowned. "We'll have to get more out of her. Where is she now?"

"Fetching her sailor. I told her to bring him straight here."

"Is he fit to work?"

"She says so, and he's sailed before."

"Good! I can use him right now."

"Without getting his story first?"

"Ma'am, we need to tend to the ship. A sheet's loose on the foretopsail, and a spar is dangling. We don't want to lose it, but even more, we don't want it crashing down on somebody's head."

Alice stared at him for a moment. "Do what you think best."

"Let's get a better light in here."

"Of course."

225

Alice took down the kerosene lantern. Gypsy lit it, then hung it up. He strode to the cabin door and flung it open. The rain still pattered on the roof, though not as violently as before, and the wind worried the ship, making the timbers groan.

"Jenny?" Gypsy called. "Come here, lass. Let's see what you've found."

CHAPTER TWENTY-ONE

Gypsy peered at the man's face, searching for clues to his character. The stowaway was tall—probably six feet, with fair, shaggy hair and a reddish-blond beard. He looked grubby, but that was understandable, as were his tattered clothes. Gypsy judged him to be in his mid-twenties, and though thin, he had some muscle. Handsome under all the hair and grime. No wonder Jenny was drawn to him. No doubt the skulker could be charming too.

"What's your name?"

"Zeemer, sir."

"Zeemer. You a Dutchman?"

"Ja. Nederlander."

"Can you lay aloft and help my sailors secure a loose spar?"

"Ja."

Gypsy nodded. "Come on, then, Dutchie. We'll see what you're made of."

Gypsy unlatched the cabin door, and the wind shoved it inward. He beckoned to the stowaway and limped as quickly as he could toward the foremast. The ship rolled, and for a moment the deck was awash. He grabbed a halyard and managed to keep from falling. When he recovered, he noted with chagrin that Zeemer had kept his balance.

They forged on to the foresail ratlines. Gypsy pointed up at the foretop and beyond, at the head of the topsail, where two women wrestled with the dangling spar.

"Can you get that?"

Without a word, Zeemer began to climb. Gypsy clenched his teeth. He hoped sending the Dutchman aloft without warning the

227

women wasn't a mistake. If they were startled too badly, they might lose their grip.

Alice and Jenny came to stand beside him.

"He's up there," Jenny said.

They all watched, the rain streaming into their upturned faces. The woman farthest on the end of the yard was Sonja, Gypsy was sure. She had more heart than most men he knew. But she had been up there a quarter of an hour, fighting the wind.

To his relief, Sonja and her watchmate, Carrie, crept to the shrouds, and Zeemer's larger form edged out nimbly. He walked along the foot rope like a cat, one hand gripping the jackstay. Within a minute, he had caught the sheet holding the flying spar and hauled it in.

"Well, now," Alice said, close to his ear.

Gypsy nodded. "He'll be worth his salt, if we can trust him."

As Zeemer and the two women began their descent, he noted that Kate and her other sailors had spotted the newcomer.

"Who is he?" Lucy asked in a lull that allowed her voice to carry.

Gypsy turned to Alice. "Let's have him back in the cabin for a chat. You'll have to inform the officers right away."

"Yes," Alice said. "And what about Jenny?"

Gypsy frowned at the girl, who stuck close to Alice's side. "You stay with your aunt, lass, unless Cap'n Alice calls for you."

"Aye, sir."

"Why did you sneak on board, instead of asking for passage like an honest person?" Gypsy faced the stowaway in Alice's cabin once more.

Zeemer met his eyes without defiance. "I am sorry. If I had money. . ."

"What are you running from?"

228

The Dutchman's eyes flickered. "I did nothing bad. Not by my choice. And I will work, if you let me. I can sail. I can climb."

Yes, they had seen as much. Alice started to speak, but Gypsy touched her arm and she fell silent.

"Answer my question," Gypsy snapped. "What are you running from?"

Zeemer lowered his gaze. "I was conquered by the sea rovers. There is another word—" He glanced about as if looking for the English term he wanted—or Jenny.

"Pirates," Gypsy said.

Alice caught her breath. "You were kidnapped?"

Zeemer frowned. "I do not know this word."

"Captured," Gypsy said.

Zeemer's eyes lit. "Oh. Ja. They take me off a ship. Degroot Trading Company. Sugar trade. Coffee. The white metal."

"You mean tin? Tin mining?"

"Ja. Yes. We carry it to Nederlands. All Europe. But the pirates, they attack the ships and steal the cargo. Our sailors dead. I live. Me and one other. They made us work and row and sail the proas."

"What's proas?" Gypsy asked.

"Small boats. With the sail, or the ... the row ..."

"Oars?"

Zeemer nodded. "They have many, like a cloud of flies. Twenty, thirty, forty, fifty proas, to attack one merchant ship. They kill, they steal, they burn the ship."

"I see. So how did you get to Moreton Bay?"

Zeemer let out a big sigh. "The English navy. They try to ... to conquer the pirates."

"Good luck to 'em," Gypsy said wryly. The Malay pirates were a notorious breed of cutthroats, too many to control.

"They found me on a proa. They hang the Malays, but they take me to Moreton Bay."

"What about your friend? The other Dutchman?" Gypsy asked.

229

Zeemer spread his hands, palms up. "I do not know. He was not there when they took me."

Gypsy glanced at Alice. She seemed eager to speak. He took her elbow and moved a couple of yards away with her—as much distance as the cramped cabin would allow.

"What do you think?" Alice whispered. "Can we trust him?"

"Probably not. He's worked with pirates. Who knows where his sympathies lie."

"Should we confine him, then? And what about Jenny? That poor girl is terribly naïve. I'm sure she meant no harm, with her tender heart, but she could have brought disaster on us all. She knows better."

"Aye, she does. I'm sorry, Cap'n. This shouldn't have happened under my nose."

"We're all at fault," Alice said. "But we can't take him back to Brisbane. We have to make the best of it."

What she said was true, but failed responsibility still weighed heavily on Gypsy. He glanced at Zeemer, who stood watching them. "If he could guide us through the Torres Straits ..." The island-strewn waters between northern Australia's Cape York and the island of New Guinea had worried Gypsy for weeks. While he'd sailed most of his life and had been through the strait twice before, he was not a navigator. The area was known as an unforgiving stretch of water, full of shoals and reefs, and home to desperate men. He had examined the charts with Alice several times, and he dreaded the passage.

"Do you think he could help us get through?" Alice asked.

"He might."

"It would be worth overlooking his past, surely."

Gypsy scowled. "There's the matter of where we'll house him."

"We have to keep the women safe," Alice said quickly.

"Of course. I'll let him know that if he touches one of our crew, it's his life to pay."

"I'll speak to Jenny." Alice's brow furrowed. "I should probably bring Hannah into this. Jenny's so young."

"Do what you must." Gypsy looked over his shoulder. Zeemer stood motionless. "I suppose he and I will trade off shifts in my cabin."

"I hate to ask it of you."

He lifted one shoulder in a half shrug, as though giving up his privacy and sharing his limited domain with a criminal was insignificant. He had put up with much for Alice. This would be no worse than close association with barmaids and soiled doves.

"Young Ned and I will not be so outnumbered."

Alice smiled. "It's good of you to take it that way. Thank you, Gypsy."

"All right, then. I'll take charge of him."

"Good. But let me address him first. She strode toward the stowaway. "Mr. Zeemer."

Gypsy held back a smile. He admired the way Alice had taken on authority since her husband's death. It suited her.

"*Ja, mevrouw?*"

"Has Jenny McKay told you that our ship's crew are all women save this man, Mr. Deak?"

Zeemer frowned. "I think … yes. The women. I saw them in the sails. And Jenny tell me you help the women."

"I am trying to do so." Alice studied him for a long moment. "We could use your strength and your knowledge of the sea, Mr. Zeemer."

He squared his shoulders. "I help."

"But you mustn't bother the women."

"Ja. I shall not … bother … the women."

"Good. That includes Jenny."

Zeemer's blue eyes clouded. "She help me. You will punish Jenny?"

"I don't know yet," Alice said. "It is wrong to harbor a stowaway."

His chin lowered to his chest. "Forgive Jenny. It is on me."

231

Alice turned to Gypsy and pulled him aside. "I want his assurance that he did her no harm, but I don't know how to ask him."

"If he's besmirched our Jenny, I'll have his hide."

"It seems she confided quite a lot in him," Alice said thoughtfully. "If he wanted to, he could have done us much harm."

"Aye. I'll get out of him what passed between him and Jenny when I take him below."

"Should we let him sleep now?"

Gypsy scowled. "He's done nothing but rest these past few days. I say put him to work tonight. One way or another, ma'am, we'll make him earn his keep."

Alice sighed. "You need to sleep, too."

"I'll talk to Mrs. Fiske. I expect she can keep him in line if I sleep through the next watch." Gypsy cocked his head to one side and listened. "The wind is easing a bit."

"Send Kate's watch back to the fo'castle if you think we're all right."

"Might we issue a ration of grog for the crew?"

Alice blinked at him. "Oh. I … suppose so. They're soaking wet and cold."

"It would take the chill off," Gypsy said. "I can have Nell mix it."

"My husband used a one-to-four mix of rum to water," Alice said slowly.

Gypsy nodded. "If you think that's too much, make it one-and-five. A pint for each sailor."

"Fine," Alice said. "Have Nell see to it. And Gypsy, you mix yours however you want."

"Yes, ma'am. I'll take him below and show him my cabin. He can help me get a keg of rum up." Gypsy frowned at the tall Dutchman. "But none for him."

"I'll see to Jenny." Alice brushed a hand across her forehead. "Oh, and please have someone fetch Hannah."

###

When Nell brought Alice's breakfast to her cabin, she entered smiling.

"There now, Cap'n. Hot coffee and some hearty damper and applesauce, with a bite of fish left from yesterday."

"Lovely." Alice looked up at the cook and tried to assess the movement of the vessel. "You've had the stove going? It's calm then?"

"Not calm, ma'am, but we're flying before a steady wind. Mr. Deak is quite pleased."

"Mrs. Fiske's watch is coming on duty?" Alice glanced at Ruel's chronometer.

"Aye, and they'll have a good breakfast after they've holy-stoned the deck."

Alice smiled. "Thank you, Nell." It seemed things were back to normal. Except for Jenny's stowaway. That thought took away her appetite.

Nell lingered, straightening the cutlery and brushing a speck Alice couldn't see from the tabletop.

"What about this man aboard?" She eyed Alice sidelong.

Alice picked up her cup, sipped the coffee, and set it down before answering. "He stowed away in Moreton Bay. Mr. Deak hopes he can be of some use to us and earn his fare."

Nell, without her makeup, was not a beautiful woman. Her face had fine lines, and her nose was a bit long. When she disapproved of anything, as was apparently the case now, her frown lines deepened around her mouth, and her brow furrowed like a cornfield under the plow.

"Mr. Deak is one thing, but that fellow … he's young and strong. The girls …"

"Mr. Deak has made it clear to him that he must leave them alone."

"I see. But will they leave him alone?"

233

"Most of our sailors want nothing to do with men." Alice broke off a piece of damper. The heavy bread was not her favorite dish, but she was getting used to it. Nell baked it in round loaves and cut it in triangles, like pie slices.

Nell eyed her for a moment. "So they say. But a handsome young limey—"

"He's not English," Alice said. "But you know as well as I do, these women want to distance themselves from the life they lived."

"True, but some of them dream of what you might call a normal life. A home, a husband, babies. And if a likely candidate comes around ..."

Alice sighed. "I have three things to say about that, Nell. First, if the stowaway tries to force himself on one of our women, he will be shot. I have no tolerance for such crimes. Second, if one of our women initiates a carnal relationship with him, she will be severely punished." She dipped the coarse damper in her coffee to soften it.

"What's the third thing?" Nell asked.

Alice sighed and gazed up into the older woman's eyes. "I fear Jenny is already attached to him."

"I heard as much. You and Hannah may have your hands full."

After Nell left, Alice finished her breakfast, delaying the inevitable. When she went on deck, she found Sarah supervising Jenny and Fiona at the ship's wheel. Alice nodded at her first mate, and Sarah gave her a little wave of acknowledgement. At Alice's request, she was keeping Jenny under her eye. Mary kept watch in the foretop while the other sailors of the first watch sat on the deck near the mainmast, picking oakum. Zeemer was nowhere to be seen.

Gypsy was leaning against the bulwark amidships, and when he saw her, he straightened and walked toward her.

"The second watch is having their breakfast 'tweendecks."

"And Zeemer?"

234

"I told him he could sleep after breakfast—since Jenny will be on deck. I took him some food in my cabin and told him to stay out of sight until I fetch him."

"I guess there's nothing to do but display him to the crew and explain the situation. Do you still think he'll abide by our conditions?"

"I do. He's grateful we're not punishing him."

"Should we? What would my husband have done?" Alice had never seen Ruel strike out at a sailor in anger, though she had seen men deprived of their grog or made to perform extra duties for minor infractions. While she had sailed with him, no incidents worthy of sterner measures had occurred on the *Vera B.*

"I think he'd have done just as you're doing: put 'im to work and count it a blessing. He could make the difference in a risky situation."

"All right, then. Will you explain his status and duties to the crew?"

Gypsy smiled sheepishly. "I'll try, so long as you let me change it if need be as we go along."

"Done."

Alice went up to the quarterdeck. She had informed Kate and Sarah of Zeemer's presence the night before, and Sarah turned toward her with an expectant air. "We're ready, Mrs. Fiske," Alice said. "Send a sailor to call all hands."

Sarah dispatched Fiona, and Alice watched as the women assembled on the main deck below. Nell came from the galley and slipped into the back row. Mary kept her post on the foretop, and Lizzie on the maintop, from where she could see aft. When the rest were gathered, Gypsy came up the companionway with the tall Dutchman behind him.

Alice caught her breath. He had washed up, and Gypsy had found him a whole, clean sailor's blouse. His hair fairly gleamed in the sunlight. She admitted to herself that he made a fine figure. All of the women stared openly at the newcomer as he marched behind Gypsy, though Zeemer kept his own eyes straight ahead.

235

Gypsy stopped at the foot of the quarterdeck stairs and indicated for Zeemer to stand beside him, in full view of the crew.

"Good morning," Alice said. "As you can see, and I'm sure you've all heard, we have an addition to our number. I present to you Jakob Zeemer, who was found hiding in the cargo hold. Mr. Zeemer has agreed to join our crew and work for his passage. He will be a common sailor, the same as you all, and must obey my rules. He will have no privileges. However, he claims to have sailing experience and some knowledge of the waters we are about to ply. Mr. Deak and I hope he will be an asset. Before I let Mr. Deak tell you more, are there any questions? We do things openly on this vessel, so speak up if you have concerns."

Several hands shot up.

"Carrie?" Alice said.

"Where will he sleep, ma'am?"

"He will share Mr. Deak's cabin. Mr. Zeemer is forbidden to go near the fo'castle, and he is never to enter any of the cabins on this ship but his own, or mine if I need him to see the charts or carry out some other duty there."

Fiona smirked, and Kate elbowed her sharply in the ribs. Alice felt her cheeks flame, but she met Fiona's gaze and stared her down.

"Mr. Deak."

Gypsy took a step forward. "You all see 'im. You'll be working beside him. As long as he obeys our rules, he gets a fair shake, same as you all. For now, he'll stick with me in the daytime. We'll do some sail drill and weapons drill today. We'll see what this lubber can do, eh?"

The women raised a cheer, some more heartily than others. Jenny stood silent, gazing at Zeemer, a smile playing at her lips. She would definitely bear close supervision. Alice caught Hannah's eye, and Hannah gave her a grim nod. She saw it too— unabashed admiration. The older women would have to tighten their ranks about Jenny.

236

"Zeemer will join the second watch," Gypsy continued. Kate nodded, accepting the addition to her team. She and Sarah knew this was to keep Zeemer and Jenny from being off duty at the same time. It might not be enough to quell the attraction, but it would make it harder for them to spend time together.

"That's that, crew. As long as this fair wind holds, let's have weapons drill for all hands," Gypsy said.

They had restocked their ammunition in Brisbane, and Gypsy had picked up a few extra pistols to replace some of those stolen when the crew deserted in Port Phillip Bay. All of the girls needed to practice loading and firing. The drill would also give Gypsy a chance to see how good Zeemer was with weapons. The tall Dutchman seemed placid now, but could they trust him with guns? Alice would have to rely on Gypsy in such matters.

"Sail ho," Lizzie cried from the trestletrees above.

Every head swiveled to stare up at her.

"Sail aft, two points to windward," came Lizzie's next report.

"Raise the staysails and royals," Gypsy shouted. "We'll make all sail and outrun her."

Alice's heart thrilled as she watched them race to their posts. Sarah's watch dashed to the mainmast, and Kate's to the foremast beyond. Gypsy said something to Zeemer, and he ran to the foremast ratlines. He hurried aloft and passed the women. He was first to the topgallants, with Sonja only a hairsbreadth behind him. Zeemer scrambled on, to the royal, where he began untying the clewlines. Oh, yes, there were advantages to having an able-bodied seaman on your ship.

CHAPTER TWENTY-TWO

Jenny tried to concentrate on loading the swivel gun. Mr. Deak had put her in charge of the crew for this weapon, and he had impressed on all of them the importance of loading quickly, without having to think about the steps. Jenny wanted to make him proud, but her thoughts kept straying to Jakob, who was giving a lesson in close combat to the women who weren't part of the two gun crews. Her aunt and Mr. Deak seemed to have conspired to keep Jenny and Jakob apart. Even so, they found a few minutes to talk when the watches changed, or at breakfast when the crew mingled.

During the two weeks since she had revealed him to Captain Alice, the crew had grown stronger and more efficient. Jakob's willingness, strength, and sailing experience had won him the favor of the officers. He was frequently allowed into the captain's cabin to examine the charts, and he volunteered for the most dangerous tasks. Mr. Deak watched him with an almost fatherly eye. He and Jakob seemed to have become great chums.

Thanks to a favorable wind, they were tearing through the Torres Strait. Since they were now in pirate waters, they all bore arms. Those standing watch, as well as the officers, wore pistols in their belts, and every sailor had a knife. Zeemer wore a cutlass on his hip. Seeing it made Jenny smile. Not only did he look dashing, but it meant he had earned the captain's trust.

She pulled the ramrod out of the swivel gun's barrel. "Ready."

Mary, who was on her gun crew with Fiona, turned the weapon out to sea.

"Aim," Jenny said.

Mary sighted at an imaginary foe.

"Fire!"

They all wore twists of wool in their ears, but Fiona still clapped her hands to the sides of her head just before the shot resounded.

"Very good," Mr. Deak said. "This time, Mary will load, and Fiona will fire."

Jenny glanced amidships. Jakob's pupils appeared to be learning how to gut a man with a knife. No use wishing she was in that group. Still, she couldn't help watching as he demonstrated on Emma how to grab an opponent's wrist and whack it down on your knee, to make the adversary drop his knife. As he stepped away from Emma, he looked her way. Jenny could swear that he winked at her, but he didn't smile or give any other indication that he was aware of her presence. He turned away immediately to answer a question from Sonja.

Even as the gladness welled up inside her, Jenny wished he didn't work closely with the other girls. Most of them were older and more experienced than she was. Maybe he would find one of them a more congenial companion. But she couldn't regret bringing his presence to light. Even Mrs. Fiske said the *Vera B.* had a much better chance of completing a safe voyage with Jakob along, and she no long had to worry that her secret would be discovered.

As they put the shot and powder for the swivel gun into a canvas bag, Jenny mulled the Bible verse Aunt Hannah had set her to learn: *For where envying and strife is, there is confusion and every evil work.* No, she would not envy those other girls. No matter whether Jakob preferred her or not; no matter that her parents were dead and gone. She could not, would not envy girls who had been forced to give their bodies to vile men.

When six bells rang, Gypsy dismissed the first watch. Jenny carried the canvas bag to the locker to stow it for their next gun drill—or, heaven forbid, for a time when they needed to defend the ship.

239

She closed the locker and walked toward the hatch. Her heart leaped. Jakob was coming toward her. This time, he smiled from his lips all the way to his gorgeous blue eyes.

"Sweet Jenny."

She couldn't help laughing. "How are you getting on?"

"It is good. Mr. Deak is improving my English as well."

She giggled. "I'm not sure if he's the best one to learn from." She looked into his eyes and caught her breath. "I miss talking to you."

Jakob shrugged. "If we do well, perhaps on Sunday, after the church, no?"

Her hope blossomed. "Do you think so?"

"It is possible. Meanwhile, I obey every rule. It is because I am thankful for well treatment, but it is also for you, Jenny. "

"For me?"

He nodded. "I do not wish you in trouble, and I wish to be allowed to be your friend. If I do behave, it can happen."

"Yes. Oh, yes."

"Go now, or it will not happen."

Reluctantly, she went to the hatch. If Jakob could control his impulses for her, she could do the same for him.

"There you are." Aunt Hannah stood at the bottom of the ladder, gazing up at her. "What kept you?"

"I had to stow the ammunition bag in the locker." She climbed down to the 'tweendecks.

"I see. You mustn't lose your head, Jenny."

"Wh—?" Jenny eyed her in the dimmer light. "I won't."

Aunt Hannah sighed. "The captain is watching you. So are Mr. Deak and Mrs. Fiske."

"I know, Auntie. I'm being good."

Hannah patted her shoulder. "I'm sure you are. It's just that men aren't always what they seem at first glance. What we *think* they are."

"Was Uncle Alton as good as you thought him at first?"

"Well, yes. He had a few rough spots, but he was a good man."

Jenny nodded. "Of course he was. And Jakob is a good man. He's done nothing to make us think otherwise."

"Oh, Jenny. You've known him only a fortnight. I knew your uncle five years before I married him. Not only that, I had his family to look at. I saw how they behaved, and I heard what other people said about the McKays. We know nothing about Mr. Zeemer. We have no one to vouch for him."

"I vouch for him myself," Jenny said a bit fiercely. "He could have done me harm when I found him, but he didn't. He could have been angry when I told Captain Alice about him, but he wasn't."

Hannah nodded with a sigh. "I know, and I thank the Good Lord for that. But you must be careful, child."

Jenny clenched her teeth. She wanted to say, "I'm not a child. I'm a woman, and Jakob knows that." But she only murmured, "I will, Aunt Hannah."

Lizzie slumped against the bulwark and lowered her head to rest on her arms. This sleeping four hours or less at a time was getting to her. Then they'd had to give up part of their off-watch time for church this morning—not that Lizzie disdained church. This disreputable lot certainly needed it. But without proper rest, they were all losing their complexions.

And the heat! London was never this bad in summer.

As they approached the Timor Sea, dodging an assortment of islands, they were not too far south of the equator. Once they crossed the line, Lady Dunbar assured her the stars would begin putting themselves to rights. They would see the Great Bear and the North Star again. It would be good to be back in the proper hemisphere.

That was if they ever got a wind to push them west and north. The *Vera B.* had been becalmed for two whole days. They sat on the flat water, barely moving, with the searing sun baking their skin.

Zeemer and Mr. Deak seemed even more upset about it than the women. Those lazy girls just lolled about when they were off watch, fanning themselves and complaining about the heat. Polly, the one who was bearing a child out of wedlock, sat under an awning Mr. Deak had rigged off the rear of the galley. She and two of the other off-duty girls listened while Carrie read from a tattered book.

The two men paced the quarterdeck and stared through the captain's spyglass at the few islands now in sight. Zeemer even took the glass and climbed to the top of the foremast this morning for a better look, and then he and Mr. Deak had huddled near the ship's wheel, bemoaning their state to Captain Alice and Lady Dunbar.

"Tired, Lizzie?"

She jerked upright and blinked. Captain Alice stood beside her, a kindly smile on her chapped lips.

"It's just the heat, ma'am. Forgive me." Lizzie squared her shoulders and faced the sea, as the watchmen were supposed to do.

"This is trying for all of us," Captain Alice conceded.

Lizzie gazed up toward the wheel. The men were still yakking away up there. "What good is talking about it? There's nothing they can do to bring us a wind."

"Actually, some captains have put boats out when they were becalmed and had their crew tow the ship, looking for a new spot where they would catch a breeze."

Lizzie stared at her. Surely she was joking. "Like we did at Port Phillip?"

Captain Alice nodded. "For hours on end."

Lizzie's hands ached already, just thinking about it. The idea sounded like a four-hour watch in a slave galley. "I'm sure the wind will pick up soon," she said feebly.

"I pray you are right."

A drop of perspiration trickled down Lizzie's temple to her cheek, and she brushed it away. "I don't suppose we could get out our skirts, ma'am? I keep thinking they'd be cooler than these awful trousers, and no one can see us anyway."

"I'm afraid not. We must be ready at a moment's notice to climb the rigging and set sail."

Lizzie sighed. "Yes, ma'am. Is it true that one of those islands out there is a stronghold for pirates?"

"So Mr. Zeemer tells us." Captain Alice frowned, gazing at the distant bits of land. "I had no idea we'd sail so close to such a place."

"I haven't seen another boat all day," Lizzie said.

"No. But he frets about them. Tells us repeatedly to be on guard. If we could just get a breath of wind..."

Seven bells rang out. Captain Alice gave her a tight smile. "Chin up, Lizzie. Only another half hour and you can rest."

The captain walked away. Lizzie ambled a few yards aft and paused to stare out at the islands again. A few yards farther, and she came to where the dinghy was stored, upside down, next to the bulwark. Its hull was too tempting. She sat down on it, but dutifully scanned the waters beyond the rail.

How long she sat, she didn't know, but she began to feel drowsy. She jerked wide awake when an acrid smell teased her nose. Peering about suspiciously, she sniffed several times. That didn't smell like Nell's cook fire. It smelled like ... tobacco. And ...

A sudden searing on her ankle made her pop up from her perch and whirl around. Wisps of smoke hung low near the deck.

"Fire!" she yelled. Mr. Deak had sternly impressed on them to call out at the first indication of fire on the ship. As footsteps clattered toward her, she stared at the upside down dinghy. The slight curve of its rail raised the gunwales a few inches off the deck, and smoke rose from beneath the small boat.

"Lizzie!" Hannah slammed into her, sending her sprawling.

"What?" Lizzie gasped, scowling up at her. "Why did you do that?" At the same moment the pain at her ankle returned, bigger and fiercer.

"Bring water," Hannah yelled over her shoulder. "Your trousers!" She rolled Lizzie over onto her side and beat her legs and back. "You're on fire! Jenny, bring that water!"

Jenny sloshed an entire bucket of tepid water on Lizzie's legs and torso. Zeemer, right behind her, grabbed the bucket from her hand and ran to the rail for more.

Lizzie sat up, shaking. "What ... " She caught the charred end of a long ribbon sash she had tied at the back of her sailor's blouse that morning, with the ends dangling down behind. She had determined that, even if she had to dress like a man, she would wear some pretty bits every day. They couldn't abandon civilization completely.

Jenny bent down and offered a hand. "Are you hurt?"

"I don't know."

"Let's get you into the galley and let Nell take a look. You may have burns."

Hannah let out a roar. "You come out of there, young man!"

Zeemer was at her side in a trice. Between the two of them, they righted the dinghy, exposing a trembling boy with one boot in his hand, trying to crush a vile wad of rolled up paper and tobacco leaves with it.

"Edward McKay! You scoundrel." His mother's face went scarlet as she surveyed the miscreant. "Fire again? And smoking?"

Mr. Deak, the captain, and several sailors surrounded them.

"What's this?" Mr. Deak demanded sternly. "Where did you get that tobacco, boy?"

"I — I found a big hank of it in a keg in the corner of the 'tweendecks."

"Ruel had it aboard for his crew," Captain Alice said, shaking her head. "I forgot all about it. But more importantly, where did he get the paper? It's a precious commodity on this vessel."

Ned hung his head, sobbing. "I took a—a envelope from—from—from Miss Sonja's pack."

"What?" Jenny shrieked. "You burned one of Sonja's letters from her uncle in America?"

"Only an envelope." Tears streamed down Ned's grimy face.

"Apologize to Miss Sonja," Hannah said sternly. "And Miss Lizzie. You've ruined her clothes, and you might have hurt her badly."

Lizzie turned her foot and craned her neck to see the damage to her trousers. "Oh! Oh!" Her leg was exposed, halfway up the calf.

"Get to the galley, Lizzie," Captain Alice said. "Jenny, see if you can find some trousers for her."

"Aye, ma'am." Jenny hurried away.

Hannah hauled Ned toward the hatch by his ear. "Get in the cabin and stay on your berth until I'm off watch. Don't move a muscle, you hear me?"

Ned went below, sobbing.

"What are we going to do with that child?" Mr. Deak muttered.

"Captain, I'm so sorry." Hannah turned imploring eyes on Alice. "I will punish him. I'll do whatever you think best."

Captain Alice looked anxiously at Mr. Deak. "What do you think?"

"I'm not the one to ask. "I'd likely say forty lashes. This is not the first time."

"No, it's not." Captain Alice frowned, and Lizzie put out a hand to stop Sonja, who was trying to lead her away. She wanted to hear what the captain would say. The boy needed a good whipping. Maybe he would get one at last.

"Five lashes, Mrs. Captain?" Zeemer said.

Hannah caught her breath.

Zeemer glanced toward the hatch and lowered his voice. "Not as hard as for a grown man."

Gypsy's bushy eyebrows arched. "Maybe so. A good spanking, given as official punishment. Take him down a notch. What think you, Hannah? I thought Ned learned his lesson the first time, but I guess I was wrong. I hate to do it, but this has got to stop."

Hannah pulled in a deep breath. "If we must, Mr. Deak. You're the bo'sun—I trust you'll make it sting, but not do him any real harm."

Gypsy nodded. "At the end of the first dogwatch, then. All hands will turn out to witness the punishment."

Lizzie turned toward the galley so Hannah and the captain would not see her smile.

CHAPTER TWENTY-THREE

Carrie savored her last bite of red snapper filet as the tropical sun slipped below the horizon. The entire crew sat about on the main deck, with the exception of Captain Alice, who had ducked into her cabin, and Mr. Zeemer and Mrs. Fiske, who stood chatting on the quarterdeck. After a day of hard work in the muggy air, the officers had allowed the entire crew to eat supper together on deck.

Anne leaned back against the bulwark, nudging Carrie with her elbow. "This would be nice, if we just had a little breeze."

Carrie chuckled. "If we had a breeze, we'd be sailing, not sitting about." She gazed up at the stars winking between the limp sails. "What's it been, three days?"

"Sounds about right." Anne eyed her empty tin tray as if considering whether to lick it clean. "That was a tasty old fish Sonja caught."

"Sure was," Carrie agreed. "Just the thing after all that scrubbing, painting, and mending."

Anne groaned. "My shoulders ache from wagging that paint brush all day." She brightened. "It's almost time to do the show, isn't it?"

Carrie had been looking forward all day to the little bit of entertaining she and a few of the others had prepared. "Kate says we're on. She must have worked some blarney on Captain Alice."

Carrie stood and stepped over Fiona to speak to Kate.

"Is it time?" Carrie asked.

Kate smiled. "I'll see if the captain is ready."

Carrie gathered Fiona, Mary, Emma, and Anne around her. Mr. Deak lit a lantern, and the crew milled about. Ned seemed a bit subdued after his whipping the evening before. He sat quietly near the foremast with Addie. Nell came out of the galley and leaned against its wall, taking in the peaceful scene.

The only person who seemed nervous was Jakob Zeemer, who paced the starboard rail, looking out toward a distant island the crew had been able to see since morning. Carrie could not see the bit of land by starlight, but its presence reminded her that they had barely moved all day.

Kate and Captain Alice came out of the cabin. The crew quieted.

"We've put in a good three days' work tidying up the *Vera B.*," Captain Alice said. "I know this calm is frustrating. Sooner or later, the wind will freshen. Meanwhile, to cheer us up, a few of our sailors have a presentation for us. Of course, we need to continue keeping watch. If any hint of a breeze picks up, we will need to look sharp to the lines. Also, as Mr. Zeemer reminded us, there could be pirates in these waters. Keep your arms handy." She smiled at Carrie. "You may proceed."

Carrie swallowed hard and drew Fiona, Anne, Mary and Emma around her in a semi-circle. She stood in the center, facing the rest of the crew. They glanced at each other uncertainly, and with a shiver of excitement. Carrie cleared her throat and started singing, "Alas my love, you do me wrong, to cast me off discourteously ..."

The other four joined in, and Carrie was stirred with the harmony. Anne had a little trouble remembering her part, but overall, "Greensleeves" went quite well. When they finished the song, the crew clapped.

Encouraged, Carrie said, "And now something from my homeland." It was her first solo since singing in the Boar's Tusk, on nights when Tom had not arranged for professional musicians. She proceeded to sing "Bold Brennan on the Moor." Her companions joined her on the chorus. Ned and Addie clapped along with the jaunty tune. By the end, even Mr. Deak smiled and clapped. Emboldened by her troupe's reception, Carrie launched into "Blow the Wind Southerly."

###

Lizzie stood against the cabin bulwark, watching with reluctant amusement as the quintet sang. She had to admit, the girls had talent. Evidently Carrie and Emma had a good bit of experience singing in public—probably only in the taverns and dance halls, though.

The tropical heat caused sweat to run down Lizzie's back even when she wasn't moving, and she grimaced. Frankly, her clothing stank, and she rarely had a chance to wash it properly. Her only consolation was the dream of dear, cool, civilized England, half a world away.

The quintet started their next song, "My Love is Like a Red, Red Rose." The tune reminded her of home. These common tavern maids and whores probably didn't know who Robert Burns was, only the songs using his poems for lyrics. She was pretty sure they got some of the words wrong.

Lizzie's eyes flew wide as Fiona and Mary opened the next song as a duet, "Will you go to the highlands, Lizzie Lindsey? Will you go to the highlands with me?" After her initial shock at hearing her name in song, she wondered whether they were singing it to make fun of her. She glanced sideways at Lady Dunbar. Her former mistress had a smug expression and seemed to find it pleasant.

Carrie's group sang several other songs: "The Minstrel Boy," "Loch Lomond," "Yankee Doodle" (a particular favorite of Mr. Deak), and "Early One Morning." Lizzie grew increasingly depressed. She hated the sea. She hated the tropics. She hated the *Vera B.* Most of all, she hated how other people could be happy when she was not. She gazed around at the rest of the crew. Polly sat on an upturned crate, swaying gently to the music. Sonja perched in the maintop like a kookaburra on a sheoak and gazed down at the show, grinning in amusement. Captain Alice smiled in rare relaxation. Even Brea, standing with hands on her hips beside the mainmast, bore a distant, contemplative expression.

Lizzie thought about going below to her hammock, but she stayed as several more songs were sung. Captain Alice wiped a tear away as the five girls sang "Van Diemen's Land," a haunting warning from an unfortunate prisoner of the Hobart Towne colony. Lizzie shuddered. The morbid song seemed a cheap solicitation for sympathy toward criminals. Still, the words gripped her, as Anne sternly sang a solo verse:

"Then when we all had landed
Upon that fateful shore,
The planters they came flocking round,
Full seven score or more;
They ranked us up like horses,
And sold us out of hand,
They yoked us to the plough, my boys—
To plough Van Diemen's Land."

There was hardly a dry eye on the ship when the song was done, except maybe Ned's. Lizzie eyed the little devil in disgust. He didn't even know when it was appropriate to be sober, but grinned at the depiction of hardship.

"Captain Alice, we have one more song," said Carrie. "This is one I learned from the British sailors, but I have modified it a little for the ladies."

Oh, gracious. Lizzie shook her head and felt sick. If there was anything worse than sentimental singing by the uncouth, it might be when they tried their hand at improvising lyrics. She scowled and arched her eyebrows. The five singers started strong and boisterous:

"Cheer up, my ladies! 'tis to glory we steer,
    To add something more to this wonderful year;
To honour we call you, not press you like slaves,
For who are so free as daughters of the waves?
Heart of oak is our ship, heart of oak our women;
We always are ready, steady, ladies, steady!
We'll fight and we'll conquer, again and again.

We never see our foes but we wish them to stay,
They never see us but they wish us far away;
If they run, why we follow, and run them ashore,
For if they won't fight us, then we cannot do more.
Heart of oak is our ship, heart of oak our women;
We always are ready, steady, women, steady!
We'll fight and we'll conquer, again and again!"

"Splendid!" Lady Dunbar cried as the crew erupted in applause. "Good old 'Heart of Oak,' one of my favorites! That's the spirit, ladies!"

The singers, flushed with exhaustion, curtsied to the applause. "Thank you," Carrie said modestly.

Captain Alice said, "Well, crew, I have enjoyed our concert, but it's time we turn in. Good night."

"I believe this is my watch," Lady Dunbar said. "I need two volunteers to stand guard with me and Mr. Deak."

Lizzie stepped forward. "I will." She may as well volunteer now, rather than be dragged out of bed for a later watch.

"And I," said Brea.

Lizzie shivered. She was more afraid of Brea than anyone else on board.

The bulk of the crew filed below. Jenny handed Lizzie the pistol she had worn on the previous watch. "Hope you don't need it," she said.

Lizzie took the gun and merely nodded in reply. She tucked it into her sash and reported to the first mate.

Lady Dunbar looked at Lizzie and Brea. "I want one of you two to stand watch on the main deck. Watch for the wind. The minute you feel a breeze or see a sail flicker, shout out. The other can go aloft. You decide how you'll share the duties." She turned to Captain Alice. "Would you mind staying on deck for a few minutes? I need to see to something in my cabin."

"Certainly," Captain Alice said.

251

Lizzie walked along the starboard rail toward the bow. Brea stalked beside her. They stopped near the foremast.

Brea looked at Lizzie. "So. That was a wee bit different."

"The singing?" Lizzie nodded. "I suppose so."

Brea shifted her weight and stared at Lizzie, moonlight reflecting off her hard eyes. "What's the matter, Liz?"

Lizzie stared at her. "Since when do you care?"

Brea didn't answer for several seconds. "I don't know. I've been doing a lot of thinking lately."

Lizzie looked away. It was ludicrous that someone like Brea would bother to do something so high-minded as thinking. She thought it prudent to keep silent and gazed out to sea off the port side. Her eyes adjusted slowly to the moon and starlight.

Somewhere to their south was the barren northern shore of Australia, which Mr. Zeemer had assured them was full of nothing but snakes and crocodiles. She stole another look at Brea, who had unsheathed her long knife and ran her thumb over its edge.

"Could use sharpening," the Irish girl muttered.

"I suppose you want me to go up to the top."

"No, I'll go. I know you haven't much stomach for the rigging."

Lizzie glanced uneasily at Brea, then walked forward to the windlass and looked up at the sails. In the dim moonlight, they all hung limp, not rustling or flapping. The stillness of the sails and the lack of waves were uncanny. The brig sat almost motionless on the water. She glanced back toward the mast. Brea was climbing the ratlines and was halfway to the maintop.

Captain Alice screamed. Lizzie whirled toward the stern, but couldn't see much past the masts and galley. Brea jumped from the rigging to the deck and dashed toward the sound. Her heart pounding, Lizzie inched along the side of the galley toward the waist. Her breath rushed out of her, and she felt lightheaded. Captain Alice lay flailing on the deck in front of her cabin while

Mr. Deak and Brea fought fiercely with several shadowy men, who growled and jabbered in some heathen tongue.

Pirates!

Brea and Mr. Deak each fired a pistol. Two pirates dropped to the deck. Brea waded into a new wave of invaders swarming over the bulwark, slashing with her knife and pummeling the men with her free fist.

"Get back, filthy beasts!" The Irish girl lashed out at the intruders, and they fell back briefly before her onslaught. One pirate sprawled on the deck, his head thudding like a coconut. Another reached Mr. Deak and the two dropped, writhing together until Mr. Deak managed to slam his opponent's head against the foot of the stairs. Mr. Deak lay on the deck, slowly lifting a hand to his head.

Captain Alice scrambled to her feet, only to be grabbed from behind by one of the cutthroats. A large pirate yelled at him, and the man holding Alice paused to reply.

"Go back to your mothers!" Brea shrieked. She flung herself at two more pirates, swinging and growling like a wild beast. One of the attackers teetered and fell over the rail. Another bashed Brea with a club. Brea flew backward and hit the deck with a thud. She lay prone, her arm twitching. Lizzie gasped and watched in horror as several pirates pulled Captain Alice shrieking toward the rail.

Jakob Zeemer burst up from the hatch with a shout. He lunged at the foes with his cutlass. Several more men clambered over the rail near the brig's waist. Zeemer advanced on them, hacking left and right. One man slashed the Dutchman's left side, and he collapsed to the deck groaning.

"Gypsy, they've got me," Captain Alice wailed. "Gypsy! Help!"

"I—I'm coming!" Mr. Deak crawled feebly across the deck and slashed at the pirates' ankles with his knife while Alice pummeled them with her fists.

"All hands on deck!" Lady Dunbar stood at the cabin door, brandishing a cutlass and a pistol. The pirates at the rail started in alarm. With a concerted effort, they heaved Captain Alice, screaming, over the rail. Paralyzed with fear, Lizzie trembled at the splash beside the brig.

"You scurvy brigands!" Mr. Deak shouted. One of the pirates stomped on his hand, making him drop the knife. The steward roared in pain, but shot to his feet like a jack-in-the-box and slammed into the pirates. He knocked two over the bulwark with the force of his impact. Lizzie gasped as one of the brigands grabbed Mr. Deak's wrist and pulled the old man over the side of the ship into the sea below.

She felt herself being lifted bodily from behind, and her blood seemed to freeze. She rose into the air, hoisted uncomfortably by her clothing, then was set down standing on the deck. Fearing a giant pirate, she whirled around to find herself nose-to-nose with Nell, whose eyes gleamed fierce in the moonlight. "Elizabeth."

"Y—yes?"

Lady Dunbar's pistol fired, and Lizzie jumped. The few remaining pirates on deck leaped over the bulwark.

Nell shoved Lizzie toward the first mate. "She froze up and didn't help."

Lady Dunbar squinted at Lizzie in disgust. "You were on watch, Henshaw! You just crouched there watching the show, while we lost our captain and who knows how many others? What is that in your hand, young woman?"

Dumbfounded, Lizzie lifted her right hand and realized for the first time that she had clasped her pistol tightly during the entire skirmish.

"A sailor on watch is expected to defend her vessel. Did it never occur to you, instead of merely observing, you could have at least fired at them? How could you not defend your comrades?"

254

A shadowy figure sprinted across the deck from the hatch, and nearly tripped over one of the bodies.

"What happened, Mrs. Fiske?" It was Kate.

Lady Dunbar looked around. "We've been boarded, and lost several of our crew. Gypsy went overboard—I saw him fall."

"Captain Alice went too," Lizzie blubbered. "It happened so fast!"

Kate swore. "Pirates? How did they sneak up on us?"

"Our minstrel show." Anne came up behind Kate, her voice quavering. "It was our fault. No one was watching. It was dark, and we were distracted. And afterward, no one was on the quarterdeck, since we were becalmed."

A moan came from one of the forms on the deck, and Brea sat up. "Oh, my head." She added an oath upon seeing several bodies lying about her.

"Fetch a lantern," Kate yelled over her shoulder as she hurried to check Brea's wounds.

Lady Dunbar snatched Lizzie's pistol away and hurried to the rail. "Alice!" she yelled.

A muffled reply came from the sea. Lizzie fearfully approached the rail beside Lady Dunbar. A hundred yards out, a large boat rowed away from the *Vera B.*

"Alice! Gypsy!" Lady Dunbar's voice cracked.

"We'll find you," Kate screamed.

"No," came Mr. Deak's reply from the boat. Lizzie trembled and burst into tears, her eyes stinging.

Lady Dunbar turned on her. "You could have stopped this. You could have at least tried, Henshaw. I cannot abide a coward. Get out of my sight."

Lizzie ran for the forward hatch, but slipped in a pool of blood. Her feet flew up and she fell hard on the deck, sinking her elbow into a dead pirate's stomach. Bawling, Lizzie struggled to her knees. Several crew members blocked the way forward, and she couldn't get by. Hannah brought a lantern as the crew gathered.

255

"Jakob!" Jenny shrieked and ran to the fallen Dutchman.

"Angel," he said, lifting his hand toward her. "I live. Not dead."

"What happened?" Jenny demanded fiercely, looking about in the gloom as she caressed Zeemer's face. "Where's Captain Alice?"

"She's gone," Kate choked.

CHAPTER TWENTY-FOUR

Kate knelt by Brea, her pulse racing. "Let me look at you, Bree. I need to see if you're hurt."

"I'm fine." Brea grasped her shoulder and levered herself to her feet, wincing. "Just got hit on the head, I think."

Kate straightened. "I don't see any blood up there. Looks like a cut on your arm, though."

Brea looked at her right forearm. Blood dripped to the deck from a three-inch gash. "That'll mend."

Most of the crew crowded around Jakob Zeemer. The Dutchman lay between two dead pirates. Jenny sat on the deck cradling his head and crying, while Hannah, Nell, and Mrs. Fiske tended to his wound. Ned squeezed in beside his mother.

"Ned, hold this rag against the cut." Hannah lifted her head. "Addie, fetch the medicine kit from the captain's wardrobe. Nell, I need you to boil some water." She looked back at the patient. "That's right, Ned, hold the bandage fast. We must stop the bleeding, or he'll die inside of five minutes."

Kate said to Brea, "We'd better see to your wound. Even a little one can get infected quickly in the tropics."

Sonja walked over to Kate, her face tense with fury. "Let's take a boat and follow them. Now. Or we'll lose them."

Kate grimaced. She understood Sonja's desire to rescue Alice and Gypsy, but she also suspected that rushing headlong after the pirates would be courting disaster. "Look, shipmate. We'd need to discuss that with Mrs. Fiske. She's in command with Captain Alice gone."

"But we need to go now, before they're out of sight. If Zeemer dies, we'll never make it to safety without them. And Captain Alice—well, they're pirates. They'll—well, you know."

Memories of hundreds of leering men flashed through Kate's mind, sending chills down her body. Alice had rescued

257

them from that sordid life. Now she might face it herself. Kate gripped Sonja's arm. "I hear you. But we need a plan, or that could happen to every last one of us."

Sonja scowled, but nodded. "I'm going to get the dinghy ready." She stalked toward the bow.

Brea huffed. "She's right."

"I know," Kate said. "But we're all in grave danger. We need to think this out."

Brea looked out to sea, where they could still see the tiny dot of the pirate proa receding in the distance. "I thought I heard the banshee earlier, when the girls were singing. They were so beautiful. When I came to, just now, I thought I had died."

Kate stared at her. "That's balderdash, Brea."

The dark-haired girl shook her head and laughed. "Old wives' tales."

Kate wasn't in the mood for superstition. "You're as bad as Sonja and her Norwegian gibberish. Let's hope nobody dies. Captain Alice isn't here to pray for us anymore."

Brea snorted. "If praying were so grand, where did it get her now?"

Kate had no answer.

Mrs. Fiske stood up. "All right, crew, we need to bring Mr. Zeemer into the captain's cabin so we can tend to him properly." She locked eyes with Kate. "I hate to ask you, Miss Robinson, but can you and Brea search the fallen pirates and throw them overboard?"

Kate shuddered. It had to be done. "Aye, aye, ma'am."

In the lantern light, she and Brea searched the four bodies. They found two pistols, three serpentine swords, several knives, a few miscellaneous tools and ornaments, three Spanish silver dollars, and some minor coins.

Brea picked up one of the swords and eyed its curved edge keenly. "I believe they call this a kris. I fancy it." She unfastened its scabbard from the dead pirate's back and added it to her belt.

"Grab hold," Kate said. She and Brea latched onto the first body and pulled it to the rail. Sonja ran up from the bow. "You aren't going to just toss them overboard, are you?"

"They'll sink," Brea said.

"But we're becalmed. They'll come up after a while and float around the ship for days, if we don't get some wind."

Brea looked at Kate, and they dropped the corpse on the deck. "Do you have a better idea?" Kate asked.

"Let's get some ballast and sink them proper."

Brea shrugged. "Suits me."

Fifteen minutes later, the thankless deed was done. The four bodies, weighted with ballast rocks from the bilge, flopped over the side and disappeared, leaving ripples on the calm surface.

Kate sighed. "I need to wash up."

Sonja shook her head in disgust. "We all do." They went to the keg and dipped some fresh water into a basin.

"Don't forget to drink," said Sonja. "Easy enough to dry out in these latitudes."

Kate took a swig from the dipper. She felt like she could use some rum, but didn't want to bring it up. "I'd better go find Mrs. Fiske. You two keep a sharp lookout on deck. You never know when those thugs will be back with friends. Mr. Zeemer said before that these pirates attack in swarms, like blowflies."

Kate poked her head in the captain's cabin, which was crowded. Mrs. Fiske looked up from helping with Zeemer and caught Kate's eye. "Miss Robinson, please open the weapons cabinet and issue pistols to those who don't have them. Then I need the crew to stand watch on deck until further notice."

Kate stepped over by the chronometer and took the key from its hiding place on the shelf that Captain Alice had showed her on her first day as mate. When she had handed out all the pistols remaining in the cabinet, she pulled one from her belt. "Here, Emma. We took this off one of the enemy. I don't know if it takes the same ammunition as the others. Get Brea to check it for you." She raised her voice. "All of you, now, out on deck. Keep a sharp eye out."

The crew filed out past Kate.

"Hannah, you will stay of course," Mrs. Fiske said. "Miss Robinson, I need to see you. And where's Sonja? Ah, there she is. Come in, please."

Sonja entered the lantern-lit cabin and closed the door. Hannah and her children tended Zeemer, who lay on Captain Alice's bed with his eyes closed.

"Well, ladies," Mrs. Fiske said. "We're in a tight spot. We've lost Captain Alice and Mr. Deak, and we're still becalmed. The first thing we must do is to establish our new roles."

"Will you be our new captain?" Addie asked from the bedside.

Mrs. Fiske exhaled heavily. "It is normal for the first mate to assume that role if the captain is lost. I suppose there's no need to put it to a vote."

Kate nodded. "If not you, I don't know who else."

"Very good. Miss Robinson, I want you to act as first mate, and Hannah, you'll be second mate. Your watches will remain the same, except that Kate's will now be first watch, and Hannah's will be second. Sonja, I'm appointing you boatswain. I'm relying on you."

Sonja snapped to attention. "Yes, ma'am."

Mrs. Fiske paced the cabin. "We need to prepare for defense. The pirates are likely to return in force. Am I right, Mr. Zeemer?"

The Dutchman stirred. "Yes, Mrs. Captain. They will come. Many proas. If you have no wind, you will not avoid it. You must shoot them with the guns. If you have the wind, sail fast away. For the women, very bad if the pirates conquer us." He moaned and gasped for breath. "All will die or be sold within—one week."

"But what about Captain Alice?" Sonja demanded, stepping closer to the bed. "And Mr. Deak. We can't abandon them!"

"No!" Zeemer spat. "They are lost. You never see them again. Mr. Deak is old. No use to them. Mrs. Captain Alice, the little chief will not harm her tonight. He will make a surprise of her for Makala. I heard him."

Mrs. Fiske stared at him. "Who is Makala?"

"The king of the pirates in this sea. I understand them, talking. The little chief came to us with his proa. I heard him to say he will take the woman to Makala. With no doubt, he owes to Makala much gold or favor, and he hopes this surprise will make Makala happy. I tried to stop them, but I failed."

"So there's time!" Sonja whirled around. "We need to rescue them, tonight!"

Mrs. Fiske shook her head. "I'm sorry, my dear, it's not possible."

"We have to try." Sonja's voice broke, and Kate put a hand gently on her shoulder.

Zeemer breathed heavily. "What would you do? If you take a boat to the island, it is certain death. If you survive from the snakes and the crocodiles, one hundred, maybe two hundred pirates you must resist. That island is their safe place. I hoped they were gone, but surely there are many."

Kate felt the blood rush to her face. She turned to Mrs. Fiske. "Please. I don't want to wait for them to come back. If we wait, we play into their hands. But I could go ashore—Sonja and Brea and I, maybe—and we could try to free Captain Alice and Mr. Deak and bring them back."

Mrs. Fiske stared at her. "You can't walk into their stronghold."

The image of Captain Alice being brutalized by the savages tormented Kate. "Please, Mrs. Fiske. Captain Alice did so much for us. If it were any two of us sailors, do you think she would leave without us?"

"But the odds, my dear." Mrs. Fiske touched Kate's arm.

"Don't talk to me about odds!"

Mrs. Fiske flinched.

"I'm sorry." Embarrassed, Kate lowered her voice. "Mrs. Fiske, I was the lone survivor of a shipwreck when I was a child. I was raised by bush people. Later, I was sold into slavery. Captain Alice helped me escape that. She took the risk, and she succeeded. I don't believe in odds, and Captain Alice doesn't either."

"She believes in God," Ned said quietly.

Mrs. Fiske shook her head slowly. "If we lose any more of our crew. . ."

Hannah raised her chin. "Please, Captain Sarah. I'm afraid, but. . . if we abandon Alice and Gypsy, I will regret it the rest of my life."

"Me, too," Ned said.

"Hush." Addie smacked him.

"Hannah's right," Sonja said. "They're our family. Our parents. The closest thing we have."

Mrs. Fiske said nothing.

Kate looked at her, willing her to surrender. "Heart of oak, Mrs. Fiske?"

The acting captain pursed her lips and sighed. "If we're going to do this, we'd better act swiftly."

"Huzzah!" Ned yelled. "I'm going with you, Miss Robinson!"

"Oh no, you're not," Hannah said, pulling him back. "I need you to stay and help me here."

Zeemer beckoned from the bed. "Come to me. I know this island. I must tell you everything."

Sonja stood with Kate, Hannah, and Mrs. Fiske outside the captain's cabin. Though she feared what might occur in the next few hours, she felt fierce satisfaction. They were doing right. She looked out over the *Vera B.'s* remaining crew, who stood solemnly in the flickering lantern light.

Mrs. Fiske cleared her throat. "Due to the unpleasant events we have experienced, we have a temporary change of command. I will act as captain of this vessel until such time as we might receive Captain Alice back on board. Miss Robinson will command her old watch as our new first mate, and Mrs. McKay will command my old watch as our new second mate. Sonja will be our boatswain. When I dismiss you, I need all hands to keep an armed watch until I give further instructions. We are especially vulnerable while we have no wind." She took a deep breath. "The officers and I are putting together a rescue plan."

A murmur of approval ran through the ranks.

"Six of our number will take a boat and sneak into the pirate encampment under cover of darkness," Mrs. Fiske continued, eyeing the women sternly. "That will leave only nine of us, not counting Mr. Zeemer and the children, on the vessel. If we are attacked again, we face much graver danger than we did an hour ago. If the members of the rescue party fail to return, I will have no choice but to sail off as soon as we have wind. We will make for Batavia, or possibly a closer port if we can find one in the charts. If we make a friendly port, we can try to send a search party back, but I cannot guarantee that will be possible." She squinted, and her voice quavered. "Mr. Zeemer assures us that no one is likely to long survive being captured by the pirates, especially women. Are there any questions?"

Sonja looked at the women's faces, wondering what they were thinking.

Lucy asked, "Who will go, and who will stay?"

Mrs. Fiske grimaced, her features stern in the lantern light. "Only volunteers who are willing to risk their lives. Miss Robinson offered to lead the expedition, and if she should fail to return, we felt the rest of you would need me here with my experience, to have any chance of making port. Now think carefully. We need five more."

Each woman gazed sternly at her fellows. Sonja saw a glint in Brea's eye. Almost in the same instant, every hand went up.

Mrs. Fiske smiled. "I only need five. Definitely not you, Ned. Addie, no. If you women can't decide amongst yourselves, I will choose. Any with doubts, put your hand down. Polly, put your hand down, sailor. I'll not have you risk that child unnecessarily. Hannah—hmm."

"I'm strong, ma'am," Hannah said, "and my children will be all right with Jenny. Alice is my friend, and I'll not leave her."

Sonja winced. She knew what it was to be an orphan, and she hated to think of Ned and Addie losing their mother.

"I think your inclusion will increase the chances of success, Hannah," Mrs. Fiske said. "Jenny, you must stay." She looked around. "Brea. Sonja. You will go. We need two more. Carrie, and Fiona. You two help row and stay with the boat while they go ashore. You six, come to the cabin with me, and we will form our plans. Everyone else, stand watch until further notice." She paused. "Ned. Go fetch Lizzie. We need her to stand watch, too."

Sonja fell in beside Carrie, who gave her a knowing look. "We're in for it now, and no mistake."

Awkwardly, Sonja reached out and patted Carrie's back. "We'll make it."

The six volunteers followed Mrs. Fiske to the cabin.

Lizzie was too dehydrated to weep anymore, but she shook in silent sobs. In the dark forecastle, swaying slightly in her hammock, thirsty as could be, she felt completely abandoned and undone. Two of the people she had come to admire most, though grudgingly, were captured and spirited off to unknown tortures. She had seen men hacked to death on the deck and two of her shipmates fall wounded. The dreadful fright of the spectacle still coursed through her frame, but the memory of a single word pierced her. That word pounded in her ears with every rapid heartbeat.

264

Coward, coward, coward, coward. *I can't abide a coward.*

Lizzie clenched and unclenched her calloused fingers, gripping the hammock's netting. I'm a coward. A blooming coward. And everyone knows it.

Round and round in her head spun a scenario—the first few seconds after she had come across the skirmish. She had hunched up by the galley wall with a clear view of the pirates and crew fighting at the foot of the quarterdeck stairs. In hindsight, she had several clear opportunities to fire her pistol. If she had done so, might she have saved Zeemer from being wounded, possibly unto death? Might Captain Alice and Mr. Deak have been spared? The fight replayed itself again and again, taunting her. Dereliction of duty.

A hesitant knock on the forecastle door startled her. Her dry throat seized, and she said nothing. Who could it be? The women who slept in the dark, smelly chamber didn't knock when they entered. The door opened, the hinges creaking. "Lizzie?"

"Who is it?" She couldn't place the whisper.

"It's me."

Ned. Great. The only thing that could go worse, just did.

"Mrs. Fiske said you need to go up on deck now."

Lizzie sighed darkly. "I'm not going."

"What happened to you, Lizzie? Are you hurt? Are you feeling crook?"

Lizzie groaned. "Go away!"

"I'm not going until you tell me what's wrong. Are you wounded? Did the pirates cut part of you off?"

"No! I said, go away."

"I don't want to. You're my enemy, Lizzie."

"What?" She was about ready to roll out of the hammock and throttle the little brat, but she lacked the energy. And the nerve. She was a coward, after all.

"You're my enemy. You hate me. But Addie was reading the big Bible to me. It says I have to love my enemies, and do good to people that hate me. The Bible also says that giving someone a

265

cup of water for Jesus is showing love. So, I thought maybe I would give some water to my enemy. That's what the Bible says."

Lizzie stared into the dark, blinking her itching eyes. "You brought me water?"

"Yair."

"Ned. What has gotten into you?" She had read the passage before and heard Lady Dunbar quote the "Love your enemies" part more times than she cared to think. She wasn't ready to love Ned. But she was extremely dry. "How did you know I was thirsty?"

"In this heat, everybody's thirsty all the time."

"Ha." Lizzie sat up and swung her legs over the side of the hammock. "Isn't that the truth. Well, thank you for bringing me the water." She reached out in the dark, and he found her hand and gave her the cup. The water soothed her parched tongue and aching throat.

"So. Does this mean I don't have to be your enemy anymore?" Ned asked. "Can we be friends?"

Lizzie frowned. "Don't you ever set me on fire again, or I'll keelhaul you."

"What's that?"

"I'm not sure, but it doesn't sound like fun."

"Why is everybody up there cross with you?" Ned asked. "They don't seem to like you anymore."

Lizzie felt a chill, even in the stuffy heat of the forecastle. "It's hard to explain."

"Well I'm not cross with you."

"That's good of you."

"Mrs. Fiske is going to be stroppy crook if you don't go up on deck. She says the pirates might come back anytime, and we all have to get ready to fight. Or we might die. The pirates might skin us like bullocks—"

"I'm afraid to go up, Ned."

"Afraid of the pirates? They're not here yet. We need to get ready. To shoot them with the guns, and cut them in little pieces

266

with swords. If you hide down here, you won't be any help, and the pirates will just find you here alone in the dark."

The boy's naïveté, combined with the stark truth of what he was saying, galvanized Lizzie into action. "Fine. If we're going to die, I might as well die fighting."

"Huzzah! Look, if we're friends now, I have a grand idea for how you and I could fight the pirates. . . ."

CHAPTER TWENTY-FIVE

The proa glided through an opening in the island's reef and approached the sandy beach edging the lagoon. A fire on shore drew Alice's attention. Half a dozen other boats were anchored in the shallows, and fifty or more men lolled about the beach. The nose of their proa crunched sand. The crew shipped their oars, and most of them jumped over the side to wade ashore.

One of the pirates, a large, swarthy fellow to whom the others kowtowed, pulled Gypsy up and shoved him toward the bow. He extended his hand to Alice. Her throat tightened, and she shook her head vigorously. On her own, she managed to stand, though her hands were bound.

The leader, who had made them understand during the hour's journey that he was called Ramu, jerked his head toward shore. A dozen other men rushed to the waterline and waded out, chattering in a tongue totally meaningless to Alice.

She understood that she was to disembark, so she made her way to the low bulwark. Gypsy was already on the beach and being pushed rudely toward the circle of firelight. Alice gasped as strong arms enveloped her from behind and lifted her bodily. Ramu, it seemed, thought she moved too slowly. He hoisted her over the side and into the arms of a stocky, brown-skinned man whose grinning face sent shudders down Alice's spine.

He bore her to the edge of the beach and set her down. She had barely regained her balance when they were surrounded by jabbering, hooting men. Several reached out to touch her dress, her hands, her hair. Alice tried to shake their hands off, but they crowded closer. Even she could hardly understand her own fractured, silent prayers. *Lord, let them be merciful to Gypsy!*

Ramu shouldered his way through the throng and spoke sharply. The others stepped back and quieted, still staring at Alice. For once, she was glad for the man's interference. He gave commands, and several men hurried off to do his bidding.

Alice spotted Gypsy, sprawled on the sand, with several pirates jabbing and kicking at him. One rifled his pockets, but Alice knew they were too late. Ramu's men had already plundered Gypsy's pipe and a few coins in the proa.

Ramu took her arm and propelled her to a rug spread on the sand. He nodded toward it, and she sat down cautiously, still the object of gloating stares. Another man hauled Gypsy over and shoved him down beside her.

"Gypsy!" Alice touched his shoulder.

He gave a little moan and sat up. A cut near his left eyebrow oozed blood.

"Are you all right?" Alice asked.

"A little worse for the wear, ma'am."

"I'm so sorry."

To her surprise, a small man wearing nothing but a sarong tied about his waist and a bright red head cloth knelt before her, offering a brazen dish. The concoction in it gave off a savory, pungent smell.

"What's this?" she asked.

"They want to feed us," Gypsy said. "Or you, anyway."

"How do we know it's not tainted?"

"We don't."

Alice's stomach already churned, and she had eaten her supper two hours past. She shook her head and pushed the dish away. "No, thank you."

The giver frowned and extended it again.

"No," Alice said firmly.

With a confused expression, the man looked at Gypsy and hesitantly offered him the dish.

"Take it away, you dog," Gypsy snarled.

The man stood and scurried away, jabbering in his own language. Pirates surrounded them on all sides, but most of them seemed to lose their fascination for the prisoners and began to eat and converse. Several jugs were passed around. Alice had the feeling that, while no one was dedicated to watching them, all were aware of their presence and none would let them make a move.

She glanced sidelong at Gypsy. "What do you think?"

"I think we're in for it."

She let out a deep sigh. She fully expected the leader to claim her and haul her off somewhere for his own pleasure. They hadn't killed Gypsy yet, for which she was grateful.

"They might think they can ransom us," he whispered.

"Do you think so?" Hope leaped in Alice's heart.

"Not really. Truth be told, I don't expect I'm long for this world, ma'am. You, I don't know. A handsome woman ..." Gypsy shook his head. "To them, you're exotic. I hope they won't make it unbearable for you. If they take you off this island ..."

"What?" Alice stared at him.

"The British might be your best bet. Hong Kong ..." He shook his head. "The Dutch maybe. Any Europeans you can get to. But this lot ... Oh, Mrs. Packard, I'm so sorry I couldn't stop them."

"You did everything you could, Gypsy, and I fear it will cost you your life."

"I hope they make it quick, that's all."

Ramu stalked over to them and gave a command. Alice stood, and two men hauled Gypsy to his feet. Ramu led the way, and Alice followed. She kept her steps slow for Gypsy's sake.

Half a dozen pirates, all formidably armed, surrounded them as they entered the jungle and climbed a path that grew steeper with each minute. Gypsy grunted behind her, and she turned to see him sprawl on the ground. One of the men prodded him until he staggered to his feet. Finally they emerged onto a rocky overlook above the beach. Ramu waited for them to catch up. Alice walked to within two yards of him and stood panting. What now? Would they be cast over the sheer cliff?

She gazed out beyond the beach, the proas, and the smooth lagoon, to the sea beyond. Was the *Vera B.* still becalmed, floating helplessly where they had left it? She had no doubt the cutthroats would summon more of their kind and return to strip the brig of its crew and cargo.

Let not one soul be lost on the Vera B., Father in Heaven!

Gypsy lurched to a stop beside her. Ramu allowed them perhaps a minute to breathe then gestured toward the path on the dark mountainside.

"What, farther up?" Gyspy said.

Alice squinted in the moonlight. "It looks like a cave." She lifted her chin as a slight movement in the air tickled her cheek. Gypsy followed her gaze to the treetops. The fronds of the tallest palms shivered.

"A breeze," Alice said softly.

"Aye. We are high up, but maybe ..."

"Maybe they'll catch a wind."

Gypsy nodded. "And sail away before these devils go back with their friends."

"I pray God they do," Alice said.

Their captors herded them toward the dark opening. Ramu turned and addressed his followers. Two of the men, one a giant towering above the others, walked over to a place where a pile of ashes bespoke other evenings spent on watch and began to lay a fire.

Ramu took Alice by the wrist and drew her forward. At the entrance to the cave, one of his men kindled a torch. Two other followers lit brands off the first one and proceeded inside. The cave opened with a good-sized chamber, which narrowed toward the back and became a passageway. Along this route, Alice and Gypsy were guided for about fifty feet. The torchlight revealed a widening in the cave, resulting in a room about thirty feet in diameter. Crates and boxes of all descriptions were piled about the walls, and a pyramid of kegs stood to one side. Bolts of cloth and bulging sacks sat in heaps about the chamber. The men put two of the torches in brackets on the wall. Ramu gestured toward one side of the cave.

Alice caught her breath. On a pile of woolen blankets lay sets of shackles and chains. She turned to Gypsy.

"Easy," he whispered.

Alice sent a plea heavenward as Ramu's men pushed them to the spot and fastened the chains to their ankles. When they were done and stepped back, she realized they had hooked her and Gypsy together with a chain about three feet long between them. She exhaled slowly. They weren't going to kill him, at least not immediately.

Ramu stooped and reached toward her. Alice jerked her head back, but his hand aimed lower, and she saw that her locket had fallen free from her bodice during their odyssey. Ramu's sinewy hand closed about it.

"Please," she whispered.

He beckoned a torchbearer closer and studied the pendant. He smiled and lifted it, trying to remove it over her head.

Alice held her hands up in protest. "No, no. You'll break the chain. Let me do it." With trembling fingers, she undid the clasp and handed the locket to Ramu. He gazed at it and nodded in satisfaction. Alice's heart sank. The lock of her precious husband's hair was inside, and she would never see it again. She held back a sob and met her captor's gaze unflinching.

With a quick command, Ramu led his band of men out of the chamber. They took the torches with them, but one still flickered several yards along the passageway after the men had left and all was silent. By its faint light, Alice could see Gypsy's weary face.

"We are safe," she whispered.

"No, not safe," he said. "We will never be safe again."

"For now, though."

"I'm sorry he took your necklace."

Alice pulled in a shaky breath. "My husband's gift. But God will comfort me. Gypsy, we must pray."

"I'm sure you will, ma'am."

"You too. We must pray for deliverance."

"You think that's likely?"

Alice considered for a moment. "God can deliver us, even now. Even as he delivered Daniel from the lion's den."

Gypsy wriggled a bit on the blanket. "I suppose so, if he wanted to. I wish it, for your sake."

"I am ready to meet my Creator, Gypsy. I am not so sure about you." Alice peered at him. "If you believe your end is near, you must make your peace with God."

"I'm sorry. I just can't believe. Not the way you do. I've seen too much in this world to trust God. If he really controlled things, he would never let a fine lady like you be in the hands of such evil vermin."

"Don't you see? It doesn't matter if they kill me. I'll go to God and see my Ruel again. But you … You must believe. God's Son died for you. You know that."

"Aye, I've heard it many times."

"Believe it then. Our mortal bodies may not survive this, but our immortal souls surely will. Trust Him, Gypsy." Alice closed her eyes and sent up fervent petitions. "Lord, save us from this awful place. I pray it not for my own comfort, but that Gypsy would see Your power, and Your love for us."

Carrie pulled on her oar, straining her eyes for any signs of life on the island a hundred yards off the starboard beam of the jollyboat. The only clue she had that this was the pirates' lair came from a speck of fire gleaming on a mountaintop near the east end of the island. A signal fire?

273

A fish jumped ten feet away, startling her. She looked at Fiona, whose eyes glinted in the moonlight. The Scottish girl grimaced at her and kept rowing. They kept careful time with their muffled oars, matching the pace of Brea and Hannah on the thwart ahead of them.

Sonja stood motionless in the stern, her knees flexed and a hand on the tiller. The moonlight reflected off her pale face below the dark bandana she wore. All the women wore dark clothing, in an attempt to blend into the night. Sonja tensed, then raised her left arm to the height of her shoulder.

At the prearranged signal, Fiona and Brea stayed their oars while Carrie and Hannah kept rowing in silence.

Behind Carrie, Kate leaned forward and whispered. "There's the rock Zeemer told us about." The tide was coming in. Now they only needed to get into the lagoon and find the inlet, with a channel between the mangrove trees.

The hint of a breeze rippled over them. Carrie looked back at Kate, who nodded vigorously. The light wind was a very welcome change. Assuming Mrs. Fiske was able to take advantage of it, she would sail the *Vera B.* a little closer to the island, so they wouldn't have to row five miles back to the ship after completing their mission. Carrie's arms ached, but she was pleased that she had held up well. Sonja and Kate had spelled Brea and Hannah earlier, to conserve their energy for use on land. Carrie and Fiona, however, as dedicated rowers, were to have no rest until the search party was safely ashore.

Sonja peered ahead. "Here's the reef," she breathed. Carrie heard the intermittent lap of the tidal swash. With the wind so calm, they had no trouble rowing through a gap in the coral reef. If only they were not discovered by the people on shore.

Within the lagoon, all hint of waves was gone, and a flat surface reflected the moonlight like crystal. The boat skimmed along. Carrie figured it was well past midnight. She hoped they could find Captain Alice and Mr. Deak and escape before dawn.

They rowed around a mangrove-covered promontory, and Sonja pointed. They held the boat steady near the widespread mangrove roots. Across the lagoon, nearly dead ahead of them, a bonfire blazed on a rise overlooking a beach. White sand fairly glowed in the moonlight, an easy path beckoning toward the fire. Raucous singing drifted across the water.

"Look at the proas," Sonja breathed, squatting down in the bow. Carrie saw the dark shapes of a jumble of boats to the left of the beach.

"Hug the shoreline," Kate admonished. "We'll blend with the mangroves."

Carrie and the others steered the boat closer to the roots to avoid being silhouetted in the moonlight.

"There," whispered Sonja, extending her right arm. "I think that's it." She turned the rudder to starboard and Carrie and Brea stopped rowing to allow the boat to turn sharply to the right. They glided into a shadow tunnel beneath the spreading, spidery mangrove trees, which infested the shallow water along the shoreline.

"Go easy," said Sonja.

Gently, they rowed through a labyrinth of exposed roots and limbs. Branches brushed against them. Now and again the boat's hull rubbed on roots that stuck up under the water like bristles on a brush. Carrie could barely see the moon now, for the natural canopy above her. She hoped Kate could see well enough in the bow to avoid obstacles.

"I think we're coming to the end of it," Kate said after a minute.

Carrie could barely see anything, but kept rowing until Kate said, "Enough." The boat hit the bank and Kate leaped out.

"Looks clear." She tied the boat to a tree. Brea, Sonja, and Hannah gathered their gear and got out of the boat.

"Say a prayer, everyone," Kate said softly. "We got this far, but this is going to be tough. Carrie, Fiona, you stay put and wait for us." She drew a deep breath and pulled her cutlass. "Let's go, women. Heart of oak."

"Good luck be with you," Carrie said, her heart in her throat.

The four infiltrators disappeared into the jungle.

CHAPTER TWENTY-SIX

Sonja gripped her cutlass firmly as she followed Hannah's shadowy form through the jungle. A dozen yards ahead, she heard Kate slashing the occasional vine or limb out of the way with her sword. Sonja did her best to watch behind them, in case they were followed.

Hannah tripped and fell to her knees. Sonja caught up to her. "You all right?"

"Yair, I'm fine." Hannah hooked her axe on a tree limb and pulled herself upright. She stepped over the log she had tripped on and followed Brea's fleeting form.

Sonja looked around the dark jungle warily. Kate led them on solid ground parallel to the mangrove swamp. Besides pirates, any number of dangerous creatures could inhabit the island, but nothing stirred at the moment.

She and Hannah caught up to Brea and Kate, who had paused to survey the terrain. Sonja scanned the darkness. The moon peeked through the overhead foliage. Drums began beating in the pirates' camp, and occasional shouts drifted through the trees from afar.

"I think there's a bit of a trail here," Kate said. "Let's follow it toward the camp, but be careful. There could be traps or sentries."

Sonja felt an insect scurry up her leg, and moved quickly. "Anthill!" she hissed, pushing Hannah toward Brea. Kate moved out along the barely discernable track. Sonja followed, reaching down to crush the two or three ants tickling her leg.

They moved quickly for several hundred yards. The eerie drumbeats grew louder. The pirates chanted, sang, and laughed. Sonja hoped they weren't laughing at Captain Alice.

Kate stopped abruptly, and the others came up behind her. Hannah bumped into Brea. The four women stood motionless. Sonja barely breathed.

"Sentry," Kate breathed. "Let me get closer to him, and then you make a little noise. When he walks by me, I'll get him."

Sonja's heart beat so loudly, she feared the sentry would hear it. As Kate glided into the darkness, she crouched by the trail with Brea and Hannah. After a minute, Brea coughed quietly.

A grunt came from farther up the trail, followed by heavy footsteps. The whoosh of a sword arcing through the air was followed by a loud crack, a gurgle, and the rustle of leaves. With a thud, the sentry hit the ground.

"All clear," Kate whispered a few seconds later.

Sonja followed Hannah and Brea to join Kate beside the dead pirate. She could barely see the body on the ground, but a faint light glinted off the barrel of a pistol. She stooped and pulled it from the man's sash.

Kate puffed out a breath. "I think we should split up."

Sonja nodded. "Zeemer said they'd probably hold Gypsy and Alice in the cave."

"Right. It's halfway up the mountain, and that should be to our right, through the woods." Kate pointed in that direction. "I'll take Brea and head overland. You two … hmm …"

"Could we get off the trail?" Hannah asked.

"Just don't get lost," Kate said. "I've kept us within sight of the mangrove swamp for a landmark. Try to get close to the camp and create a diversion for us, like we talked about."

"We will," Sonja said readily.

" Don't get caught. We all need to survive this."

"Girls," Hannah said. "I just want you to know, before we part … I can't speak for Mrs. Fiske, or anyone else, but if any of you are missing, and I escape, I will do whatever it takes to come and find you, if there is any hope at all you're alive."

Kate exhaled heavily. "I would do the same. Never lose heart. The women of the *Vera B.* do not abandon each other."

"Aye," said Brea.

"Aye," Sonja repeated with a shiver.

"Make your way toward the noise," Kate said. "Give us an hour before you begin your diversion." She paused. "Can you find your way back to the boat?"

"I reckon," said Hannah.

"Just don't get caught. Let's go, Brea."

Sonja watched as Kate and Brea disappeared off the path into the dense foliage.

"Well," said Hannah. "We can follow the trail, or get off it."

"Let's risk it a little farther," said Sonja. "We'll keep alert." She led off along the path, willing her eyes to discern details.

A couple of minutes later, she saw an orange light ahead. She stopped and drew Hannah's attention to it.

"A small fire," Hannah whispered. "Not the main one. An outpost, maybe."

"Right." Sonja stared at the flickering fire. "Let's go around it."

"Ha!" a guttural voice sounded barely ten feet away. A large body crashed toward them.

Instinctively, Sonja leaned back and kicked the pirate in the chest, her nerves delivering extra force. The man flew backward into the bushes and groaned.

Hannah leaped toward the ruffian and sunk her axe into his body with a plunk. With another blow for good measure, she rose and eyed Sonja in amazement. "Did you—kick him?"

Sonja smothered a chuckle. "Not bad, eh? A little trick I learned from my Chinese friends at Port Phillip." She listened warily for any sound that might betray more foes nearby.

"Good job. But it's time to get off the trail," Hannah said.

"Come on." Sonja veered off to the left and led Hannah downhill toward the mangroves. Carefully they skirted the edge of the water. The small sounds of the jungle rang in her ears. Frogs croaked, leaves rustled, the water lapped quietly against tree roots. Somewhere among the mangroves, she heard a loud splash, followed by something wallowing in the water.

Hannah gasped. "Is that a man?"

279

Sonja listened a few seconds. "I don't think so."

"Crocodile, maybe."

"Could be." Sonja's flesh crawled. She set her jaw and continued along the bank, slicing the occasional vine away with her cutlass and hearing no sounds of pursuit.

After a few yards, she peered around a massive tree. Water shimmered ahead, as well as the orange glow of the pirates' bonfire above and to the right. "Nearly there," she whispered to Hannah. The drumbeats sounded clearly now.

"Move your hand!" Hannah yanked her back from the tree. With a loud whack, she sank her axe head into the trunk just above where Sonja's hand had been. A dark object fell to the ground. A shudder jolted Sonja.

"Snake," Hannah panted. Sonja jumped back as the flailing body of the reptile slid out of the branches and flopped to the ground at her feet.

Kate jumped behind a big tree, hauling Brea with her. She peeked around the tree trunk at the trail a stone's throw away. Four swarthy pirates sauntered past them. The light from the bonfire reached into the jungle, etching shimmering patterns on the men's leather and silk outfits as they walked. The men were in a good mood, laughing and slapping each other on the back.

Kate turned to Brea. "That was close. I don't know how to get to the cave. What do you think?"

Brea looked around, pursing her lips. "Up above the huts, Zeemer said."

Kate frowned. "Right. I think that's where we are. Above the huts, above the bonfire..." She looked up at the mountainside. "We can go higher."

"Maybe we should follow those pirates," Brea said.

"Hmm." Kate didn't think the pirates were headed to take care of prisoners, nor to exploit them. Her observations of men in Melbourne and elsewhere had made her a fairly good judge of people's intentions. Usually she could tell by a man's posture and demeanor what his mind was bent toward. These four looked like they were simply ready to turn in.

"Unless you know something else to do." Brea grimaced.

"Fine. We'll follow them." Kate scanned their surroundings, and sneaked toward the trail. At least it was ground she and Brea had not covered yet. She froze. Fifty feet ahead of them, a pirate stood with his back to them. He held a jug in one hand, and raised it to his lips.

Kate turned to Brea and put a finger to her lips then led her away, intending to make an arc around the lone pirate. They painstakingly sneaked through the jungle, listening for any sound that might be out of place. The incessant drums thumped in counterpoint to her heartbeat.

Brea seized her arm. Kate drew up abruptly and crouched with her in the underbrush. They watched through the foliage as a slight-framed pirate approached the one with the jug. The two spoke for a minute, then the newcomer grinned at his companion, shifted his eyes as if wary of being detected, then made another remark in his incomprehensible dialect. The man with the jug chuckled and made a sly comment in reply. His friend gave him a knowing grin and slinked away.

"That's it," Kate breathed. "I know that kind of talk. He's the one we need to follow." Not waiting for Brea's response, she stalked through the jungle, trying to avoid being seen, but not wanting to lose the buccaneer bent on mischief. She could still see him trudging purposefully up the trail.

Risking a little more exposure, she darted from tree to tree. Brea followed. The man trudged steadily up a path along the hillside. Once he looked back. Kate froze in mid-stride. The man scanned the jungle, his eyes wide. Reassured, he turned and trotted on.

Kate let out her breath, glanced around, and trotted after him. She came to a flat spot from where she could see the big

281

bonfire below. She grasped a sapling and leaned over the side of what was nearly a cliff. Down on the beach, about a hundred men milled around. Several thumped in unison on wooden drums. One clump of men appeared to be deep in conversation, while a few danced around the fire and others chanted and laughed. Food and drink seemed to be in abundance. Kate looked at Brea.

"Not much different from Melbourne," Brea said. "Do they have any women?"

Kate looked over the scene. "If there are any, they must be hidden."

"They probably have a 'Dame Nell's' hut somewhere."

Kate grimaced. "Come on, we're losing our quarry." She looked around the mountainside, then sprinted up the path. She rounded a rock and jerked to a halt. Fifty feet ahead, the man picked his way up the dim trail.

At a soft cry behind her, she whirled. Brea wrestled on the ground with a long-haired man in a leather tunic. Kate pulled her sword and scrambled down the path. She hacked the man on the shoulder and he flinched. Brea erupted like a volcano from beneath him, flinging him against a small tree. Kate tried to aim a blow, but feared hitting her friend.

Brea punched the pirate in the throat, and his eyes glazed over. She cursed him and ran her sword through his chest. "No man who touches me survives," she fumed. "I am done with that."

Kate scanned their surroundings, her heart racing. "Where did he come from?"

Brea grimaced and pointed upward. "He jumped out of that tree. He must have seen you go by and thought he could take me without a sound."

Kate grabbed one of the man's ankles. "Let's get him behind the tree." When he was out of sight from the path, they headed on up the trail. This time Kate made a point of scanning the tree limbs overhead. She should have known better than to get caught like that.

Ahead, the flickering of another fire warned her. She paused and drew to the side of the path, Brea close behind her. The pirate they had followed approached the fire, and a massive man stood up and addressed him in a booming voice. The newcomer cringed and whined before him. They continued with a lengthy exchange, the big man's low bass voice contrasting with the smaller one's whinging tenor.

"David and Goliath," Brea whispered in Kate's ear. "Don't tell me Goliath is guarding Captain Alice and Gypsy."

Kate sighed. "That's what I'm thinking."

Sonja eased along the moist ground on her hands and knees, keeping below the cover of the underbrush. She moved with extreme care, doing her best not to shake the shrubs and ferns. The edge of the clearing lay just ahead. Warily she raised her head and peered around a sheoak bush to assess the scene.

The pirates maintained a bonfire on the beach, fifty paces or so from the water's edge. Scores of dark-skinned men milled about, most of them wearing colorful sarongs and batik shirts. A few men beat their drums, and some sang. Several roasted bits of meat on sticks over the fire. The ruffians passed bottles and jugs among them, and some of the partakers staggered about, shouting and laughing. A group of men stood around three pirates whose dress and bearing proclaimed them as leaders. The crowd conversed in strident tones. One of the leaders kept pointing out to sea. Were they talking about launching an assault on the *Vera B?*

High above the beach, occasional flames could be seen from a smaller fire partway up the steep mountainside. At the mountain's peak, maybe five hundred feet above the sea and a mile or so beyond the lagoon, another bonfire burned brightly.

283

Sonja gritted her teeth. According to Zeemer, the mountaintop fire was a beacon to summon any proas that were out prowling for miles around.

On the far side of the lagoon, a dozen proas were anchored. A few were pulled up on the beach. Even this small number could be deadly against the *Vera B.* Swivel guns studded their rails. Sonja wondered how big a cannonball it would take to pierce their thick hulls.

A shout went up, and the pirates' attention was drawn to the reef at the entrance of the lagoon, where three more proas glided toward the beach. The men around the bonfire cheered as their numbers increased. Sonja shook her head. All they needed were more enemies. Maybe this little distraction would give her an opening, though.

She glanced back at Hannah, whom she could barely see hiding behind a tuft of ferns, then peeked warily past the sheoak. A stretch of open ground lay between her and a small, partially enclosed hut. It was time to act. She rose beside the feathery sheoak and ambled across the open space, forcing herself to walk casually, as if she belonged there. She looked straight ahead and strode across the open space as if she owned the hut and was returning home to it.

It went against her nature not to look around, but she knew that any furtive actions would draw attention. She peered in the hut's open doorway, fearing what she might find. Enough firelight illuminated the space for her to see that it was unoccupied, but some bedding and clothing were strewn about, along with a basket of nuts, a coconut, and a jug. Sonja ducked inside and looked out an opening in the side wall. As far as she could tell, she had not drawn any attention.

Several other openings broke the woven sides of the hut. Sonja gazed out each one in turn. She needed to find something flammable. She could burn the hut, but she wanted a bigger diversion, preferably a keg of gunpowder.

Behind the hut was a bigger structure. Several palm trees grew in between, in a slight dip in the sand. Sonja went to the doorway and looked out. The pirates were still at the beach, talking loudly and waving at the proas, most with their backs to the huts. She grabbed a discarded sarong from the floor of the hut and tied it around her waist, then stepped outside as if she had done it a thousand times and sauntered around to the larger hut.

She stepped into the doorway in a show of confidence. The fire was to her back, so she knew she would be silhouetted to anyone within and they could not see her features. Her eyes began to adjust to the darkness. A man's voice asked a question in a foreign tongue.

Sonja's heart raced, but she shifted her weight authoritatively and grunted in reply. Her blood flowing cold, she searched the hut's interior. Movement toward the back caught her eye.

The man repeated the question, a hint of indecision in his voice. Sonja growled in disapproval. She stepped aside and gestured for the man to leave the hut.

The occupant sighed and stumbled toward the door. Sonja moved inside, giving him plenty of room to exit and hoping he wouldn't be able to see her clearly.

The light from the bonfire played over the man's face, showing bleary eyes. He was short and slight and wore a plain cotton shirt and a ragged sarong, his only apparent weapon a sheathed karambit knife worn at his belt. He squinted in the firelight, chuckled, and made an amused comment, gesturing back into the hut. He punched Sonja playfully.

"Ha." Sonja punched him back and shoved him out the door. She watched breathlessly to see what he would do. The pirate shook his head and stumbled toward the bonfire. Her heart in her mouth, Sonja watched until he was a good way toward the pirates on the beach, who were chattering, yelling, and gesturing toward the approaching proas.

A clink of metal behind her caused Sonja to whip around. She held her breath and tried to maintain an air of confidence. Maybe she should just leave while she had the chance. The metal clinked again, and she made out a figure on the floor in the back corner.

Stealthily, Sonja pulled her seaman's knife and held it close to her hip. She had been seen. Should she leave, or investigate?

The clinking came again, and Sonja recognized the sound of chains. The person in the corner was a slave. Warily, Sonja approached, cautious of tricks.

"*Siapakah anda?*" The person said in a clear, high voice. A woman. Sonja winced. She should have left when she had the chance. Could she trust the slave woman to keep quiet? She turned to leave, knowing she would spare this hut from the fire.

"*Tunggu, tunggu,*" The woman called desperately from the corner. Sonja paused, facing the door. She didn't want to go back. It had been nearly an hour since she had left Kate, and it was time to make the diversion.

"*Sila, tunggu,*" the woman pleaded, her voice breaking. Sonja swallowed. How long had this poor woman been chained in the hut? Was she an unwilling concubine to all these men? The pirate who had left the hut seemed like an underling, and had easily submitted to Sonja's confident bluffing. The woman must be very bad off indeed.

Slowly, Sonja turned and stepped to the back of the hut. "Easy now." She reached for the woman's hand. The corner smelled horrible. Sonja hoped the woman had been brought here only recently. Zeemer had suggested the island was not a permanent settlement, but an outpost.

The captive grasped Sonja's arm and chattered earnestly.

"I'm sorry, I can't understand you," Sonja said. She repeated it in Norwegian, but still got no response.

The unfortunate woman wasn't wearing anything but a ratty shawl on her upper torso. Sonja slipped off the sarong she was wearing and handed it to her. Then she felt the chain that held

286

the slave's leg to the hut's corner post. If only she had Hannah's axe, she might be able to sever the chain. It wasn't very thick, but too stout to break with her knife or cutlass.

Sonja straightened and fumed in silence. How could she possibly free this woman? She didn't have all night to think of a solution. She leaned against the post, and the shelter swayed slightly.

She smiled. The chain was wrapped around the bottom of the post, and the post was stuck in the ground. Maybe—

Sonja forced her hands past the woven palm fronds of the wall, hugged the post with both arms, and heaved upward. The post moved a little, but it was stuck deeply in the sand. She pushed it back and forth a few times and tried again. With a mighty effort during which she fleetingly thought of Samson in Captain Alice's Bible, she lifted the post a foot. It was just enough for the woman to pull her chain out with an exclamation of triumph.

Sonja let the post drop and gasped as a sharp pain shot through the small of her back. She put a fist to her spine and rubbed it.

The woman grabbed her arm and jabbered. Sonja sighed and stepped toward the doorway.

"Come."

The slave followed her to the doorway, where Sonja scanned for pirates. Most of them were a hundred yards or farther away, at the beach. Sonja winced. Now she doubly needed to make the diversion. The pirates must be kept from launching their proas, and Kate needed the chance to release Captain Alice and Gypsy. Had Kate and Brea even found the hostages' hiding place yet?

She looked at her new friend, who gazed out the doorway beside her. The girl was a little shorter than her, but might be a bit older. The resolute expression on her pretty face said she was ready to conquer any challenge. She glanced at Sonja and grinned.

"We're not safe yet." Sonja pointed at the pirates and mimed crushing them with her fist. The girl nodded enthusiastically.

Sonja hesitated, trying to think of the best way to communicate. If she could just find where the pirates kept their gunpowder, she might be able to blow up their stash. A terrible thought hit her. What if the gunpowder was stored where Captain Alice and Gypsy were being held?

"Sri," the girl said, pointing to herself.

Sonja touched her chest. "Sonja."

Sri smiled shyly, and jabbered in her language.

Sonja pulled a pistol from her belt and showed it to the girl, who looked at it with understanding. Sonja put it back and took out the powder horn and lead balls from her leather pouch. She opened the horn and showed the black powder to Sri.

"I need to find more." She closed the horn and put it away, then indicated an explosion, spreading her hands. "Boom!"

Sri looked at her quizzically, then spoke urgently and tugged at Sonja's sleeve.

"Good." Sonja scouted warily from the doorway, but could see no one watching them. Sri stepped out, carrying her chain in one hand.

Sri waved up the hill at another hut. Sonja followed her, stealing from bush to fern. She had never been one to pray, but Captain Alice was beginning to rub off on her. She mouthed broken prayers to the Almighty as they sneaked along. It couldn't hurt.

Sri took Sonja to the secluded structure. Sonja pulled her down in the underbrush a few yards from the door and peered out cautiously. It looked safe enough, and she crept around to the back and found a window hole. She stood on tiptoe and looked inside. Sure enough, there were a number of wooden barrels inside, as well as sacks, kegs, and crates. Ropes and other goods were stacked neatly along the far wall.

Sonja handed her knife to Sri. "Keep watch." She stepped back and assessed the building's construction. Like the other huts, it had a framework of wooden posts with woven palm frond walls. She pulled off her pack and emptied it on the ground. Glancing around furtively, she grabbed tufts of wool and wove them into the dried palm fronds, near the ground. Then she opened the little flask of whale oil and poured it on the wool and the hut wall. Sri gasped when Sonja produced a lucifer and struck it, catching the wool on fire.

Sonja jumped up, grabbed Sri's hand, and ran, retracing her steps past the other huts and across the open ground toward where she had left Hannah. They had nearly reached the sheoak bush when a shout came from the jungle to their left.

Sonja dove behind the sheoak, pulling Sri with her. Ignoring the pain that lanced her back, she sat up and pulled her pistols from her belt.

With a bloodcurdling yell, five pirates dashed out of the jungle toward them.

CHAPTER TWENTY-SEVEN

Kate stood against the rocky mountainside with Brea and gathered her wits. Captain Alice and Gypsy could not be far away. Brea gazed out to sea.

"Look. Proas coming in."

Kate looked down at the lagoon, some hundred feet below. Three pirate boats skimmed toward the beach. She sighed. "Reinforcements."

Brea nodded. "They're probably coming to help attack the *Vera B.*"

Kate peeked around the rocky outcropping at the campfire on the ledge. The scrawny pirate they had followed up the trail continued talking with the huge man Brea had dubbed 'Goliath.' A third man roasted a small plucked bird over the fire. Kate could just see the opening of a cave in the mountainside behind them.

Brea nudged her. "What do you think?"

"We need to get past those three men, into the cave. I wish Scrawny would leave. There's no cover on the other side of the path, but maybe I can sneak around down the slope and come up on the other side of their fire. It looks like there's more space on that side between them and the cave."

"Along the cliff?" Brea asked, frowning.

"There looks to be enough of a foothold. I might be able to make it in without being seen. Can't be worse than the royal yardarm. You'll stay here and keep an eye on things, right?"

Brea nodded slowly, moonlight glinting off her keen eyes. "Maybe I should get their attention, once you're in place."

Kate frowned. "Sonja's supposed to make a diversion down near the beach. I wonder what's keeping her." She put her hand on Brea's shoulder. "Very well. I'm going to sneak around. Whatever you do, Bree, don't let them get you."

Brea fingered the edge of her sword. "They won't take me alive."

"Don't let them take you dead, either." Kate scowled. "I'm counting on you."

She peered around the outcropping again. The pirates stood on a broad rock shelf before the fire, intent on the proas entering the lagoon. Kate stealthily scuttled to a bush on the near side of the fire and hid there.

The pirates stepped closer to the fire. Goliath made an exasperated remark to Scrawny, who chuckled in glee, grabbed a burning stick from the fire, and padded into the cave.

Kate hauled in a deep breath and started feeling her way down the steep mountain slope below the fire. Her toes groped for solid footholds on the treacherous hillside. The cliff face lay before her. She grasped the protruding root of a scraggly tree and used it to help her swing across a sheer surface. In the moonlight, she could barely see what she was doing, but grasped clumps of grass and fissures in the rock. Above her, but out of sight, the fire crackled.

A fist-sized rock broke off beneath her boot, careening down the mountainside, clacking on hard surfaces. Kate froze, hoping her foes didn't hear it. Gingerly, she felt for a new foothold, found one, and eased along. Finally she found a tough vine growing straight up the incline, grabbed hold of it, and pulled herself upward. The vine rustled a tuft of grass farther up. She imagined Goliath whacking the vine off with a kris, and herself tumbling helpless to the beach below.

When she gained enough height to see the campfire again, Goliath sat on a rock across the fire, nearly facing her. His comrade knelt by the blaze and gnawed at the roasted fowl. Kate clearly saw the cave's opening, but she didn't feel safe climbing any closer, for fear Goliath would see her. She looked back toward where she and Brea had hidden a few minutes earlier. She couldn't see Brea. Hardly daring to breathe, she waited.

###

Sonja stared at the pirates charging her in the dusk. Lying where she had landed, she aimed her pistols and fired. The closest man tripped and fell on his chin in the sand, but her other shot went wide. She rolled to her knees, tucked her spent pistols in her pack, and brandished her cutlass.

Two loud reports sounded behind her. Hannah's aim was deadly. Two more pirates fell, one screeching from a hit to the arm. Sonja leaped to her feet, her mouth dry, a sharp pain in her back. The two remaining pirates slowed and looked at her and Sri, and beyond.

"For Alice!" Hannah yelled, and charged out of her hiding place. When her friend came close, Sonja sprinted with her toward the remaining enemies, shouting a Norwegian insult. A clinking sound told her that Sri was not far behind. Facing their charge, the two remaining pirates fell back.

"To the boat!" Hannah yelled, and led them along a path leading into the jungle above the mangrove swamp.

Hannah ran, carrying her axe and huffing, and Sonja followed, checking on Sri from time to time and wondering if the powder stash in the hut would ever blow. Surely the fire had taken hold. It ought to reach the powder kegs by now.

The glow of the bonfire faded behind them, and she could hardly see the trail. Ahead, she glimpsed the dying embers of the outpost fire they had seen earlier. Hannah approached it warily, but they had killed the one guard, and no one was nearby now.

Shouts came from behind them.

"They're coming," Hannah said. "Maybe we should hide and reload."

Sri tugged at Sonja's shirt, and pointed to some banana bushes a few paces beyond the dying fire. Sonja flinched and prepared for a pirate to jump out, but Sri ran over to the bushes and stepped behind them, beckoning with her thumb for Sonja and Hannah to take cover with her.

Sonja crouched behind the bushes with Sri and stuck her cutlass in the ground so she could reload. She hurried to rearm her pistols, fumbling with the powder. Hannah growled softly as she dropped something on the ground. Footsteps came crashing through the woods. Sonja got the powder into one of her guns, popped the wadding in, and pressed the ball in with the little ram rod she carried with the powder horn.

Sri looked at Sonja, then put a hand on her shoulder, and one on Hannah's. They all crouched behind the banana bushes, listening to the shouts and footfalls. Sonja thought maybe they should run for the boat, but Sri grinned at her, then tossed back her head and wailed, eerily mimicking the cries of an infant.

"Ah-a-awah-awah! Ah-awah-awah! Awaaaaaaaaah!"

Sonja looked at Hannah in alarm. What on earth was Sri doing? She would give their position away!

A knot of pirates crashed toward the women, but stopped short upon hearing the sound of a crying baby. About fifty feet away, they stood jabbering in confusion.

Softer and softer Sri cried. Sonja's hair stood on end. How the girl could sound so like a baby, she couldn't guess.

Cautiously, seven or eight pirates approached from the other side of the fire. The Malay girl's wailing grew quieter, then she was silent a few seconds. She pulled the knife from her belt. Slowly, she stood, presenting a confident face toward the fire.

"Sri!" Sonja mouthed, paralyzed with fright. One look at her new friend told her, however, that she was carefully working through a plan.

Chain clinking, Sri glided out of the bushes and showed herself in the firelight, her long dark hair flowing around her shoulders. The pirates hesitated and trembled, the fire reflecting off their wide eyes and drawn blades.

"Oooo," Sri crooned, swaying gracefully before the fire. She waved the knife above her head, then in front of her body. "Oooo!" She beckoned slyly to the pirates.

"*Pontianak*," one of the thugs shrieked. The pirates roared and ran back toward the beach. The jungle resounded with their caterwauling.

Sri chortled, nearly doubling over with laughter as they fled. Hannah shook her head. "Must be a local superstition."

Sonja nodded. "Head for the boat now?"

An ear-splitting explosion sounded from the direction of the beach. The shockwave shook the jungle and nearly knocked them off their feet.

Sri stopped laughing. She turned wide eyes on Sonja, a mischievous grin splitting her face. "Boom!"

Gypsy had dozed off with his head on his bent knees, but he jerked awake as footsteps approached through the cave's passage.

"What is it?" Alice whispered.

"Someone in the tunnel." Gypsy's mouth was so dry he could barely form the words.

Flickering light came closer and illuminated the rock cave and the piles of stores. A slight-boned man wearing a sarong and loose shirt entered and stole toward them, holding his torch high. He stopped a few feet from them and stared. Slowly, a grin distorted his face.

He took a step nearer to Alice. She caught her breath and lowered her head. The man laughed.

"What do you want?" Gypsy asked sternly. Drawing the cutthroat's attention might bring dire consequences, but anything was better than having him touch Alice.

The man snarled and glared at Gypsy. His hand jerked to his shoulder. From a sheath on his back, he whipped out one of the long, wavy knives the Malay pirates favored.

Gypsy opened his mouth, prepared to hurl an insult, when the rock floor beneath him shuddered and a muffled explosion echoed through the tunnel and the chamber.

The man yelped and dove between two stacks of crates.

"What's happening?" Alice clutched Gypsy's wrist. "Is it cannons?"

"I don't know. If we could just get these hobbles off." Gypsy reached down with his bound hands and felt the link that attached the chain to the shackle on his ankle.

"If we could overpower him," Alice whispered. "Get his knife."

A flutter near the tunnel opening caught Gypsy's eye, and he sucked in a breath. "Shh. Someone else is there." The back of his neck prickled.

"Where?"

"Near the passage."

They both sat in silence, watching the shadows. The pirate remained concealed and seemed to be worming his way farther from the light, between the crates.

"I see it," Alice whispered. "Someone peeked in."

"Sneaking, ain't they?" Gypsy's heart thumped. They both stared at the tunnel opening so long he was nearly convinced he'd imagined it.

Ever so slowly, a head poked out from beyond the wall of stone, and the torchlight gleamed red on the hair.

"Kate!" Alice struggled to get up.

She was right, Gypsy realized.

"Beware," he cried as Kate showed herself and walked into the light, her face tense. "There's a scoundrel in here. Behind those boxes." He raised both hands and pointed, but he could no longer see the thug.

Kate said nothing, but ducked low behind a row of casks. Gypsy and Alice stood, but their shackles tethered them to the floor near the woolen blanket the pirates had given them.

"Pray, Mrs. Packard," Gypsy whispered. "Now is the time for your God to deliver."

Alice's lips moved in silence.

295

Gypsy hauled in a gasp of air and froze once more, listening. To his surprise, something like a prayer formed in his mind. A plea. *God, if you're real, let that girl survive!*

A rustling sound came from the gloomy depths of the cavern. Kate's head jerked toward it, and she crept toward the sound, her sword drawn.

The pirate leaped from behind the crates and slashed at her with his kris. Kate swung back but missed, and a moment later, her sword rattled to the floor. The man advanced on her slowly, and Kate backed away.

"Watch out!" Gypsy pulled at his chain, helpless.

Kate backed into a large wooden box and put her hands down to feel it. A moment later, she sprang forward with a shriek, swinging a two-foot iron bar. The man staggered back, but Kate pressed toward him and brought the bar down with both hands. Alice let out a small scream. Her fingernails dug into Gypsy's arm.

The pirate folded slowly to the floor, and Kate stood over him for a moment, gasping, then dropped the bar as though it were hot. It clattered on the stone floor. She stooped to retrieve her sword and came to stand panting before them, dark stains covering her sailor's blouse.

"Thank God," Alice murmured. "Are you hurt badly?"

"No," Kate gasped.

"I told you not to come," Gypsy said.

Kate did not reply but held out her knife. Alice raised her hands so Kate could cut her free.

"We're chained together," Alice said, "and Gypsy's shackle is hooked to the floor." Her hands came loose, and Kate turned to Gypsy.

"No time to get the shackles off," he said as he held up his bound wrists. "Maybe we can pry open the link that hooks me to the floor."

"Yes. Then we must fly." Kate sliced the ropes on Gypsy's wrists and handed him her knife. "Hold on."

296

She dashed over to the lifeless pirate and returned with the crowbar she had found with the crates. She handed it to Gypsy. One end was sticky. He fumbled with the chain but couldn't get purchase on the ring or one of the links.

"Bring the torch closer." Kate dashed to get it. When she came back, Gypsy said, "Give it to Alice. I'm afraid my strength is spent, but the link next the ring seems the most likely to give."

For a tense minute they waited, fearing more pirates would swarm the cave.

"We heard guns or thunder," Alice ventured.

"A hut exploded. I think Sonja found their powder magazine."

"Sonja's ashore too?" Gypsy asked.

Kate grunted and heaved on the crowbar so hard that when the ring gave, she fell over backward.

"Are you all right?" Alice asked.

"Yes. Come on!"

Kate stood and seized the torch, then led them along the tunnel. Alice and Gypsy hobbled along behind, the chain between them scraping on the floor and tripping them up if they went out of step.

Gypsy put an arm around Alice's shoulders. "Beg pardon."

"Of course," Alice said. They quickly found a rhythm and hurried after Kate.

As they approached the entrance, she held up a hand. They halted, and she whispered, "Wait here until I call you." She laid down the torch and crept toward the opening.

Gypsy couldn't stand not knowing what was happening. He eased forward, and Alice went with him, past the smoldering torch. The stars still glittered above, and the moon hung low in the west. From close by they heard panting, moaning, and a sickening thud.

Kate stepped outside, and Gypsy and Alice emerged on her heels.

297

On the ground a few yards away, a huge pirate struggled with Brea McDonovan, who writhed under him, trying to elude his grasp. She held a kris, but the pirate's meaty fist was locked about her wrist. As they wrestled for control of the blade, they inched closer to the cliff's edge.

CHAPTER TWENTY-EIGHT

"We are going to regret this." Carrie followed Fiona gingerly through the jungle. She clutched her pistol in one hand and felt ahead with the other. She hoped she wouldn't fall into the mangrove swamp.

"We must find the baby," Fiona said. "Poor wee bairn is out here somewhere."

An explosion boomed from the pirates' camp, so loud Carrie tottered a step and grabbed a branch to keep her steady on the path.

Fiona shrieked with joy. "Sonja! She foxed them, but good!"

Carrie wanted to share Fiona's enthusiasm. The explosion would be a great diversion, but with all the strange sounds she had heard in the past few minutes, she didn't know whether to hope that any of their friends were still alive.

Fiona scampered on through the jungle and Carrie followed, determined not to let her out of her sight.

Fiona stopped and waited for her to catch up. "A little fire."

Carrie looked past her and saw campfire embers smoldering in the woods. "Hush. I see it."

Movement between them and the fire caught Carrie's attention. "Get down!"

They hid in the underbrush. Cautious footsteps approached them. Carrie peered out and saw three shadowy figures.

"Halt!" Fiona popped up, her pistol aimed toward the new arrivals.

Carrie jumped up beside her. "Halt."

"Carrie?" It was a familiar voice.

She lowered her weapon. "Hannah. Thank God. Put your gun down, Fiona."

Fiona stowed her weapon and leaped out to greet the newcomers. "Hannah, Sonja, you're all right! Grand explosion! But where's the baby?"

"Baby? There was no baby," Sonja said. "Only our new chum, Sri. She just sent a pack of seadogs running back to their mums!"

Fiona eyed the small Malaysian girl in the starlight. "Ha! That wee thing turned Wallace on the pirates? I declare."

Carrie studied the newcomer. "Glad to meet you, I'm sure." She could barely tell anything about the new girl in the dark.

"Let's get back to the boat," Sonja said.

They returned the way Carrie and Fiona had come. A few minutes later, Fiona halted. "The boat's just down there."

"Maybe we should wait up here for Kate," Sonja said.

Hannah added, "And we could make a stand if they're being chased. How many pistols do we have?"

A quick count revealed six guns, but one recovered from the pirates would not accept their ammunition.

"Five shots, well-placed, can make a big difference," Hannah said. "But I think Sri could be onto something. Swords and pistols may not be our greatest weapons."

"Sri scared the pirates off by crying like a baby, and then showing herself like some kind of ghost," Sonja explained.

"She fooled us," Fiona said. "We thought it was real."

"And Fiona liked to have killed me, traipsing about the jungle searching for it." Carrie took a deep breath. "So what do we do—all weep like babes if we're attacked?"

Sonja grunted. "Maybe. Sri will know. She must know their superstitions. Let's follow her lead if there's trouble. I'll show her the boat, though, so she knows our plan."

As Sonja took Sri down an embankment to the mangrove swamp, Carrie shivered. The darkness concealed all but the vague bulk of trees and bushes. "Hannah, do you think Kate has a chance?"

"We separated before reaching the pirates' camp. We can't know how she and Brea fared. From where I stayed, I could see nothing of them, or Alice and Gypsy."

Sonja and Sri returned stealthily. "She really likes the boat," Sonja confided. "I wish we could understand each other better. There's a lot she could tell us."

Carrie extended her hand and touched the short girl's shoulder. "I'm Carrie."

"I'm Carrie," Sri repeated dutifully.

Fiona giggled. "She thinks 'I'm' is part of your name."

Carrie took a deep breath. "Carrie." She touched her chest.

"Carrie." Sri touched her hand to her own chest. "Sri."

"Good to meet you."

"Gootameechu." The voice was high and playful.

"I wish I could get her chain off." Sonja knelt down and felt about the girl's feet. The chain clinked.

Sri tapped Sonja's shoulder and spoke in her musical language.

"What are you trying to say?" Sonja stood.

Sri continued to talk, gesturing toward the looming jungle. Carrie studied her in the near darkness, doing her best to imagine what the girl's fluid motions meant. Beckoning gestures seemed to indicate people coming toward them. Jabs might mean directions the women might go, or that they should fight. Then Sri leaned her head back and made a muted wailing sound. "Oooo, oooo. . . ."

Hannah sighed. "One of two things. Either she's telling you how she scared away the pirates, or—"

Carrie finished the thought. "She's telling us what to do if they come back."

Kate gasped as the giant pirate yanked the kris from Brea's hand and raised it to skewer her. The dark-haired girl stared up at

301

him wide-eyed, pinned to the rocky mountainside by the huge man's arm and knees.

"No!" Kate lunged at Goliath, swinging her cutlass at his upraised arm. She barely nicked his forearm as he jerked it away, but the move broke his concentration. Brea wriggled her left hand free and slammed her fist into her aggressor's throat, stunning him.

Kate recovered her balance and kicked Goliath's temple. Brea shrieked and pushed up with both hands. Kate dropped to her knee and shoved against the pirate's side. She gasped as the thug slipped off Brea's body and fell over the ledge with a yelp. His free hand grasped at Brea, dragging her after him.

"Bree!" Kate lunged for her friend, but Brea slid from sight. Goliath roared, and Kate heard his body crash on rocks and bushes as he tumbled down the mountainside.

"Oh, Lord God, no!" Captain Alice squeaked.

Shock coursing through her body, Kate leaned over the ledge to look.

"Cooee. You didn't think you lost me, did ya?" Brea stared up at her from where she clung to a scruffy bush a few feet below the ledge, where Kate had scooted across the rock face a quarter hour earlier.

"Brea!" Kate choked. "You lucky roo. Hang on, we'll get you!"

She dashed into the cave and came back with a rope from the pirates' stash. Gypsy grasped the coil, and Kate tossed the end down. Captain Alice joined their efforts to pull against Brea's weight, and she clambered back onto the ledge. "I'm all right," she said. "He took my boot with him, though."

Kate eyed her critically. "Looks like your shoulder got in the fire." A hole was burned through her shirt.

Brea touched the spot and swore. "No time for that now. I dropped my kris, but I think there's another one over yonder." She strode to the path they had traveled to reach the cave. Kate followed, and caught up with Brea as she knelt beyond a rock.

"I killed this beggar," Brea said. "The man that was eating the chook. Ah yes, he has a nice kris stowed on his back." She retrieved the serpentine sword and its sheath, and fastened it over her shoulder. "And here's another pistol. Oh, what have we here?" She plucked something from his belt and held up a key.

"Maybe that goes to the shackles," Kate said.

Alice and Gypsy had caught up, and Brea swiftly put the key into the keyhole on Alice's shackle and twisted. The metal band fell off. A moment later, Gypsy was also free.

"Let's go," said Kate. "Before the ones from down below come to see why Goliath fell."

"Wait," said Captain Alice. "Gypsy can hardly walk."

"I ain't that bad off," he protested.

Kate stepped back and put her arm around the old sailor's waist. "I'll help you, Mr. Deak."

Brea led the way down the path. Kate let Captain Alice follow and took up the rear with Gypsy.

As they labored down the dim pathway, an uproar arose from the beach. From the mountainside overlook, Kate saw five more proas entering the lagoon. On shore, huts and bits of debris burned in a pattern radiating out from a hole in the sand where timbers and other mangled remnants glowed red hot. The stench of burned gunpowder hung thick in the air, along with a smoke that drifted away in the breeze.

"Wind's picking up," Gypsy grunted. "If we can just get back to the ship. . . ."

"We'll make it," Kate said.

By the time they neared the bottom of the mountain, Gypsy was panting. "I don't know how far I can go," he gasped. "If they jump us, just leave me and run."

"No sir," Captain Alice said. "We will not leave you. And let's not talk about it anymore."

"Yes, ma'am."

A loud exclamation sounded ahead of them, and a pirate dashed out of the darkness, cutlass raised. Brea jerked her pistol

303

from her belt and fired without seeming to aim. The pirate fell in the trail. She turned to the others. "We'll have to run for it! Mr. Deak, climb on my back!"

"I couldn't—"

"Yes, you could!" Captain Alice scolded him. "We'll all die otherwise."

Gypsy relented and let Brea carry him piggyback, and Kate led them through the jungle. She glanced back in the gloom to make sure Captain Alice was keeping up. Brea strode purposefully, huffing under her burden, though her missing boot gave her a limp. Kate chose her way carefully. They had to go slower than she and Brea could have gone alone, but she was pleased with the progress they made. She found a trail heading down the slope in the right direction and followed it.

Behind them, shouting filled the night.

"They're following us!" Captain Alice cried out.

"The boat isn't far," Kate said. She quickened her pace, but didn't dare get too far ahead of Brea.

"Put me down, before you kill us both!" Gypsy blustered. Brea obliged. Kate wanted to give everyone a rest, but shouts and crashings of pursuit sounded from behind them.

"Run!" Brea gasped.

Kate led off. Above the jungle canopy, patches of sky seemed lighter now—soon the sun would burst on the horizon. Ahead were the coals of a small fire. She remembered seeing it before and watched warily for sentries, but met none. The pirates clamored after them, shrieking and yelling.

"Oooo, oooo!" an eerie voice screamed ahead of her. Kate stopped in her tracks, her flesh crawling. Her companions halted, looking around.

"Oooo, oooo!" additional voices joined in, louder and louder. Several voices—Kate wasn't sure how many—faded in and out like specters in the night. She stood transfixed with dread.

The pirates fell quiet behind them, a few uncertain voices muttering in confusion.

Brea reached for Kate's arm, trembling uncontrollably. "Banshees."

"Don't be ridiculous!" Kate snapped. "I hear them too, and I'm not Irish!"

"You could be," Brea whimpered.

"That's stupid." Kate pulled herself together. "The pirates are afraid, so this is our time to escape!"

"Oooo, oooo!" Several of the voices crossed over each other, sliding up and down and sometimes harmonizing.

Gypsy guffawed. "It's the ladies. They're helping us. Come on!" He grabbed Brea's hand and dragged her on. She pulled away from him with an exasperated mutter and followed.

Kate sucked in a deep breath and forged ahead. "Heart of oak!" she yelled toward the voices.

"Heart of oak," a voice sang in reply. Carrie.

Knowing the phantom voices were her friends, Kate plunged confidently along the trail toward the swamp.

"Kate?" Hannah's voice.

"It's us," Kate panted.

"Come, quick!" Sonja stepped from behind a tree. "To the boat, hurry!"

The women and Gypsy clambered down toward the jollyboat. Below the shelter of the bank, Fiona lit their one lantern briefly so everyone could see to safely enter the craft. Kate did a quick count to make sure everyone was present. Her gaze met that of a spritely, waif-like girl with big eyes in a brown face.

"Sri," the girl said, pointing to herself.

"Not now," Sonja said. "Into the boat, everyone! We've a ways to go through the swamp."

Kate helped Gypsy and Captain Alice into the boat. Gypsy tumbled into the bottom and lay there gasping. Kate jumped in, and Sonja pushed off. Fiona put out the lantern, and everyone was blind for a few seconds, until their eyes adjusted.

Howls went up from the pirates as they realized they had been tricked. Clamoring loudly, the mass of men stormed toward the swamp.

"Row!" Sonja said.

Kate grabbed an oar and obeyed, her heart in her mouth.

Sonja knelt in the bow and guided them along the channel between the mangroves, toward the open sea. The jollyboat scraped on a submerged root, but their oar strokes pushed them onward. The pirates thronged the bank above the swamp, hooting and threatening. Little flashes accompanied booms as several men fired muskets or pistols at them, but their aim was vague in the murk. None of the balls found a mark.

"We're going to make it," Sonja said, encouraging the rowers.

A big splash sounded a hundred feet or so behind them, and a pirate screeched with pain.

"One of them fell in," said Fiona.

They continued out the channel, leaving the pirates' ruckus behind.

Beneath them, another root scraped the boat's hull.

"Why are we hitting so many things?" Carrie asked. "It wasn't like this on the way in."

"Tide's going out," said Gypsy. "These mangroves have thousands of roots sticking up like spikes in the water. At high tide, there's plenty of water over them. At low tide, the root tips stick up above the surface."

Sonja muttered in Norwegian. "Row faster! We have to get clear of these roots before we're stranded like fish in a bucket."

Kate rowed with all her might. Her chest ached, and it was hard to fill her lungs. She glanced over her shoulder. At the end of the tunnel of mangrove trees and dark water, the dawn shimmered on tiny waves below a brightening sky.

"Almost there," Gypsy said. The boat scraped more and more. Little Sri stood behind Fiona and Carrie and helped them row, a hand on the end of each oar.

The boat shuddered near the end of the tunnel, but Kate and the other rowers pushed against the barely-submerged roots with their oars, and the jollyboat scooted out into the open water.

Sonja cheered. Kate looked to see what had drawn her attention. Less than a mile outside the reef, the *Vera B.* bobbed on gentle waves, her sails backed and a single anchor keeping her in place.

"Huzzah!" Carrie shouted. "We'll make it yet."

Sonja grabbed the boat's mast and set it in place. Gypsy rose and helped her raise the sail. Sonja handed the sail's foot line aft. To Kate's surprise, Sri grabbed the line and quickly belayed it.

Sonja gawked at her. "You've done that before."

Sri smiled modestly and shrugged. The sail filled with wind, and relief washed over Kate's aching frame.

Gypsy cleared his throat. "I hate to be the bearer of ill tidings. . . ."

Kate looked aft, and her heart sank. Proas were launching from the beach like ants swarming from a mound.

CHAPTER TWENTY-NINE

Alice sat in the bottom of the jollyboat with Gypsy, overwhelmed with emotion. They were only a short distance from the relative safety of the *Vera B.* Sonja and Hannah spelled Kate and Brea at their oars. More than a dozen proas pursued them, brown sails catching the wind, oars slicing relentlessly through the small waves. The jollyboat would reach the brig before the pirates overtook them, but Alice wondered whether the last of their nine would make it on deck before they were overrun.

After all the anxiety of the past ten hours, her head swam. She had barely dozed since dawn the previous day, but the urgency of their flight kept her wide awake.

Brea manned the tiller while Kate crouched beside her, keeping a pistol trained on the nearest proa. Both women were dirty, sweaty, and disheveled, their hair matted, their clothing torn and bloody. Brea glanced at Alice, haggard lines creasing her cheeks. But the girl had a new look in her eyes—an earnest purpose to work toward a necessary goal.

"I never dreamed you girls would come for us," Alice choked. "I never thought you would try."

Kate smiled wearily. "We couldn't leave you. But I'm amazed we pulled it off. I'm starting to think there might be something to all your praying and Bible reading."

Alice smiled. "God has truly delivered us. But we will need His strength in the next hour." She looked beyond Kate to the advancing proas.

"Boat ahoy!" Jenny yelled from the *Vera B.*'s deck.

"Good," Gypsy said. "They have the boarding nets up, and it looks like they got the cannon moved to the starboard side. Aye, they're in good shape."

Several anxious faces lined the brig's rail. The flowing boarding nets extended up and away from the bulwark, forming an impediment for pirates trying to board.

Someone on the brig let the rope ladder down as they neared. Sonja used an oar to push off against the ship's hull and turn the jollyboat sideways. "Drop us a line to secure the boat," she yelled.

Kate and Hannah helped Gypsy toward the rope ladder. In spite of his good spirits, the old sailor trembled from fatigue. Alice offered him a steadying hand as he grasped the ladder and started upward.

"Here's a line!" Mary shouted from above. She let a rope down beside the ladder. Sonja deftly snatched the loose end and tied it to the boat's painter. "We won't be able to ship the boat with the nets out."

"It can't be helped," Alice replied. "We don't have time anyway. If we survive this attack, we can think about boats and such later."

Sonja held onto the rope ladder to keep the boat steady. The long line Mary had thrown over hung limply. Sonja scowled. "I hope the other end's attached to something. But the pirates will probably steal it anyhow." She shook her head in disgust at the approaching proas, which were now barely a half mile away.

As soon as the women on the brig helped Gypsy over the rail, Alice climbed the rope ladder. Despite her fatigue, she hustled, knowing every second mattered. At the top, Jenny and Anne helped her through the gate and under the boarding net. She clumsily stepped onto the deck.

"Welcome back, Captain!" Sarah stepped up and embraced her.

Alice sighed. "It's good to be back." She looked at Gypsy, who sat panting on a coiled line. "Thank God, we escaped and the pirates held off."

"Mr. Zeemer gave us his knowledge," Sarah said. "He thought we might have a little time." She paused, a shadow crossing her face. "Neither he nor I thought we could do anything for you, but Kate and Sonja insisted. I apologize for my lack of faith."

"No need," Alice said. "Let's see to our defense. And have someone bring Mr. Deak some water."

"Aye, Captain." Sarah shouted to Nell to fetch water for the steward. "With the wind picked up, I've prepared to slip our anchor for a quick getaway, with your permission."

Alice glanced at Gypsy, who nodded. "By all means," she said. "Good thinking."

Alice looked back to the rail in time to see Sonja clamber over. As she had expected, the Norwegian was the last to leave the boat.

"Are your party well enough to take their battle positions?" Sarah asked. "We await your command."

Alice grimaced. "Gypsy's probably the worst off. He took a beating."

"I'm fine," the old man said. Wincing, he stood up. "Those dogs are in range now. Mrs. Fiske, have your women slip that anchor and trim the sails." He gathered his breath. "Gun crews, to your battle positions! Aim and fire at will!"

Jenny dashed to the swivel gun, where Mary stood waiting, ramrod in hand. Fiona, looking a little the worse for wear, staggered after her. Jenny rotated the gun and aimed for the nearest Proa. "Fire!" she yelled.

Fiona pulled the cord, and the little cannon fired with a huge *boom*. The solid ball struck the water just aft of the proa.

"Reload!" Jenny commanded, swinging the gun around. Mary swabbed the barrel, and Fiona plunged powder, wadding, and shot down the muzzle. Mary rammed it home, then Jenny swung the gun around and found her aim. "Fire!"

This time the ball hit the proa at the waterline.

310

"Huzzah!" Fiona shouted.

They reloaded and fired again. In the bow, Emma's crew kept the cannon smoking. The pirates began firing too, the swivel guns of the nearest proas booming away.

Jenny glanced to her right, where Hannah, Kate, Sonja, and others secured the main sheets to belaying pins. The *Vera B.* shivered and swayed as the sails worked to gather the fresh breeze and send her forward.

The proas swarmed closer now. A ball whistled past Jenny's head. She gritted her teeth and aimed her weapon. The solid shot hit a proa's hull. Jenny was pleased to see one of those she had hit previously arc out of the pack and head back toward the island, settling lower in the water.

"Keep firing!" she said. "We can stop them! Switch to canister, Fiona!"

As the proas drew close, the brig's sailors not assigned to a gun crew fired small arms toward the pirates. Two proas simultaneously slammed into the side of the *Vera B.,* and pirates used ladders they'd carried and boat hooks to swarm up the side. Other proas circled the brig to attack from the port side.

The noise and swift action engulfed Jenny, but she kept at her post. A filthy pirate's head appeared on the opposite side of the boarding net right next to the swivel gun's mounting as Jenny ordered Mary to fire the weapon. Jenny flinched as a pistol sounded behind her. The pirate loosed his grip and fell. Jenny whipped around to see Nell fling her pearl handled pistol, still smoking, across the deck and into the open door of the captain's cabin for reloading.

As she turned back to the fight at hand, Jenny tried not to think about Jakob, lying in the bed in the captain's cabin. She had spent much of the past ten hours by his side, tending his wound, holding his hand, and praying for his survival. He had a fever now. Polly and Addie were to tend him the best they could while reloading pistols and muskets for the crew on deck.

311

She set her jaw and aimed the swivel gun at a proa beyond the one bumping the *Vera B.*'s side. The canister shot mowed down two pirates caught in the act of jumping from one proa to the other.

Something whizzed down from overhead—an arrow. Mrs. Fiske had positioned Lizzie in the maintop to make best use of her bow. A long-haired pirate slumped over the proa's tiller, the arrow protruding from his back.

The proas scraped and bumped against each other as the wind propelled the brig away from the smaller craft. Those in the brig's lee couldn't fill their sails. Others, however, sailed and rowed circles around the ship, seeking targets for their guns and jockeying for a chance to come alongside and board. Gunfire on all sides filled the air with deafening reports. White smoke hung over the deck, making Jenny's lungs itch and obscuring potential targets.

"Kate!" she heard someone cry out behind her. Above her, something snapped and Jenny lost consciousness.

Upon hearing her name shouted, Kate instinctively whirled and ducked, in time to see a pirate fire a pistol through the port-side netting at her. The ball flew past her shoulder.

Fury building inside, she threw herself at the man and jabbed her cutlass through the netting. The tip found his shoulder and he howled and dropped into the sea.

She turned to see Jenny hit the deck with a thud. Fiona gawked at the girl, stunned. Kate ran to Jenny's side. There were no visible wounds on the girl's body.

"She got hit by a line," Mary yelled. "A sheet broke."

Kate swore. "She's breathing. You two keep firing, I'll get her to the cabin."

She sheathed her cutlass and dragged Jenny by the shoulders to Mrs. Fiske's cabin and left her on the floor. Drawing her

312

sword again, she stepped out on deck to find a mass of pirates clawing their way up the netting on the port side. Brea, Carrie, and Sonja fought to keep them back.

"Kate." The voice came from behind her, and she turned. Polly stood at the door to Captain Alice's cabin. She handed Kate a pistol.

"Thanks." Kate pulled a spent gun from her belt and tossed it to her.

With a newly loaded pistol, she dashed to help the others. She fired the gun point blank through the netting, hitting a big pirate in the stomach. He shrieked and fell to the proa below.

Though Brea and Carrie had inflicted some damage on the invaders through the net, several of them flung themselves over the top and sprang down to the deck.

Brea cursed and lunged at them, followed by Carrie and Sonja. Kate hurried to help them. Beyond them, Gypsy dropped one scoundrel with a shot from his fowling piece. Kate rushed at the pirates, lunging and slashing as Zeemer had taught her.

Brea took the brunt of the onslaught. The Irish girl fought with a raging fury that shocked Kate. She howled and taunted the men as she mowed them down—three in rapid succession. Her wavy kris was a bloody blur as she whipped it about.

"She's berserk," Sonja said in astonishment. She leaped to Brea's side as fresh pirates dropped from the netting. Kate plunged after her, but was careful to stay clear of Brea's whirling blade. Together they fought back a knot of several cutthroats. Carrie defended their flank and got in a few jabs, keeping the men from getting past them.

A huge pirate leaped down and landed on his feet, swinging at Kate with a war club. She deftly raised her cutlass to deflect his blow, but he snatched at her with his free hand and clasped her throat, nearly breaking her neck with his steely grip. Kate reached for her knife as the pirate knocked her down, but he pinned her hand to the deck with his knee. The brute knelt on top of her and raised his club to bash her skull. Suddenly his eyes went wide and

313

his mouth fell open. His club clattered on the deck next to Kate's head. The big pirate slumped over and fell off her.

Kate gasped for breath and put a hand to her throat. She propped herself on her elbow and looked stupidly at her enemy's body. A knife stuck in his back.

Warily, she stood up. Sonja and Brea finished off a pair of rangy-looking miscreants. A flicker of motion at the end of the galley caught Kate's attention. Sri winked at her and ducked around the corner. Kate yanked the knife from the pirate's back.

Carrie looked at Kate. "She threw it. I tried to get to you, but. . . " Blood dripped all down Carrie's shirt and trousers. "I had me own pirate to clobber."

Kate looked around. On the starboard side of the brig, Sarah, Hannah, and Gypsy held their own against the thugs attempting to swarm over the side. An arrow whizzed from above and found its mark in a pirate who was rounding the top of the net. Lizzie was still at work in the maintop.

The Vera B.'s sails fluttered as the wind propelled them. On the quarterdeck, Captain Alice held the wheel steady while the gun crews fired round after round.

"Look out!" Carrie cried. Kate whirled to see another seven or eight pirates scaling the port side netting.

Brea roared and ran to the nets, jabbing through them with her kris. Kate and Sonja followed her. Kate hacked through the netting at a pirate with a red cap. A pistol went off right beside her, and Brea dropped to the deck with a shriek, blood flowing from a fresh wound at her waist. Kate's stomach lurched.

She raised her cutlass and rushed the netting, jabbing through with her blade. A pirate reached through with a kris and slashed at her, cutting her left upper arm. Kate swore and backed off, hacking the man's arm. The blow hit bone. The pirate dropped his blade and pulled his bleeding arm back. Kate jabbed at his midsection and didn't stay to see if he fell.

She grabbed Brea and pulled her over against the mainmast, trailing a wide swath of blood on the deck. Brea moaned as

314

several pirates got over the netting and jumped down, landing on bodies of their comrades. One of them went after Sonja, who parried a blow but was knocked to the deck. Fury drove Kate, and she lunged at the men.

Nell stepped out of the galley, a meat cleaver in one hand and a skillet in the other. "Come to me, you meat-heads!" she crowed. "If it's tucker you want, I'll carve y' up some!" She rushed the pirates from abaft, which distracted them enough for Kate to skewer one in the side. The rest fell back toward her and Sonja, who struggled to rise from the deck. Two of the pirates stumbled over her, and Sonja grabbed one's foot, toppling him just before the other tripped over her.

Kate braced herself as three pirates rushed at her, fleeing Nell. Kate jabbed her cutlass at the first one, catching him in the arm. He howled and swung at her, but she deftly backed away, and his kris sliced empty air.

Nell caught one of the men on the back of the neck with the meat cleaver, nearly taking his head off. The second man succumbed to a bop on the head from the skillet. Kate lunged at the pirate who had swung at her, but Nell brought the cleaver down on his collarbone, and he slumped to the deck.

"Ha! Never row with a cook!" Nell said, bringing the skillet up across her chest.

A pistol fired from the netting, the ball hitting Nell's skillet and ricocheting off into the rigging. Nell gaped at Kate. "Maybe I better stick to cookin'."

Spotting a lull in the conflict, Kate strode over to Brea. Carrie was kneeling beside the injured girl.

Kate crouched by them. "I'm sorry, Bree. You put up such a good fight. You're a real warrior." A tear trickled down Kate's cheek. She and Brea had been through so much together.

"I'm sorry, Kate. I—should have seen that one coming."

"Nonsense." Kate cut off a strip of Brea's pant leg and handed it to Carrie. "Hold that in the wound. It will stop the blood."

More pirates streaming over the nets yanked Kate's attention back to the fight. Sonja heaved herself to her feet, blood streaming from her nose. "Those dirty Hottentots!" she muttered. "We'll take'm yet."

CHAPTER THIRTY

Lizzie knelt on the maintop platform and checked her supplies. She had eighteen arrows left. Below her, the proas crowded on every side of the brig. She could hit them easily, but the arrows would do little damage unless they hit a man. Where was Ned? The rascal ought to be up there with her. Was he cowering below decks? Lizzie doubted it. Nothing seemed to deter him, and they had laid intricate plans.

She laid down her bow and took her pistol from her belt. She had powder and shot, and could save the arrows. She looked around, port, starboard, and aft. A pirate on deck headed toward the quarterdeck, where Captain Alice grimly held the wheel. Lizzie aimed and fired. The seadog toppled down the stairs and lay still.

Lizzie sat with her back to the mast for protection and reloaded her pistol, hands trembling. The noise of the battle surged below her—shouts, groans, gunfire, splashes, and thuds. As she rammed the lead ball home in her gun, a face popped up at the edge of the platform. She jumped and dropped the pistol, slapping a hand on it as it nearly fell off the edge.

"Ned! You startled me. Get up here."

The boy hoisted her leather satchel onto the platform and scrambled up. "Here it is, Lizzie. Sorry it took so long. Mum told me to stay below decks, and then I had a hard time opening the hatch."

Lizzie scowled. "Your mum's probably right, you should be safely below. Well, you're here now, so let's get to work. Sit back against the mast where you'll be safer, and give me space."

While Ned nestled in against the mast, Lizzie looked for another target. Kate and Sonja battled two pirates on the port side, while Sarah, Hannah, and the new girl fought with boarders through holes in the net on the starboard side. Gypsy wearily climbed the stairs toward Captain Alice, his shirt ripped and bloody. Lizzie aimed at a pirate hacking holes in the starboard net and fired. The man fell off the net into the sea with a splash.

She glanced at Ned, who had opened her satchel and had the stopper out of the glass bottle of whale oil. He carefully slipped a piece of wool into it. "You ready, Lizzie? Get your bow."

She stashed her pistol and handed Ned an arrow. He pushed the small target point through the oil-soaked wool as she reached for her bow.

"Now we need the slow match." He fumbled in the satchel. "There it is." He pulled out a coil of fuse. "And—the match sticks." He grinned as he showed her a pepper shaker full of lucifers.

"Hurry up." Lizzie looked about for targets. If Ned could get her arrow lighted quickly enough, a proa on their port side was coming into range.

Ned struck the lucifer and caught the end of the slow match burning, then lit the oily wool on the arrow. It caught and burned brightly as he handed it to her.

Breathlessly, Lizzie nocked the arrow to the bowstring, knelt on one knee, and pulled the string back. She aimed at the nearest pirate boat and released the arrow, but jerked as the heat singed her fist.

"Drat!" The arrow flashed toward the proa but fell short into the water.

Ned scowled. "You missed by a mile. I thought you could aim."

"The confounded thing burned me." Lizzie fumed. "Get me another."

A few seconds later, she aimed at another proa on the brig's starboard side. She anticipated the heat and didn't flinch. The arrow zinged down onto the deck of the boat, where a startled pirate stomped on it and put it out.

318

"Aim higher," Ned said, hustling to ready another arrow.

"I don't need your advice." Lizzie grabbed the flaming arrow and tried again. She was gratified to see it pierce the center of a proa's sail. The flames quickly engulfed the canvas.

"Hooray!" Ned cheered. "We did it, mate! Have another!" He lit another missile.

Lizzie sent arrow after flaming arrow into the sails of the surrounding proas. Five of the little war craft turned away from the *Vera B.,* their rigging ablaze.

Lizzie looked aft over the taffrail. Proas, some on fire, and some not, littered the ship's wake for a mile.

"They're giving up!" Ned shouted. "We did it! We did it, Lizzie!"

Something on the horizon caught Lizzie's attention, just below the rising sun. A tall white sail, and barely five miles away.

"Sail ho!" she cried. "Sail ho, dead aft!" Her spirits lifted. In these waters, pirates didn't sail large ships. The new arrival could only be friendly. The fleeting thought of Con Snyder's schooner crossed her mind, but it seemed implausible that he would follow them for two months. Help was at hand!

"Lizzie, look out!" Ned shouted. She glanced down, to see another proa off the starboard rail. She took the arrow Ned handed her, and shot it deftly at the enemy's sail. The canvas fairly exploded into flame. A little red flash at the proa's rail came at exactly the same instant a massive pain erupted from her shoulder. She fell on the platform, nearly tumbling over the edge. She screeched and grabbed for the top shrouds, catching them with her right hand. She could not feel her left hand, but unbearable pain shot through her body.

"Lizzie! Lizzie, they got you!" Ned scrambled on top of her. His mouth and eyes wide open in terror, he straddled her body and gaped at her shoulder. "You're bleeding bad!" All she could do was gasp and sob.

319

"No, Lizzie, don't close your eyes. You can't die! We clobbered those pirates, and it's gonna be all right. Lizzie, do you hear me?"

The boy sobbed. She wanted to tell him to get off, but couldn't form the words. A fierce look came over his face. He leaned over and grabbed one of the swatches of wool they had prepared a few hours earlier for the fire arrows. Unceremoniously, he jabbed it into her wound, bringing a new level of pain.

"I'm gonna stop your bleeding, Lizzie—you can't peg out on me now. You gotta make it!"

The boy's earnest blue eyes dissolved in a mist of gray bubbles.

"Captain! Begging your pardon, sir."

Josiah rolled over and blinked, then sat up.

"What is it, Chase?"

"The wind's freshened sir, and we're making good headway at last. Mr. Stark asked if you could step on deck for a moment."

"I'll be right there." Josiah tossed down a glass of water, raked a hand through his hair, and put on his coat and hat. Too hot for these clothes, but after all, a captain had to maintain his dignity.

When he reached the quarterdeck, a sailor manned the wheel and Stark stared ahead with the spyglass.

"What news, Mr. Stark?" Josiah said.

"Something ahead, sir. I'm not sure, but it appears to be gun smoke."

"Let me see."

Stark handed him the glass, and Josiah put it to his eye.

"One point to starboard, sir, drifting to leeward."

"I see it." Josiah watched the cloud for a long minute. "It's probably a ship burning."

"No!"

320

"See what you think." He passed the spyglass back to Stark.

After perhaps half a minute, Stark said, "I believe I see it, Cap'n, sitting low in the water. And beyond it, there's something else. Another burning sail?"

As Josiah reached for the glass, muffled thunder reached him. "I hear guns. We may be coming up on a skirmish. Better call all hands."

Within a short time, they were certain. Occasional booms from ships' guns sounded across the waves, and several smears of smoke marred the horizon.

"More flames," Stark reported.

Josiah stood granite steady beside the binnacle.

"Fire ship ahead," called the lookout in the foretop.

"It's a small craft," Stark said.

Josiah nodded. "Likely a proa." He had spent the interval working out the most likely situation ahead of him. "They've attacked a ship and taken a drubbing."

"Aye. Several more are heading off to windward, sir. Oh! Another's sails just burst into flames. Do you want to get into it, or shall we back sail?"

"If we can help them, we must." Josiah didn't want his clipper pummeled, but if he were on the other ship, he'd be forever grateful to a captain who came to his aid. All along the deck, his men stood ready at the guns, Mr. Reiner rallying the crew.

He could clearly see a square-rigger now without the glass, outdistancing the smaller Malay boats.

"There must be thirty or forty proas," Stark said. "The brig seems to be making a successful run for it, though."

"Yes, and they've pounded the scum." Josiah could now observe clearly that several proas had burnt to the waterline. Two still blazed, abandoned by their crews. As the *Jade Maiden* came closer to the small craft, several of them came about and faced the tall ship. "Give those dogs what they're worth," he told Stark.

321

"With pleasure, sir." Stark walked to the quarterdeck rail. "Mr. Reiner!"

"Aye, sir."

"Allow the gun crews to aim and fire on the pirates at will."

The guns were soon in action as the *Jade Maiden* skimmed the water and flew among them, pursuing the brig now a mile head. Oh, it was good to have a fair wind at your back after days of dead, sweltering calm!

Josiah put the glass to his eye again and caught his breath. "She's American. By George, it's the *Vera B.*!"

In another hour they overtook the brig, and both backed sail to speak. Josiah's heart leaped when he saw Alice at the wheel. Someone else took over for her, and she came to the rail.

"Ahoy, *Vera. B.*," Josiah called through his speaking trumpet.

"Ahoy, Captain Howard! You're a sight for sore eyes."

"We saw the proas and sank a few. How have you fared?"

"Badly, sir. If you've a surgeon aboard, we would be most grateful for his services."

"Aye, Dr. Benet of Geneva is aboard. I shall bring him over."

"We'll take down our nets and welcome you."

Alice lowered her trumpet. She waved to him, standing tall and straight, wearing her husband's sword at her side. Her long, chestnut hair had lost its pins and tossed about her face. Josiah thought he had never seen a more beautiful woman.

Alice met the visitors at the rail with Sarah and Kate at her side. The sight of Josiah on her deck, so solid and competent, nearly brought her to tears.

"Welcome! You are so welcome."

He took both her hands in his. "Alice! I hardly know what to say." He glanced about the gory deck. "I've brought two sailors to help clear things up."

322

"Thank you very much. Mr. Deak and I spent a harrowing night in the blackguards' den, and our crew rescued us at great risk. I shall tell you all that later, however. We came back aboard just in time to face the onslaught. Mr. Deak is in charge of getting rid of the slain."

Josiah gave his two sailors orders to assist Mr. Deak in any way he wished and turned back to Alice. "I'm pleased to present Dr. and Madame Benet." Both the surgeon and his wife carried satchels, which Alice hoped contained medical supplies. Josiah smiled gravely at the Swiss couple. "Mrs. Packard, or perhaps I should say, Captain Packard."

"Madame, I am so pleased to meet you." Dr. Benet, an elegantly-garbed man with silvery hair, bent over her hand. "Allow me to be of service to your wounded."

"Thank you. This is my first officer, Mrs. Fiske, who can take you to the cabins where we've placed the most seriously wounded. And this is Miss Robinson, my second mate, who needs to have the gash on her arm attended to."

"Of course." Dr. Benet smiled at his wife. "Helenie, I give the lesser wounds over to your care. Perhaps you can help Miss Robinson first?"

"There are other girls worse off than me," Kate said quickly. "Doctor, please see to Brea McDonovan first."

"Mum! Mum!"

All eyes turned upward at Ned's piteous cry from the maintop. Knowing Hannah was in the cabin trying to help Brea and Zeemer, Alice shouted up to him, "Ned! What is it, child?"

"Lizzie! I've been holding onto her, but she's shot bad. We need to get her down!"

"Good heavens," Josiah said. "You've a wounded woman up there?"

"I'm afraid so," Alice said. "The boy is only eight years old. He must be terrified. Could your sailors …?"

"At once." Josiah strode to where his men were helping Gypsy and Emma salvage anything useful from the dead pirates'

323

possessions before heaving the bodies overboard. "Mr. Deak, my men need to lay aloft and bring down one of your wounded sailor girls."

"Help is coming, Ned," Alice called to him. "You're a brave lad! Captain Howard's men will be there soon."

Jenny staggered toward Alice, holding her head. "What's wrong with Ned? Is he all right?"

"He's fine, dear. What about you?"

"Something hit me on the side of the head. I feel sick."

"Sit down, dear," Alice said.

Mrs. Benet eyed the girl with concern. "She must remain quiet. Have my husband look at her before he goes."

Alice nodded. "I will."

"Perhaps you have a place where I can wash and bandage the cuts."

"Of course." Alice laid a hand on Sarah's arm. "You must stay on deck, Mrs. Fiske, but I'll assign Fiona to take Mrs. Benet to the galley and help her dress the lesser wounds."

Alice walked the blood-stained deck, examining the wounded. Sonja, whose nose had been broken and still bled freely, followed Kate to the galley under protest. Hannah, Carrie, and Anne also had minor injuries.

"You must have it disinfected," Alice told Anne firmly after removing a neckerchief the girl had knotted about her forearm. "Infection will set in if you don't. Mrs. Benet might want to take a few stitches as well."

Josiah's sailors eased their way down the mainmast ratlines with Lizzie bundled unceremoniously over the first man's shoulder. Ned scampered down behind them, his face streaked with tears.

Alice met him as he made the last hop to the deck.

"Ned, my lad, you fought valiantly."

He buried his head in her skirt and hugged her waist. "Is Lizzie going to die?"

"I don't know." Alice watched as Josiah directed the men to carry the wounded woman to the cabin.

"I want my mum," Ned sobbed.

Alice patted his shoulders. "She is very busy, helping those who are hurt. In fact, she will probably be helping Lizzie."

"Will she die?"

Alice crouched and looked into his eyes. "I haven't seen her wound, Ned. But Captain Howard brought a doctor aboard. He will know what to do."

Ned sniffed.

"Why don't you go and sit with Jenny?" Alice pointed her out, sitting forlornly by the dinghy. "She bumped her head, and she's supposed to sit quietly for a while. Can you talk to her and keep her from trying to get up and work?"

Ned nodded.

"Good lad." As he hurried toward Jenny, Alice walked to the door of her cabin. From inside came the doctor's calm, accented instructions and Hannah's terse replies.

Alice took a deep breath and walked in. Both her side of the cabin and Sarah's had been taken over as a clinic. Zeemer, who had occupied her own bed the last time she had been there, now lay on a quilt on the floor, his long legs stretched out beneath the table. Her bed held Brea, whose face was white against the linen pillowcase, her dark curls spilling around her forehead. On the other side of the bed, to Alice's surprise, lay Polly, seemingly unconscious.

"Polly's hurt!"

"Aye," Hannah said, glancing up for a moment. "Knocked out by a blackguard, poor lass. Dr. Benet's afraid she'll start her labors early."

"Oh, dear." Alice stepped closer. "And Lizzie?"

Hannah nodded toward the doorway to Sarah's cabin. "Yonder with Mary and Nell. She's next."

Dr. Benet stood and beckoned Alice to the bedside. Looking down at Brea, he said softly, "There is nothing I can do, madame.

325

My condolences. She has asked for you, and it is time to say *au revoir.*"

Tears filled Alice's eyes. "I feared as much. Thank you."

He nodded. "I go now to attend the mademoiselle with the shoulder wound."

"Lizzie Henshaw? It's not too serious then?"

"I think she will live, but I must remove the ball." Dr. Benet picked up his satchel and went into the other half of the cabin.

Alice sat down on the stool he had vacated and took Brea's hand. The linen was stained with blood, and the bandages on her abdomen were saturated. Blood seeped through the patches of cloth on her neck and arm.

"Brea, my dear, I'm so sorry."

Brea's eyes fluttered open. "Cap'n Alice ..."

"Yes, I'm here."

The girl swallowed with difficulty. "I tried to do good, but I'm wicked."

"We're all wicked, Brea. God loves us anyway."

"Can Jesus do anything for someone as bad as me?"

Alice gazed down into the pleading blue eyes.

"Oh, yes, darling. Jesus is the only one who can. He isn't like us, you see. He never sinned. And so, He could take our sin upon Himself and die in our place. Trust in Him, Brea. He's waiting for you in heaven." Alice pushed the unruly curls off the girl's brow. "He loves you. Can you believe that?"

"I'll try."

"I know you've repented of your sins, Brea. You've said you were bad, but you don't want to be that way, do you?"

Brea shook her head.

"Trust in God. He gives you His gift of life."

"I'll believe," Brea whispered, her eyes wide. "Thank you, God."

"Yes, dear Lord, thank you," Alice said.

Brea closed her eyes and drew a shuddering breath. After a moment, she exhaled and lay still.

Alice met Hannah's eyes. "Is it …?"

"I fear so, ma'am. She's gone."

Alice wiped at the tears rolling down her cheeks with her sleeve. "Oh, Hannah, we've lost her."

Hannah came around the bed. "There now, Cap'n. She died a good death, saving her friends."

Alice stood and embraced her. "I've prayed so hard for this girl."

"I know, and she's with Jesus now. She believed, like the thief on the cross."

"Yes. Thank you, Hannah."

Alice broke free and strode to her wardrobe. She opened her handkerchief box and took one. It struck her how odd it was that she had two dozen fine lawn handkerchiefs embroidered with flowers when all around them people were bleeding and dying. She took the box to Hannah.

"Here, sweet friend. Use one yourself, and offer these to the girls. They can use them for bandages if they like, or wipe their tears with them. We are all sisters now."

Hannah took a delicate cutwork square embellished with sprigs of pink roses. "Now, isn't that lovely?" She glanced at the bed. "I reckon we'll have to move Brea out and put Lucy there."

"Lucy?" Alice stared at her. "What's wrong with Lucy?"

"One of their little cannon balls struck her leg. Broke a bone at least. The doc said she might need an amputation."

"No!" Great sorrow washed over Alice.

"He'll try to save it. But you'd best sit down, Cap'n."

"No, I must see to my girls. But we'll give Brea a proper burial when everyone's been tended."

"Yes, ma'am." Hannah resumed her seat beside Polly and laid a gentle hand on her stomach. "I don't feel any cramps now. Maybe she'll carry this bairn."

"I pray God she will." Alice went to the connecting doorway. In Sarah's cabin, Dr. Benet and Nell bent over Lizzie's form. Lucy lay moaning on a palette of blankets on the floor, with Mary kneeling beside her, holding a cup of water.

"What's the word, doctor?" Alice asked as she approached the bed.

"This one will mend. I am stitching her now. Then I will see to the leg wound."

"It's very bad?" Alice asked.

"Not so bad as I thought at first. A ball shattered her fibula, the small bone. She will walk with a limp, but she will recover."

"Oh, thank heaven. I'm so glad to hear that."

The doctor nodded and clipped the ends of his sutures. "If Madame Hannah can aid me with that operation, I would be so happy."

"I'll tell her," Alice said.

"Thank you." Dr. Benet smiled at Nell and nodded. "You, my dear lady, may go. I thank you very much, but since you are the chef for this fine vessel, you may be needed to prepare sustenance for all these people."

"A grand thought, doctor," Nell said. "I'm peckish myself."

"Oh, Nell, Mrs. Benet has set up a bandaging station in the galley," Alice said as she passed. "I hope she won't be in your way."

"That's fine." Nell paused and smiled. "It's grand to have you back, ma'am."

"Thank you." Alice went back into her own cabin. "Hannah, Dr. Benet wishes you to assist him with Lucy's leg—if you don't mind."

"Of course not." Fatigue lines rimmed Hannah's mouth and eyes. "Polly's sleeping peacefully now. Mr. Zeemer's a little feverish. No complaints from that one. He just says, 'Tend to the girls.' Oh, say—" She paused and looked at Alice. "Are my kiddies all right?"

Alice blinked. "Ned is fine. He's with Jenny. I think she may be concussed, but she'll mend. Addie, though ... I don't think I've seen her since the attack."

Hannah's face blanched. "Dear God! She was in here with Polly, reloading for us all. They can't have got her!"

CHAPTER THIRTY-ONE

Kate flinched as Mrs. Benet inserted a needle into the skin of her arm. She didn't wish to have stitches, but the prim Swiss lady had insisted. "You'll need to keep it clean," she said. "Wipe it with rum or some kind of spirit every day, and use a clean bandage."

"Yes, ma'am. Will I still be able to go aloft?"

The doctor's wife gave her an incredulous look. "Aloft? Up the sails? Not a good idea, until this heals."

Kate exhaled slowly and let Mrs. Benet finish the sutures. How many of their crew would be fit enough to climb the shrouds now? She wanted to get to Brea's side and say her farewells. She glanced at Sonja, who held a cloth to her bloody face.

"Do you think we'll have enough crew left to sail?" Sonja asked.

Kate ticked people off in her head. "We'll know shortly." Through the open galley door, she could still see a dead pirate on the deck.

"At least we have Sri," said Sonja. "She came through without a nick."

"Yes, and she saved my life." Kate sighed. "She knows about boats. She may be a real help."

"Where is she?" a voice boomed from farther aft.

Kate frowned at Sonja. "Who was that?"

Sonja poked her head out the door. "I think it was Hannah."

Kate jumped up, nearly knocking Mrs. Benet over. She followed Sonja out the door.

"Where's my baby?" Hannah wailed. People swarmed in and out of the captain's cabin like bees.

Ned ran past Kate and nearly bowled Gypsy over as he came out. "Mum! Mum!"

Gypsy stepped aside to let Ned in and Captain Alice out.

"What is it?" Kate asked.

"Addie," Captain Alice replied. "We can't find her. Everyone needs to help."

A scream came from the cabin, and Hannah pushed past Alice, blubbering wide-eyed. "She's not there."

Kate's blood chilled. She ran to Hannah and grabbed her hand. "We'll find her." Hannah collapsed on the deck sobbing.

Alice's face was white as she explained, "Addie was in the cabin during the fight, and there's no sign of her now."

Ned came to the doorway. "At least she's not lying there bleeding, like Lizzie. It could be worse."

Sonja put a hand on his shoulder. "Hush, Ned. That doesn't help."

Hannah gasped. "I should have known, when I saw Polly unconscious. How could I have not thought of my little one?"

Alice knelt and put her arm around Hannah's shaking shoulders. "We've turned the cabin inside out. She's not hiding in there. Do what you can, Kate. Search the ship."

Kate put all the able-bodied hands to work, searching the *Vera B.* It was a thankless, grim task. Within a few minutes, the vessel had been combed thoroughly, but no trace was found of Addie.

Kate ended up on the quarterdeck with Sarah, looking out to sea. The jollyboat trailed fifty yards behind them. Kate was glad they had not lost it to the pirates, but it was a bitter consolation.

Captain Howard approached them. "I just noticed that the cabin's rear windows are open. You say the young girl was in there. Maybe the pirate who knocked that woman unconscious took Miss Addie and jumped out the window with her."

Kate stared at him. "There's one person who might know."

She tore down the stairs and ran into the cabin, stopping short when she saw Brea's bloody form in the bed, still as a stone.

331

Heart in her mouth, Kate approached the bedside, unable to tear her eyes away from Brea's face, which bore, perhaps for the first time ever, a peaceful smile.

Kate gasped as she remembered her mission. She looked about the dim cabin and found Zeemer lying on the floor. She knelt by his side.

"Mr. Zeemer, do you hear me?"

"Who is it? Miss Kate?"

"Yes. Mr. Zeemer, you need to tell me what happened in the pirate fight. Was Addie in here?"

Zeemer breathed heavily. "Little Addie, yes. But not now."

Kate swore. "What happened to her?"

"Water, I need water."

She found a jug nearby and put it to his lips. "Where is the little girl?"

Zeemer shivered. "The sea rover came in. He hit Miss Polly and chased Miss Addie. She jumped out in the water. I—think. Then—I tried to shoot him with the gun. But I—I think—I don't know. Maybe he went out the door."

Without a word, Kate jumped up and burst out the cabin door to find Captain Alice, Gypsy, and Captain Howard conversing, faces subdued.

"She's not on the ship," Kate said. "She jumped out the cabin window to escape a pirate."

Captain Alice gasped, and Gypsy looked ill.

Captain Howard asked, "Can she swim? The water is calm enough, she might have had a chance. We can come about and search for her."

Captain Howard's first mate approached, shaking his head sadly. "We could try, but I doubt. . . ."

"It's not you we're looking for," Captain Howard said sternly. "It's a little girl. If there's even a fleeting chance we can find her, we must."

The first mate stirred an uneasy memory in Kate's mind. He nodded and cast his eyes downward. "Aye, aye, sir. I'll put out our boats."

Captain Howard and his mate rowed back to the *Jade Maiden*, leaving their two sailors and the Benets on the *Vera B.*

"Mademoiselle, your stitches," Mrs. Benet said, coming up to Kate as she tried to bark orders to the crew. "They are only half complete."

Kate looked at her arm and laughed wryly. Mrs. Benet's needle still dangled from the thread attached to her arm.

"I'll handle the crew," said Gypsy, "You go get your stitchin'. All hands!"

For an hour, the *Jade Maiden* and the *Vera B.* plied the sea at the scene of the battle. Several pirates were found floating, dead or alive, but there was no sign of Addie.

Kate, trying not to flex her throbbing arm, stood at the port rail, looking out to sea, hoping against hope for good news. Behind her, Hannah, Ned, and Jenny clung together. Kate didn't want to look at them—their sorrow was too great.

Dr. Benet came out of the cabin and approached her. "Miss Lucy's surgery is complete."

"Thank you, Doctor." Kate smiled at him. "I don't know what we would have done without you."

The *Jade Maiden* approached from the starboard quarter and came up alongside the *Vera B.* The clipper's crew cheered and waved to them.

Captain Howard produced his speaking trumpet. "Ahoy, *Vera B.* You may want to bring in your jollyboat!"

Kate stared at him across the waves, her mouth open. What was this? She turned and sped up the stairs, her feet barely touching the quarterdeck as she rushed to the taffrail.

The jollyboat trailed behind them as it had before, but something was different. Kate's jaw dropped.

A small figure sat in the boat, blearily rubbing her eyes. Addie was safe!

###

Jenny sobbed with joy as Aunt Hannah lifted Addie over the bulwark. The girl looked around at all the people gawking at her. Ned ran over to his sister and hugged her fiercely.

"What's all the fuss?" Addie asked.

Jenny hurried up to her. Her headache was nearly gone now, though she had a tender spot. She hugged her cousin and kissed her on the cheek.

"We thought the pirates ate you up," Ned said. "Even though you're mean to me sometimes, I'm right glad we got you back."

Addie gasped as her family engulfed her in a fervent hug.

"I was fine the whole time," she said. "Well, I was scared when the pirate came in the cabin and bopped Miss Polly on the head. I didn't want him to do that to me, so when he saw me, I jumped out. Good thing Pa taught me to swim, Mum."

"Yes, thank God." Tears streamed down Hannah's face.

"I found the rope behind the ship, and I grabbed on," Addie said. "Then I saw the boat, so I let go and let it come up to me and climbed in. I lay down in the bottom so the pirates wouldn't see me. I reckon I was so tired, I fell asleep." She looked at Jenny. "You have a black eye."

Jenny chuckled. "Yair, I'm glad that's all I got. I'm sure glad you're all right, Addie!"

Now that her cousin was safe, Jenny thought of Jakob once again. She dashed into the cabin, flinched as she saw Brea's body, but went to kneel beside Jakob.

"Jakob, we found her."

The Dutchman grasped her hand. "Splendid, my angel. I suppose she must have swum a long time."

Jenny laughed. "No, she got in the boat we were towing. She's all right!"

Jakob sighed. Jenny wasn't sure how clearly he was thinking, though he seemed fairly coherent.

"Angel, I wish to ask you something."

"Yes?"

"If I survive this wound, will you wish to marry me?"

Her heart skipped a beat. A vague, uncertain future swarmed her mind.

"I—I want to. But please. You must give me more time. We have to talk about it more. When you are feeling better."

"I understand. But I want you to be my wife. Take the time you need. We can discuss it later."

"I'll consider it, for sure. I just don't know what plans you have—but I'm in favor of hearing them."

"In time, my dear. If we go to Batavia, we will make our plans there. Perhaps my cousin will have a post for me."

Jenny squeezed his hand gently. "You plan to stay in Batavia?"

"I don't know yet. I can work there. It is a good place. If we can get a little house, you will like it."

She hesitated. She had never had a proposal before. She had known Jakob only a short time, and he had never even kissed her, but she loved him fiercely. Aunt Hannah would say she was too young—and yet, Aunt Hannah was married by this age. She nodded. "I'll speak to my aunt."

"I love you, sweet Jenny."

Startled, she stared into his eyes. What she saw there made her stomach swirl. She could trust this man. He would take care of her for the rest of her life. She reached out and smoothed his fair hair off his brow.

"I ... want to say yes."

He smiled and drew her hand to his lips. "You think about it."

"I will. And you sleep. Get better."

"I must. You have given me hope, so I must become strong again."

###

As the sun sank, all hands of the Vera B., along with Captain Howard, his officers, and Dr. and Mrs. Benet, assembled on the main deck to bid farewell to Brea McDonovan. One of Josiah's sailors manned the wheel, and another stood watch in the foretop.

Alice's voice broke as she read the committal service from her husband's prayer book. Josiah stepped forward to give the final prayer over the canvas-wrapped body, and she bowed her head. The women stood in silence, except for an occasional sob or sniff. All held Alice's fine handkerchiefs tight in their fists and used them to swab away errant tears. Earlier, Kate had tucked one of the prettiest bits of embroidered lawn under Brea's cold fingers, whispering, "My sister." She had helped Hannah weight the canvas shroud with ballast and stitch it up.

Josiah had volunteered four of his sailors to carry out the actual disposal of the body. They lifted it on a plank and tilted the head end upward. The canvas bundle slid over the bulwark and hit the water below with a subdued splash. A flood of tears escaped Alice's eyes. At least they were now many miles from the scene of the skirmish that had taken Brea's life. The valiant young woman would not share the same water as her slain enemies.

They all stood in silence for a moment as the *Vera B.* ran on. Her sails full, the little brig seemed sprightly, almost joyful before the wind. At any other moment, Alice would have reveled in the breeze ruffling her hair. But now, she could think only of the young woman she had lost.

What could she have done differently if she had the last day to do over? They should have been more vigilant. Perhaps have cut their concert short, or kept more sailors on watch, or fixed their boarding nets as soon as they hit the calm.

She let out a pent-up breath. Sarah slipped an arm about her waist.

"She is in God's hands now."

"Yes." Alice lifted her chin. "Carrie O'Dell, would you lead us all in a hymn?"

Carrie's clear soprano rose in the opening strains of "Amazing Grace." The women had practiced it each Sunday, and it was perhaps the one they knew best. Several of them wept openly as they joined in the melody.

When they had finished, Alice smiled at the group. "Thank you all. We will miss Brea. Now those of you off watch may go below and rest. I believe Miss Robinson's watch has another hour to go."

The women of Kate's watch went to their stations, and the others filed down the ladder to the 'tweendecks.

"Mr. Deak," Alice called to Gypsy, who stood forlornly near the mainmast, "would you kindly join me and Captain Howard and his mate in the cabin?"

She led the way to her cabin door and ushered them in. Nell and Jenny had scrubbed the decking inside until the bloodstains were only faint smears. Zeemer had been removed to his cabin, and Lizzie, Polly, and Lucy were settled in the 'tweendecks, where the doctor and his wife could tend them easily. Alice glanced about.

"I only have two chairs, gentlemen. Mr. Deak, the stool is in Mrs. Fiske's cabin, and I believe she has a small bench in there as well."

Mr. Stark helped Gypsy retrieve the items, and Alice and Josiah took the two chairs. Their seating arrangement crowded them against the wardrobe and the end of the berth, but they could manage.

"What are you plans?" Josiah asked. "You have some damages."

"Yes, but not severe," Alice said. "Gypsy thinks that, with help from a couple of your men, we can swap out our main topsail during the morning watch."

"Aye," Gypsy said. "It's not beyond repair. I'd have had it down tonight, but ..."

"I'll leave two men aboard," Josiah said. "Do you think that's sufficient?"

Gypsy nodded. "The ladies and I could do it, but it will be much easier with them."

"We've some other damage to the rigging and several holes in the hull, but those are mostly above the waterline," Alice said, looking to Gypsy once more.

"Aye. There's two small leaks in the hold. I've patched them temporary like, but we need to put in somewhere and have 'em fixed proper, or we'll have more trouble soon. I'll check again and see if we need to start the bilge pump."

"So ... do you have a port in mind?" Josiah asked. "You won't go back to Australia?"

"No," Alice said. "I was thinking we could make it to Batavia."

Josiah's brow furrowed. "Yes, they've plenty of shipwrights there. And Java is practically on my way to Bombay. I could see you safely there."

"That would put you behind," Alice said. "The *Jade Maiden* can fly compared to our progress."

"Nonsense. I won't leave you out here unprotected with the damages you have. That wasn't the only flock of pirates in these waters."

Alice took a deep breath. Depending on a man for protection had seemed normal to her three months ago. Now it ruffled her feathers for some reason. She and her misfit band of women had learned to be independent. But a friend was a friend, and she knew Josiah spoke truth.

"Thank you. I'll accept."

He nodded graciously, but Mr. Stark's smile held a triumphant gleam Alice didn't like.

"Two of my best sailors can stay with you until we drop anchor in Batavia," Josiah said. "And you'll want Dr. Benet as well. I'm sure he will want to stay with his patients for a week or so."

Alice wanted to say that wouldn't be necessary, but thought better of it. "Mrs. Benet is welcome to sail with us until her husband rejoins you."

Gypsy said, "Thank you, sir. We'll be short-handed until some of these ladies heal up, and we'd appreciate having a couple of extra seamen. We might need to hire on a few more hands in Batavia."

Alice hadn't thought of that.

"The Malaysian girl, Sri," Gypsy went on. "She helped Kate's watch trim the sails this afternoon. She knows about such things. Kate and Sonja think she'll stay with them as crew if you'll allow it, ma'am."

"Well, I ... suppose so. We can't just leave her off in a strange place with no one to look after her."

Gypsy smiled. "It wouldn't surprise me if Zeemer could speak her lingo, him having sailed with the scurvy devils."

"You may be right," Alice said. "When he's feeling better, we can ask."

"Do you trust that man?" Josiah asked. "I know he's laid low for the time being, but really, my dear."

"A pirate among your crew," Mr. Stark said, shaking his head.

"He isn't a pirate," Alice insisted, surprised at her own passion. "He was forced into it, and he helped us a great deal before he was wounded."

"I'll leave that to your judgment," Josiah said. "But do you intend to take him with you to Boston?"

"He has connections in Batavia. If he wishes to stay there, I will give him my blessing. However, I'm not against having him aboard when we sail for England and home."

A knock at the door brought Alice to her feet. "Enter."

Nell came in with a tray. "Begging your pardon, Captain, but I've got brandy for the gentlemen and a cup of strong tea for yourself."

"Bless you, Nell."

Alice and her guests enjoyed their refreshment as they settled the details of their course and arranged flag signals they could use if trouble arose.

Josiah sent Mr. Stark out to give orders to their men and ask the Benets what arrangements they wanted to make. Gypsy also left to show the borrowed sailors where they could sling hammocks.

"My dear," Josiah said.

Alice looked up at him, her heart accelerating. How much did that "my dear" mean? Josiah gazed down at her, his eyes full of tenderness.

"It grieves me to go even so far as my own quarterdeck from you. This has been a very trying time."

"It has," Alice said.

Josiah reached for her hands. "Let me beg you once more, though I fear unsuccessfully, to come aboard the *Jade Maiden*. You could sail in comfort, with the company of Madame Benet. Mr. Stark could take command of the *Vera B.* and bring her to Batavia." Her dismay at this suggestion must have shown in Alice's face, as he quickly amended, "Or your Mrs. Fiske, if you prefer. She seems competent."

"No, but thank you, Josiah. I will stay with my ship and my crew. The women need me now."

"I thought as much, but I had to try."

She smiled. "You are most kind."

He drew a deep breath. "I should like to be more than kind. Alice, we have known each other for many years, and Ruel was a very dear friend of mine. I know your gentility, and now I know your strength and your courage."

Alice caught her breath. Was he winding up for a proposal? The idea was not the shock it would have been a few weeks ago, and that in itself surprised her. But she wasn't ready for that, not nearly, though she liked Josiah and respected him as a sailor and a businessman. But romance … her bruised heart was far from prepared for romance.

She pulled her hands away. "Thank you, Josiah. And you've been most staunch, a truly loyal friend. Perhaps we can dine together ashore when we reach Batavia."

"Uh … yes, I would like that."

Alice nodded and looked away. "I'm still getting used to being … a widow, my friend."

"Of course." Josiah picked up his hat and smiled tightly. "We shall speak again. And do not hesitate to fly your signals when you wish for aid. Or even … simply for company."

"I'll keep that in mind."

They walked out onto the deck. Night had fallen, as was wont to happen suddenly in the tropics. Mr. Stark saw them and brought the sailors who were not staying to the bulwark.

"Our boat is ready, Captain."

"Thank you, Mr. Stark." Josiah gazed wistfully at Alice in the moonlight. "We shall meet again soon."

Alice bid her guests good-bye. Josiah went last over the side, and she watched as their boat pulled away, toward the tall clipper.

"That's a beautiful ship," Hannah said, coming to stand beside her.

"Yes, one of the finest on the seas," Alice replied. The companionable silence lengthened.

"Jenny's saying she might want to leave us in Batavia," Hannah said at last.

Alice whirled toward her. "What on earth for? Oh! Zeemer, I suppose."

Hannah nodded. "I didn't know what to say. I want to think he's a fine young man, and that he'll take care of her."

"Has he offered marriage?"

"Apparently so. Jenny says he wants to speak to me when he's up to it."

341

"This fever," Alice said. "If he can't throw it off ..."

"Jenny will be heartbroken," Hannah finished. "But he's strong. Dr. Benet thinks he'll beat it."

Alice eyed her friend keenly. "Would you stay with her?"

"I haven't had time to even consider it, but I think not. I want to take the children back to England. I can't see raising them by myself in a heathen land."

"And leaving Jenny there worries you, of course."

"My, yes. But if he can support her and provide decent lodgings ... Well, we'll see, won't we?"

"A lot can happen between here and Batavia," Alice said.

"Aye, so it can." Hannah gave a brisk nod. "Well, I'd best get back to my patients."

As she walked across the deck, Gypsy approached. "A word, ma'am?"

Alice smiled. "Of course."

He leaned on the rail and looked across at the *Jade Maiden*. "Good to have company."

"Very good."

Gypsy turned toward her and fished something out of his pocket. "Earlier today, when we was cleaning up—well, there wasn't time to speak much, and I didn't want to upset the work detail, but while we was taking care of those blasted pirates—clearing the deck, you know—"

Alice nodded, trying to make sense of this rambling narrative.

"Well, old Ramu was among 'em, ma'am."

"Ramu himself?" Alice's throat tightened. "Among the slain?"

"Aye. So we ... we done the same with him as with the others. Took his weapons and checked for anything else useful."

"Did you find anything?"

He held out his hand and opened it. Caught in the gleam of the moonlight lay Alice's gold locket.

"Oh, Gypsy!" She seized it and held it up close. Her fingers trembled as she sprang the catch. The lock of her beloved's hair remained safe within. She snapped the pendant shut and threw her arms around Gypsy's neck. "Thank you so much, my friend! You know what this means to me."

"Well, I – I think I know summat—"

Alice chuckled and pulled away from him. "Now I've embarrassed you. I'm sorry, but it was so unexpected. I never thought to see it again."

Gypsy cocked his head to one side. "It's a matter of comparison, ma'am. This time last night, we never expected to see the dawn."

Alice gazed up at the billowing sails. "Aye. It's good to be back on our ship again, Gypsy."

He ran his hand along the bulwark. "Indeed. Well, I reckon I'll turn in. I've had enough adventure for one day. Week. Year."

Alice chuckled. "For some reason, Gypsy, I have a feeling we're in for a whole lot more."

THE END

Dear Reader,

Thank you for reading our book. We hope to bring you more in the Hearts of Oak series soon, so you can continue Alice and her crew's adventures. We hope you enjoyed *The Seafaring Women of the Vera B.* You can help get the word out about this book by writing a review. A sentence or two on your favorite website can make a big difference.

To keep up with our writing endeavors, visit Susan's website at: www.susanpagedavis.com. You can sign up for a free, occasional newsletter there that will let you know as soon as the next book is ready. You can also read more about Susan's other books there. Thank you!

Susan and James Davis

About the authors

James Samuel Davis grew up as the oldest of six children in the rugged forestland of central Maine. His parents are a novelist and a retired newspaper editor. Homeschooled from first grade through high school graduation, he has always been an avid student of history and geography. Writing and researching have been a lifelong passion. Add a vivid imagination and an aversion to thinking inside the box (what box?), and you have the beginnings of a new paradigm for fiction writing.

James completed an agricultural degree at Bob Jones University, then undertook an agricultural exchange through the University of Minnesota. This included a 4-month internship on a dairy farm in Australia, where he broke his leg in a dirt bike accident while trying to intercept an escaped herd of cattle.

His writing credits include articles for *Green Magazine* and special sections of a daily newspaper. In addition to Australia, he has traveled to China and Alaska, and he made a mission trip to

Micronesia in 2012. He resides in rural Travelers Rest, S.C., with his wife and seven children.

Susan Page Davis, James's mom, is the author of more than sixty Christian novels and novellas, which have sold more than 1.5 million copies. Her historical novels have won numerous awards, including the Carol Award, the Will Rogers Medallion for Western Fiction, and the Inspirational Readers' Choice Contest. She has also been a finalist in the More than Magic Contest and Willa Literary Awards. Her books have been featured in several book clubs, including the Literary Guild, Crossings Book Club, and Faithpoint Book Club, and have been named Top Picks in Romantic Times Book Reviews and appeared on the ECPA and Christian Book Distributors bestselling fiction lists. Susan lives in western Kentucky with her husband, another Jim. She's the mother of six and grandmother of ten. Visit her website at: www.susanpagedavis.com and follow her on Twitter at: @SusanPageDavis.

Some of Susan's other historical novels you might enjoy:

The Outlaw Takes a Bride
Captive Trail
Cowgirl Trail
The Prairie Dreams series: The Lady's Maid, Lady Anne's Quest, and A Lady in the Making
The Ladies' Shooting Club series: The Sheriff's Surrender, The Gunsmith's Gallantry, and The Blacksmith's Bravery
The Crimson Cipher
And many more!